CASSANDRA CLARK lives in London. She is passionate about history and is often found haunting ruined abbeys and castles by night. Her childhood in the East Riding of Yorkshire was her inspiration for the Abbess of Meaux series.

www.cassandraclark.co.uk

By Cassandra Clark

The Law of Angels
A Parliament of Spies

A Parliament of Spies

An Abbess of Meaux Mystery

CASSANDRA CLARK

Allison & Busby Limited
12 Fitzroy Mews
London W1T 6DW
www.allisonandbusby.com

First published in Great Britain by Allison & Busby in 2012.
This paperback edition published by Allison & Busby in 2012.

A CIP catalogue record for this book is available from
the British Library.

10 9 8 7 6 5 4 3 2 1

ISBN 978-0-7490-1213-7

Typeset in 10.5/16 pt Sabon by
Allison & Busby Ltd.

The paper used for this Allison & Busby publication
has been produced from trees that have been legally sourced
from well-managed and credibly certified forests.

Printed and bound by
CPI Group (UK) Ltd, Croydon, CR0 4YY

A Parliament of Spies

Part One

Prologue

Eltham Palace. Morning. A tall fair young man strides down the narrow corridor towards the sound of splashing water. Steam billows through the half-open door ahead.

He is wearing soft kidskin ankle boots that make no sound on the polished tiles. His brocade gown, wide sleeved, embroidered with silver harts and gold crowns, is swinging loosely open as he hurries towards his bathhouse.

The flickering fires of the cressets that line the corridor are not more bright than he is. He glitters, sheds light as he strides along, his red-gold hair, his lucent skin, his shimmering garments, brighter than fire. Tapestries on both sides sway with his urgent haste, their own gold thread bringing the scenes of the hunt to life, a falcon stooping to its prey, a stag among the trees with huntsmen closing for the kill. The embroidered leaves seem rustled by the wind as the tapestries billow from the wall.

A real wind from an open window tuckers underneath as he reaches the door and one of the tapestries bulges to meet him.

He catches a glimpse of it out of the corner of his eye and gives a shout. A narrow-bladed knife appears in his hand. He launches himself at the unseen assassin. Stabs wildly into the swirling fabric. Stabs again and again. The gold and silver threads protect his assailant like thin armour. Then from within the folds a shape lurches forward and he raises the knife to finish them.

But a shout stops him. Knife raised.

'My Lord! No!'

Swivelling, he sees Robert.

White-faced, he is lunging forward, arms outstretched. 'Stop! Dickon! My Lord! Stop!'

The newcomer throws himself against the King regardless of the knife, yelling again, 'Stop! Stop!'

'What?'

'It's Agnes!'

The tall young man, fair and pale anyway, blanches. Sky-blue eyes darken. He steps back in horror.

The bundle behind the tapestry struggles to free itself. Topples towards the two men. Robert tears the tapestry aside. 'Agnes?'

A figure resolves itself into a young woman with long pale hair and a gorgeous gown of yellow silk.

She falls into his arms.

The King steps forward, the knife useless in his hand. 'Is there blood?'

Agnes is sobbing with fear and relief. 'You missed me, Your Grace . . .'

He slams the knife back into the jewelled sheath on a gilded belt under his gown.

Without another word he pushes on into the bathhouse and vanishes into the billowing steam.

Agnes is still sobbing in her saviour's arms, shaky with relief, furious with herself. 'I thought I was dead . . .'

'Fool. You know he fears assassins.' He kisses her roughly, with relief, with lust. 'No harm, angel – you're safe. But what were you thinking?'

'I just wanted to jump out and surprise him,' she whispers, allowing herself to be kissed. 'I meant it as a joke.'

'My mad Bohemian,' he whispers. 'We have to look after him. This is the one place he feels safe and then you frighten him like that. Oh, sweeting . . .' He holds her more tenderly and begins to laugh.

'I'll never ever do anything like that again.' She is still shaking.

'He'll never forgive you.'

When they enter the chamber with the wide tiled pool at its centre and a blonde-haired girl gravely swimming in the water, the King himself is already stepping down to join her. He smiles when he notices their expressions.

'What else can we expect when we surround ourselves with mad Bohemians?' he asks Robert. 'Anne is quite as crazy.'

11

He glances over to his wife where she floats serenely on her back, long hair flowing in elfin knots around her head making her look like a mermaid.

'You may leave us.' He dismisses them both, calling, 'I forgive you, Agnes. I'm greatly at fault. I pray you forgive me.'

He is already planning to give his wife's madcap lady-in-waiting a balas ruby in recompense for the scare he gave her. For the scare he himself received, he will give thanks later in his private chapel to his protector, St Edmund.

He turns back to his wife. Then stares in horror.

Her face is deathly white.

She is floating in a pool of blood.

Chapter One

Bishopthorpe Palace in the county of York. Three days after the feast of St Giles. Dawn.

Alexander Neville stood in the great courtyard watching his servants load his sumpter wagons. In the pale light of early morning they scurried about the yard, readying for the long journey ahead. The wagon boards groaned as goods were packed into every available cranny. One cart carried fresh bread racked in warm rows under crisp linen cloths. Behind that was a wagon loaded with cheeses, another with dried fish, and one with salted pork. There was a water wagon. An ale wagon. And one for the archbishop's wine. There was a wagon for the hawks, hooded falcons, peregrines, merlins, followed by a wagon for the falconer and his men, and behind that, strangely, a small cart with a wicker cage on board and inside the cage a brood of pigeons, softly cooing.

After that came the dog cart, wet muzzles poking between

the corded withies. A wagon loaded with swords, shields, body armour, racks of mail, hauberks and helmets, greased and ready for use. A cart full of arrows, sheaved twenty-four together. Steel-tipped. Barbed. Then a cart for spare wheels followed by a string of pack horses.

At the head of this convoy stood Archbishop Neville's own char, its gilded hood glimmering in the light of flares. Finally, after the line of sumpter wagons came those for the archbishop's retinue, his chaplain, his page, his steward, his chamberlain, his personal servants, his grooms, his cooks and kitcheners and his yeomen of the board and their necessary cutters and broilers, choppers and spit boys. His ordained. And his unordained. His inner circle.

'Forty persons in all, Your Grace,' murmured his chamberlain with satisfaction. 'Are we into Mass now?'

The archbishop glanced round the yard at his well-appointed cavalcade. 'We are. Conduct the Pope's fiends in before everybody else.'

With this he strode off some way for a word with his secretary, Edwin Westwode, all the while maintaining an eye on the papal envoy and his tax-gathering henchmen.

As soon as he saw them enter the church and the rest of the York retinue disappear inside, Alexander Neville superstitiously touched his cross and his mitre and followed them.

Hildegard and her priest, Brother Thomas, both ready to join the convoy on its long journey to London, were standing at the back of the church swamped in billowing clouds of incense, with Thomas trying not to cough and

Hildegard praying that his asthma, the coughing spasms, would not assail him before the service ended.

Fortunately the archbishop, swift in his incantations, eager to be out on the road and down to London, eager for battle to commence, offered up swift prayers. 'And for King Richard,' he concluded, 'pray God guide and bless him all his days. May this forthcoming Parliament bring peace and purpose to our realm. May all factions be joined in amity. May the Queen be delivered of a son. May the French invasion be thwarted by the power of your divine hand. O Lord, have mercy on us all.'

'Amen,' sang the congregation without dissent.

A young woman with a pert and pretty face was standing at the door as they came out, craning her neck to see inside. As the last of the servants left she turned away with a puzzled frown.

By now the sky was the colour of polished pewter. A stiff breeze had sprung up and seemed likely to keep the rain off. It brought the scent of woodland into the courts and chambers of the palace, evoking a lingering nostalgia for the waning summer. But that was the past. It was autumn now and momentous times lay ahead. Everyone flocked to the carts to find their places if they had one and check their boots if they hadn't. The red-haired blustering cook inspected his char with misgivings while his personal servant, stifling a groan, bent with cupped hands to heave him inside.

'Hold it!' The chamberlain, after a hurried word with

the papal envoy, held up one hand. Silence fell. Thomas, a tall, gangling young man with a bony intelligent face, stood on tiptoe in his sandalled feet and peered over the heads in front.

'What's happening, Thomas?' Hildegard asked.

'It seems the envoy wants a recount,' he told her. 'There's been a mistake.'

'I would have thought counting was the one thing he was good at, given the practice he's had adding up our taxes.'

The envoy, attired in garments of sumptuous elegance, was counting heads himself now. He took his time.

Eventually he turned to the archbishop with a thin smile of triumph. 'Forty-one, Your Grace. I'm sure your chamberlain agrees?'

The latter, after another swift tally, reluctantly nodded.

Nobody moved, except for a few corner-eyed glances to see who was present now who hadn't been present before.

The kitchens at Bishopthorpe Palace were empty. The fires were out. The spit unturned. The stone flags swept clean.

The retinue destined for London was eager to be on its way.

Now this.

The archbishop, famed for his rages and fully justifying his nickname of Fiery Neville, walked off a few paces, stared hard at the ground, then walked back, his face blank save for a jumping nerve at the corner of his mouth.

He took a swift step forward as if to strike an assailant,

but instead folded his hands inside his voluminous sleeves and in familiar fruity tones announced, 'I beg Your Holy Eminence to revolve this matter in the court of your mind.' He inclined his head with a judicious display of respect. 'I beg you, pray arrive at a more accommodating conclusion. One only?' He raised his eyebrows and paused for a full beat before adding, 'My retinue is pared to the bone, Your Eminence. There is not one servant I can travel without.'

It sounded final. But, strongbox bulging with the tax he had extorted from this – in his opinion – barbaric outpost of Pope Urban's empire, the papal envoy showed that he was impervious to special pleading no matter how sonorously delivered.

'I don't make the rules, Archbishop. I merely apply them. You are one too many. You must leave one of these men behind.' His glance shifted round the growingly hostile servants. He assessed them with his dark foreign eyes, glance flickering this way and that. It swooped past Hildegard in her white habit but then just as suddenly swooped back.

'Is that a nun? Get rid of her.'

Archbishop Neville didn't so much as glance in Hildegard's direction. 'The nun comes with us.'

Meaningful glances were exchanged among the lower servants.

The envoy gave a very foreign shrug. 'Choose somebody. Anybody. But choose you must. Forty persons in your retinue. No more. The Pope wishes it so. Humility in all things, Your Grace.'

Neville scowled. 'You choose, Master Fulford,' he addressed his red-faced master cook. 'Get rid of one of your kitcheners. We'll have to survive the journey with a little less fine dining.' He shot a mean look at the envoy.

Fulford was just about to heave himself down from his char when there was a high-pitched wailing and a ragged lad came stumbling into the courtyard from the direction of the kitchen gardens. His wild glance alighted on the archbishop and he ran forward as if to sanctuary to throw himself at Neville's feet.

He was in such a panic he could scarcely get his words out and the archbishop had to reach down and raise him up to standing. Then, in a tone of surprising kindness, he asked, 'Now then, little fellow, what's all this that can't be sorted?'

The boy clung onto the archbishop's arm, his grubby fingers all over the embroidered satin, and his mouth worked until at last he stuttered, 'My Lord Archbishop, forgive me – I beg forgiveness . . .'

'You are forgiven, lad. Now come on. Out with it. We're waiting to leave.'

'In there, My Lord . . .' The child, trembling, pointed back towards the kitchen yard. 'In the brewhouse, Your Grace. Something in the vat. A monster. A hideous thing that leered up at me and would have dragged me in as well had I not fallen back and thus escaped its clutches.'

He began to sob.

The archbishop gave a despairing glance. Everybody was pressing forward to peer at the boy and assess the truth of what he was saying. Before panic could erupt the archbishop held up his free hand. 'Who knows this lad?'

There was a murmur from the outer ranks and an alert-looking servant pushed to the front.

'I know him, Your Grace. It's my kid brother.' The servant, despite his rough clothes, dropped with some grace to one knee.

'Is he given to fantasy?'

'Never, My Lord.'

'You had better go and inspect this so-called monster. And then you may as well stay behind. Meanwhile . . .' Neville turned with an angry rustle of taffeta-lined velvet, 'my retinue of forty persons . . .' he glared in the direction of the pontiff's man, 'will proceed without further delay to London!'

There was a spontaneous cheer. The wagons refilled with travellers.

'Doesn't he want to know what this monster is?' murmured Thomas in Hildegard's ear. 'I know I do!'

'It'll be some trick of the light. The boy shouldn't have been in there in the dark, should he, the little scamp?' She noticed the envoy turn to his groom, so she climbed onto her palfrey and jiggled the reins.

There were one or two murmurs about the monster but boys will be boys, and hardly anybody gave a backward glance as they headed for the arch under the gatehouse that would lead them at last to the open road.

No more than a couple of wagons had passed underneath

before they were halted by the return of the servant and his kid brother.

'My Lord!' The servant dropped to his knees with the same grace as before. 'I crave your attention . . .'

'You have it.'

'There is no monster in the vat, Your Grace.'

'Of course there isn't.' Neville glowered.

He stood. 'But there is, albeit, a man.'

'What's he doing there?'

The servant crossed himself.

Neville took a step forward. 'Is he dead?'

'It looks like it, Your Grace.'

'What, drowned?' The archbishop, with his bone-achingly distant destination in mind, his irritation at the delay to their departure, the nit-picking of the envoy, suddenly let out a roar. 'Nobody drowns in my vats! I won't have it!'

There was dead silence.

The servant who had brought the news stared at the ground.

More temperately Neville asked, 'Do you know who it is?'

'I do. It's Martin the saucier, Your Grace.'

While Archbishop Neville consulted one of his bailiffs there was a horrified uproar of questions from his retinue.

Travel cloak billowing behind him, Neville marched at the head of a group of officials into the kitchen yard, down the path to the bakehouse, crossed into the brewhouse and stared into the vat.

It was true. A youngish man with thick curly hair was

20

lying in the water among the crushed barley. His eyes were shut. His clothes floated round him giving him buoyancy. He looked peacefully asleep.

'Get him out.'

Two servants struggled to lift him over the side of the wooden tub then deposited him on the floor in a puddle of ale. Neville bent, felt for a pulse, evidently failed to find one and rose to his feet looking grim.

Hildegard pushed her way through the onlookers. 'May I?'

She knelt and lifted the man's eyelids, checked his pulse to make sure, looked inside his mouth, scrutinised his body for knife wounds, found nothing to arouse any comment other than to confirm the archbishop's verdict. 'He's dead, certainly, Your Grace.'

Water was dribbling out of the man's mouth. He was turning an odd colour. His jaw lolled open.

'Perhaps you might turn him over to see if you can empty his lungs.'

The bailiff's men did as she suggested. Water spewed out of the man's mouth. He remained motionless, showing no sign of life.

'Bailiff?'

'Your Grace?'

'We must leave. Take him to the mortuary. I charge you with finding out how this mishap occurred.'

When they followed the archbishop outside morning had broken. Standing in the pearly light Neville delivered a

21

short prayer for the redemption of Martin's soul then ordered everybody into the wagons.

Hildegard went back into the malthouse. The bailiff and a few men who were staying behind were already lifting the body to carry it away. She stared at the vat. Wide enough for a man to lie in full length. About three feet deep. With enough liquor in it at this moment to drown a man. She leant over the side. It would be easy to topple in should you be trying to stretch out to reach something, or if somebody came up behind you without warning and tried to force you over the side.

Apart from the door they had entered there were two other doors on the other side of the chamber with an unglazed window between them through which trickled a little light from outside. She went over and gave one of the doors a push. It was locked. The second one opened easily, however, and led out into a garden that stretched down a shallow slope towards the beck. There was a wall round it, high enough for anyone agile to climb over, but then they would find themselves on the bank side and it led nowhere.

Bending, she peered at the bushes growing close by. Herbs. It was a herb garden, then. They lay in undisturbed rows, the dew unshaken from the leaves.

A path led alongside the building to a wicket gate in the wall. Beyond that was a lane and the high wall of the abbey infirmary with the dark huddle of the other abbey buildings beyond that. The sky behind them was beginning to lighten.

'Hildegard!' It was Thomas. 'We're going to be left behind if we don't leave now.'

'I'm coming.' She closed the door and went back inside. Light was beginning to slant in through the window slit, illuminating the clean swept tiles.

She followed him out.

The papal envoy and his tax-gatherers were dropped off a few hours later as they passed Selby Abbey and would presumably inflict the same indignities on the brothers there. By evening the convoy was approaching the river to make the Humber crossing at low tide before descending into Lincolnshire. A few trees straggled beside the road, beyond them, thick woodland. The sun had disappeared behind a wreath of evening mist.

It was then they sighted the wolf.

It was running between the trees, a silvery shape moving in the same direction as themselves. At first it was thought to be a hind, as it was at the time of day when they came out to feed, and already one of the huntsmen was standing up in a moving cart with his bow unslung and an arrow fixed to the string.

'There, look!' someone shouted as the creature wove in and out of the boles of the trees. 'I told you it was a wolf.'

It moved like quicksilver, fleet and fast. The arrow, however, was faster. They saw the animal leap in an arc as the barb hit. Then it fell and lay still.

Half a dozen men were already out of the carts and running into the woods. The man who had shot the creature drew a long hunting knife and crept up on it with warning shouts from the others not to trust it, but when he reached it the animal was dead, the arrow having pierced its skull. He hacked off the head and with the help of the kitcheners gutted the creature there and then, fed the innards to the hounds, flensed the skin as well as they could in the falling darkness, and returned to the waiting convoy. There were cheers when he stuck the wolf's head on a pole and fixed it to his wagon. The skin was hung up to dry like a shirt.

'Barbarians.' Hildegard sighed. 'It seems a shame to kill a creature of such grace and beauty when there's no need.'

'Dangerous, though, with winter coming on,' Thomas replied.

Hildegard had no idea why she had been summoned out of her grange at Meaux to attend the archbishop. In August King Richard had announced his intention to summon a Parliament at Westminster. From all parts of the realm dukes and earls, barons and burgesses, and every shire knight with a piece of land to his name were forced to set out to reach Westminster for the first day of October.

The Abbot of Meaux, Hubert de Courcy, had sounded serious when he informed Hildegard of the archbishop's decision. 'Don't ask me why he wants you to go. He'll have to tell you himself. I hope you'll take care on that long journey.'

Now, having crossed the Humber and being well on the road towards Lincoln, where they were to spend a few days with Bishop Buckingham, she was no wiser.

It was on the following morning, after the first night's stop in a clearing by the roadside, with Thomas riding beside her picking hazelnuts as they passed, that a smartly dressed indoor servant came out from the verge as if he had been waiting for them. He drew his horse up in front of their own forcing them to a stop.

'Domina, I beg leave to speak.'

'Please do,' she replied.

'His Grace invites you to travel in his char with your priest.' He turned to include Thomas. 'Ride on and I'll come with you to take your horses when you dismount.'

Thomas beamed. 'What's made him ask for us?'

The servant disdained the young monk's gaucherie with a flick of his hair and murmured, 'I'm sure His Grace will enlighten you, Brother, you may be sure of that.'

He rode alongside Hildegard for a little way, long enough to tell her he was the archbishop's secretary, Edwin Westwode. Dressed in a dark tunic, he wore a wide belt with a leather bag hanging from it. There was a writing box tied to the pommel of his saddle. His hair was thick and hung in the latest fashion as far as his shoulders. She noticed his habit of flicking it back every now and then in a languid and courtly manner, even when it wasn't in his eyes. After he spoke his horse gained speed to take the lead and she and Thomas followed him to the front of the swiftly moving wagon train until they reached the four-horse char of the archbishop. A halt was called while steps were put in position to allow them to climb aboard.

Inside it was as well appointed as Hildegard had expected. Metal hoops supported a leather canopy to keep out the rain, and instead of having to sit on an uncomfortable wooden bench as they bumped along as in the other wagons, there was a padded platform piled with cushions and furs.

The archbishop reclined there now with a goblet in one hand and an enamelled silver dish containing sweetmeats on his lap.

He beckoned them inside. 'May as well travel in comfort,' he greeted, and while they found space on the cushions he started to talk of this and that: the weather, fine enough though the wind was strengthening; the misery of the Selby monks at having to suffer the same punishment as themselves over the papal taxes; the harvest, good; wool yield up, and so forth, requiring little more than the occasional nod of agreement from them.

At one point he leant forward. 'I am not unmindful that a member of my household has met with an accident. A Mass will be said for the fellow. His body decently buried. His wife provided for.'

Relieved to hear it, Hildegard replied, 'To judge by what your servants say about him, he was a devout and honest man. But how he came to be in the brewhouse is some kind of a mystery, isn't it?'

The archbishop crossed himself. 'I believe we can trust my men to sort it out before we return north.'

He closed his eyes. They carried on for some miles in silence. It was certainly more comfortable in the well-padded char than on horseback. The regular rhythm as it bounced along was soporific. Hildegard felt Thomas lolling more heavily beside her. Neville himself was lying back among his furs, to all appearances asleep.

He was about forty, heavy-jowled, unbearded, florid of complexion. His air of authority had his staff jumping to obey. He seemed well liked. The only doubt she had was about his allegiance. They were living in a time of faction. The Great Rebellion was scarcely five years away. Memories were not so short that people had forgotten the bloody aftermath of that event. Feelings still ran deep. The perpetrators of judicial violence continued to hold power. It was a sure thing that even now choices had to be made.

Impatient to find out why she had been prised out of her cloister and summoned to London, Hildegard leant forward to see if it would be advisable to wake him, but the rustling of her cushion must have alerted him because he opened his eyes, glanced across at Thomas, and whispered, 'Get rid of your priest, Domina. I have something to impart which you may not bother to confess to him. I take it he is your confessor?'

'Indeed, yes, Your Grace, and to be trusted—'

'Not with this.'

Hildegard felt her mouth open in astonishment. 'But Your Grace—' she whispered to match his own discretion.

'Do as I say.'

Hildegard gave Thomas a nudge. He woke with a start and looked round, dazed, before pulling himself together.

'Thomas,' she asked, 'would you care to go along to the sumpter cart to replenish His Grace's wine flagon?'

When they were alone the archbishop spoke in an undertone. 'I know you trust him but he's one of Abbot de Courcy's men. These are dangerous times, Domina. The French monasteries are unreliable.' He fixed her with a hard glance. 'You understand me?'

'I'm as aware of the French threat as everyone else.'

He nodded. 'Your prioress at Swyne – my sister in blood – has used you in the past on secret business. Now she commends you to me.'

'Commends?'

'Most strongly, although not without a warning to have regard for your safety.'

'I'm just a nun with no useful skills or connections—'

He cut her off. 'You are loyal.'

'Of course I am.' She held his glance.

He regarded her steadily for a few moments while she, in her turn, tried to work out which of the many rumours circulating about him were true. His lands were surrounded by those of the Duke of Lancaster, which might mean he saw it as prudent to regard his neighbour as his ally. His own brother, in fact, was married to one of the Duke's cousins. On the other hand the prioress was his sister, as he had just reminded her, and she was well known for her support for the young King. The bitterness

28

between the two sides of the royal family was well known. The Lancasters were active in drawing allegiance to themselves. They had allies in every corner of the realm, not just in the north, and they had active supporters at court.

'The kingdom is at a dangerous crossroads,' Neville warned when he eventually spoke. 'Apart from factional interests threatening to tear the country apart we're in immediate danger of invasion. That young hothead, King Charles, together with the support of his French dukes, has been rearming ever since he signed the last truce. We, on the other hand, have not. We're unarmed and vulnerable.' He gazed angrily into his wine goblet. 'Taxes have been squandered on inconclusive skirmishes against the Scots when they should have been directed to our southern defences. The French know this. They see us as a ripe plum, ready for plucking.'

'And you believe they really intend to invade?' There had been rumours all year about the build-up of French forces along the coast of Picardie but so far their ships had shown no sign of leaving port.

'They've delayed throughout the summer months, that's true, but our informers tell us it's because their Spanish allies are still bringing their ships up the narrow seas to Sluys to join the French fleet. The Constable of France is having a ship built that's bigger than anything ever seen before. There are other signs of their readiness. We'd be fools to ignore them.' He frowned. 'The question is, will Parliament grant King Richard the money to pay for our defence? The rumour is it will not. Lancaster's son, Harry Bolingbroke, the Earl of Derby, and his uncle the Duke of Gloucester, are refusing to grant permission to raise taxes. This is why we're being called to Westminster. The King will have to plead with them to vote for sufficient resources to defend the realm. And you can be sure,' he warned, 'his enemies will pack both chambers with placemen in order to defeat him.'

'You mean they'll vote as they're paid to vote? But if they do defeat the King and leave us undefended the French will swoop.'

'There are rumours . . .' he frowned. 'It's not merely a question of raising a war fund. The King has personal enemies. Members of his own family. They want nothing more than to get rid of him. The fear is this: they may use the invasion as a way of ridding themselves of him once and for all.'

'What do you mean?'

'They will use the invasion as a pretext.'

'A pretext . . . ?'

He gave her a long stare. 'You recall what happened to King Jean of France after we captured him and put him up for ransom?'

'Why yes, everyone knows. He was held for twenty years and died in the royal apartments in the Tower of London simply because the French dukes would not pay up.'

The archbishop was silent.

Hildegard could only stare. 'You mean there's a plot

to exchange Richard for the price of peace? To allow the French to hold him to ransom – and never redeem him?'

Neville nodded.

'But that would be diabolical.'

'Indeed.'

'First he would have to lead an army into France. And this is precisely the course of action they seem to want to block by refusing to grant him the funds . . .'

He gave a humourless smile. 'There are other ways of offering a king for barter.'

Neville was staring hard at her as if trying to read her thoughts. 'All I require of you,' he murmured in an urgent undertone, 'is your observing eye when we reach London. It's a cesspit of conspiracy. Plot and counterplot prevail. If we're to survive we need to know who our enemies are, the ones who work in darkness against the realm.'

He lowered his voice further. 'There are names at court you will need to learn. Medford. Slake. Several others. They may mean nothing now but they'll come to mean more over the next few weeks. They're attached to the Signet Office. Mr Medford is King Richard's personal secretary. He has use of his Signet, the royal seal, without which no business can be conducted. It bestows great power on him. Remember that.'

She made a mental note of both names. 'Is their loyalty in question?'

Neville leant back. He made no answer. 'There's more—' With some abruptness he changed the subject. 'I understand you know something of herbal lore, Domina?'

'A little,' she admitted, startled by his sudden change of topic. Then she heard a noise outside.

His expression had not altered. 'There's a curious garden outside the city walls at a vill called Stepney. You may care to visit it while we're down there. See if you can find a cure for my arthritis.'

He raised his voice a fraction and now she glimpsed a shadow behind the swinging flap at the entrance.

'They say the Dominican who runs it grows over two hundred different kinds of herbs,' he continued smoothly. 'I can imagine he supplies most of the city's apothecaries with cures and the necromancers too. An extraordinary idea, don't you think, to grow plants for the purpose of commerce – oh, there you are, my dear brother. My thanks.'

He reached for the flagon Thomas was holding out, refilled all their goblets despite the lurching of the char and raised his own. 'The King!'

So I'm to be his spy at Westminster, Hildegard said to herself. What an unexpected commission. There was a lot more she needed to know before she would be content with the situation.

They were in Lincolnshire now with many miles still to go.

Thomas sounded as puzzled as everyone else. 'They're still wondering how Martin got himself into the vat of ale,' he told her, having just come from a walk around the wagons when they stopped beside the road.

Hildegard had heard them talk too. 'He had had no reason to be there in the brewhouse. It wasn't his job to interfere with the work of the brewers. That little pot boy shouldn't have been there, either. What was he up to?'

'Kicking a pig's bladder around. Those lads are always being chased out of there, I'm told. They say it's the only level floor.'

'Presumably he thought he'd have a scoop of ale while his elders were out of the way.'

'He won't be doing that again in a hurry.'

'As for Martin,' she continued, as he'd raised the subject, 'what do they say he was up to?'

'No ideas. They can't make it out.'

'He must have been leaning over the side of the vat and lost his balance. I still don't understand what he would be doing in there. It makes no sense. Not when we were just about to set off.'

There was a lot to see that was new on the journey down into the southern shires. It pushed to one side fruitless speculation about the activities of one unlucky kitchener.

On the road. Evening. A woodland clearing.

The wagons drew up in a circle away from overhanging branches and a cooking fire was built in the middle. Fulford had his chair brought out so he could preside over the preparations. Tonight they were roasting a hind. It was skewered on a spit. The flames sizzled over the dripping meat sending the smell of burning flesh into the air. Sparks flew up and fell back like dying stars. The sky darkened.

The men, their faces glowing in the firelight, seemed to edge closer together as if threatened by something unknown beyond the perimeter of light.

Usually when they stopped to rest and the men went off into the woods for a piss they would return with whatever they could forage. Some were coming back now, breaking into the circle of light, throwing down their findings – toadstools, crisp and sweet, thrown into the pot; a rabbit, quickly gutted, thrown in after them. One man had an arm full of herbs and threw those down but Fulford stopped them from going in before he had had a proper look at them.

'What's that, rat fodder?' somebody quipped.

'Piss off,' the man said good-humouredly to a few cackles from the rest of them. He walked with a kind of swagger to where the falconers were sitting. They made room for him without comment.

Forty people fed. Forty-one including the archbishop, who sat alone on the running board of his char, deep in thought, wearing his black wool night-cloak. His page sat cross-legged on the ground in his own little cloak, a wooden bowl filled for a third time on his lap.

The men. Eating like wolves. Made ravenous by the long miles.

Everything soon done. Ale finished. A song or two bawled into the night.

The others were getting up, like Hildegard, to make for their own private sleeping corners. Under a wagon. Inside a wagon if they were lucky. As they went, somebody happened to mention Martin again.

It was almost too soon to reminisce. She guessed they were still coming to terms with his death and after the first bout of questions there was a strange kind of silence over the matter. They were too shocked, she supposed. Later they would start to question again the how and the why such an accident could occur.

One of the falconers left the group and went over to the caged hawks. She heard Fulford ask, 'Is he all right?'

'Leave him, master.'

'It's this talk about Martin that's getting to him,' somebody explained.

'He's hit hard.'

'They were mates.'

'Always ready for a laugh, was Martin.'

'Not recently. He must have had a premonition. Remember that time he could only throw "ones" and somebody said "your luck's gone, fella", and he nearly throttled him?'

Hildegard said her goodnights then went over to climb into her sleeping space in one of the small baggage wagons. She was just drifting off to sleep when she heard a group of men walking slowly past. Voices clear on the still night air. Conversation had turned to London. It was the first time down there for most of them. They had no idea what to expect.

'They say the streets are paved with gold, don't they? Do you believe it?'

'Nah, paved might be true. With gold? Never.'

'Maybe one or two, outside the palaces?'

'Outside the Duke of Lancaster's, maybe.'

'I bet King Dickon walks on gold.'

She heard a third voice. 'Aye, at our expense.'

'You don't like Dickon, do you, Jarrold?'

'Why should I? What's he ever done for me?'

'He's well enough.'

'God save him, say I.'

Murmurs of agreement followed. Their voices faded.

After that Hildegard drifted off to the sound of distant snores, the clink of metal as the guard shifted at his post, and that strange wrenching sound as horses crop grass.

By now they were travelling through a landscape that was flat and bleak, a no man's land, with mile after mile of nothing but scrubland, the straight Roman road cutting through it, and a huge sky full of curlews.

The huntsmen began to grumble. They wanted to bring down some game. The archers strung their bows. They wanted wolves.

The skin of the one shot before they left Holderness was dry now. It hung from its pole and the head, boiled in cummin as a favour by Master Fulford, gazed sightlessly towards their destination. The drivers geed their horses and made the wagons bounce on the track in their eagerness to reach somewhere more interesting.

'Woodland up ahead,' somebody muttered at last, staring hard at the skyline to the south after a few more uneventful miles. 'We'll get sport there, enough at least to fill our bellies.' There were grunts of agreement. Somebody peeled off to the wagon carrying the sheaves of arrows to prepare to bring them out.

The dogs in their wicker cage whined with frustration.

The woods were a dark blur from one side of the road to the other and there was a cheer when the chamberlain called a halt.

Holding up his white stick so everybody could see he had something to say, he bellowed, 'It's not for your benefit. His Grace wishes to stretch his legs!' He turned to the kennelman. 'Might as well get a brace of those dogs out, see if you can raise a few rabbits?'

'We flying the hawks, sire?'

The chamberlain shook his head. 'Not unless you want to follow on foot to Lincoln. This is a short stop. We aim to be there before nightfall.'

The long line of wagons squeezed up one by one as the command to halt was passed down the line and eventually, with a creaking of harness, the whole convoy groaned to a stop. Several people jumped down at once, following the archbishop's example, and walked about, stretching their legs and trying to ease the aches out of bruised joints, while others leant wearily against the wheels of the carts they had been forced to run alongside. Someone produced a reed pipe and struck up a tune, bringing several cheerful souls to stamp their feet in a rough-and-ready jig.

A couple of huntsmen whistled up the dogs as they

were released from their cage and led them purposefully towards the woods.

The archbishop looked round for his master of horse. 'Bring Pegasus up, will you? I'll ride into Lincoln. It's not far now.'

While he waited he glanced up at the sky as if checking for rain. It was awash with flat grey cloud from one side of the horizon to the other, but with a fresh wind from the coast that had been blowing for several days now, keeping the rain off.

Hildegard saw him scrutinise the convoy spread back along the narrow road. There was a ditch on one side full of water, a clump of trees, then miles of empty moorland. His cook, from the canopied comfort of his wagon, was ordering parcels of bread and cheese from the vittling cart behind and a few servants were scurrying along handing it out to a forest of eager hands.

Hildegard watched all this with a mind as empty as the sky, thinking, Lord I'm tired, I wish we were there. Munching on her own portion of bread and cheese, she wandered over to have a look at the hounds. Her own two, Duchess and Bermonda, too old to travel, had been left behind in the kennels at Meaux. She ruffled the heads poking between the bars. 'Is anybody going to let the rest of them have a run?' she asked the kennelman.

'We're not stopping long. Chamberlain says it's only to give the lads a chance to raise a few rabbits while His Grace stretches his legs. '

Hildegard was about to return some bantering remark

when there was a shout up ahead followed by more shouts from the tail end of the line. An oath followed and some further altercation that ended in a howl of pain. Out of the corner of her eye she saw the cook, Master Fulford, rise magnificently to his feet on the running board of his char only to sink down again as an arrow winged past his head.

A voice somewhere in the thick of the commotion shouted, 'Nobody move unless you want your throat slit. This won't take long.'

There was a jangling of chain mail, more cries, stifled this time, and then a sudden ominous silence over the entire convoy as three crossbowmen rose from the ditch beside the road followed by two foot soldiers in chain mail.

Hildegard, caught between the dog cart and the one next to it, craned her neck to see what was happening. Word was filtering back that the wagons were being searched.

'By whom?' she asked a man standing next to her.

'Dunno. Some armed band it looks like.'

'Whose insignia do they wear?'

'None so far as I can see.'

The man climbed onto the running-board of the wagon loaded with arrow sheaves and peered back down the line. 'They're chucking things out onto the road,' he reported. 'They seem to be looking for something.'

Just then Hildegard turned her head and to her astonishment saw the archbishop being helped into the saddle by his groom. He was carrying a leather bag under one arm and as she watched he kicked his horse on and vanished soundlessly into a brake beside the track. No one else seemed to have noticed.

Meanwhile the wagons were being searched one by one, all the carefully packed stores hurled out, the chamberlain wringing his hands and making polite protests, the master cook growing redder in the face and saying nothing. The chamberlain turned to the members of his household. 'I advise everyone to do as we're told until we find out what these fellows want.'

His surprising lack of resistance was the result of having a crossbowman aiming an arrow straight at him from a hand's breadth away.

There was a subdued grumbling, but with another couple of bowmen coming into view, it was enough to make everybody do as he suggested.

'What are the archbishop's bodyguard doing?' Hildegard whispered to the man on the running-board beside her.

'Bugger all,' he growled.

She noticed the hunting bow slung across his chest and indicated the sheaves of arrows in the wagon. 'Can we work our way round behind their line without being seen?'

He showed his teeth in a grin. 'We'll have a bloody good try.' He slipped quietly down off the wagon. 'I'll get a couple of the lads.'

No one was paying any attention to the middle of the convoy, cowed into submission by the one bowman. The looters, with short swords raised, and protected by the other bows, were laboriously working their way towards the centre while their commander, his face concealed by the nosepiece of his helmet, sat astride a grey destrier and looked on.

Hildegard reached for one of the bows used by the pages. They were shorter than the hunting bows the bodyguards carried. There was no way she would have been able to draw one of those. She found the strings and took one out and, snatching up a few arrows from the sheaf, strung the bow as she followed three archers into the gully beside the road. They began to work their way behind the line of wagons. Once under the cover of the trees, the men spread out.

Hildegard edged further into the trees with the intention of coming out behind the crossbowman with his bolt aimed at the chamberlain. After that she had no idea what the plan was, maybe to give the impression that the men were surrounded in the hope it would scare them off.

She found a vantage point with a good view of the chamberlain's wagon. The crossbowman was half concealed by the trunk of an oak, clearly expecting to be safe from retaliation. His broad back was an easy target. I must not draw blood, she reminded herself.

She tightened the string, fixed the nock of an arrow into place, drew back and sighted the target. A long time had elapsed since she had handled a bow.

Pull, aim, release.

That had been Ulf's teaching in the old days at Castle Hutton during the long hours when he had made her practise at the butts.

She saw the others get into position then waited for the signal.

It came.

Pull. Aim. Release.

She did so.

There was a grunt from the man behind the tree. He jerked his head round to find himself pinned by the sleeve of his chain mail to the trunk of the oak.

There was a chuckle behind her. 'Neat work for a nun.'

She turned. It was the man she had spoken to earlier.

'There's no way he can get out of that without dragging his hauberk off,' he chuckled again.

Then he drew his great hunting bow and aimed.

The power of the longbow meant it could cut through mail and even through plate armour. It was the instrument of war that had led to England's victories at Crécy and Poitiers against far greater odds of mounted militia. Hildegard was well aware of all that.

The bowman, so neatly pinned by her small bow without bloodshed, finished up clutching an arrow that pierced his steel shirt and reappeared through the front in the middle of his chest. He staggered, looking down in astonishment at the arrow tip between his fingers. Then blood gushed from his mouth and he toppled forward.

The other bowmen were dispatched with no more than the loss of an arrow apiece. As the last one fell, the men-at-arms penned in their cart by the looters erupted with a roar, snatched up their weapons from the armoury wagon and turned to attack the horsemen.

In the melee that followed Hildegard searched for a sight of Thomas and Edwin. The last she had seen of them was when they jumped down from the char to walk back along the line towards the tail end to see what was happening. Now she glimpsed a flash of white and saw Thomas, unarmed except for a hazel switch, staring up at a horseman whose sword was arching towards him.

Hildegard had automatically slipped an arrow into its notch and now, without thought but with a whispered, 'Forgive me', lifted her bow and loosed an arrow into the nearside shoulder of the swordsman's horse. It reared with a scream of agony as the arrow hit. When it fell it toppled onto its rider, who scrambled to escape. A nearby man-at-arms finished the job. The body was kicked into the ditch.

Hildegard closed her eyes. When she opened them Thomas was rushing to the aid of one of the kitcheners, lashing out with his hazel stick at the face of his assailant and managing to hook his fingers into the servant's belt to haul him out of harm's way.

In a hand-to-hand skirmish with the now armed bodyguard the attackers were beaten back. Their leader had already ridden off and one by one the survivors streaked after him across the wasteland and into the woods.

The York captain roared at his men to fall back.

'Too late now, you losels! Save your arrows! From now on you keep a proper lookout.'

There were some cuts and bloody noses but nothing serious. The attackers had abandoned their dead and wounded and the captain ordered his men to find the one least likely to die and have him bound in ropes and brought along as a hostage. The man was barely conscious but he was dragged off, groaning in pain, to the back of the convoy and thrown roughly onto a cart among the spare wheels.

It was all over by the time the two huntsmen who had gone off earlier emerged from the woods carrying a dozen or so rabbits on poles across their shoulders. They looked askance at the partially unloaded carts.

'I thought we weren't stopping?' one of them asked.

When they were told what had happened they said they were sorry they'd missed the fun. One of them added that they had heard horsemen crashing about in the woods and thought it was a local hunting party and best to give it a wide berth.

'Who the hell were they?' asked Edwin while everything was being packed in again. Nobody knew.

'There's that manor over at Kettlethorpe,' somebody suggested. 'On the rampage from there, you reckon?'

'I don't see what they were after. They didn't take so much as a crust.'

'We'll get the truth from that hostage,' the captain

snarled. 'Meanwhile,' he turned to his men, 'sharpen up unless you want your ears off. We're not on a bloody pilgrimage.'

It had all happened too suddenly for the kitcheners, who were unused to anything more violent than a pan whizzing past their heads in the palace kitchens at Bishopthorpe. There were white faces. An air of faintness. No one said much.

The chamberlain returned to his char and sat within, fanning himself with his sleeve. When he asked for news of the archbishop, a servant came back looking puzzled. 'Gone on ahead, My Lord.'

The chamberlain closed his eyes and it was Master Fulford who rose to the occasion.

'Break out the ale, Gufrid. We'll catch up with him. Meanwhile let's stiffen our sinews, then back on the road to Lincoln.'

The archbishop was waiting for them on the far side of some woodland astride his horse Pegasus, with the leather bag strapped across his chest. He offered no explanation for his escape as he handed the reins to his groom.

Edwin, climbing back into the char after him, spoke with a tinge of disapproval in his voice. 'I trust Your Grace is unharmed?'

Neville growled a response and they travelled on in an uneasy silence.

Edwin had shown himself to be useful with his sword

and when Hildegard made a remark to that effect he nodded. 'Why do you think I was thrown out of Oxford?' He looked quietly pleased with himself.

Licking his cuts, Thomas cuffed Hildegard on the shoulder. 'I didn't know you'd been keeping up the old skill. I'm in your debt.'

'Nonsense, Thomas. I'm truly distressed that men were killed. Even if they did invite a tough response. And the poor horse . . .' she shuddered.

'I saw it gallop off after the survivors,' he told her. 'Those boys' bows don't penetrate deep tissue.'

This mollified her somewhat but the fate of their attackers preyed on her mind. As did the reason for their ambush and Alexander Neville's uncharacteristic flight.

They thundered on towards their destination and it was shortly before curfew when they poured at last through Lincoln's northern gate on Ermine Street into the narrow cobbled lane leading to the bishop's enclave. With the archbishop, true to his original intention, riding at their head on Pegasus, they filled the town with the noise and excitement of their arrival.

Judging by the number of armed guards patrolling the city walls and visible at the top of the great keep on its hill above the town, the whole place was on high alert.

'News of the invasion?' asked their own constable, taking in the presence of the militia as soon as he arrived. He stood alongside the city guards and counted everybody in.

'Nothing fresh. It seems King Charles is having to wait for the Spanish to bring all their ships up.'

Then the attack on the York contingent came out and men were roused from the guardhouse to get out after them, more as a show of goodwill to the visitors than in the hope of stumbling across the band, for they would be long gone by now. The hostage was thrown into the castle jail for the night until he recovered enough to denounce his comrades.

Unable to talk confidentially to Thomas in the turmoil of carrying in their baggage, Hildegard looked for a chance as soon as they were being conducted towards their separate quarters. They were lodged in the guest house across the garth from the bishop's palatial abode, with the large Saxon hall between.

She tugged urgently at his sleeve. 'Has anybody said anything to you about why we've been asked along?'

'By "anybody" I suppose you mean Hubert?' Thomas gave a wry smile. 'Whatever the abbot might know he would surely have told you above anybody.'

'I need to know, Thomas.'

He became serious. 'Rest assured, Hildegard, I would tell you if there was anything to tell.'

'Even if you were sworn to secrecy?'

He took her arm and turned her aside from the toing and froing of servants bringing in the baggage. 'Do you suspect some secret motive?'

His grey eyes were as guileless as a child's.

'I wondered if you'd heard anything?'

'Only that you have knowledge of herbal lore. Hubert mentioned something along those lines. Not that I asked. It's not my business.' He smiled down kindly. 'No one's sworn me to secrecy. There are no secrets. Even the archbishop's arthritis is known to every soul in the shire. I'm here to be your shadow wherever you go. You can trust me.' He smiled reassuringly. 'I expect that ambush has made you uneasy? I believe it was merely a chance attack.' He watched her closely. 'Do you think there's more to it?'

Chapter Two

Lincoln. The bishop's enclave. Early morning. Rain.
They were scarcely out of prime when a messenger arrived. His horse came splashing into the foregate, and by the time everyone had turned to stare, a man in Neville's livery was tumbling from the saddle. A group of excited servants hurried him towards the guest quarters.

Hildegard was called into the archbishop's audience chamber after the messenger was sent down to the kitchens for a reward of cheese and ale. She was joined by Edwin and Thomas.

Neville began without preamble. 'It seems that my unfortunate kitchener did not drown as we believed, or, at least, not before receiving a blow to the back of the head.' He glowered at the three of them. 'What d'you make of that?'

Edwin bit his lip.

'An accident?' offered Thomas tentatively. 'He hit his head on the side of the vat, maybe?'

Neville raised his eyebrows.

Hildegard spoke up. 'It sounds to me like foul play.'

Neville was grim-faced. 'And so it sounds to me as well. My bailiff has questioned the few servants who remain behind. He has decided not to mention that he found a stout stick lying in the herb beds not far from the door of the brewhouse until he has learnt more. So you're right, Domina. Indubitably foul play.'

Edwin spoke up. He sounded shocked. 'Somebody hit the fellow on the head with the stick, then tried to dispose of his body in the vat?'

They glanced at each other. But Neville continued. 'What you're going to do, Edwin, is look at this list here and tell me what you think.'

He handed the clerk a piece of vellum with the seal of the Bishopthorpe bailiff dangling from it. Edwin scanned it and looked up. 'These are the old servants who stayed behind at the palace, Your Grace.'

'They are indeed. And when you call them old you're right again. Can you imagine any of them picking up a club and bludgeoning a man to death with it?'

Edwin threw his head back and gave a musical laugh. It relieved the tension. 'Only with the greatest difficulty, Your Grace.'

'You think it a ridiculous idea?'

'I do.'

'So do I. And it suggests one thing: the man's assailant must be one of these blackguards here and now in Lincoln skulking in my retinue. Now . . .' He took the piece of vellum, screwed it up into the shape of a dagger and stabbed it angrily at the air to emphasise his words. '. . . the second thing you're going to do,' his voice rose, 'is question every man we have with us!'

'Every single man?' gasped Edwin.

'Yes,' he snarled. 'I want to know who was where and when and why. You'll be helped by the domina and her priest.' He glared at Hildegard and Brother Thomas, who flinched. 'The three of you can comb through their lies and find the fellow without a plausible story. We do not leave Lincoln until the matter is resolved!'

He turned with a furious rustle of embroidered brocade. 'He's here. He's got to be. It's one of these lying devils. I want him nailed forthwith. And, I do not need to remind any of you' – he paused ominously – 'the words "blow to the head" or "murder" will not pass your lips. Let them put two and two together. The one who makes four is our man.'

Shrugging his cope into place he raged out.

'Well, well,' said Edwin glancing at the two monastics. 'This is a turn-up. I can still hardly believe it. In the palace of all places!'

'We'd better start now if we want to get to Westminster,' Hildegard suggested.

'Who are we going to call first?'

'We could start with your head cook, Master Fulford. He should know exactly where everybody was.'

'After him I suggest the cook's clerk, to check that their

versions tally, then the brewmaster and the baker.' He added, 'We'll give them all a good going-over. The bailiff must have done the same at Bishopthorpe with what's left of the staff up there.'

'They're going to guess something's up,' muttered Thomas as they took their places.

Rain was blowing in through the eye slits. It was a miserable day and not a good one for travel. The bishop's yeoman of the chamber ordered his underlings to light a fire for them. 'Useful things these fireplaces,' he murmured as he went about his task. 'I don't know what we did without them.' Thomas went over to warm his hands when he left.

Word had been put out that Master Fulford was required to attend His Grace's clerk in the privy chamber next to the guest hall. They took their places on a bench close to the hearth with another bench placed opposite to give them a good view of those they called. They were just waiting for Fulford to show up when Edwin eyed Hildegard and Thomas in a somewhat cynical manner. 'I hope you two are ready for a pack of lies?'

'It's everyday life for us,' replied Thomas, unperturbed. 'You've no idea the lies they tell us in the hope of gaining pardon by the back door. As if their sins are not already known!' He sighed and looked as if he was about to enlarge on the subject.

Hildegard was used to this. She turned quickly to Edwin. 'While we wait for the archbishop's cook, why don't you tell us something about him?' She recalled the red-faced, angry-looking fellow who had almost swamped his fellow travellers in the wagon reserved for himself and other members of his kitchens.

Edwin looked pleased to tell what he knew. 'Of the lot of them I'd take his word first. He's been with His Grace for about twenty years. Stuck with him through thick and thin. I expect they get on because they both have vile tempers. It allows them to understand each other. I'm surprised neither of you two have been bawled out by His Grace yet.' He raised his eyebrows. 'Maybe it's the power of your Order that makes him rein in the worst of it.'

'I'd like to see him shouting at Hildegard,' said Thomas.

Edwin gave her a sidelong glance. 'Anyway,' he continued, 'Fulford, despite his rages, has acquired a measure of respect. Maybe it's the nature of his calling. There's no quicker way to men's hearts than through their bellies, as they say, and he knows what he's doing in that department. He's a real craftsman. A taskmaster, true, but fair-minded after he's let fly.'

'"Let fly"?' asked Thomas with interest.

Edwin nodded. 'Anything that comes to hand.'

'We had a cook at Meaux like that but he seems to have calmed down since the abbot took him aside.'

Hildegard looked impatiently towards the door.

Edwin continued. 'Fulford prides himself on it – "I tell them what for" and "I speak as I find". They call it talking plain. He's just an old Saxon, of course.' He made a dismissive gesture with one hand. 'Be that as it may, he runs a tight ship. No complaints from His Grace.

And when people come to work for him they tend to stay. Nothing much else to say about him. Unmarried, of course. His work is his life. His kitcheners are his family.'

'Can you see him hitting anybody over the back of the head?'

'Never. No matter how riled he was.'

'Where's he from originally?'

'Some village near York. He worked for the Bishop of Durham as an apprentice after a stint as a scullion with a York merchant when he was a lad back in the Dark Ages. He boasts he's never been further south than Doncaster.'

'Not even when His Grace was called to attend previous Parliaments?' Hildegard asked.

Edwin shook his head. 'Left to hold the reins at Bishopthorpe. This time His Grace insisted. Something to do with putting up a good table for guests in Westminster.'

'With his commitment to His Grace, then, his testimony should be reliable.'

'I'm prepared to trust it.'

A page boy poked his head round the door. 'The master of the kitchens approaches.' He bobbed back out of sight.

A few moments later Fulford hove into view. He addressed the two men as if Hildegard were invisible.

She didn't mind, of course. It was a lesson in humility and gave her chance to observe the cook more closely than she would otherwise have been able.

She noticed how he groped around behind him to find the bench before settling his vast bottom on it, and once firmly seated, began folding and unfolding his hands until eventually they found a resting place on his paunch. He was breathing hard as if having run up a flight of stairs. She couldn't imagine him being able to hit a man. No wonder he threw things instead.

Edwin opened the questions with an invitation to tell them when he had last seen Martin. 'We're just trying to establish how he came to fall into the vat,' he explained.

'I can't rightly remember when I saw him,' Fulford admitted. 'We were run off our feet that morning. I know I saw him near the wagons at one point. Mebbe putting his stuff on board.' He shrugged apologetically. 'There was more on my mind than the whereabouts of one servant.'

'Don't know, then,' Edwin made a note. When he stopped scratching his quill over the vellum, he asked Fulford to explain where everyone was meant to be from matins to prime on the day they left the purlieus of Bishopthorpe. The dead man had been found just after prime when they all came out of the service and assembled in the main courtyard ready to leave.

'And so they were,' replied Fulford. 'Remember, we had all that tomfoolery with the Pope's man and his vultures, counting heads?'

'Run us through everybody's movements, then.'

'At matins they'd still be in their beds. No necessity to go and pray at that time of night. We're not monks.' He bowed his head courteously towards Brother Thomas.

'I can verify that none of the kitchen staff was in church at matins,' agreed Thomas. 'In fact there was just myself, His Grace and his acolyte, the sacristan, a priest from—'

'We'll get your testimony later, Brother, if you don't mind,' Edwin cut in. He turned back to the cook. 'The period of time we're more interested in is after that, closer to prime itself. Your staff must have been up and about by then. What time do they rise?'

'The bakers are on with their bread before first light. My clerk personally assigns the tasks as I've instructed the day before. On a normal day he makes sure all the produce is checked in and everybody's allotted their duties—'

'That's on a normal day. Was this day what you'd call normal?'

'No, it wasn't. Anything but normal. There was no call for our usual fare that day. It was all vittles to be carried and eaten on the road, most of it prepared and packed previous, like. Cheese, dried fish. All except for the bread, of course.'

'Tell us more.'

'The only place functioning was the bakehouse. It was going full blast. You can't have any idea how much bread folk eat, and it takes a lot of organisation to get enough for forty on a journey of near on three hundred miles not knowing when we'll be able to get fresh bread again. We buy it in when we can, of course, but it all takes planning.'

He sat back with his hands clasped over his stomach and a look of challenge on his face.

Edwin nodded. 'I'm sure your skills are up to it, master. So,' he continued, 'the bakehouse going full blast. Everybody else still in their beds. What I'd like to know is who was in the bakehouse at this point? Who was first in?'

Fulford ticked them off. 'Kitchen lad to stoke the fire, couple of spit boys, under-baker and his two assistants, pot boy.'

'The bakehouse adjoins the brewhouse where the body was found,' Edwin explained in an aside to Hildegard and Thomas.

'So who was in the brewhouse?' she asked.

'Nobody had any need to be in the brewhouse.' The master cook was emphatic but he addressed Edwin. 'We'd already loaded the casks of ale the night before. There was nothing in there for anybody. The mash could be left to do its job by itself.'

'I do apologise for asking this but I'm a stranger to Bishopthorpe. Can you tell me where exactly the brewhouse is in relation to the bakehouse?' Hildegard asked.

Fulford addressed his answer to Brother Thomas. 'The bakehouse and the brewhouse are one linked building. There's a wall inside to separate one from the other. You go in over the small footbridge across the stream. It takes you in through the main door into the bakehouse. From there you go under an arch on your left and on into where they do the brewing.'

'And how do you approach the bridge over the stream?'

Again the same avoidance of her glance, his eyes fixed on the monk. 'You come at it down a path behind the infirmary. It takes you past the herb gardens across the side of the bakehouse and round the front. As I say, there's a little wooden bridge over the stream – it's no more than a sluice. The bridge leads you right in through the main door and you turn left if you want the clerk's office, otherwise you're right there.'

'Is that the only way in?'

He fixed Thomas with a firm glance. 'There are another couple of doors,' he admitted with a sidelong glance at Hildegard as if afraid she had almost caught him out. 'One is the brewmaster's chamber and the other leads into the brewhouse from the herb enclosure. But it's private. It's for the use of the brewmaster and nobody else.'

'But anybody could enter through the enclosure, into the brewhouse itself, without coming in by the main door over the sluice?'

'No, definitely not. It's forbidden. Unless you want the brewmaster to say something to you.'

'Was he there that morning?' asked Edwin.

'As I said. He was overseeing the casks, marking them up and making sure his ale was fit for travel. He was with me in the yard from getting up until His Grace said Mass, and he was standing right next to me when the lad came shrieking out with the news.'

'To go back to the garden you mention,' said Hildegard. 'Is it overlooked?'

'Only from the infirmary windows – oh, and by anybody walking along the path.' Glance still averted.

Brother Thomas had a question. 'Where does the path go?'

'It continues towards the watermill – although there is a branch before that that'll take you up to the main gate.'

'And from there it joins the road the convoy took when we set out,' concluded Edwin. He glanced at the other two. 'Do you have any more questions for the moment, Domina?'

She shook her head.

'And you, Brother?'

Thomas frowned. 'Surely it would have been easy for somebody to go from the bakehouse through into the brewhouse at any time, wouldn't it?'

The master cook was emphatic. 'Not with my kitchen clerk overseeing matters. They'd have had to leave their stations, for one thing, and he wouldn't stand for that in working hours. Not without leave and with so much to be done before we set out. Definitely out of the question.'

'We need to talk to your kitchen clerk,' remarked Edwin.

'He'll say the same as me.'

'Are you suggesting, master, that we can discount your bakers altogether?' Thomas leant forward.

Fulford frowned. 'What exactly is this?' He looked from one to the other. When nobody answered his colour rose. 'Are we talking foul play here?'

He began to struggle to his feet. 'Now look here, if you think any of my lads are capable of . . .' He sat down again. After a moment he asked, 'What really happened to the poor devil? Are you going to tell me? Because if there's—'

'He drowned, as you know,' Edwin cut in. 'We simply want to find out how it happened. It strikes us as odd,' he continued, 'that nobody knows what he was doing in the brewhouse nor how he made his way there, whether alone or with someone. And of course,' he added, 'I have to prepare a report for the coroner.'

Looking doubtful, Fulford sat down heavily on his bench. 'So you're trying to work out how Martin got into the brewhouse without being seen? And why he bothered to go there in the first place?'

'That's about it,' agreed Edwin.

'Your guess is as good as mine.'

'I wonder,' Hildegard interjected, 'just for clarity, will you confirm that someone could have got into the brewhouse from the herb garden, whether forbidden to go in that way or not?'

'I'm confirming nothing.'

'Very well. But, from what you've just told us, the only conclusion to be drawn is this: in order to get inside the brewhouse through the master's private door, you'd have to approach by the path under the infirmary windows?'

Reluctantly he went on to agree that it would be easy to slip out through the back door of the main kitchens and take the path through the enclosure wall.

'And then, if you didn't want to be seen, all you'd have to worry about is a short walk under the windows?'

'Even then it's not likely you'd be noticed,' he reluctantly pointed out. 'Them windows is high up. You'd have to stand on tiptoe to see out, or be some kind of giant,' he added.

'Putting aside the question of giants, it must be possible for somebody to slip into the brewhouse unnoticed through the brewmaster's door, even when the bakehouse is going full swing?'

'Possible.'

Edwin looked pleased.

'Possible,' Fulford repeated. 'But forbidden.'

'You can leave us now, Master Fulford. Many thanks for your help.'

After the cook had heaved himself off his bench and before leaving the chamber he stood by the door with a fierce look. 'You think Martin was done in. It's not one of my lads. I'll lay my life on it. And if it is, I'll want to be the first to see him hang.'

After he'd gone Edwin said, 'Hell, it's like getting blood out of a stone. Now all we need to know is whether anybody saw Martin going off in that direction and whether he'd had words with anybody that morning. It's my bet he had a falling-out with someone and they followed him down to the brewhouse to show him what for.'

'That may be so, but why would he go sneaking in there by the back entrance anyway?' Hildegard still puzzled.

'His job could entail a visit to the herb gardens, I suppose,' Thomas contributed, 'but, you're right, why enter the brewhouse?'

'Unless to meet somebody in secret,' Hildegard suggested.

'It was all confusion that morning, with everybody preparing to leave for London,' Edwin pointed out. 'But they were all busy in the yard. It might have been the only empty place they could find if they wanted to settle something in private. He'd have had to carry his personal stuff from the lay brothers' dormitory to the wagons like the rest of us, so somebody will have noticed him.'

Edwin scribbled rapidly, the quill flying over the parchment with a harsh scratching sound. 'We'll find out,' he murmured.

Hildegard was frowning. 'Do you remember that argument over the number of people in the entourage? There was one more when they had a recount.'

'So the chamberlain wasn't wrong, after all. He was adamant there were only forty, as permitted. "I learnt to count when I was a babe in arms!" I heard him say.'

'There were forty before we went into Mass,' Thomas pointed out, 'and forty-one when we came out. Someone – I mean, the murderer – must have rejoined us then.'

The kitchen clerk entered as soon as the page announced him. In contrast to his master he was a thin harassed-looking individual with a groove-line of worry down his forehead and a habit of biting his bottom lip. It was clear from his manner that he knew he was going to be questioned about more than an accidental death.

Before anybody spoke he waved a vellum roll and said, 'It's all down here. Anything you want to know, it's here recorded. Who, where and when. That's my job. And you'll agree, Edwin, I know my job.'

'Indeed,' Edwin murmured. 'But it can't all be down there, can it?'

'Everything that happened that was above board.' He leant forward and mouthed, 'So it's true, he was done in?'

'We don't know. Why do you ask that?'

He looked confused. 'Master's said so just now. He's still out there trying to get his breath back. He's in a terrible state.'

'Well, he is right, insofar as we do have a few questions to ask. As he may have mentioned, I have a report to make. More than that we can't say.'

The kitchen clerk turned to Hildegard. 'Domina, permit me to read it to you—'

Edwin broke in. 'My gratitude, master, but that won't be necessary.' He eyed him as one professional to another. 'We'd be more than grateful if you'd leave your written testimony to one side for a moment and tell us in your own words what you remember of the morning in question.'

With the wind taken out of his sails the kitchen clerk glanced at his records then reluctantly stuffed them back inside his jerkin.

'You can let us have a look at them later. Pray proceed,' Edwin encouraged.

'Well, it's like this . . .' He paused as if at a loss now the written word had been forbidden him. 'We get up at the usual hour.'

'At what time?'

'You know what time, Edwin. You were there yourself, overseeing the archbishop's morning tisane as usual.'

'It's by his special request,' Edwin came back with some asperity.

'I'm saying nothing about it. I'm simply saying you were there. You must have seen everybody that came into the kitchens at that time.'

'I certainly didn't make notes. What about Martin? Let's keep to the point. Did you see him then or not?'

'He came in, yes. The bakers were just starting to bring their bread over. I remember breaking a piece off for you and you making some comment about not wanting the coals of hell in your gob. Anyway, Martin did come in. It was soon after you left.'

'Was he alone?' asked Hildegard.

'Aye. Alone. He took a lump of bread and made no untoward comment.'

'It had probably cooled somewhat by then?' suggested Thomas, automatically spreading oil on troubled waters.

'Aye, it would have. It would be not much later but enough for bread to cool.' The kitchen clerk gave them all a pitying look at wasting time with the obvious. 'Then the bread was loaded into wicker baskets to be stowed on racks in the sumpter wagon. Martin helped with that until I told him he didn't have to.'

'Why did he help you? Was it his job?' asked Hildegard.

'It wasn't. But he was like that. He felt it was his duty to help whenever he could.'

'A penance of some sort?' Thomas queried.

The kitchen clerk looked surprised. He cleared his throat and seemed to have forgotten what he had been about to say.

'And after you told him not to help, what did he do next?' Hildegard encouraged.

'I advised him to make sure he had everything with him he'd need for the journey.'

'So he was to come with us, then?' Hildegard asked just to be sure.

'Aye. Somewhat reluctant, like. He didn't want to leave his wife by herself.'

'Was she ill?'

'No. She was new. What's that Latin word? Uxorious, aye, that's the one. Martin was still at the uxorious stage. Been handfast less than three months. Tried to persuade the steward to allow her to come with us. "What! A woman in a retinue of menfolk? I hardly think so!" You know the steward, Edwin,' he turned to his counterpart in the inner household.

'So did he leave you then to go and get his things?' Hildegard asked, her status as a woman clearly in abeyance.

The kitchen clerk's face was suddenly set in stone. 'He left. I don't know where he went. That's the last time I clapped eyes on the poor devil.'

'He left alone, presumably?' asked Edwin for neatness.

The kitchen clerk nodded. 'Quite alone. He went out by way of the lay brothers' refectory, if you're asking.'

Edwin's glance sharpened. 'I was just about to ask

you that. Why would he go out that way? He must have known there would be nothing to eat in there that morning. His dormitory lies at the opposite end of the building, adjoining the kitchens on the other side.' He turned to Hildegard and Thomas. 'I should explain that there are quarters for our married laymen in a wing leading off the lay brothers' dormitory. Martin's wife worked as a laundress for us.'

The kitchen clerk was frowning now. 'You know, at the time I thought it unexpected but I assumed he was maybe going out through yon door to fetch some herbs from the enclosure. I thought maybe that was his intention,' he frowned, 'but we'll never know now, will we?'

Edwin was again scribbling furiously and broke off with a muttered curse to sharpen his quill with a little penknife.

'Just for clarity's sake,' murmured Hildegard. 'This back door leading out of the refectory into the herb garden near the bakehouse – is it inside or outside the enclosure wall?'

The kitchen clerk looked mystified. 'It's just inside. There's a door in the wall leading out to where the gardens are.'

'Thank you.'

The kitchen clerk took his sheaf of notes from his jerkin and placed them on Edwin's writing tray. 'Look after them. I must be getting on if that's all, masters, Domina.' He inclined his head towards Hildegard. 'Work to be done. People never stop eating.'

'Thanks, Cedward,' Edwin barely looked up. 'Tell us if you think of anything else.'

'You can count on it. I want this sorted as quick as you do. I tell you, nobody's going to dare walk alone when this gets out.'

The door closed softly behind him.

There was a long silence. 'From the murderer's point of view the safest time was when everybody was busy loading the wagons. Then he could slip back to join us afterwards, probably when we were all in church.' Thomas let out a sigh. 'Sadly it's no good asking me who I saw in there. Not with all that incense and my eyes streaming with tears.'

'So was anybody else likely to be in the kitchen gardens at that time in the morning, Edwin?'

'Gardeners?'

'But it was scarcely light at that point,' she reminded.

Edwin sniffed. 'Always pottering at unlikely hours, aren't they?' He threw down his quill. 'Let's call one of them.'

'Good idea,' agreed Thomas. 'But how? Surely they're all still in Bishopthorpe?'

'You'll find out. We'll have something to drink while we wait for him to scrape the mud off his boots.'

Not much later, and energised by a jug of something from the bishop's cellar, they were confronted by the man in charge of herbs and spices. 'Confronted' being the appropriate word in Hildegard's opinion.

He strode in with a determined manner and folded his

.

67

arms across his chest before subjecting each of them to a penetrating stare from beneath black brows. Afterwards his glance returned to Edwin.

'I've nothing to tell you,' he began without invitation. 'I don't know why I've been brought here.'

'I'll tell you why,' replied Edwin with youthful dignity, outfacing the older man. 'It's because, as you've probably heard by now, one of our friends and respected servants has died and we intend to find out how. Anything and everything that happened the morning of his death is of interest to us and will shortly be known to us. You can count on that. Now give us your version if you'll be so good.'

The man was unfazed. 'I have no version. I wasn't there and I know nothing.'

'*Where* weren't you?' Thomas asked quietly enough.

'*There*,' he snarled in response. 'In the brewhouse where the body was found.'

'Did you see the body?' asked Hildegard.

'No. I did not.'

'Then how do you know where it was found?' Edwin demanded.

The herberer let his arms drop to his sides and then refolded them. 'Am I deaf? Everybody knows.'

'And you weren't there. What is your name, my friend?' asked Edwin, moving on. 'I need it for my records.'

The man eyed the clerk with antagonism and looked as if he would refuse to have his name recorded, but then, seeing the three of them staring him out, he muttered, 'Jarrold.'

'Jarrold of . . . ?'

'Kyme.'

'Now where in the world is that?' asked Edwin in a pleasant tone.

'South of Lincoln.'

'So we'll be passing your home territory as soon as we're back on the road? You'll be stopping off to visit your kinsfolk, no doubt?'

'Not likely.' Jarrold the herberer plainly thought as little of his kinsfolk as he thought of his questioners.

'Well, Jarrold, if you'll be so kind, tell us where you were on the morning in question. You'll have heard when that was, won't you?'

Sarcasm didn't bring out anything helpful.

Grudgingly he told them that he left the lay brothers' dormitory to get a bite to eat in the adjoining kitchens with everybody else, then returned to the dormitory to fetch his gear. He then went down into the kitchen yard to find out which wagon to put it in and then he'd hung around just like everybody else until it was time to leave.

'And were you present when the papal envoy did his head count?'

'I was.' He stared straight ahead without blinking.

'And was this before or after we went into church?' Hildegard asked.

He gave her a startled look and mumbled, 'Same as everybody else.'

'And did you notice anybody missing in the yard

whom you expected to see present?' Edwin leant forward watching him intently.

Hildegard turned at this unexpected line.

The herberer was already shaking his head. 'I didn't notice Martin being there, if that's what you mean, but nor did I notice he wasn't there neither. I wasn't especially looking to see who was there. It was all the usual crowd. And it didn't matter a tinker's cuss who they took. It was all one to me. Except I was more likely wondering whether I'd be the one to be left behind when the Pope's man said we were one too many.'

'Why would you wonder that?' Hildegard queried.

'Last in, first out,' came the retort.

'Explain.' Edwin dipped his pen in the inkhorn and glanced up.

'I only joined the household a while back. Yorkshire folk here, aren't they? I'm a Lincolnshire man myself.' He paused and insolently added, 'As I've just told you.'

'Do you thereby feel excluded?' asked Thomas in an interested tone.

Jarrold looked at him as if he were mad and didn't bother to reply.

'What is your function in the household, exactly?' Hildegard asked him.

'I'm an outdoor-indoor servant. I'm an expert on herbs. I oversee the ones grown and check that the right ones get given to the cooks.'

If Martin had been poisoned, here would be their prime suspect, she thought, a man with all the shiftiness and ill-humour you might expect in someone evil enough to kill a man in cold blood. But Martin had not been poisoned. 'So did you go into the herb garden that morning to pick herbs for the journey?' she asked.

'I told you what I did.'

'We'll take that as "no" then, shall we?' Edwin scribbled something in his notes and looked up. 'You might beg the domina's forgiveness for your tone.'

Jarrold stared at the floor and made an almost imperceptible movement of the head that seemed intended to mollify. Edwin dismissed him with a shooing motion.

When the door closed Thomas turned to him. 'What do you think?'

'Insolent bastard. But that doesn't make him our man. We'll have to see if anybody can vouch for him.' He pushed the plug into the inkhorn to stop it from spilling, replaced it in its notch in the tray and closed the whole thing up. 'I expect you've both got to attend the next office. Let's stop now and reconvene. We've already got a few questions for the constables at Bishopthorpe. If Master Jarrold or anybody else was near the brewhouse at that time somebody must have seen them. It's just a question of combing through their depositions and finding a discrepancy.'

Thomas gave a hollow laugh. 'Finding a needle in a haystack might be easier.'

Hildegard reminded Edwin to ask about the weapon that had battered the back of Martin's head in. 'I wonder what happened to his travel bag?' she asked as they got up to go. 'Do we know whether it turned up here with all the others? Or didn't he get around to fetching it from his chamber on the morning?'

Despite their efforts, speculation was rife. An air of suspicion prevailed. Word was out that questions were being asked and no one would be exempt.

It was disturbing to everybody to suspect that they were harbouring a murderer in their midst. The ambush on the road had startled many of the staff into a state of fear. With word out about this new danger, the killing of the wolf was seen as an omen.

It distracted them from the threat of invasion, despite the fact that the castle garrison was on full alert. Previously the knowledge that they were staying in a garrison town had given everyone a feeling of security: groups of armed militia on duty at the perimeter of the bishop's enclave, archers visible on the battlements of the castle. With the view from the keep stretching for miles over flat country to the south there would be no element of surprise should an army come marching up the shire from that direction. Lincoln would be impossible to take.

Even so, with a murderer within the enclave, the mood of the men from York became volatile. Scuffles broke out. Old vendettas were revived. Eating knives sharpened as if the meat in Lincoln required it. Some people stopped speaking to others altogether. Suspicious cliques stood around in the belief there was safety in numbers.

* * *

Martin's bag, packed for the journey, was discovered in one of the wagons. The contents looked pathetic as they were tipped out onto a table – a clean tunic, some woollen hosen, and a trinket wrapped in a piece of cloth, presumably a memento from his wife – not much as the sum of one man's life.

'No clues there,' murmured Edwin as if he expected an incriminating note as he sifted through the things.

During the rest of the day Master Fulford's other kitcheners were called in to give an account of themselves.

It was as the master cook had told them. Everything was on the record – he had waved his clerk's parchments to prove it – but with such a lot of coming and going it was impossible to know who had been able to slip away without being spotted. The brewmaster confirmed what the cook had told them, the cook's account was confirmed by the chamberlain, the steward's by the sub-steward, and so on. What was clear was how the chamberlain had arrived at a figure of forty in his first head count and the Pope's man at forty-one in the second. The extra man was the murderer.

Archbishop Neville was given a full account of what they had discovered – precious little, Edwin complained – and one of his pigeons was dispatched at once with a message seeking additional information from Bishopthorpe: had anyone been working in the herb garden at any time that morning, was anyone at all seen near the garden or on the path under the infirmary windows?

The baker and his clerk were recalled but could only repeat their story. The murderer had to have entered through the garden. But neither Martin nor anyone else had been noticed around there. In the confusion of departure everybody had been too busy to notice anything exceptional.

The herberer was not mentioned because there was nothing to report other than a dislike of his manner. In none of the accounts did anyone say they had seen Martin other than in the yard helping to load wagons.

Now resigned to staying in Lincoln until more information turned up, the three of them went separate ways: Thomas to the scriptorium to talk shop about the chronicle of Meaux his abbot was planning, Edwin to continue his duties on behalf of his lord, and Hildegard to have a look at the famous vines in Bishop Buckingham's garden now there was a break in the rain.

Chapter Three

She plunged her hand in among the wet leaves and tugged at the roots. They came up easily. Short and straggly. Wet earth clinging to them. A herb of some sort, perhaps.

The woman she had seen just now had collected an entire scripful before hurrying back up the garden to greet a young man just coming out of the bishop's hall. The leaves were clearly useful for something.

She sniffed one. It had no distinctive smell. She crinkled a leaf and tasted it. It had no particular taste either. Fern-like, it looked undistinguished but clearly it had a use.

Regretting that the woman had disappeared before she could ask what it was, Hildegard decided to take a sample. The gardener Archbishop Neville had mentioned, who ran the gardens outside the London walls at the place called Stepney, would be the one to identify it – if he lived up to his reputation.

She got up off her knees. It might be something she could add to her cures.

An uneasy couple of days elapsed. The delay, the suspicion, set everybody on edge.

Neville was also beginning to fret about being late for the opening of Parliament. It was now three weeks away and he had to be constantly reassured that he would be in Westminster well before then.

Hildegard met Edwin as she was crossing the yard to go onto the cathedral close shortly after Lady Mass that morning. She had decided to visit St Hugh's shrine before hordes of pilgrims turned up and turned it into a bunfight. But Edwin detained her.

'I was just coming to find you, Domina. His Grace wishes you to go to his chamber.' He added that he had no idea what it was about but to watch her step, his mood was worse than that of a baited bull.

When she went in, Neville gestured irritably for his servants to leave, and after even his little page had slipped out he trod over to the great door of his chamber and pushed a stool against it. Hildegard stared.

Dressed in his usual opulence, he wore scarlet and purple beneath a silvery cope and the insides of his full sleeves were lined with viridian silk. The hem of his many-layered vestments made a slithering sound as they trailed after him along the floor tiles as he padded over to his reading desk. He beckoned her, then gave her a considering stare for one long drawn-out moment.

'Domina – in future I'll address you as Hildegard. Why? As a token of our complicity.'

She stared at him in confusion.

'Two years ago, you most admirably travelled across the Alps to Tuscany in order to retrieve a powerful relic at the behest of your prioress in Swyne. Your courage has not passed unnoticed. You may be wondering . . .' he paused and his blue, somewhat red-veined, eyes fastened on her face '. . . why I claim complicity? It's in recognition of our shared support for the King. It has come to our ears that a conspiracy is being hatched to destroy him. But as you know, we possess something that may save him and confound his enemies.'

Without saying more he reached across to a small leather-covered chest banded in iron that sat prominently on the desk and, fishing inside his vestments, brought out a key which he fitted into a complicated lock in the lid.

He invited her to come closer and she watched while he listened for the key to turn in the lock. Then, slowly and reverentially, he lifted the lid.

Inside was a gold reliquary about twelve inches long and four inches deep. Hildegard had never seen it before but she stared in astonishment as the archbishop removed the reliquary from the chest and pressed a secret catch in the design of little figures that ran round its rim, and made the lid spring open.

Inside, on a velvet bed, looking like nothing much, was

a T-shaped piece of blackened wood. She recognised it at once. On the back an inscription would be found: *In hoc signo vinces*. It had been the Emperor Constantine's battle cry when confronting the enemies of his fledgling Christian empire at the Battle of the Milvian Bridge near Rome many centuries ago. God, went the legend, favoured Constantine and bestowed victory on his army to prove it. The cross he carried into battle was said to be this very one and because of that its power was believed to be immense.

It went without saying that it was priceless to anyone with ambitions to steal a crown from a king. It would legitimise their theft in the eyes of the people who believed in such things.

Last time Hildegard had seen it, her prioress was keeping it safely and secretly at the priory of Swyne.

Expected to hand it over to the archbishop, whose gold had financed Hildegard's expedition on the quest to fetch it back to England, the prioress had point-blank refused. Even though Alexander Neville was her brother, she had doubts about his loyalty. She suspected that he intended to offer the cross to the Duke of Lancaster's eldest son, young Harry Bolingbroke, who had offered a vast sum for it. But, suspected of plotting to depose the King, his cousin Richard, he had been refused. The cross, with the legend to impress the superstitious, would clearly have bolstered his claim.

Now, Hildegard registered, it confirmed the hope that the archbishop had recovered his sense of loyalty and the prioress had handed the cross into his keeping. His intention must be to deliver it to the King in Westminster.

He did not lift it from the reliquary and nor did he touch it. Instead he gazed long and hard at it, and finally, when he raised his head, she saw tears in his eyes. 'I would lay down my life for this.'

Hildegard said softly, 'So now I understand, Your Grace. It was to protect the cross that you abandoned your household, leaving them to defend themselves against those men lying in ambush.'

'Precisely so.'

He snapped the lid closed, replaced the reliquary in the small chest, then pulled a linen bag over the whole thing.

His voice shook. 'This morning,' he told her, 'I discovered that those who seek the cross are now within the bishop's enclave. Who they are, I know not. I decided that someone should be told what I possess in case anything happens to me and the cross is stolen.'

'What makes you think they're inside?' she asked in astonishment.

'During the night my guards disturbed someone trying to gain entrance to my privy chamber. There's only one reason anyone would want to break in here.'

'Surely you don't suspect someone in the bishop's household?'

'Buckingham himself is loyal. I'm sure of that. But he spends so little time here in Lincoln these days he must have failed to keep a close watch on the loyalties of his household. It's my guess it was somebody allied with those armed men my men routed on the way down.'

'We can find that out by closely questioning the prisoner we took.'

He nodded. 'Be it so, although he may be in ignorance of the greater lord from whom his captain receives his orders.'

'No doubt they'll make another attempt?'

He agreed. 'It goes without saying. I shall increase the number of armed guards.'

'Your Grace – may I make a suggestion?'

When he nodded she said, 'Armed men often provoke attack. Their presence creates interest in the value of what they've been instructed to guard. Mightn't there be some more unobtrusive way of conveying the cross to Westminster?'

'Such as?'

'Remember how I carried it all the way from northern Italy back to Yorkshire? No one suspected the value of the object in my old travel-scarred bag.' She smiled, remembering the ease with which she had carried the cross past the guards collecting the customs tolls at the port of Ravenser on her return. 'Might I offer my services in like fashion?'

Neville looked startled. 'God's teeth, I would never hear of such a thing! Carry the cross yourself? Think of the danger if they attacked – no! Never!'

'But Your Grace, I beg you to consider it.'

He shook his head. 'I promised my sister I wouldn't put you in danger.'

'My prioress is ever flexible in her actions, Your

Grace, as I am sure you already know. She would appreciate the problem and come to an accommodation with any promise made in ignorance of the present circumstances.'

'She would?' He cocked an eyebrow. 'She would.'

He glanced down at the linen bag with its priceless contents. It looked as if it might contain clothing, a nun's book of hours, spare leggings, or whatever nuns carried when they travelled from their cloisters.

With a sudden gesture, half gratitude, half reluctant submission, he placed the bundle in her hands.

Without speaking she slipped it inside a capacious leather bag – her scrip, where, among other things, her cures were stored. There, under the fern-like leaves from the bishop's garden she hoped to identify later, she concealed the cross.

It was raining by the time she came outside, the sort of rain that floats on the wind like a mist but still drenches and finds a way inside the thickest cloak. Undeterred, she pulled up her hood and hurried across the garth towards the west door of the cathedral. The bag was safely hidden underneath her cloak. From now on she would not let it out of her sight.

Inside the entrance the pilgrims had already started to gather, joyful at this extra penitential inconvenience, shaking the rain from their woollen cloaks and glorying in the mud that fell from their rain-sodden boots.

Hildegard gave a groan. There would be no hope of

getting near the shrine this morning. The pilgrims had beaten her to it.

The cathedral was the centre of a diocese that stretched from the border with Yorkshire down through the midland counties as far to the south-west as Oxford. It possessed extremely profitable lands and displayed its wealth with spectacular soaring arches, perpetual chantries, and a hundred gilded carvings placed up and down the long nave. Expensive beeswax candles flickered on the altars, the continual sonorous chanting of the monks filled the airy caverns with sound, and the susurration of slippered pilgrim feet was like the brushing of a thousand wings. Today the coloured glass in the tall lancets was darkened by the gloom outside and rain clattered incessantly against the quarry panes.

Already there was a huge crowd round the elaborate gilded shrine dominating the east end. The heady scent of incense billowed from the censers carried by a little army of acolytes as they marched up and down the nave, passing the winding queue of those waiting to crawl inside the shrine. For a moment the scent of frankincense reminded her of the Abbey of Meaux, of Hubert de Courcy, the abbot. His handsome, haunted features swam before her.

He would be riding down to Westminster soon, as would all the other prelates summoned to attend Parliament. It was to be no ordinary gathering. It was intended to put the country on a war footing in order to repel the invasion when it came, and the abbot would be expected to speak in the lords' chamber. Those for and against the King would have their votes counted. Where his loyalty lay would become apparent.

Carrying her bag she slipped into a small chantry away from the crowds, driven by the urge to pray for Hubert, his judgement, his safe journey and for the defeat of the King's enemies.

The place was empty when she entered. There was barely room to kneel, as a large fretted screen separated the altar from the rest of the little place. She knelt in a wedge of shadow to one side and turned her thoughts to what was important: the safety of the abbot, of the King and of England.

After a few moments she was reminded of the little panicked boy when he saw the contents of the vat and she prayed for him too, that he was safe in York with the rest of his family and friends, and then, about to rise to her feet, she heard a commotion in the doorway and two men entered.

They had their hoods up and had evidently just come in from the rain, because they dripped water all over the tiles. One of them was wearing a waterproof cloak and his companion, in fustian, was holding onto his arm and being half dragged towards the painted effigy of St Hugh on the other side of the screen.

The man in the waterproof dropped to his knees, forcing the other man down with him. A muttered conversation followed as they knelt in front of the effigy and it continued more viciously when the first man forced his companion's head and shoulders down towards the floor as if to make him kiss the base of the pedestal where the saint's effigy stood. The man freed himself with a curse and scrambled to his feet.

He was panting with fury, she saw now. 'You bloody have to!' he was muttering. 'I'm in enough shite already!'

The kneeling man ignored him and there was a fierce silence until he stood up, made the sign of the cross, then turned, grabbing his companion by the front of his cloak. Both still had their hoods up and their faces were in shadow but the venom of their exchange carried to where, momentarily transfixed, Hildegard was still kneeling.

She could not help but hear him say, 'Listen to me, you bungling shithead! I've got bigger fish to fry! Don't waste my time with your piddling problems!'

'You bastard! Are you just going to leave me in the lurch?'

The man laughed without humour. 'I've told you I'll sort it!'

'Sort it?' the other demanded in disbelief. 'How the hell are you going to sort it now?'

'I will do so. There's only one thing you have to do. Give me a sign. It's as good as done. And then you can bloody get on with the other business!'

She saw him release his grip and ask, 'What the hell is it about anyway?'

There was a brief pause, then grudgingly, the reply, 'A woman.'

'You bloody fool!' His companion gave a jeering laugh and began to stride back through the opening in the wooden screen, snarling over his shoulder, 'I've heard it all now!'

'What are you going to do?'

'Everything can be sorted. I know what I'm saying! Now do it!'

The other man followed him out, leaving wet footprints down the centre of the tiles.

The chantry was lit by a slant of light from one small window. Not enough to make out who they were. They could have been anyone. They could have been two men from the town. Anyone at all.

She saw them mingle with the congregation in the nave.

Even after they left the air seemed full of venom.

She got up and went out. A group of York men were queuing outside the shrine waiting to pay their respects to the saint. It was only as she approached that she noticed that one of the men who had just been arguing in the chantry, the one in the soaking-wet fustian cloak, was pushing his way through the crowd towards them. She watched as he went over to join them, pushing back his hood as he did so. Then she stared. It was Jarrold of Kyme.

She searched the crowds for his companion. He had gone to lean against a nearby pillar. He was difficult to pick out because he was still wearing the grey woollen hood half over his face with the waterproof draped across his shoulders.

Jarrold went up to the line of men waiting to crawl inside the niche under the sarcophagus of St Hugh and flung an arm round one of them. She saw him say something and the man laughed and clapped him on the back. The others shuffled up to make space and he fell into line with them. The man near the pillar turned and began to thread his way towards the exit.

Hildegard decided it was time to leave too. The scene had been unpleasant and it was stifling here, now that the crowds had grown as more and more people came in to shelter from the rain. When she reached the west door she was temporarily stalled by the influx of a fresh batch pushing in. Jarrold's companion was halted as well and she found herself standing close to him in the porch. He pulled the waterproof hood up. She was close enough to smell it. He had had it treated with a mixture of pig fat and rosemary oil. She had seen the mercenaries wear such garments in the Alps.

With one hand holding the hood over his face he plunged out into the rain and she watched him splash across the garth towards the row of tenanted houses within the enclave.

Reluctant to get wetter than she already was she hung about in the entrance for a moment or two, waiting for a lull in the storm, and was surprised to see Jarrold appear. She greeted him by name. 'So you decided not to wait to enter the shrine?'

He looked confused.

'I had the same intention,' she continued, 'but the queue put me off as well.'

He realised what she was saying and gave a brief nod. 'That's right, Domina. Yes, that's it. Too many people. Better to come back later.'

He was about to step outside when she said, 'There seems to be some excitement in the close today. Is it just the storm or is there fresh news of the invasion?'

'Nothing on that score as far as I'm aware.'

'I saw a good number of your companions inside . . .' she indicated the cathedral. 'What's bringing them out in such numbers?'

'Confused by a more local kind of panic, maybe.' He raised his eyebrows.

'Are they?'

He gave her a sardonic smile. 'Fear over the manner of Martin's death is sending them back to God. Don't you find it's always the way? Nothing like a good scare to fill the Church's coffers. And they're also in a ferment at the thought that one of their boon companions will shortly hang for murder.'

'Shortly?'

'With so many educated persons hot on his trail?'

Without delaying a moment longer he ducked his head and made off into the rain.

'Well liked. Is that all they're saying about him?' She had found Thomas in the cloisters with a prayer book in his hand.

'A strong sense of right and wrong.' Thomas sighed. 'Also, too honest.' He gave her a sharp look. 'Too honest? How can a man be too honest?'

'Too honest for his own good?'

'Do you suspect him of knowing something he shouldn't?'

Hildegard gazed out across the cloister court. There was a stone well in the middle. The bucket on the parapet was brimming with rainwater. Above their heads water was jetting out of the mouths of the gargoyles as if it would never end. On the far side of the yard the passage into the hall was busy with diners going in for the first sitting.

'What sort of thing could a kitchener know?'

News from Bishopthorpe, or rather the lack of it, dampened everyone's spirits as if to mimic the weather. The archbishop's retinue broke up into rival factions and their Lincoln hosts, with the knowledge that there was possibly a murderer among their guests, eyed them with growing resentment. Bishop Buckingham, like one oblivious to the darkening mood, presided late that afternoon over a succession of dishes produced by his own cooks and conversed at length with his illustrious guest. Neville frowned and looked glum and stared deeply into his goblet. As the shadows lengthened cressets were lit and placed in brackets along the wall. They cast a flickering smoky light that somehow only seemed to add to the gloom.

Thomas was sitting at the end of one of the trestles, working his way through a pile of meat, it not being a fish day. 'Edwin has made a list of everybody at Bishopthorpe,' he told Hildegard. 'By crossing off those the constables are dealing with and cross-referencing the others with the testimonies of those we've spoken to he's been able to establish everybody's movements and work out who has an alibi and who hasn't. They all have. Until we get word from the gardeners, in case they saw something, it's the best he can do.'

'The usefulness of his approach depends on two things: the accuracy of people's memories and their honesty.'

Thomas wiped his mouth on the back of his hand. 'What about this Jarrold fellow?' Hildegard had told him about the odd little scene in the cathedral. Now he was frowning. 'He comes on like a villain in a Corpus Christi play. Too bad to be true.'

'Several people say they saw him in the main courtyard that morning, helping load the wagons.'

'I must say,' Thomas continued, 'it would take ingenuity to find the privacy to carry out a murder in somewhere like the palace. It's always so busy. The brewhouse must have been the only empty place that morning.'

'Does it mean the murderer simply took his chance?'

'He was lucky, then.'

'Or,' she picked at her fish, 'maybe he was unlucky?'

'What do you mean?'

'Maybe he planned it expecting that if he waited until just before the convoy set off the body might go undiscovered for days?'

'But then that mischievous little lad with his pig's bladder got into the picture.'

'If the murderer did plan the whole thing with such attention to detail, he must be a patient type, able to wait for the right moment to act.'

'To plan so carefully, then kill in cold blood. Chilling.'

'You can mix with these men more freely than I can, Thomas; who's likely to be able to think like that?'

He shook his head. 'They're mostly a bunch of ribalds with no thought for the morrow. Of course,' he frowned, 'the falconers have to have patience. They need it, in order to train their hawks.'

'All accounted for?'

'It seems so.'

'Well, our man is the one with the cunning to plan ahead and the patience to bide his time.'

News arrived while they were still dining. Due to some bungling by the custodian, the hostage thrown into the castle jail had been released.

Edwin was fuming. 'How on earth? The sot wits. You don't just open the gates and tell prisoners they can walk free!'

'How did it happen?' Thomas asked.

'Somebody went to the guard with a release note and the fool failed to verify the signature. Now the document can't even be found. The constable's in hot water – he should never have let it happen – but it won't bring the prisoner back.'

The news was soon all round the refectory and a buzz of conversation broke out. A murderer on the loose. And now this. Nobody to be brought to book for the ambush. What sort of world were they living in? The end days were approaching, that was for sure. Next thing: the apocalypse.

The archbishop's earlier remark that the enemy was within the gates came back to Hildegard with greater force. The sooner they left Lincoln the better.

She reached for the bag beside her on the bench and slipped her hand inside it, just to be sure the contents were safe.

It was then there was a flurry of activity at the great doors. The herald blew a quick phrase or two and a woman appeared. In the silence that fell she made quite an entrance.

To be fair, thought Hildegard, watching as the newcomer made her way to a seat below the dais, she didn't look as if she was trying to make an entrance and few women would fail to draw all eyes in such a world of men. Her gown, however, was the sort seen more often at court than in an ecclesiastical establishment. Her little page was attired in a tunic of silver thread.

Thomas had eyes like saucers.

'Who is she?' Hildegard touched him on the arm.

'The Duke of Lancaster's mistress.'

'Katharine Swynford?'

He wrenched his glance away. 'She's a tenant here within the cathedral enclave. And that's her son Thomas beside her.'

Hildegard had not noticed the son. He was an unhandsome youth with an untidy beard and strange crinkly hair like sheep's wool. She turned to the monk. 'You know Thomas Swynford?'

'Know of him. I've seen him on previous visits to Lincoln. He must be here visiting his mother. I believe she has several manors around here. He probably has charge of them.'

Hildegard watched them both for a few moments. Katharine Swynford was notorious. Her long-term relationship with the Duke of Lancaster throughout both his marriages was a great scandal. She had borne him several children but despite that she had been in charge of the upbringing of his legitimate children – his eldest, Bolingbroke, the Earl of Derby, included. They said there was a rift between the Duke and his mistress now and she had been pensioned off to live here in Lincoln, distanced from court and favour.

In contrast to his mother, young Swynford was dressed unshowily in grey with a black capuchon pushed down round his neck.

Now, clearly unbothered by her reputation, she beckoned her page, whispered something in his ear, then sent him with a little push towards the dais where Bishop Buckingham was sitting in an ornately carved chair with Neville on his right-hand side.

From the end of the table Hildegard could hear the page's piping voice as he begged leave to ask a boon of the archbishop.

The archbishop cupped a hand to his ear. 'Speak up, boy. Ask away.'

Everybody stopped talking.

'My Lady Swynford begs to present her son, Sir Thomas Swynford, Your Grace.'

'Tell her she may.' Neville exchanged a barely perceptible glance with Bishop Buckingham.

The page conveyed this message and with a poorly pretended air of reluctance Thomas Swynford rose to his feet.

He made his way to the dais and stood before it until Archbishop Neville acknowledged him.

Buckingham rose to his feet, made some excuse about needing to retire, and with a servant on either side, was helped out through his own private door into his apartment.

'Listen to this,' Hildegard whispered to Brother Thomas.

Neville was regarding the newcomer with a genial smile that did not reach his eyes. 'So, Master Swynford . . .' he invited.

'*Sir* Thomas Swynford, Your Grace. I've been knighted since you last saw me.'

'I beg your pardon. I didn't catch what the little page said.' The archbishop, known to have hearing like a bat, inclined his head no more than half an inch. 'And your boon, sir?'

'Your Grace, I beg leave to offer you the strength of my sword arm on the road south.'

'So you're itching to get down to London to join the fight against the French?'

'I am, indeed.'

'Or is Westminster your destination?'

Swynford, checked, murmured, 'As the King commands, Your Grace.'

'Then your offer is most gratefully accepted.' Neville was at his most smooth. 'You were a shield-bearer for the Duke of Lancaster, our putative King of Castile, I believe?'

'I was indeed, as a boy.'

He's a boy now, judged Hildegard, and surely no more than nineteen or so, not yet of age.

'And who is your lord?'

'I have the honour to attend the Duke's son, Henry Bolingbroke, the Earl of Derby,' Swynford replied, unable to conceal a smirk.

Hildegard stared hard at him. Neville was offering some polite platitude or other about the difference between being a retainer to the Duke and to his son, a harmless remark, but Swynford evidently thought otherwise.

He gave the archbishop the benefit of a curled lip and replied, 'The difference is, the son is the future. He's in his prime, not his dotage. This is no time for old men to cling onto power, neither in Church nor State.'

Neville took the insult to his forty-odd years – the same as the Duke's – with a placid smile. Hildegard was astounded. He was noted for his flying rages, aroused at the smallest slight, but now he looked almost benign as he observed the grinning youth and after only the briefest pause replied, 'I expect we old men can show you young fellows a thing or two if it comes to it.'

Swynford gave a barking laugh. The disparaging glance he gave the older man was undisguised.

Two of Neville's men-at-arms standing behind his chair moved not a muscle.

But Swynford hadn't finished. 'No doubt you would have welcomed a fully trained knight by your side during the unfortunate incident on your way here. You might have been less likely to invite attack.' There was a gasp from those close enough to hear.

Neville's colour rose. But even then his reply was carefully modulated. 'My men struggled on as best they could. I've no doubt we can struggle on to London, too, without any help. My gratitude for your offer, Swynford.'

He picked up his goblet and drank the contents before turning to the dining companion on his other side.

Swynford's jaw dropped, but before he could make matters worse his mother appeared below the dais where she had been hovering.

'My dear Lord Archbishop,' she cooed. 'Your Grace, forgive me my temerity in interrupting but we don't stand on ceremony here in Lincoln. It's a simple place—'

Neville lifted his head. 'Madam?'

'Lady Swynford, at your service.' She sank in a billowing curtsy and remained in this submissive posture while looking up at the archbishop with the full brilliance of her green eyes fixed on his face, and when she was sure she had his full attention she rose to her feet with slow grace. 'I am deeply honoured and full of joy now that you've agreed to include my son in your retinue on the long and dangerous road to Westminster. You are most generous, Your Grace, and quite live up to your reputation. Unfortunately for my poor dear son, he has only one servant with him, having had to leave Harry Derby to attend to business at our manor of Kettlethorpe. He is eager to rejoin his lord in London as soon as possible.' She gave a dazzling smile. 'I know he will make himself most useful to you in any way he can.'

Hildegard saw Neville's eyes harden but he was sympathy incarnate.

'The pleasure will be mine, dear lady.' And as if Swynford wasn't listening in, added, 'Pray tell him so.'

'That's settled, then. He comes with us,' muttered Thomas in Hildegard's ear. He gave her a quizzical glance.

'I know no more about him than you do except that it's lucky for him his mother knows how to get her own way.'

Chapter Four

The morning sun, low in the sky, was just beginning to cut a swathe through the banks of mist shrouding the close when the York retainers came stumbling out from the fetid stew of their bedstraw. It was quickly kicked into a corner of the stone passage where most of the servants had been sleeping, and one by one they staggered out into the cold damp air.

'On the road again,' somebody yawned, still half asleep.

'Aye, it's a dog's life,' another complained.

'Even so, shift this water barrel and set it on that third wagon, Jack. Stop moaning and jump to it.' The man who last spoke scratched his groin while he waited for his instructions to be carried out.

Hildegard had her leather bag over her shoulder inside her travelling cloak. She had slept uncomfortably with her head resting on the bag instead of a pillow. She too was yawning.

Thomas appeared. 'This is a sudden change of plan. What's made His Grace decide to leave all of a sudden?'

'Urgency in getting down to London,' she told him. 'That's all I know.'

'Nothing to do with Swynford, then?'

She shrugged. Swynford. Bolingbroke. The cross.

Soon the wagons were reloaded and the dray horses were backed into the shafts. People stood around in little knots. Suspicion of each other made them more silent than usual.

During the night it had come to Hildegard why she had been compelled to stare so hard at young Swynford. He was the same build as the man who had the argument in the cathedral yesterday with Jarrold, the same way of walking, the same swagger and, above all, the same voice, with that unmistakable Lincolnshire accent. She had seen him again as well. The scene in the bishop's herb garden came back. The unknown woman pulling up armloads of the mysterious herb was Lady Swynford, and now she knew that the young man who had taken her arm in that familiar fashion was her son.

She recalled the fact that the herberer hailed from a place a little way south of Lincoln. Kyme. It could be one of the manors held by the Swynfords along with Kettlethorpe and some other holdings in the region. Jarrold still had kin down that way, so he claimed.

Eventually the archbishop appeared. After checking that Hildegard was carrying her bag he walked briskly to his char without greeting anyone, climbed in and had his grooms pull the hood forward to close the leather flap. Clearly he wanted to be alone. His was the first vehicle to rumble out over the cobblestones followed by his longbowmen in a brisk little cart beside which some of them preferred to run. The men-at-arms were in evidence too, one allotted to each wagon this time and all of them carrying arms. The vittling wagons followed, and the water wagon, the kitchen servants' wagon, with the red-faced Master Fulford taking up more than his fair share of space as usual, and finally, after one or two more rumbled by, including the high-sided wagon bearing the falcons, came the wagon loaded with picks, shovels and a spare wheel or two, to take up the rear. Many servants chose to run and only jumped aboard the wagons when they felt they'd had enough exercise.

In this formation and at a steady pace equivalent to a horse's trot, they made their way down the steep hillside to the flat country beyond, passing over heathland for many miles and wending their way eventually down onto the wetlands, skirting dykes and watercourses and passing many mills along the way, following the old Roman road that would lead them down to London.

Hildegard and Thomas decided to ride and Edwin joined them. He had news of a sort.

'When I took in His Grace's tisane this morning and happened to make some casual remark about the murder and how we seemed to be no further on, he really snapped at me. "I haven't time for servants and their quarrels," he said, practically snarling in my face. It's my view he intends to wash his hands of the whole affair if we don't get a lead soon.'

'Poor Martin,' remarked Hildegard. 'I expect his wife, for one, would still like to know who killed him.' She recalled the young woman standing outside the church the morning they left and the anxiety on her face as she peered inside.

'We'll get a statement from her when the Bishopthorpe messenger catches up with us. She should know if he had any enemies.'

The roadside. Day. Morning. Hildegard and Thomas.

'It's made ten times more difficult by being on the road. If we'd remained in Bishopthorpe we'd have solved the mystery by now.'

Thomas agreed. 'There are too many laymen working at Bishopthorpe. Grooms, stable lads, the blacksmith, his apprentices, the saddler, the assistant falconers, the dairymen, and so on and so forth. Most of them living just outside the enclave or at home farm and none of them with any need to be up around the palace. But,' he concluded, 'you wouldn't know if one of them hadn't taken it into his head to stroll up to the palace to commit a murder.'

A day passed, a night, and then another day, and they had travelled a fragment of the journey that had taken Harold, the great Saxon king, only five days to accomplish. But he had his victory at Stamford Bridge behind him and dreams of future glory against the Norman threat in the south to goad him forward. His men must have been half dead on their feet by the time they staggered to Hastings.

They themselves journeyed in comparative comfort but still had many more miles to go and were staggering with exhaustion too.

Every day the hawks were flown and they ate well. The rule against meat for the two Cistercians was relaxed. The falconer was running alongside the archbishop's char now and called up to their driver. When the horses were pulled to a trot and Neville poked his head out he produced the latest kill with a smile. It was a young hind, no larger than a dog.

'Well done, Willerby. Who brought her down?'

'Pertelot, Your Grace.'

'Ah, sweet creature. Make sure she gets her portion.'

'I certainly will, Your Grace.'

Whistling to himself the falconer stood by the side of the track with the animal dripping blood until the butcher's wagon rolled up.

They reached the vast woodlands in the shire of Nottingham.

It was a savage territory, rendered dark and gloomy by the storm-contorted trees. A dead trunk blasted by lightning now and then emerged like a ghost out of the darkness of the undergrowth. The track became more and more twisted, full of ruts and potholes and sudden drops. They were forced to wind their way round tree roots that lay like snakes across their path. It was a perfect lair for outlaws.

Nobody mentioned the ambush at the beginning of their journey but it was remembered in every sidelong glance into the trees.

All this time Swynford had been riding with the convoy accompanied by his page. Sometimes they rode on ahead, sometimes they lagged behind. When the cavalcade stopped to enable cooking fires to be lit late in the afternoon, he remained aloof, as if afraid of catching some contagion. He had his own supplies, noted Hildegard, today augmented by a rabbit which his servant tried to roast on a spit over the small fire.

The burnt offering he produced was evidently not to Swynford's liking because when it was put into his hands he inspected it disdainfully then hurled it into the grass.

A servant from the archbishop's party loped over to retrieve it. 'Chucking good food away,' he scoffed as he rejoined his companions. The rabbit was hacked into pieces and added to the stew they were heating over their own fire.

Swynford made an ill-judged remark about shit being what they were used to, which the others piously ignored, and eventually they were back on the road again after no more than the exchange of a few black looks. Hildegard noticed, however, that one or two hands slid to knives and she wondered how long it would be before a fight broke out. Swynford would be idiotic to provoke it when he was so greatly outnumbered.

The weather took a turn for the worse, just as Bishop Buckingham's weather prophet had predicted, and the trees shut out what little light there was, so that they rattled down the narrow track into the heart of the woodland in an ever darkening gloom.

Earlier the leather canopy over the archbishop's char had been rolled back to its first hoop to make the most of the fine weather, but now it was rolled forward again. Summer was fading to nothing.

Hildegard was sitting with Thomas, Edwin and the archbishop's page on the running board next to the waggoner while Neville himself remained in the shelter at the back where he could sleep undisturbed beneath his furs, and it was now so quiet in this thickly wooded country that it began to cast a spell over the entire retinue. Gossip ceased. The only things audible were the sounds of the straining harness leathers, the squeak of the wooden wheels turning on their axles and the occasional clink of metal. Now and then a bird sang but mostly they fell silent as the convoy passed by.

They were bowling down the side of a shallow hill when a shout came from behind, and when Hildegard turned she saw that one of the drivers had hit an obstacle damaging one of the wheels. The passengers were climbing down with glum faces to have a look. The vehicle hung at an odd angle and could be driven neither forward nor backwards.

'A wheel,' she reported.

'We've been lucky so far,' observed Thomas, sleepily. 'Last time I went by cart to Pickering Castle we had no less than three changes of wheel.'

'The track is bad up there on the moors,' agreed Hildegard.

Everybody else began to climb down to see what they could do and a servant was sent back to the end of the line to get hold of the wheelwright. Neville's bodyguards got down one by one from the wagons where they had been separately posted and jogged back to lend a hand. Their own guard looked uncertain then decided to follow suit.

'At least they've got plenty of beef,' Thomas murmured as he watched the brawny fellows manhandle the great wagon onto a support so the wheel could be taken right off.

Neville gave a shout from his haven under the canopy, demanding to know why they'd stopped.

'A wheel off, Your Grace,' called Thomas over his shoulder.

'Tell my man to drive on. They can catch up with us. Let that Swynford fellow scout ahead. May as well make himself useful.' He pulled his furs round himself again and went back to sleep.

The driver clicked the horses on and they trundled forward.

By this time Swynford, after a quick look, had remounted and soon overtook them. His little page trotted quickly along behind him and they descended a dip in the track. A few minutes later they disappeared from view.

The trees clustered more thickly on both sides hereabouts and the scent of autumn was thick on the air. The hoof thump of Swynford's horse dwindled then faded.

The char continued on down the dip to the bottom where it levelled out before the next corner and they reached a point where the track dropped deeper into the trees round a slow curve. The rest of the carts were out of earshot by now.

Rain began to fall in big single drops making the few leaves that remained bounce and glisten on the branches. Hildegard pulled her hood up and wished she had a waxed cloak like Swynford's. They were just turning the corner after coming out of the dip when their driver gave a shout.

He cracked the whip as one of the lead horses reared, and the char juddered to a halt, the four horses snorting and jostling in their traces.

As if by magic the woods were suddenly bristling with men. Bowmen rose from the undergrowth on both sides of the track. Hildegard gripped her bag in alarm. Edwin gave a curse.

Swynford's riderless horse was cropping grass nearby. Its owner, his scabbard empty, was in the grip of two ruffians dressed as labourers in brown fustian.

One of them was gripping him by the hair while another held what looked like Swynford's own sword within inches of his exposed throat.

Thomas scrambled down off the running-board, picking up his stave as he went, but a couple of men armed with hunting knives materialised on both sides and pinned him against the char, saying, 'If you know what's good for you, Brother, start praying.'

Hildegard jerked to her feet. She kicked a fold of her

cloak over her bag and reached to her belt for her knife but a man's voice addressed her from across the grove.

'Stay where you are, Domina. You're in no danger if you do as you're told. We're here for this fellow.' He indicated Swynford, whose face was deathly pale, his lips trembling.

'Why the devil have we stopped again?'

The irritable voice of the archbishop broke the tension. The wagon tilted as he rose from his furs and lurched forward to see what was happening.

Clearly the men had not expected anyone else in the char and now the man holding Swynford called out, 'Who the devil are you?'

Neville stood to his full and considerable height on the running-board then shrugged his great fur-lined cloak from off his shoulders to reveal his vestments and his gleaming pectoral cross.

'I,' came his reply, filling the grove with its sound, 'am the Archbishop of York.'

'It's Alexander Neville,' one of the gang exclaimed in awe.

'Indeed,' agreed Neville pleasantly, turning towards him, 'and who, pray, are you?'

There were subdued mutterings but no clear answer.

'You're not those devils from the other side of Lincoln are you?' Noting their blank stares he demanded, 'Where's your master?'

'We have no master but our own true will,' replied the man holding Swynford.

'And why does this "true will" instruct you to have the audacity to halt my wagon?'

'We've been burnt out of our vill by this captive here.'

'Captive, is he?' Neville, bunching his robes in one hand, started to climb down. Nobody stopped him. 'I rather imagined he was my guest.'

As he strode through the grass towards the group he made no attempt to conceal the hefty sword on his belt. He came to a stop in front of the spokesman and now ostentatiously rested his right hand on the hilt. The gesture left them in no doubt he knew what a sword was for.

He eyed the spokesman for the group with genial interest. 'Where is this vill you mention, sir?'

The man uttered a name that meant nothing to Hildegard but Neville nodded. 'It's in the diocese of my good and reverend friend the Bishop of Lincoln. Why not take the matter up with him? A court is the place where you can sort out your grievances, not here in the wildwood abducting my guests.'

'Are you trying to tell us we'd get a fair hearing?' asked the leader. He laughed in disbelief. 'It was this fellow's master who gave him the orders to get us out. He's the law, not the bishop.'

'Indeed?'

'Indeed! He has use of arms which the bishop has not!'

'Why would this "master" want you out?'

'He wants our manor so he can gift it to this fella in return for some piece of dirty work.'

The man failed to bow or address the archbishop

107

with the usual courtesies. His face was grimed with several days' dirt and his clothes were patched things that scarcely hung together. But he seemed toughened by hard physical labour and now his outrage at what had been done gave him a dignity that won Hildegard's respect.

She watched Neville carefully to see how he would react.

He was frowning. 'You have Sir Thomas Swynford in your grasp. Do you know that?'

'We do!'

'Are you sure he was the one who burnt your vill?'

'It was Swynford all right. You want witnesses?' The man turned to his followers. 'Has anybody here seen this fellow carrying a burning brand at the head of a gang of Derby's retainers?'

'Aye. I have.' A man stepped forward. He was simultaneously followed by every man in the grove.

'And what did they do with their brands?' demanded the leader harshly.

'They set them to the thatch of our cottages.'

'They burnt our houses to the ground so we could not go back.'

'They fired them with women and bairns inside,' added another.

'It's a damned lie!' Swynford burst out, flinching from the edge of the sword. 'I've never seen these villains in my life! They're off their heads on drink!'

There was a brief scuffle as he tried to duck away

but he was dragged back to his former position with the sword in place. The men stood in a sober group giving him baleful stares. It was a tense moment. They clearly wanted to string him up from the nearest tree.

Hildegard held her breath. Their baggage wagons with the bodyguard were too far off to be of any use.

Thoughtfully, Neville addressed them. 'I have a clerk with me.' He placed his right hand over his heart. 'I make you this promise, friends. By the grace of God and the power of King Richard, if you present your case to the bishop I will guarantee that your grievance will be heard and justice delivered.'

'How do we know we can trust you?'

Neville drew his sword now. It made a rasping sound and the blade glittered as if by its own light. 'If you wish to prove me a liar, take Swynford's sword and let God be the judge.'

The leader stepped back. 'Your Grace,' he muttered, lowering his head. 'I will take the risk and accept your word if my comrades agree. What about it, men?'

Murmurs of agreement arose, albeit reluctant ones, and Swynford's sword was lowered, although his arms were not released yet. Master Edwin, still crouching with open mouth on the running-board, suddenly came to life. He fished around in his pouch for a piece of vellum and opened his writing tray. Unstopping the horn that held his ink he looked expectantly at his lord.

'Can you read?' demanded Neville of the spokesman.

He shook his head.

'No matter. I'll tell you what it says. Take it to Bishop Buckingham. He will know my seal.'

The message was scratched out, and to show that his word was true, wax was melted and the archbishop's own signet engraved with the crossed keys of St Peter was pressed into it.

'Hand it to him,' he told Edwin.

The leader of the gang took the document and looked at it with suspicion. Then he glanced at the archbishop's sword.

By now the rest of the convoy could be heard thundering down the slope between the trees.

Stuffing the document into his tunic, the leader hesitated for a moment as if to say something, then, apparently thinking better of it, he and his men melted rapidly into the woods.

In a moment the grove was empty. A bird sang. The rain stopped. The sun made shadow patterns over the trampled grass.

As soon as he knew he was safe, Swynford burst out in a rage of self-justification.

'You lying dogs!' he shouted after the vanished men. 'You have no rights. They are serfs!' he hissed, turning to Neville. 'They own nothing! How dare they impugn the honesty of a knight? The Earl of Derby gave me that land. It is mine! I will not barter for it with lying cut-throats.'

'It seems,' replied Neville, 'that you have no choice in the matter. And it seems also that if you feel so strongly about your rights you might have put up a better show in defending them.'

'One against a dozen?' Swynford spat into the grass. 'Better to go to law and get the bastards hanged!'

He went over to his horse and pulled himself into the saddle. His empty scabbard swung at his hip. Jerking his horse's head, he beat him with the whip, raked spurs hard along its flanks then galloped off up the track. His little page scrambled astride his pony and scurried after him.

'Well I'll be damned!' exclaimed Neville's own page, staring at the empty track.

'You will, varlet, if you talk like that,' growled Neville. He turned to the others. 'All aboard. To St Albans. It's now or never!'

As they were climbing back into their places the rest of the cavalcade appeared round the corner. The lead waggoner looked surprised to find the archbishop not much further on.

'Another wheel, Your Grace?' he inquired.

Archbishop Neville gave a gesture that explained nothing. 'A little local encounter. Nothing to worry about.'

Despite his words, he was plainly seething with rage. He climbed back inside the char and sat down among his furs. The focus of his ire became apparent when he called Master Edwin to sit beside him. The clerk, with his archbishop fully redeemed, hurried to comply.

'Write a letter to Buckingham,' he instructed. 'I want it sent back as quickly as possible. Use one of those homing pigeons of his. If he imagines I'm content to take Derby's hired man all the way to London he's vastly mistaken. The blundering thoughtless upstart! Swynford! He's more trouble than he's worth. Greed and duplicity rule him just as they rule his mother. I will not be party to his iniquity!'

Hildegard cradled her leather bag. She was still shaking.

The Abbey of St Alban. Shortly after nones. Rain again.

It was sheeting down over the roofs and sending the monks running to the cloisters with their hoods over their heads. Hildegard glanced out of the window. Part of the convoy had already straggled out onto the road to London.

Thomas stretched out his feet. 'Done for.' He indicated his sandals. They were hanging together by nothing more than threads.

'You should have asked Abbot de Courcy to allow you to wear boots,' she remarked. 'I don't know of anywhere in the Rule that says you shouldn't go properly shod.' Then more kindly she added, 'There's bound to be a saddle-maker here who wouldn't mind stitching them for you. Would you like me to find out?'

'I'll find him myself. I should have thought of it sooner. I expect that's exactly what you're thinking now.'

'You read me so well, Thomas.'

He smiled as he went in search.

The Abbey of St Alban was like a fortified town, host to all the craftsmen common to such places, and there were masons, blacksmiths, armourers, carpenters, leatherworkers and similar skilled craftsmen employed here. He would easily find someone to fix his sandals before they had to leave.

The abbey church itself, with the monks' quarters attached, was built on a high hill overlooking a narrow dale with a river meandering along the bottom. There was a watermill down there and a winding path back up to the abbey enclave. Even under rain it was a scene of beauty and tranquillity, a place you would long to remember in your dreams.

Yet its beauty was superficial. Underneath was a pulsing heart of black corruption, death, maimings, rape and betrayals still vibrantly within recent memory.

Only five years ago, near the time of the Great Rebellion, a gang of townsfolk had clashed with the abbot.

They were angered for good reason. He had ordered his men to smash their grinding stones in order to force them to use the abbey flour mill at whatever price the miller chose to extort. It was not an impulsive revolt. They had tried putting their case in the abbey court but it had been thrown out.

Eventually they marched out of the town and climbed the hill wielding billhooks and staves, the only arms they possessed. Their demand was modest – restoration of their ancient right to grind their own corn.

The abbot and his miller had other ideas and it was stalemate until the abbot ordered his men to go round every cottage, drag out every hand mill, cart them back up to the abbey and concrete them into the floor. Anyone found with a mill after that would hang.

The townsfolk resisted but were quickly subdued by the armed force of the abbey militia. Later, when the Great Rebellion in London was crushed and Tresillian, the Chief Justiciar of England, arrived in St Albans to inflict retribution on those who had supported it, there were many summary hangings.

Now, today, here was the York contingent, with their own memories of resistance against bonded labour, uneasy in their accommodation, doubtful about putting tainted bread in their bellies.

On top of that, thought Hildegard, aware of the labourers' smouldering discontent, the mystery of Martin's death was still unsolved. The failure of the archbishop's men to find the culprit must seem like yet another instance of the injustice meted out by Church and State to the powerless.

Unsurprised that they were keen to leave as soon as they could, and wondering how it would end, she began to check through her luggage until Thomas returned. It was impossible to believe that the puzzle of Martin's death was no nearer a solution than when they had started. Edwin was probably right when he offered the opinion that Martin must have been in a quarrel the morning they left – victim of someone's sudden rage that got out of hand. The perpetrator was probably far away by now, unheeded and unpunished on some remote manor in the Riding.

If they couldn't find the culprit soon, blame would descend on the archbishop for failing to protect his retainers.

Their last hope, that one of the Bishopthorpe gardeners had seen something suspicious, had come to nothing. Only two days ago a message had reached them to say that nobody was in the gardens at that time in the morning on the day they left. The master gardener's exact words were, 'We don't work by moonlight. We're not bloody necromancers.'

As for the rest of the outdoor servants, it was the same story. They had no need to be in the main courtyard while the convoy was getting under way. It was an opportunity to take it easy in their own quarters. And they had grabbed it.

Even Martin's young wife had had nothing to add.

So that was that.

Now, with Thomas wandering off into the rain, trailing his broken sandals, Hildegard slipped the last of the leather ties through the loops on her bag to hold everything in place, pulled the whole pack tight then sat back on her heels.

She would not be sorry to leave St Albans. Beautiful though it was, there had been too much blood shed under its soaring arches.

Before she left Meaux, Hubert de Courcy had said something about the archbishop intending to make several strategic stops on the way. She assumed this was one of them: Neville, drumming up support for the King among his brother prelates.

With thoughts on what lay ahead at Westminster

uppermost, she hoisted her bag onto one hip and started for the door.

She was no further than the top of the steps down into the main yard when Thomas materialised like a ghost at the bottom.

He was barefoot, his broken sandals nowhere to be seen, his face, as white as his robe, stark with horror.

'Hildegard! Quickly!' he croaked. 'Come at once! Something terrible has happened!'

Chapter Five

He led at a brisk run across the puddled yard towards the stables. Instead of leading her inside he quickened his pace until they reached the end of the building, where he veered off into a smaller yard enclosed on three sides by a high stone wall. He ran in through an open door at the far end of this cul-de-sac and when she followed she found they were in the mews.

It was dark. Against two, long, shadowy walls were fixed the perches where, chained, sat maybe twenty birds of prey.

They were impassive. Silent. Eyes fixed steadily on the intruders.

Thomas hurried barefoot to the very end of the passage to the lodge where the falconer kept his equipment.

It was a cramped chamber with no windows and only one door.

Hildegard could make nothing out at first.

'Brace yourself,' he whispered. 'Look!'

He pointed to a shape on the flagstones. She peered down trying to make out what it was and then she guessed. It was a body. She thought of it as a body first because of the way it was sprawled. But then she saw a movement. As she peered she thought her eyes were deceived. He had to be dead because a puddle of something pooled round his head. She knelt beside him.

He was lying curled on one side, hands across his face. From between his fingers more blood was seeping.

When she bent closer she could hear breath, rapid and shallow, as after a shock. Carefully she touched his wrists. 'If you can bear it, permit me to have a look.'

The man shuddered and cried out. For a moment she glimpsed what had been done to him and then his hands came back as if he could hold in the blood and lessen the pain.

'It's his eyes,' breathed Thomas, crouching down beside her. 'Has one of the falcons attacked him?'

Hildegard rose to her feet. She was shaking too.

'They say they go for the eyes,' Thomas went on. 'Is he blinded?'

'First we have to staunch the blood or he won't live either.'

She tugged at one of the sleeves of her habit to rip away sufficient cloth, and cursing the lack of light, persuaded the man to take his hands away from his eyes long enough to allow her to staunch his wounds. Thomas bent to help.

After a moment he took over while she opened her

scrip and it was then, as she bent to pick up her bag from where it had fallen, that she caught sight of something lying on the ground. It was a bundle of feathers.

As if everything was being refocused she realised that there was a presence detaching itself from the shadows. A man stepped out into the grey light coming in from the doorway. She saw the leather gauntlet strapped to his forearm.

He muttered, 'This is a disaster, a total disaster. I'd give an entire city for that bird.'

'Who are you?'

'Domina, I'm chief falconer here. This is one of your men from York. He brought the archbishop's hawks in here and he's been tending them ever since you arrived. There's no sense to it!'

The man seemed desperate. Something like a sob forced its way from him. He bent to pick something up from the ground and she saw that it was a dead falcon. Cradling it in his arms like a baby, his shoulders began to heave with grief.

'It was one of yours, was it?'

He nodded. 'She's new to us. Only just come over from Norway. Not fully trained. Cost the abbot over five hundred pounds. Docile as a lamb. I can't understand it. A beautiful creature, beautiful.'

The falcon's speckled feathers were crushed with blood. Her head hung at an awkward angle, the neck broken. The man stroked her feathers over and over, oblivious to the blood staining his jerkin.

In a gruff voice he told her what had happened. 'I had to club her to get her off him.' Another sob heaved from out of him. 'She was clinging on to his face. She would not let go. Oh God, oh God,' he muttered, bending his face to the soft feathers and starting to pray under his breath.

Hildegard's immediate concern was to get the wounded man to the infirmary, but Thomas had called for help from that quarter before he ran to fetch her, and a couple of burly monks showed up carrying two long poles with a canvas slung between them. With Thomas's help they managed to lift the York man onto it despite his howls of pain.

Thomas, still barefoot, was silent as he accompanied Hildegard outside.

'His blood's beginning to clot,' she remarked.

They followed in the wake of the stretcher-bearers, neither of them saying anything more until they reached the door of the infirmary. By that time they had a troop of anxious-looking followers.

Hildegard rested her hand briefly on Thomas's sleeve. 'How could it have happened?'

The wounded man had become a familiar face on the journey. As the archbishop's chief falconer, he had kept up a regular supply of fresh meat. 'He's called John of Willerby,' Thomas remarked. He looked ashen.

'I know him. I saw him in Lincoln Cathedral, lining up with everybody else to send prayers to St Hugh.'

* * *

120

The St Alban's falconer was clearly a man rarely given to tears and especially not in front of a woman. After they had got the man into the infirmary he came up to Hildegard and made his apologies. Barrel-chested, with an air of calmness about him like most of his trade, he was still grief-stricken by what had happened.

He kept saying, 'I had to do it with my own bare hands.' The violence he had done to the abbot's falcon by breaking her neck was worse than knives in his gut, he told her. He paced back and forth across the well-swept tiles of the infirmary muttering about how he had been forced to kill the bird and now he was done for.

'What's the price of a man?' he asked at large. 'Compare it to a falcon, whatever its pedigree. Wick though they are, they do not have human souls. Surely the abbot will see it that way?'

Realising that he was horrified at the amount of money the abbot had invested, and consequently frightened for the loss of his livelihood and the future welfare of his family, if he had one, Hildegard spoke to reassure him. He had obviously done the only thing possible.

And when he was calmer she asked, 'But what caused the bird to attack?'

The man ran his hand through his hair. 'It beats me, Domina. I've never known anything like it. There wasn't a sign of trouble. I would never have let your fella near our birds if I'd thought it would lead to this. He must have done something to rile her.'

'That's most unlikely,' observed Thomas, 'he was the most patient of men.'

The brothers in the infirmary were busy tending the injured man and he was howling in pain at what they were doing to clean him up. Hildegard forced herself to go over to take a closer look.

As well as the gouging to his eyes deep gashes ran down his face, opening the flesh to the bone where the bird's talons had ripped into him. Used to bringing down prey at speed, a falcon like this one had phenomenal strength in its claws. It could tear through the hide of a deer. The softer skin of a man was nothing. The scars on his face might heal with skilful stitching but their ugly tracks would be visible for as long as the man had breath. As for his eyes, it was best not to think about them.

He was in no fit state to explain what had happened but after a while it began to look as if the skill of the monks would save his life, so she left him in their care and returned to where Thomas and the falconer were watching. The latter was still going over things, protesting that it was an attack without precedent, without reason.

'It can only be the work of the Devil. We are all sinners and now we must pay.'

'Tell me,' Hildegard broke in when she could, 'what was he doing in the mews at that time?'

'That's another thing,' the man said. 'They'd had their feed. At least they should have. They were resting. There was no reason for him to be there then.'

'What was their mood while they were being fed?'

The man looked at the ground. 'Same as always. You've seen crows round a carcass?'

Something made her ask, 'Were you there?'

His mouth tightened. 'To be honest, I was there at the start – but I was called away.' He lifted his head with a puzzled frown. 'One of your little servant lads told me I was wanted by Master Fulford about some game I was supposed to have promised him.' He frowned again. 'The thing is, I never promised any such thing. I went over to try to sort it out. But he told me he'd sent no message. He had no idea what I was talking about.'

'So somebody lured you away at feeding time.'

He looked shocked but then considered the idea. 'It looks like it. But why the hell would anybody do that?' The answer dawned. 'To get at my hawks?' He thought it over. 'Why? For what purpose?' Again an answer came. 'To set her onto this poor fellow?' He stared, aghast.

Hildegard moved closer. 'Could somebody do that? Is it possible?'

The falconer frowned. 'She'd be in a rare rage if she hadn't been fed. She'd attack anything. Prey, that is.'

'So had she not been fed?' asked Thomas, sounding puzzled.

'She should have been—'

He swivelled round with an oath and called to one of the apprentices hovering nearby. 'Did you see to them at feed time?'

'Only till that fellow came in and took over.'

123

'Fellow?'

The apprentice glanced round the circle of hostile faces. 'I thought he was from York. He wore a leather gauntlet on his wrist.'

'You slack devil! Do you realise you've nearly got a man killed?' He struck him a hard blow on the head. The youth was dragged off to examine the face of everybody from York who still remained, half the company having already set out, but he failed to recognise the interloper. Snivelling, he was let go with the promise of a good beating.

When things were calmer Hildegard asked how it was possible to make a bird attack a human being.

The falconer slowly shook his head. 'It's not very likely, especially as how she already knew him as a friend. If she thought there was prey to be had, mebbe, and she was trying to get at it . . .' His voice trailed away. The facts spoke for themselves.

Archbishop Neville was standing beside his char with a scattering of servants, waiting to leave. Many of the household had set out before Willerby's accident and even Swynford had left. He had told the archbishop that he wanted to check over one of his mother's properties along the road and would rejoin the convoy wherever they caught up with it later. Neville had sent several of his trusted men with him, either to keep an eye on him or out of courtesy. Now he turned when Hildegard and Thomas appeared and his expression was perplexed. 'Don't give

124

me any nonsense about coincidence,' he greeted. 'Is the man talking yet?'

Hildegard replied in the negative. 'Does it make sense to you, Your Grace?'

Neville's eyes narrowed. 'One of my kitcheners murdered. And now a deliberate and planned attack on my head falconer.' He looked thoughtful. 'Somebody's trying to send me a warning.'

He didn't mention the cross, not with Thomas present, but Hildegard suspected that was uppermost in his mind. With a sudden gasp she realised she had left her bag in the mews. With a hasty excuse she fled.

The bag was where she had let it fall. She fumbled around inside the linen sleeve to make sure the little leather-bound chest was still there. The threat against the cross loomed larger than ever now.

She was just about to go back outside when she nearly tripped over something on the ground. Bending she recoiled with revulsion. It was a dead rat. Then she had a closer look. It had a string round its neck.

It was with much relief that the stragglers finally left the Abbey of St Alban. Hildegard and Thomas were the last to leave. They had been forced to leave the patient too. He was in good hands, however. One of the brothers had trained with the renowned royal surgeon, John of Arderne, and if he did not know what to do for the best to save his sight then nobody did.

Before following the others Hildegard paid a final visit to the infirmary. The monks had applied clean bandages to Willerby's eyes and he was sleeping peacefully after a draft of white poppy.

'Has he spoken yet?' she asked the monk in charge.

'Only to tell us that someone came up behind him and hit him on the head. He remembers nothing more.'

'There is something,' she said before leaving.

'What is it?'

'A dead rat. It was near to where he was lying when he was found.'

'Those yards are plagued by rats.' He gave her a careful look. 'What you suggest is that this attack was diabolically conceived?'

He slid his hands inside the sleeves of his robe.

Thomas still looked ashen-faced. 'What malice,' he kept saying. 'How could anybody do a thing like that?' She had told him about the rat and the piece of string that looked as if it had been tied to something.

'I don't understand it.' Hildegard was riding along beside him. 'Is it to do with the present political unrest? The archbishop sees the attack as a personal warning.'

'It'd take some nerve to attack him,' Thomas replied. 'He's the second-highest prelate in the land. Physical retribution would follow, public beheading, and also, for a believer, there'd be the risk of eternal damnation.'

It would only be worth it with an enormous prize at stake.

She could not fathom how the falconer could be involved in anything of such magnitude.

'If His Grace is right, the man must have been chosen at random,' he concluded.

It was late in the day, shortly before vespers, when the entire baggage train drew to a halt on the summit of a hill. There were exclamations of awe. Below them lay the wide valley of the Thames. A servant who had been here before shouted, 'There she lies!'

The walls and turrets and steeples of London's great buildings could only be guessed at. They were concealed under a pall of fog.

Undaunted, the lead waggoner raised his whip and pointed into the milky whiteness. 'Journey's end at last! Aim into that bank of cloud. It hides the portal to heaven or hell!'

Cheers and shouts rang out again as the wagons began to roll one by one and with ever increasing velocity down the side of the hill towards the invisible city.

It became a storm of sound, wheels churning over the rough track, pots, pans, harness, armour jangling and rattling in the sudden turning speed as the cavalcade hurtled down the last hill to their destination.

And then, as they drove beneath the clouds, the Thames revealed itself like a silver snake winding from one side of the horizon to the other.

'London!' Thomas stood in his stirrups and cheered.

* * *

They took the cattle drovers' road through a vill called Islyngton where the herds from the mid-country and the wild mountains of North Wales were marshalled before being driven across the moor to slaughter at Smithfield.

Everybody was in a jubilant mood, even though they were forced to waste a night at an inn called the Angel while armed escorts were found to guide them through the territory north of the city. Cut-throats abounded, they were warned, and they should not attempt to cross except by light of day with an armed escort.

The men gave in to a spirit of celebration that night.

No earthquakes, no plague, no torrents of frogs, nothing but the grinding endless miles and the discomfort of the saddle, the char, the feet. But they had done it! They were invincible! Now they were ready for anything.

To northerners it was as near London itself as to make no difference.

Part Two

*H*ildegard blinked into the glare of light from the cresset. Wedges of shadow still obscured the knight's features.

Then the light moved. It picked out, first, an unkempt beard, then small, darting eyes, then a familiar broken nose.

She stared aghast.

It was not her long-time enemy Escrick Fitzjohn as she feared.

It was worse.

Far worse.

And now she believed in ghosts.

'No . . . it can't be . . . !' She put out a hand to ward off the apparition. Then she fell in a dead faint to the floor.

Chapter One

The threat of invasion was everywhere. Armed militia filled the streets. They clattered about in groups of four or five, sharpened swords swinging at their hips. Bowmen were constantly arriving from the shires. There were horsemen. Contingents of foot soldiers. Liveried armies pouring in to the town houses and palaces of the magnates.

The soon to be opened Parliament brought other kinds of incomers to fill the streets. Shire knights accompanied by their own small henchmen of liveried conscripts from the manors. Convoys of the nobility with armed guards wearing the signs of their allegiance. Bishops with sumptuously attired retinues of acolytes. City dignitaries, aldermen, burgesses, guildsmen of every description, all accompanied by servants and apprentices. There were clerks by the shoal, lawyers and serjeants-at-law plying for trade, general assistants to fetch and carry, and scriveners, parchment sellers, purveyors of wax for seals and candles, craftsmen in wood and leather, stone and glass and precious metals; along with bow makers, fletchers, saddlers, carters, grooms, lorimers, stable lads and horse traders, there were wheelwrights, there were cloth workers, all accompanied by a hurrying, ever-changing crowd of servants, pages, messengers, go-betweens and attendants and, everywhere, the necessary marketeers to pander to all needs and desires.

The alehouses and wine shops were doing a roaring trade.

The armourers worked all hours making the streets ring with their clangour.

Young women in and out of the taverns schemed to make enough money to move to the country.

Apothecaries and leech women were in great demand.

Bakers, butchers, candlestick makers – name it, there were traders of every description enjoying the fruits of their foresight in stockpiling foreign goods as the blockade of the narrow seas continued.

On top of this, the streets were full of carters bringing produce in from outside. Grain was being brought from the manors of Essex and Kent. Fruit was brought. Cheeses. Fish, dried and salted in immense quantities. Eels, jugged or jellied. The mayor, Nick Brembre, swore that if the French got off their arses and sailed across to lay siege to London they would have a long wait before they starved the Londoners out. As for Parliament, down the road, outside the safety of the walls and the protection of the city militia, there was a similar seething influx of persons and goods from afar.

A mood of grim purpose was apparent in both places, and a sense of solidarity gave rise to the incessant chanting of war songs and raucous battle cries. 'Engelond! Engelond!'

Into this the York contingent rode that morning like lambs to the slaughter.

Chapter Two

The archbishop had his own substantial palace outside the city walls near Westminster. York Place was the first great house outside the abbey enclave. It was a formidable building, the largest on this side of the river and only outshone by Canterbury's palace in Lambeth on the other bank. Scarcely a stone's throw from the Great Hall in Westminster Palace where Parliament was due to meet on the first of October, it could not have been more conveniently close to the seat of power.

A small group of servants remained there through the archbishop's long absences in Yorkshire and when his cavalcade arrived they lined up outside to give the northerners a warm welcome.

The archbishop had no sooner arrived than he whisked Edwin away with his inkhorn and writing desk to attend a private conference with his inner circle of advisors.

Hildegard was to stay in the guest house in the Benedictine

abbey near Westminster Palace. Before leaving she went into the great courtyard to see what she could do to help unload the wagons.

Thomas was on the point of going to his own lodgings on the other side of the city.

'I'll be spending all my time being ferried up and down river,' he commented when he saw her. 'You'd think they could have found somewhere closer.'

'Who instructed you to stay over at St Mary Graces?' she asked.

'Neville and Hubert must have cooked it up between them.'

'You'll be glad of the peace and quiet. Westminster's going be a seething cauldron with all the shire knights and their armies piling into town. And,' she added, 'it can't help but be good for your career to be living in the English headquarters of your Order. You'll be an abbot in two blinks, I shouldn't wonder.'

He smiled at that. 'I'm happy as I am.'

As he turned to go, keeping her tone casual, she asked, 'Do you happen to know when Abbot de Courcy is expected?'

'He may be here already for all we know. He's riding down with only a clerk and his page in attendance. Knowing him it won't take long.'

When she went to join them, the northerners were strolling around the palace and venturing as far as the warren of streets outside the gatehouse to see what was what. They were in no way allowing themselves to look impressed.

'I thought York was big but this is madness,' she heard one of them comment.

'I wouldn't like it. Swarms of folk all on top of one other?'

'Like maggots in a midden,' somebody disparaged.

Before they had even started on the wagons one of the pastry cooks went out to find a pie shop. 'Just to compare them against our own.'

He came back when they had almost finished unloading, ages after everybody had forgotten he'd left. 'You won't believe it,' he announced. 'There was a queue about a mile long just to get near the bloody place.' He held up a steaming pie like a trophy. 'Imagine having to wait in turn like that every day, just for a pie!'

'What's it like?' somebody asked as he bit into it.

He chewed for a moment looking thoughtful. Then he held it up to peer inside the envelope of crust. 'I tell you what, even one of Martin's concoctions could never have made this shite edible.' He gave a flick of the wrist, landing the pie neatly near the muzzle of one of the dogs roaming in from the street. 'London cooks? London pisspots!'

Roaring with laughter, the men watched as the cur, knowing no better, ran off with the pie in its jaws.

Thomas Swynford had lain low ever since his sword had been taken from him in the woods, but he had acquired a substitute from the blacksmith at St Albans, and at Islyngton he had not stayed with them overnight but had ridden on with his page – unafraid, he said, of a few lawless men now he was rearmed. They had seen neither hair nor hide of him since. Everybody assumed he was in a hurry to get to his patron's house so he could start law proceedings against the fellows whose vill he had destroyed, and the common hope was that he was lying on Clerkenwell Moor with his throat cut. 'And good riddance' was also the common view.

After the pie incident Hildegard heard one or two of the men talking in this manner as they were carrying in sacks of produce from the carts. 'Do you fellows have any personal grievance against Swynford?' she asked, going to help them.

One of the men pursed his lips. 'Personal? It could get personal, Domina.'

'Why so?'

'It's his manner. Who the bloody hell does he think he is? He's no better than us. *Sir* Thomas!' The man spat. 'Everything he has is gifted from Bolingbroke. We might ask why the great Earl of Derby should be so generous in raising this nobody to such heights.'

'And what answer would we get?'

'We'd get an answer that says maybe he's not all he seems. Maybe he's more closely related to Bolingbroke than it appears? Is his name really Swynford? Or would it be more honest to use another name?'

Hildegard gave him a sharp glance. 'What name do you have in mind?'

'Any name you want to give to the bastards of the

139

Duke of Lancaster, I reckon. The ones he spawned with Mistress Swynford are running around with the name Beaufort now. A name plucked from the air.' He gave a jeering laugh.

'You're suggesting Swynford is brother to the Earl of Derby – and that he was born outside the marriage?'

'We shall never know now, with his supposed father, old Hugh Swynford, dead. Unless his mother's confessor spills the beans!' The servant gave her an amused smile. 'The old man's death was lucky timing.' He lowered his voice. 'Very lucky indeed. They say it was *she* had him poisoned because he was in the way of her ambition to be the Duke's whore.'

'This is slander . . .'

'No smoke, Domina. They say old Swynford discovered the truth. The midwife sold him the information, looking to enrich herself—'

'More likely the midwife to be poisoned, then—'

'And maybe she was! She vanished and he died in France – so how are we to know the truth of it?'

'This is preposterous . . .'

The man was laughing. 'They say even Gaunt isn't what he seems. He was born of a butcher in Ghent. His mother, Queen Philippa, God bless her, gave birth to a girl but when she rolled over in bed she smothered her. She was so frightened of old Edward she bought a newborn from a butcher's wife and claimed it as King Edward's own. So you see, Lancaster is a bastard too, his begettings are bastards and—'

'What? His son, Bolingbroke, as well?' She, too, was beginning to laugh. The man was outrageous. He was clearly enjoying the idea of shocking her and no doubt saw her as nothing but a pious nun foisted on them for no good reason. 'I've heard it all now!' she scoffed, hoisting one of the smaller sacks onto her hip.

'What our masters get up to, oh, you wouldn't believe, there in your cloisters with your holy sisters! But no, I'll concede that one point. Bolingbroke is likely to be his father's son, seeing as the Duchess Blanche was ever reckoned to be a virtuous woman. Nobody disputes that. But you can see why he's so generous to Swynford, can't you? Bolingbroke, or Harry Derby if you prefer, is Swynford's half-brother.'

They dumped the sacks of flour they were carrying on top of the ones that were already stacked up in the storeroom.

Another servant came staggering after them with one more and now he chipped in as well. 'You're as mad as a bat, Jack. You've got it all wrong.' He grinned at Hildegard. 'Don't heed a word he says, Domina. Swynford stands high for one reason only.'

'And what's that?'

'He's such a useful little toad. It's this way, see. If the price is right, Swynford'll fall over himself to oblige. And why? Because his mother pulls his strings. His *ma*, get it?'

'What the hell's Kate Swynford got to do with it? She's out on her ear, they say.'

'Yes, but it's like this. She's desperate to get back in with the Duke. And her son is the means to do it.'

'What the devil can he do?'

'Think about it! You'd oblige a man if he'd scratch your arse for you, wouldn't you? Harry Derby's no different. Swynford does the scratching and Derby obliges him – by putting in a good word for his ma with the Duke.'

'Aye, I like it.' He was beginning to grin.

'And don't forget,' his companion added, 'Kate Swynford was Harry Derby's wet nurse. She's as close to being his real ma as spit. I reckon he's still in the nursery, jumping when she says jump.'

'I'll tell you one thing, you bat-eared losel, if I wanted my arse scratching, I'd employ somebody with bigger tits than Thomas Swynford's!' They both roared and, punching each other on the shoulders, strolled off to unload more sacks from the wagon.

Well! Hildegard thought, watching them for a moment.

She considered Swynford and his connections. She thought of the ambush and the cross the archbishop had taken to safety. Now it was in his privy chamber where no thief would ever find it.

And then came the business of the rats. Before they even began to settle down for a much-earned meal the first one showed its muzzle. Five, ten, a swarm of them appeared from out of the stores. With no fear of the humans they ran all over the sacks of meal and began biting at the threads with their vicious teeth.

Hildegard hurried outside with everybody else when she heard a din of shrill squeaking. The place was overrun. A few men armed with clubs were setting about the vermin and a hunt and hullabaloo started up when the creatures swarmed into the yard to escape. With a lot of shouting the men pursued them and blood and guts and torn flesh were soon being spattered everywhere. Hildegard felt sick.

A falconer came out to see what the commotion was with one of his birds on his wrist and when he saw what was going on he loosed her. She made several gyrations to gain height and then fell to earth like a stone and flew up at once with one of the struggling rats in her mouth.

But there were too many for one hawk and not enough space in the yard for more so the men tried to scare the rats towards the river. To the horror of those watching, the remaining ones turned on their pursuers. One man had two or three clinging to his garments, biting, devouring, while he screamed for help to get them off him. He fell to the ground and rolled around until they let go and turned to another victim.

The battle continued until the men got the upper hand and were chasing the last one, a particularly large cunning creature, round and round the yard unable to dispatch it until somebody stepped forward and whacked it over and over until it was pulp. He picked it up by the tail and, with a shout of triumph, hung the mess on the tip of his knife and paraded it round the yard as a trophy. There were cheers and shouts: 'It's the Duke of Gloucester!'

Somebody standing next to Hildegard muttered, 'If clever methods don't succeed, try the old one Jarrold.'

There were knowing guffaws from those who overheard him.

The rest of them were shouting for Gloucester. It was known that the Duke carried a fox's tail tied to his lance. It was his symbol. A sign of his brutal cunning, as Hildegard saw it.

She went to the cart to pick up her bags. The threat of being in a strange city seemed to have unleashed a mood of violence in the men and she was glad to get away.

A couple of more temperate servants escorted Hildegard from the landing stage at York Place to the busy quay near the abbey. 'Safer to go by water, Domina,' they warned her. 'We've been instructed not to set foot on the Strand at night without a few men-at-arms with us.'

'I'll remember that.'

It was only a short boat ride but their wherryman had to row against the tide and the servants marvelled at the strength of it, comparing it unfavourably with the slower more tranquil River Ouse that swept past the edge of the woods near the purlieus of Bishopthorpe Palace. They dropped her bags on the quay when she alighted, then stayed in the boat for the return journey, leaving her to make her way by herself up the path and along to the porter's lodge where she had to show her pass and wait to be admitted.

Westminster Abbey had been built long ago in wood, rebuilt by King Henry II in stone, and was now being added to yet again by the King's master mason Henry Yevele. Situated in marshland on a hummock called Thorney Island, the only reminder now was the watercourse that encircled the abbey complex like a moat.

Bridges gave access at three points. One went over a stream to the west and led to the horse ferry. This served travellers, especially pilgrims, who wanted to cross the Thames to go south to Canterbury, to Rome, to Jerusalem even. It also gave access to a group of fortified buildings on the opposite bank set amid meadows and pleasant-looking copses. After Archbishop Sudbury's murder during the rebellion it was now William Courtenay who wore the mitre in Canterbury and lorded over there at Lambeth.

The second bridge was a small wooden service bridge leading north from the gardens and used mainly by servants for conveying produce in and out of the labyrinthine kitchen quarters serving both the abbey and the palace.

The third and busiest bridge was the main thoroughfare from the city of London.

The abbey and the palace were separated by a wide yard. Today it was seething with onlookers waiting for a glimpse of the King, as well as with the usual lawyers, clerks, couriers, parliamentary officials and servants. They in turn had attracted an army of pie and ale sellers, as well as jugglers, acrobats, card sharps and a muzzled bear on a chain that sat disconsolately outside a nearby tavern.

Hildegard was just making her way through this crowd after depositing her belongings in her chamber in the guest quarters when someone pushed a scrubby piece of parchment into her hand. By the time she looked down, noticed the unfamiliar seal and looked up again, the messenger had vanished.

She peered at the seal again. It looked vaguely like a mitre and a sword but was so smudged it was difficult to make out. She began to prise it off as she threaded her way across the yard. A single piece of much-rubbed parchment opened out to reveal a message written in black ink.

'*My dearly beloved lady mother,*' it began. '*It is with much pleasure and delight I inform you that I have the honour to accompany my liege lord His Grace the Bishop of Norwich to the opening of Parliament and am now lodged at his house in the city. However, I beg a boon and would do so in person and beseech you to meet me privily at the church of All Hallows by the Tower after nones this day, when I may see your beloved face again.*'

It was followed by a few more filial endearments and signed in her son's name, Bertrand.

She felt her heart leap. Her dear boy, the beloved child of her youth, fifteen now, for the last five years a squire to the bishop's captain of guards – it had been an age since she had held him in her arms. To his disappointment, he had been passed over as too young when the bishop made his recent ill-fated march into Flanders and been so utterly routed. Because of this the bishop's temporalities had been withheld for a time – putting her son's future in jeopardy – but the bishop was restored to favour, her son rejoined his retinue. And now he was close at hand.

She smiled as she put the note safely in her bag. He must have got one of the bishop's clerks to pen it – either that or his handwriting was much improved since she had last seen it.

'Still not showed his face!' The porter was cheerful when she reappeared. 'If King Richard hasn't arrived from Eltham there's a good reason for it.' He had been jubilant when he had first signed her in, confident that today the King and Queen would put in an appearance, even though Parliament was not to open yet.

Hildegard made some non-committal remark as she passed.

He called after her. 'It looks as if the French are going to be here before him. They're running round like headless chickens in there.'

She turned back.

When he nodded towards the chapter house she asked, 'Is there news, then?'

'So they say. Some intelligence just come in. You should go across there if you want the latest.' He was envious of her freedom, it seemed, and added, 'I can't get away from here until compline.'

'I'll see what I can find out then send someone to keep you informed, if you wish.'

'Grand. Let's hope it's not a false dawn. Let 'em come!'

* * *

The crowds, those who could not get inside the building, now milled around the porch.

'Is it true?' she asked a couple of pilgrims leaning on their staves close by.

'Invasion? It sounds like it.'

'And where are the French supposed to be?'

'Halfway up the Thames,' one of the pilgrims said, smoothing his beard nervously with one hand.

'They've been saying that since midsummer,' Hildegard pointed out.

'Yes, but our spies have been watching Sluys,' the shorter of the two men replied. 'They say it's a forest of masts. You can walk half a mile out to sea by stepping from one deck to another. And now it's moving this way.'

It was known by now that the French had paid the mercenaries in the Low Countries to bring their ships to Sluys to join the armada they were gathering. It was said that there were one thousand three hundred and eighty-seven, and that if you looked out to sea the masts were like a vast stretch of woodland floating on the water.

There were other stories as well, that the Constable of France was having an enormous warship fitted out in Brittany, bigger than anything ever built, and that every ship from the port of Seville, right round to Prussia, had been bought by the French for their invasion fleet. No expense had been spared.

'Every port has had its ships requisitioned,' one of them told her now. 'You name it, Bruges, Blankenberghe,

148

Middleburg, right round to St Omer – and what do we have in all this?'

'Calais,' his companion chipped in.

'And allies?' The man gripped his stave more tightly. 'Not one. We're on our own.'

'Backs against the wall.'

'As usual.'

'What's going on inside the chapter house?' Hildegard asked. She could not dispute their claims. England did stand alone except for the support of a handful of Welsh bowmen. Ranged against them was all the might of France, Spain, Scotland and Flanders under the Duke of Burgundy. The Queen's brother, Wenceslas of Bohemia, the Holy Roman Emperor, offered no practical support either.

One of the pilgrims said, 'They're making an announcement soon but they won't let us in for fear of people being crushed to death.' He glanced at his companion and they both shrugged their shoulders.

The execution block on Tower Hill had a handful of well-armed guards posted beside it. They were bristling with weapons and eyed Hildegard and Thomas narrowly as they approached.

Aware of the bloody events that regularly took place in the vicinity, the two of them were in a subdued frame of mind as they walked past on the way to All Hallows to meet Bertrand. It had taken an age to find a ferry willing to take her downriver to the Tower landing stage and then she had had to find Thomas in the rambling Cistercian headquarters, but she had not wanted to walk about alone with the city in such turmoil.

They were just discussing the invasion and the likelihood of London being under siege when they were alerted by the sound of running footsteps. A gang of youths appeared, soon filling the narrow street opposite the Tower and swarming towards the block. They were running in some kind of formation, military style, banging cudgels against their bucklers in an ominous rhythm. A little drum started up behind them with a rapid warlike beat, urging the gang to quicken its pace. A few dogs, growling and slavering, galloped at their heels. They avoided the armed men near the block and ran on with a look of grim purpose.

Hildegard and Thomas were about to cross the green when a second group appeared from one of the lanes on the other side. They too had a drum which was being beaten to a martial rhythm.

The first gang, in red and white livery, and the second, dressed in lovat green with black slashes on their sleeves, continued to sprint towards each other.

'Apprentice boys,' murmured Hildegard in alarm. 'What are they up to?'

It was soon apparent. With wild shouts the two groups met head-on, wielding their cudgels and beginning to crack each others' heads open. The first victim fell, blood pouring from a wound above his eye, and Hildegard automatically made as if to help when Thomas gripped her by the arm.

'Let's get out of it! Look!'

He was pointing to a line of constables marching out of one of the side streets and as they watched others appeared from the alleys and lanes leading onto the green. Properly armed with swords and shields, most wore chain mail under their tunics, heads protected by steel bassinets. They were a disciplined force and quickly surrounded the green and everyone on it. The din of swords banging in unison against their shields drowned out the sound of the apprentices' little drum. An armed man on horseback followed behind the biggest cohort as it came up the lane from beside the Tower.

Soon the lines of armed men began to close in. The apprentice boys, lashing out randomly to protect themselves, were being brought down with howls of pain. Blood began to slick the cobblestones. The apprentices slipped and fell under a hail of blows and the constables attacked the fallen with batons flying, pinning them to the ground. Hildegard cried out as mailed boots thudded into the boys' ribs. The constables methodically set to work dealing out the same fate to everyone until, as at some prearranged plan, they began to close in on the two groups, meting out punishment indiscriminately as they went.

Thomas dragged Hildegard into the safety of an alley.

With the odds turned against them, the apprentices in green and black began to scatter. Some made a run for the same refuge where Thomas and Hildegard were sheltering but the constables pursued them, cudgels, swords and batons flailing in every direction.

'Stop! We are not of these people!' shouted Thomas, trying to shield Hildegard from their blows as they charged into the alley.

'Then get the fuck out of it!' snarled one of the constables as he ran past.

'Come on!' Thomas gripped Hildegard by the sleeve and dragged her out onto the green again. 'Run for it!'

Together they headed as fast as they could towards a street on the other side of the green, away from the main fight, but a line of constables appeared from one of the lanes. Behind them stood a reserve of a dozen more armed men.

'Permit us to come through?' Hildegard asked, throwing a glance over her shoulder at the battle as it spilt out of the alley and spread onto the green again. The apprentices seemed to be gaining the upper hand.

When she tried to push her way through the line she noticed that the constables had linked arms, barring the way like a Saxon shield wall, and when she asked again to be allowed through they stared past her without responding.

She called out to the man on horseback patrolling behind the lines but he ignored her and moved on, checking that the wall of men was firm.

'This is ridiculous!' Thomas argued with the constable standing nearest. 'You can see by our garments we're not apprentices. We're monastics from the Abbey of Meaux.'

'We don't care if you're monastics from bloody Jerusalem, you can't come through, so piss off!'

'By what right can you keep us kettled up here?' Thomas demanded with unaccustomed force. 'We are free citizens. We have a right to walk where we please.'

No one answered.

He glared. 'Come on, Hildegard, let's try further along.'

They began to pass down the line in the hope of finding a constable who looked more open to reason but they hadn't gone far when Hildegard found herself whisked through an opening that suddenly appeared. It happened without warning so that she was out on the other side before she realised Thomas had not followed. The shield wall re-formed. 'Thomas!' she shouted, turning and trying to push her way back.

'You're wasting your time, lady,' muttered one of the men.

She shook his arm. 'He's my priest! Let him through!'

By now the constables were beginning to tread forward, a pace at a time, moving inwards just as the first wave of constables had done earlier, converging on the two gangs and pushing Thomas and several other men who had been caught inside closer to the fighting.

'Please!' she shouted as they moved in.

'You can find him later,' she was told. 'Nobody crosses the line.'

Thomas had been pushed into the thick of the conflict as everyone was forced into one brawling mass.

The same constable advised her to get along to the next street. 'He'll be sent along there.'

She didn't believe him. It was chaos. There was no way

Thomas would know to do that. And why would they let him out there instead of here? She saw the bloodstained apprentices being kicked to the ground, the battle lines surging now this way, now that, heard the crack of clubs on the backs of unprotected heads, saw green and red liveries mixed together. The constables were protected by steel helmets, by chain mail, well armed. It was not an equal fight.

They must have had prior knowledge of the apprentices' plans, she surmised, bewildered by the violence.

Reluctant to leave Thomas to his fate, she made her way into the next street as she had been advised, but it was the same: lines of constables, everyone inside one fixed battle zone.

Unsure what to do for the best, she turned down the hill towards All Hallows. Her fear now was that Bertrand might have become embroiled in the riot as well.

With the raucous shouts of the combatants in her ears she hurried down to find him.

Chapter Three

It was an impressive church. Not for its size, nor even for its slender spire and wide porch, but for its sinister reputation.

It was where the victims of the axe were taken after judicial beheading on Tower Green. It was where prayers for their tormented souls could be offered up and their mutilated bodies laid to rest.

Finding no one waiting outside she hurried in. It was empty.

Candles burned at the far end illuminating an effigy of the Holy Mother with the twisted corpse of her son in her arms. Every contorted muscle was revealed. It looked horrifyingly lifelike.

No sign of Bertrand.

She went further in. Massive rafters loomed over the nave. Stone pillars cast shadows across the uneven floor. It was an eerie place. Knowing what she did about it, she shuddered.

Worried, now, that Bertrand was in trouble of some sort to want to meet in a place like this, she forced herself to go in search of the sacristan. She was already halfway down the nave when the big iron-bound door slammed behind her. The noise of fighting up the street faded to distant howls and the barking of the dogs.

In the silence she could hear the sound of her own footsteps.

A flight of steps seemed to lead into the crypt. Noticing candlelight at the bottom, she went over, confident there would be somebody down there who would be able to tell her if one of Norwich's squires had been asking for her.

It was well after nones by now. She and Thomas had been caught behind the lines far longer than she had realised. Hoping that Bertrand had not simply given up and left, she began to descend.

She called his name when she was halfway down.

The light at the bottom went out.

She came to a halt.

'Bertrand?'

Her voice echoed round the stone vault. When there was no answer after she called again, she took a step forward into the muffling darkness. Drops of water fell onto the flagstones. She steadied herself against the wall, feeling flakes of lime fall away beneath her finger tips.

There was no glimmer of light from below now the candle had gone out. Cautiously she stretched out the toes of one boot and found a step. She lowered her foot onto it, then the next one, and down, carefully descending.

Turning too quickly at the bottom, she bumped into a wall then realised it was the slender column of an arch. She stretched out a hand in front of her but encountered nothing but cool, subterranean air in the blackness of the void.

She edged forward. There had been a light, a candle or taper of some sort. It had lured her down here, giving a glimpse of tombstones at the bottom of the steps before it had suddenly gone out. She should have stayed where she was but, now she was here, she had no choice but to find the tinderbox and get some light.

She began to edge forward again but then stopped. A small current of air came out of nowhere. Ghostly fingers seemed to brush her face.

'Is that you, Bertrand? . . . Are you playing games?'

Before she could say more she was pitched backwards, cold steel crushing over her face, dragging her against something that felt like chain mail as she clawed at it to free herself.

The thing that had caught her was everywhere and she was unable to lay hold of it.

A sudden irrational thought came that it must be a ghost. The risen dead! There was the smell of death everywhere.

Her hair stood on end.

She could not breathe.

Struggle as she did, she was held in a grip like a vice.

Her bag fell to the floor. Her cross was ripped away in the struggle.

She managed to find her knife in the folds of her cloak, but then the thing slammed her hard against the wall and she heard a chuckle from out of the darkness.

It was no ghost.

Hot breath slid down the side of her face and a voice grunted, 'Some welcome this is, my lady!'

'Who are you?' she managed to croak. Her knife was unsheathed now but she had no idea where to thrust as her assailant began to rip her garments aside, now here, now there, never still.

When he felt the strength with which she resisted, he growled, 'I'll get light.' He moved away.

On the other side of the crypt a spark suddenly glinted then light flooded the whole crypt. In its brilliance she saw a monstrous image. It was an armed knight, his visor raised. His grotesque shadow leapt across the wall behind him as he turned back to her.

With the light held high above him his face was still in shadow.

'Don't you recognise me, Hildegard?'

She froze. He knew her name.

Terror made her open her mouth but she could force no sound from between her lips. It must be Escrick Fitzjohn, she surmised feverishly. He had tracked her down as he had vowed he would. Now he was here to wreak vengeance on her.

She blinked into the glare. Wedges of shadow obscured the knight's features. Then the light moved. It picked out, first an unkempt beard, then small darting eyes, then the familiar broken nose. She stared. It was not Escrick after all.

It was worse.

Far worse.

'No . . . it can't be . . . !' She put out a hand to ward him off. Then she was falling into darkness.

Only seconds elapsed, because when she came round she was still being held in a grip of steel and the apparition was staring into her face, the flare held high, its light flooding over them.

'It's me!' The thing gave a harsh laugh. She felt its mailed body crush her against the wall, mauling her, rough and determined, growling, 'I thought you'd guess!'

'How could I?' she replied weakly.

'It doesn't matter. Now you can greet me as you should. It's been long enough, my dear wife.'

Hugh de Ravenscar. It was impossible.

He disappeared, believed killed in the French wars, more than ten years ago. As his wife, Hildegard had been given papers to prove it. She had believed herself a widow for over ten years.

He became violent when he realised she was going to resist, and with the advantage of his coat of mail her struggles were having little effect. In the tussle that followed she tried to feel around with one foot for her knife where it had fallen but it was too dark and instead she tried to find a weak point to counter his attack.

Remembering Hubert in all this turmoil, she recalled how he had defeated Sir William atte Wood at the shrine of John of Beverley when the knight, fully armoured, had broken into the minster to abduct the minstrel Pierrekyn Haverel. Hubert had defended the boy's right to sanctuary and, unarmed, had defeated atte Wood by wounding him in the throat just above the top of his breastplate, where armour gives the least protection.

Now her fingers grappled at Ravenscar's chain mail but it was pulled up tightly under his chin and she could find no opening.

'Leave hold!' she cried hoarsely, 'I can't believe it's you. Why did you let me believe you were dead?'

He gave a wild laugh, but when she put her hand on his forehead in something like a caress, but in reality to hold his lips away from her own, he lifted his lust-bleared eyes and in the flickering light she saw a wish to boast about his deceit.

'Tell me, husband, why did you leave us to mourn?' she whispered.

'I sent two men,' he rasped, drawing back a little. 'I paid them for the journey. Did the bastards take the money and run?'

'Two Genoese arrived at Castle Hutton with a ring and some documents to show they were from you. They spoke no English. We guessed they were trying to let us know you were dead.'

'That's so. I sent them.'

'But why?'

He laughed harshly, as if only a fool would ask such a question. 'I didn't want anybody to come looking for me. I was safer where I was.'

'Safer? But where? How? The last I saw of you, you were going to join Woodstock in Normandy. Tell me what happened.'

'We were on *chevauchée*. Hungry. Looking for loot. We'd been holed up in some godforsaken town for weeks, neither able to take the castle at Caen, nor anything else worth a pig's whistle. We came across a small town which we ransacked. Good pickings. I broke into a fish-merchant's house, biggest in the village, with plenty of gold and silver in it and a woman—' he broke off. 'I was wounded. I caught a fever. I decided the woman was useful and if I played it right I could have both the loot and the woman and – what was best – a safe bed to lie in. Luckily she thought it worth her while to keep me alive so she could claim the ransom. After the English army moved on I recovered and put my plan to her and she agreed. It suited us both. Her man had been killed when we took the town. So, off with the old, on with the new! Good business!'

'You mean you changed sides?'

'What choice did I have? The English army was making a push towards Rouen. What did you expect me to do? March through Normandy alone? It was infested with mercenaries. I was wearing valuable armour. I was safer where I was.'

'But you let us believe you were dead . . .'

'Was I supposed to offer myself as a hostage and trust somebody to pay up?'

'You know Roger de Hutton would have paid. You were his vassal.'

He made a mocking sound at the back of his throat. 'I'm damned sure I wouldn't pay up if one of my fellows was fool enough to get himself caught.'

'Roger is not like you.'

Ravenscar braced his shoulders and his lip curled. There was a small scar beneath his nose that she had forgotten about. It made him look pathetic. He must have seen the change in her expression because, misunderstanding it, he pulled her towards him again.

'I've waited a long time to regain what's mine. You owe me a hell of a lot of duty—'

'That's surely not why you're here . . . ?' Her heart gave a sickening plunge, a physical response that happened before she had time to acknowledge what it meant.

His touch repelled her.

It had begun to do so long before he left for Normandy. She had felt guilty about it but had been unable to help her feelings. Now the old, secret repugnance surged back and she flinched away from him, attempting to run towards the steps leading out of the crypt, but he lunged after her and brought her to the stone floor with a crash of steel and a turmoil of tangled limbs.

She screamed then. As loud as she could. As long as she could. Until his hand clamped over her mouth and he hissed in her ear. 'Stop your racket! Do it again and you're dead. I'm here in secret. Until I've got the lawyers to sort out my claim nobody can know I'm here.'

She was on her back, crushed under his great armoured weight, but her eyes widened in disbelief. 'Claim?'

'My lands, of course. France is an expensive country. Ma belle dame has sent me to get back what's mine—'

'But your brother inherited your land. The rest passed to the children – and I took my dowry back and gave it to my Order—'

'Your dowry!' he derided. 'It belongs to me. Everything you have belongs to me. You belong to me.' He gripped her by the jaw. 'You can't be a bride of Christ, Hildegard, you're *my* bride. Now open your bloody legs and let me prove it.' He began to fumble under the edge of his chain mail shirt for the belt holding his breeches.

'Let me go!'

The letter she believed came from her son had been a fake. She felt sick. His ruse had taken her in completely.

Rage at her own stupidity made her fight back strongly, gasping with every blow and shouting for help whenever she managed to free her mouth from the suffocating pressure of the mail gauntlet he held over her face. It was hopeless. He was too strong. She was weakening. Then, when all seemed lost, suddenly, like a miracle, the entire crypt was flooded with light.

Ravenscar jerked up his head, blinking towards its source. His weight shifted. Somewhere behind the light a voice demanded, 'Who are you?'

Ravenscar was gawping at a figure standing in the doorway.

Hildegard scrambled free and got to her feet.

Someone was descending the steps.

He wore a white habit and was tall enough to have to stoop under the low ceiling. His torch revealed a dark foreign-looking face, with large liquid eyes that took in the scene with one quelling glance.

'Well?' he prompted.

Ravenscar, with extraordinary speed, pulled up his breeches and hurled himself past the stranger to the top of the steps without looking back. The man watched him go without trying to stop him. Then he turned to Hildegard.

They stared at each other for a moment without speaking. She took in his white habit similar to her own and noticed some sort of red and gold symbol on the shoulder. An alien friar, then.

His observant honey-coloured eyes alighted on her long enough to suggest he knew everything about her.

Shaking, she crumpled to her knees. 'My thanks, my deepest thanks, Brother. You arrived just in time to save me from a most horrible—' Then she could not hold back the tears of relief. They coursed unchecked down her cheeks. She raised her tear-stained face towards her rescuer. 'Please escort me out of this place.'

He held out a hand. 'Come. I didn't realise you were a Cistercian nun. Come, Domina. You're safe now.'

* * *

Hildegard alighted at the wharf near the horse ferry and made her way along the busy path to the bridge. There she had to produce her pass. The strap of her bag was hanging off and she had forgotten to search for her cross when it had been wrenched from round her neck in the crypt. Her knife had gone as well.

The porter recognised her from earlier that day when she had set out with Brother Thomas to meet her son. Then she had spoken to him in a mood of joyful anticipation. He waved her through now with a puzzled smile.

When she offered no explanation for her appearance he exclaimed, 'Still no sign of him, Domina. Not long to go now, though.'

His excitement at the prospect of seeing King Richard arrive to open Parliament exceeded his curiosity about her appearance. 'The royal barge is going to be berthed just down there at the wharf.' He gestured across the palace green towards the river. 'We're all agog. They say there's going to be an announcement as soon as he arrives.' He lowered his voice. 'A royal birth! There'll be dancing in the streets then all right!'

She could scarcely understand what he was saying. Her head ached where Ravenscar had banged it against the wall and her thoughts were in turmoil.

She muttered something along the lines of, 'The birth of a baby is usually a cause for rejoicing,' and started to move on.

But his eyes lit up and he said, 'It'll be more than that! The succession will be assured. No more crown-hungry uncles trying to oust poor Dickon! He'll be able to sleep in safety at last, St Margaret be praised!'

'Ah, the succession. Yes, but what if Queen Anne gives birth to a girl?'

The porter frowned. 'I, for one, would not object to a queen if she was for the good of all – as I'm sure any daughter of Queen Anne would prove. Others might object.' He gave a sniff. 'It's not a Norman custom to respect women. They prefer their monarchs to be warlords. We're more reasonable.'

With a vague acknowledgement that what he said was true, she made her escape, crossing the west front of the abbey, where the scaffolding was rattling eerily in the wind. It looked as if the enlargement to the nave had come to a stop. Labour was being redirected to the defences against the invasion. Signs of abandoned works were everywhere and wind whistled through the half-built vaults with a constant wailing sound.

A watchman sat on one of the measured-up blocks of stone paring his nails with a knife. He did not look up when she passed. Hildegard was sharply conscious of her dishevelment. The friar who had rescued her had offered a cup of wine but she had declined. Driven by a desire to get away she had allowed him to guide her to the nearest landing stage so she could get a ferry straight back to Westminster. Now arrived, she could not bear the thought of going back to her chamber.

Instead she made her way through the building site and out into the cloisters on the other side. Here was an air of peace and she sat for some time in a quiet corner where no one would bother her.

Ravenscar's reappearance made no sense.

She could not bring herself to call him Hugh.

What did he hope to gain by coming back? He could not claim control over her children's small inheritance. If he tried and by some mischance succeeded, he could ruin them. Even he could not want that. And could he really claim restitution of her dowry as he threatened? Surely he could only do that if they were still legally married. And what about this French woman he had been living with? Were they married? It was all confusion.

Whatever happened, her own life would be different from now on.

With a start, she remembered Thomas.

The last she had seen of him had been in the thick of the fighting, with the constables pressing in more menacingly and lashing out with their clubs.

I should go along to York Place and see if there's news, she thought guiltily. Pray the saints he's safe.

Better still, she could take the ferry back to the Tower and go up to St Mary Graces to find out for herself if he had been brought in. If anyone knew what had happened to him, his fellow Cistercians would.

Her thoughts flew back to her son and the disappointment of not seeing him. Her hands clenched.

There were many people who needed to know that Hugh de Ravenscar still lived. Her son was only one of them. Her daughter, almost too young to remember much about her father, would also have to be told, a message sent to the house in Shropshire where she attended the wife of one of the marcher lords.

And then there was Roger de Hutton, recently arrived with his retinue from his Yorkshire castle to stay in his London town house so he could attend the forthcoming session of Parliament. There was Archbishop Neville, too, and many others who would have something to say about the unexpected reappearance of the Lord of Ravenscar.

But she did not move. She could not. The thought of returning to the city alone and unprotected filled her with an uncharacteristic fear. She could instead send a message to St Mary Graces and ask for news of Thomas that way.

But still she could not make herself get up.

The sun was hidden behind a vaporous cloud and the easterly wind was strengthening. It blustered at the hem of her robe and fallen leaves eddied into the corners of the garth. A swaying file of black-robed Benedictines eventually came singing from out of their cells and padded towards the chapel.

Her thoughts flew to Abbot Hubert de Courcy. He, too, would surely have arrived from Yorkshire by now.

She imagined how he would look riding into the forecourt of St Mary Graces – hot and travel-stained, a few days' growth of dark stubble on his jaw, eyes flashing with intelligence, his strong fingers playing lightly with the reins of the spirited mare he rode. She imagined how his face would light up when their eyes met.

Then came a picture of his reaction when she told him

the news that she was still a married woman and no widow after all – that her monastic vows were a lie and a sham.

Everything that had passed between them was a sham.

Forcing herself to her feet, aching somewhat, bruises where she did not expect them, she made her way out of the cloisters and back to the guest wing where she would take off every stitch of clothing and sponge herself all over to get rid of the memory of Ravenscar's malign touch. Then she would put on fresh garments and venture out to do what had to be done.

The Strand. The house of Earl Roger de Hutton.

'*What?*' Earl Roger de Hutton could scarcely get the word out. He stared at her for some moments, then, mouth still open, dropped heavily onto a cushioned bench in front of his blazing fire and gazed violently into the flames. His colour was always high, somewhere between scarlet and vermilion, now it clashed with the fiery red of his beard.

Hildegard had expected a roaring hour. Knowing of old what he was like, she was surprised now by his single strangled exclamation and even more surprised when, after a long silence, he lumbered to his feet, clanked over the tiles in his metal boots and dropped on one knee in front of her.

'My dearest Hildegard,' he began gruffly. 'I've foolishly put your soul in everlasting danger. First by permitting you to be betrothed to the smooth-talking blaggard when you were scarcely old enough to know your own name and second by not making sure the reports of his death were properly verified. I can do nothing to assuage my guilt but to track him down and kill him.' He placed one hand across his chest. 'And this I vow to do, so help me God.'

'Roger,' she put out a hand. 'You cannot blame yourself. I was headstrong in those days. I thought I loved him. If you had tried to prevent me, I would have absconded with him.'

'You would?'

'He would have insisted and I would have eagerly complied.'

Roger was still on one knee. 'But now he's lied about being killed in France, breaking his vow of fealty to me, and he's put your soul in jeopardy. Your vows – for heaven's sake, Hildegard! – what about those?'

'I shall take advice from Abbot de Courcy when he arrives,' she told him, feeling faint at the very thought. 'He'll know the Church's view on the matter. I acted in all innocence. That will have some bearing on my Order's judgement.'

Roger laid his right hand across his chest again. 'I promise my protection if they decide on punishment. I make this vow.' He peered at her with a quickened glance from under his brows. 'What can they do to you? Excommunicate you? My dear Hildegard!' He rose massively to his feet. 'That on top of all the rest!'

He stood four-square with his back to the fire and rammed his thumbs into his sword belt. 'We have a king likely to lose his crown. We have a city about to be overrun by armed Frenchmen. We have a mayor and aldermen intent on tearing each other to pieces and dancing on the remains. We have plot and counterplot by the nobility such that you can't even trust your own mother. And now, to crown it all, Hugh de Ravenscar, the Devil take his black soul, rises from the dead!'

After a heavy pause he asked, 'What state's he in these days?'

'Not much changed. He's been living quite well, I gather. Older, of course, as are we all.'

'Did he have any excuse?'

Ulf, Roger's steward, who had been silent throughout all this, now erupted with a snarl. 'If I may say so, My Lord, that's a damnable question. His deceit is inexcusable.'

'Of course it is!' Roger exclaimed vehemently. 'God's bollocks, I know that! But to himself – he must have had a reason that would square with his own conscience.'

'If he's got one.' Ulf gave a strangled oath and went to fling himself in the window embrasure, where he stared savagely out into the yard.

'I believe,' explained Hildegard, 'he was wounded during a *chevauchée*. You remember, he was with Arundel's failed expedition to Normandy, and during a raid on a minor town there he found himself in the house of a woman whose husband had just been killed. She tended his wounds. By the time he felt able to rejoin the army they had moved on. He stayed.'

'With the woman?'

'So he tells me.'

'Faithless bastard. A deserter and an adulterer. What do you think to a man like that, steward?'

'What do you imagine I think, My Lord? Do you want me to put it into words while Hildegard is still present in your chamber?'

Roger turned back to her. 'So he decides to stay? Just like that.'

'I gather the woman had been married to a comfortably-off fish merchant, so it must have been an irresistible opportunity to step into the dead man's shoes.'

'Irresistible? To an outright bastard, maybe.' Ulf had taken out his dagger and was staring at the blade.

Roger started to prowl about and now he came to a stop in front of her. 'You sound remarkably calm about it.'

'I'm not sure whether I'm a nun or not.'

'And if you're not?'

'Then I'll be able to rage and curse to my heart's content and do whatever else I please.' She paused. 'But I won't. I feel benumbed.'

Ulf slapped the flat of his dagger down on the stone sill. It made a crack that echoed round the chamber like bone breaking.

Before she left, Roger had already started to marshal his forces and had decided to send Ulf, his steward, to All Hallows by the Tower to hunt Ravenscar down.

'The double-dealing devil must have had a reason for choosing to meet you at such a place,' Roger claimed. 'He'll have gone to earth nearby. We'll dig him out,' he vowed. 'Or I'll know the reason why!' There were fellows whose job it was to keep an eye on other people, he told her; all the barons employed men like that, as he did himself. They would pool their intelligence. No baron would support a knight who broke his oath to his lord. Ravenscar would be dragged out by his heels and punished.

'What's His Grace saying about it?' he asked Hildegard before she left.

'I came to tell you first.'

She dreaded having to inform the archbishop almost as much as she feared to tell Hubert. She had been included in his retinue precisely because she was a Cistercian nun, with the privileges of her calling, a woman to be trusted. Now what would he do if her vows were invalid?

There was also her prioress at Swyne to answer to.

Ulf followed her out when she left. He was already on his way to the church of All Hallows by the Tower with a small band of armed men. He detached himself from them and caught up with her in the courtyard before she reached the gatehouse.

'Where are you going?'

She turned and pushed the back of one hand over her face. 'I'm not quite sure.'

'You look dazed. Did anything else happen when you met him?'

She avoided his glance. 'Not much.'

'What does he want?'

'He wants his lands back. This woman he's with insists.'

'You didn't tell Roger that.'

'I didn't get a chance.'

'You were holding it back.'

'That as well. I thought on top of what I'd told him already it might be too much in one go.'

'What else are you holding back, Hildegard?'

'Why should I be—?'

'Come on,' he interrupted savagely, backing her into an alcove. 'We've known each other ever since we were bare-legged little heathens running wild in the woods round Castle Hutton. There is something – what is it?' He turned her face up to his. 'Is that a bruise on your cheek?'

Her eyes filled. 'Ulf. It's all such a mess.'

'Did he touch you?'

She knew what he meant. She avoided his glance. 'Please – don't . . .'

'Did he? Tell me, Hildegard. If he did I'll break his balls.'

'It was nothing . . .'

'He's come back for you, hasn't he?'

'Never!'

'You said you loved him, you'd have absconded with him—' His voice was harsh.

'It was true . . . long ago. I was headstrong. That's what I was like in those days. But I was a fool. A child. I was fifteen! I thought I knew everything!'

'But when he left for the war . . . ?'

'It ended long before that. I realised I'd made a mistake

174

almost straight away. There was no love in it. What I felt to begin with was like a mist. It dissolved at the first sign of reality. I realised pretty quickly he was no good. His violence. Self-pity. The cruel games he played. It was a marriage of convenience. Nothing more. I tried to accept it. It was what I was expected to do.' She twisted away. 'I didn't love him, Ulf, not after that first rush of romance. I could never love a man I didn't respect.'

'I wish you—' he clamped his lips together and his eyes were splinters of blue as they searched her face. 'You know what I wish.'

'Everything might have been so different. I know that.'

He reached for her and pulled her powerfully into his arms. 'If Roger fails in his promise, Hildegard, I shall not fail in mine. I promise I shall kill him.'

'No!'

'What?'

'If I say spare him, will you?'

Ulf stepped back as if she had slapped his face. 'Would you want that?'

'It depends on who I am, doesn't it?' She looked at him in open confusion. 'As a nun I must not draw blood or cause it to be drawn. Ulf! I don't know who I am or how I'm bound until I've talked to—' She could not say his name.

'Damn him to hell!' Ulf ground out between his teeth. He knew whom she meant and what prevented her from naming him. Hubert de Courcy. Always her abbot standing between them.

He gazed bleakly into her face, then after a moment of indecision reached out and crushed his mouth against hers. His lips moved hotly, drawing a response she could not resist. She tasted blood. She weakened in his arms. He released her, all the time staring into her face to read her expression with his piercing blue gaze.

'Damn them both,' he intoned hoarsely after an agonised pause. His eyes flashed murderously as he turned and stalked off.

Chapter Four

As soon as she went out she found herself in the middle of a huge crowd. It was no apprentices' brawl this time. It was mostly pilgrims and sightseers and for some reason they were singing a *Te Deum*. Loud voices bawled the Latin to the skies. Hats glittered with saints' badges. Cloaks flapped in the wind.

'Has the King arrived?' she asked somebody standing nearby.

'Not yet. But any time now!'

As usual the yard around the Great Hall was seething with people as well. The pungent aroma of food being cooked on open spits floated on the air. Rabbit. Wild duck. Teal. Song thrush. Chestnuts roasting in shallow pans. Eel pie, too hot to handle. And the constant smell of ale. The drift of woodsmoke. Watching over all this, like a brooding spirit from another world, the dancing bear, now sitting on its haunches staring dully at its chains as if wondering how to free itself.

Scarcely a cobblestone was without somebody standing on it. Necks were craning at a procession approaching across the bridge.

A herald appeared in the thick of the crowd.

Trumpets shrieked.

A high voice made an inaudible announcement.

The trumpets blared again.

Hildegard turned to a fellow with a cockleshell in his hat. 'Is it him, master?'

He was standing on tiptoe. 'It's somebody in red and gold,' he told her, overcome by excitement. Then he stood down again. 'Not the King, I'm afraid, just somebody from the Lancaster affinity. I can't see who it is from here. Doesn't your abbot tell you what's going on?'

'He hasn't arrived yet. And I expect when he does he'll be as much in the dark as I am.'

'It's a constant show just now. All the nobles! Both archbishops! Every magnate in the land. The guildsmen in their regalia! God bless them all! May the saints provide wise counsel!' The pilgrim smiled and moved off to find a better vantage point.

A path was being opened by some rough-and-ready men-at-arms with pikes coming in from the direction of the wooden bridge leading down from the city. Hildegard was pushed back with the rest of the crowd as someone strode towards them through the path that had been carved for him.

She looked askance. She knew him all right.

He headed for the open north door of the church.

It was the Duke's son, Harry of Derby, young Bolingbroke. The subject of the York servants' ribald comments.

It wasn't the first time she had seen him.

It had been a year ago at Bishopthorpe Palace when he had tried to buy the Cross of Constantine from the Archbishop. She remembered his brusque manner, the way his eyes had hardened when he had been refused.

About nineteen years old, the same age as his cousin the King, he was still short but he had filled out and even started a little reddish goatee beard, maybe an attempt to give himself some *gravitas*.

And a pace behind him, Thomas Swynford.

She could see no family similarity between the two men except maybe in their swaggering self-importance.

At least Bolingbroke can be forgiven for throwing his weight around, she thought, watching him march inside with great pomp and accompanied by another brassy blare of trumpets. His father was said to be the richest man in England. Soon, if the Duke won the crown of Castile by means of his second wife, he would be one of the richest in Europe.

Young Harry had a weight of responsibility now his father was away on campaign. He was heir to the Duchy of Lancaster and would need swagger to carry it off.

The gowns of the court ladies fluttered as they followed after him.

She joined the stragglers.

Harry Derby and his inner circle filled all the standing

room at the front near the altar and she had to press in among the rest of his retinue at the windswept open end of the nave where the missing west facade was filled with scaffolding. Craning her neck she could just make out the figure of the abbot near the high altar. Nicholas Lytlington.

He looked frail and aged but his voice carried clearly to every corner of the building.

They had three or four small boys to sing the anthems and a vicar choral with a deep bass voice to add weight to their soaring trebles. It was all done without fuss, the responses right on cue. To Hildegard it sounded somewhat chilling, no more than a merchant's bargain: sell us a seat in heaven then we'll build you a church.

She guessed the rest of Henry Derby's bargain. He had made that clear when he committed the sacrilege by trying to purchase the Cross of Constantine after she brought it from its hiding place in Italy.

His father might have accepted that the English crown was not for him.

His son was another matter.

So far he had not got his hands on what he might see as the stepping stone to the crown and Hildegard pondered the lengths he would go to get the cross.

What was it worth to him?

She remembered the ambush when nothing had been looted and the marauders had ridden away, stealing not so much as a crust of bread.

She remembered Neville, handy with a sword, riding

away from the battle scene with the bag under his arm. And she recalled his suspicion that a thief had tried to steal it from his chamber at Lincoln.

From where she stood she could see the back of Bolingbroke's head. He removed his velvet, jewel-encrusted cap. His hair was short. It was red like a fox's pelt.

She made her way outside. It was still busy in the palace yard. The wind was howling upriver making the flags on the towers snap.

The arrival of King Richard and Queen Anne had been greatly exaggerated. The royal barge, apparently, had come out onto the water, but instead of turning upstream to the seat of government, it had turned and headed down towards the mouth of the river.

Nobody knew where it was going.

Down to the docks at Rotherhithe maybe.

Escaping to France, some joker suggested before he was set on by a couple of the King's supporters.

The crowd judged that there was nothing here for it and began to disperse. Hildegard decided there was nothing to stay for either and was just turning away with the intention of going back up to her guest quarters when someone murmured in her ear.

'How did we ever get into this situation?'

She felt hot breath on her cheek. With it came a scent of sandalwood reminding her piercingly of Hubert de Courcy and her cheeks flooded with colour. She spun round. Then her lips parted.

It was her rescuer from All Hallows.

He was smiling, his expression wolfish, his large brown eyes exploring her features with a liquid softness that was ambiguous coming from a friar.

She could not step away, the crowd was too pressing, and as a consequence she became sharply aware of the scent of his clothes, his skin. It was unfamiliar, enticing and disconcertingly intimate.

'This situation?' she asked more sharply than intended, trying to draw back. The sense of having been followed swept over her.

'Battle after battle won against the odds,' he murmured. 'Crécy, Poitiers. No one to beat our heroic archers. And now – people on the very streets of London quaking with fear at the prospect of being overrun by an enemy they despise?'

'I see, yes,' she agreed. 'Once so strong. Now so weak.'

'The old King, God save his soul, gave too much away when he gave his heart to Alice Perrers.'

His lips were only inches from her own and as he spoke he seemed to mould the words with a sort of caress. She found she couldn't take her eyes off them.

'Now we have the boy King reaching manhood to the alarm of his uncles. A recipe for disaster, wouldn't you say?' He was smiling. 'Our beloved and gracious King Richard, surrounded by the ambitious and thwarted brothers of his poor war hero father. How can he hope to live up to an example like that, withstand them, and fulfil all our hopes and dreams of victory?'

'Perhaps if he had control over the war chest he could assign resources for our defence,' she countered sharply.

'Indeed. That would be a solution.'

He seemed to look at her with some kind of assessment in mind but she had not said anything seditious. It was most people's view that the King needed money – but they would rather he took it from those who could afford it than from the poor who scarcely had enough to put food into their mouths. She said as much.

The friar laughed exposing long even teeth. Like a wolf, she thought. But his soft lips came together again and he ran the fingers of one hand over his mouth with a meditative gesture, half closing his eyes as he considered her words.

'What is your interest in these secular affairs, magister?' she asked.

He chuckled. 'Matters of state are everybody's concern if we have a care for our own survival.' Bending over her he adopted a tone of concern. 'But tell me who that man was – the one who tried to defile you in the crypt?'

Despite the softness of his voice she felt it was a thrust of some kind – attack was too strong a word – but there was an edge. Her fault. *She had only herself to blame.*

'It was the man I was married to before I joined the Order.'

'So he was your husband?'

When she hesitated he went on staring at her until she was forced to reply. It was a mere nod of the head.

A crowd of newcomers were pressing all around them,

heading for the hall, and she allowed herself to be swept along with them, and when she looked back the friar was staring after her with that enigmatic expression that could have been kindness – or an invitation to a confession to be used against her.

She shook herself free.

'Master Edwin!' she exclaimed. The archbishop's clerk was waiting with his page in the lodge. She had changed her clothes again, had another look at the bruises Ravenscar had inflicted, and moved in a miasma of balsam.

'Domina, you've saved me the trouble of getting out my inkhorn.' He smiled and made a bow. 'His Grace sends his warmest greetings.'

'Where is he?' she asked guiltily, knowing she would have to face him as soon as possible.

'On the King's business. But I have a message for you. We are to visit a prisoner in the Tower.'

'The Tower?'

'There's a man there wrongfully locked up on an accusation by Thomas Swynford. We have to obtain our permissions from the King's secretary, Mr Medford. If you'll follow me?'

Crossing the yard they arrived at one of the side doors leading into Westminster Hall, where the porter checked a docket Edwin handed him and waved them through.

The great raftered hall where all the business of the realm was conducted lay to one side of the passage. Through an open door Hildegard glimpsed a gloomy and forbidding place where rows of clerestory windows slanted grey light across the floor and the oak pillars were wide enough to conceal assassins. Bunched at the far end near the king's dais was a crowd of lawyers and clerks, the former gaudily dressed, the latter in more sombre colours, attending to matters in the courts of Chancery and the King's Bench.

The distant echoing noise of their activities receded as a servant led them up a staircase to the first floor and came to a halt outside an iron-studded door.

Two young men were sitting at a long trestle heaped with documents. They rose to their feet when Hildegard and Edwin entered.

Using what prior knowledge she had, she turned to the one with a pale clever face dressed entirely in black. 'Mr Medford, I presume?'

He was the most important clerk of the Signet Office, controller of King Richard's personal finances.

They stood eye to eye. His attitude seemed to be to face her down. She was determined not to be so faced. There was a brief silence while he took her measure.

'Domina,' he murmured then, 'so good of you to bestow on us the grace of your presence. Mr Westwode has briefed us on relevant matters.' He glanced over her shoulder at Edwin who had followed her inside.

When she turned, Edwin had a dazzled look on his face. Medford must represent the pinnacle of his world, she realised. To Hildegard the King's secretary looked like nothing more than a tall child in adult clothing. A handsome wilful child. He could be no more than twenty-two. The power he wielded was enormous and, of course, the King himself was only nineteen – little to be wondered that he should surround himself with young men of a similar generation.

We are governed by children, she decided, turning her gaze to rest on Medford's companion. An open-faced, fair-haired fellow, he looked even younger than Medford.

'And this is the Dean of the Chapel Royal and head of the Signet Office,' explained Medford languidly.

'Will Slake.' The young man gave her a pleasant smile and bowed. 'Another fellow from King's Hall, Domina, do forgive us. We Cambridge men have rather taken over the King's affairs these days.' He grinned, friendly and unapologetic.

Before she could reply Edwin stepped forward. 'If I may, Mr Medford . . . Dean . . . there *is* something – now we're here to pick up our permits to visit the prisoner in the Tower, perhaps we can discuss a related matter?'

'The problem of Sir Thomas Swynford? Quite. I was coming to that.' Medford gave Edwin a reproving glance. 'On that topic we may have something for you.' He called to the servant by the door. 'Bring him in.'

While they were waiting Slake cleared some rolls of parchment off a chair and offered it to Hildegard, then went to sit on the edge of the trestle, swinging his legs.

He wore leather boots with embroidery of gold thread down the sides. Medford took up a place in the window embrasure where he could brood. Edwin, more nervous than she had seen him before, paced restlessly towards the door and back.

The servant returned. With him was an abject little figure, snivelling and ill-kempt. The servant had him by the scruff of the neck and dropped him at Slake's feet like an unwanted kitten.

Silence fell while they all looked at him.

The boy cringed and kept his head down.

'Come on, then, tell us who you are.'

Slake was still swinging his legs in a nonchalant fashion but the boy stayed on his knees. He muttered a name but the sound caught in his throat and Slake got up, raised the lad by one ear and said, 'Again! I can't hear you!'

'Turnbull, sir.'

'Is that what you do? Turn bulls?'

'No, sir.'

'What do you do?'

'I'm page to Sir Thomas Swynford, sir.'

'He's a dirty-looking young devil to be a page to anybody,' remarked Medford, looking him up and down. 'Do you ever wash, boy?'

Slake still had him by the ear. 'I'll tell you what he does, Mr Medford, he carries messages. You carry messages, don't you, Turnbull?'

'Yes, sir, when Sir Thomas demands, sir.'

'Obedient little fellow, aren't you?'

The boy hung his head and Slake let him drop suddenly so that he fell to his knees.

Medford leant languidly in the window and in a bored voice instructed him to tell them about the message he had delivered at the Abbey of St Alban not this week past.

The boy, still crouching on all fours, stared silently at the floor.

Slake grew impatient. He slid a long silver knife from out of the tooled-leather sheath on his belt. 'If you won't talk to us, Turnbull, maybe I'd better cut out your tongue as you don't seem to need it.'

'No, please, sir!' The boy crouched at Slake's feet and began to sob.

'I will. I've a mind to. I like tongue. Fried nicely on a piece of white bread. What do you say Mr Medford?'

'No accounting for taste, Dean. You eat it. I'll have his fingers, one by one.'

'No! Please, don't!' The boy was shivering in terror and Hildegard stepped forward.

'I think perhaps he might like to tell us what we want to know if we ask him in a more straightforward manner.' She knelt down beside the child and asked soothingly, 'What do you have to tell me, Master Turnbull?'

'I can't say. He'll kill me, My Lady.'

'You were at St Alban's with your master, Swynford, weren't you?' demanded Medford.

The boy was so frightened the words stuck in his throat.

'No harm will come to you,' Hildegard told him with a

glance at the two clerks. 'I'll see to that. But tell me, were you at St Alban's Abbey when the archbishop of York's retinue were in residence?'

The boy nodded but would not look at her.

'Ask him about the message,' urged Slake.

'Well, what do you have to say?' she whispered. 'You can tell me.'

'I can't! I daren't – please, My Lady!'

'Is it something to do with the falconer and what happened to him?'

Between sobs the boy nodded.

'Then make it easy for us all by telling what you know. You're quite safe here with us.'

'He'll kill me,' the boy sobbed. 'He said he would beat me within an inch of my life then leave me to die.'

'Does he beat you?'

'All the time.' The boy was still crouching abjectly on the floor and every few moments a sob would shiver through his thin body. He needs a good square meal or two, thought Hildegard, wanting to gather him up.

'By "he" I suppose you mean Sir Thomas Swynford?' demanded Medford.

The boy nodded. 'He swore he would chain me in a tower like a baited bear and starve me to death.' He turned a tear-stained face towards Hildegard. 'He said he'd block up the door so I couldn't get out and I'd dwindle away like a wraith and then die and nobody would ever know what happened.'

'I think Mr Medford would have something to say

about that. Isn't that so?' She raised her head and gave Medford a challenging look.

Medford's black eyes were boring into hers but he lifted one hand and let it fall. 'We'll spirit him away out of Swynford's reach if we feel he deserves it. Let him tell us about this message first.'

'Was it from your lord?' she asked.

He gave a resigned nod.

'Who did you take it to? Just his position will do. There's no harm in that, is there?' Hildegard coaxed.

'It was to the head falconer at St Alban's,' he mumbled.

'And did you tell him that he was wanted by Master Fulford over some matter to do with the Yorkshiremen's kitchens? You may nod if it is so.'

The boy gave a small nod then raised his head. 'I don't want to starve to death, My Lady.'

'And nor shall you. Mr Medford will make sure you have plenty to eat. But tell me, did you also give a message to Archbishop Neville's falconer that he was needed in the mews?'

Again the boy agreed, with a reluctant terrified nod.

'And tell me, have you heard the name Jarrold of Kyme?' She felt Medford and Slake lean forward as if taken by surprise at the question.

She looked into the child's eyes. He was shaking his head and staring straight at her. 'I'm sorry, My Lady. I've never heard of him.'

Hildegard stood up and encountered Medford's brooding stare. 'So it's as we suspected, but why Swynford should involve himself in such diabolical activities remains a mystery—'

'The victim's name at St Alban's is John of Willerby,' Edwin interrupted. 'So far he can't remember much and but for divine intervention he'd have bled to death and Swynford would therefore be guilty of murder.'

'Don't worry about him. We're dealing with him. Who's this John of Willerby? Never heard of him. Is he from some place in Yorkshire?'

'His family was. He himself used to work for the old abbot at St Alban's, so I'm told.' Edwin looked pleased to be able to supply an answer.

'And what is his importance to the King?'

'Is he an informer?' asked Slake, bluntly.

Edwin shrugged.

'We have not been advised on that,' Hildegard told them. 'If he is, it still makes no sense,' adding, 'so far.'

'So far?' Medford cocked an eyebrow.

'It will, master. We shall make sure of it.'

Medford gave a faint smile. 'Good.' He got up. 'Then I'll leave it with you. Meanwhile we'll see what else we can get out of this snivelling brat.' He gestured to Slake. 'Their documents, Dean.' He turned to Edwin. 'You will return here after speaking to the prisoner, Westwode. And you'll report to me in person.' He toyed with the papers Slake had thrust into his hand then offered them to Hildegard. 'Domina.' He bowed.

Dismissed, Edwin was already moving to the door but Hildegard hesitated. 'I take it the boy will not now be returning to Swynford. If it is discovered that he has helped us, his life will be in danger. I trust, therefore, that your house servants will take steps to keep him safe and fed?'

'See to it, Dean.' Medford yawned.

'Oh I will, Mr Secretary, I will!' Slake laughed as if Medford had cracked a good joke.

'You can't aspire to such a position, Edwin, even if you had been trained at King's Hall and your path was open. It involves too close a kinship with cruelty.' Hildegard turned a worried look on him.

He was uncomfortable. 'It's how things are done here. That's how the Signet Office gets results.'

'Did they beat the boy before they brought him to us? Is that why he confessed?'

'I've no idea.'

She saw him frown. He knew the answer as well as she did.

'At least we know the truth,' he mumbled.

'The truth?'

'That Swynford deliberately attacked His Grace's falconer.'

'But he had already left when the attack took place. We'd have great difficulty in proving it.'

'Either he came back covertly and did it himself, or he hired a servant to do it.'

'And his purpose – to punish Willerby or silence him?'

'What do you think?'

She frowned. It must be to do with the cross. Neville already suspected that he was being given a warning by having his retinue terrorised. Now it looked as if he was right.

Hand it over or else.

But she could say nothing of the cross to Edwin, and besides, he was already continuing on another tack.

'I think Swynford wanted to maim Willerby as a warning,' he said slowly. 'If he'd wanted to silence him, he could have had him knifed in a back alley somewhere. I think Willerby must know something he shouldn't. And if it is a warning, it's to tell others to keep their mouths shut.' He scowled. 'If only he'd regain his memory and begin to talk!'

'We can only be patient.'

Then Edwin surprised her. 'Mr Medford is treating it as a direct plot against the King.'

'How so?' she asked cautiously.

'The archbishop is close to His Majesty. His enemies plan to attack the King's supporters first, one by one, then attack the King himself.'

'Is that what he told you?'

Edwin nodded.

'Then we're all in danger.'

Edwin's hand went to his sword. 'But what if it's more complicated than that? Why Willerby?' he mused. 'Why him? Is there something more that made them choose him—?'

'We certainly seem no closer to knowing if there's more

behind it,' she interrupted, pulling her cloak more securely round her shoulders as a sign that the conversation was ended. He could not know about the relic Neville was carrying in secret but if he continued to speculate he could stumble across the truth.

He was frowning and seemed determined to tease out the problem until he had a solution, and then he took another path. 'What if he knew who killed Martin?' he demanded. 'And what if Martin had told him a secret that led to his own murder?'

Hildegard was silent. Swynford could not imagine that the falconer knew about the cross. Willerby was surely too far down the scale to have access to such a secret. It must mean that the attack on him had been random, designed to scare Neville into giving them his support. It must be as Medford had suggested.

'I hate to find myself agreeing with Medford,' she told him, 'but the Duke had Neville's allegiance in the past. Now Lancaster's in Castile maybe his son might feel he can't count on His Grace as formerly? Bolingbroke won't be sure which way Neville will vote when Richard asks Parliament for support. Tough measures might seem the only way to encourage his allegiance.'

And, she told herself, to frighten him into handing over the cross, because certainly they knew it was in his possession.

Edwin kicked at a corner of the step where they were standing but made no reply.

'We'd better get along to the Tower,' Hildegard suggested. When he did not move she asked, 'What is it?'

'I hate being taken for a fool,' he said slowly. 'There's something I'm not being told.'

While Edwin went to fetch his cloak from the lodge Hildegard retraced her steps to Medford's office. A page was holding the door open. Distinctly she heard Slake saying, 'But that bloody nun will guess what's happened—'

She turned back.

When they came down a few moments later she was standing on the opposite side of the courtyard in the shelter of a stone buttress. They had Swynford's page between them, Medford on one side, Slake on the other. As they drew level she stepped out towards them.

'Well met, masters. I see you've brought the little fellow with you. Would you like me to take charge of him? A nun is probably better used to caring for children than you gentlemen.'

Both men stopped abruptly and stared at her with their mouths opening. Medford was the first to recover. 'Most kind and in keeping with the compassion of your Order, Domina. What would you intend doing with him?'

'A good meal, a dry bed, a wash and change of clothes? When he's presentable I believe His Grace the Lord Archbishop of York may find a suitable use for him.'

Medford cleared his throat. He gave a quick glance at Slake. 'Dean, are you in agreement?'

Slake shrugged. 'So be it.'

Medford put his hand on the back of the boy's neck and squeezed. 'Any trouble from him, Domina, inform me.' He gave the boy a push.

She watched Medford and Slake walk off and, when she glanced down, little Turnbull slipped his hand into hers.

Chapter Five

'Unfortunately, I have no page with me,' Hildegard told him as they walked across the great court towards the landing stage where she was to meet Edwin. 'You may stay with me and run errands for me, and I promise that if you do your work well and honestly I will not beat you nor threaten you with starvation in a tower and later we will decide on more interesting work for you, in keeping with your skills. How does it sound?'

'Like heaven, My Lady.'

'I shall, of course, have to ask His Grace's permission after explaining how you come to be in my care.'

'I hope he won't punish me for what I've done.'

'I'm sure he won't. He is a kind person with a strong sense of fair play. All you have to remember is that his bark is worse than his bite.'

* * *

Edwin had already summoned a wherry and was waiting by the steps when she turned up. They took Turnbull on board with them but instructed the oarsman to let them off at York Place. While Edwin stayed in the boat Hildegard escorted the boy to the steward's office and explained what was needed.

Servants were summoned. The yeoman of the wardrobe took over. He told Hildegard little Turnbull would be washed and combed and told to try on several clean sets of clothes until he found some that fitted, then he would be fed and found some useful work to do. She walked back to the ferry with a lighter heart.

Through the eye slit they could see a group of aldermen in their bright gowns come out of the White Tower and make their way to the nearby Salt Tower.

There were five of them. They had their hoods up as they crossed the yard, but before they passed one by one in front of the guard on the door, they pushed them back so he could see their faces before allowing them through. The prisoner had taken out a lens of polished glass and, cupping Hildegard's hand in his, he angled it so that it was focused on the entrance to the tower and on the men's faces as they went inside. He named them as they appeared and disappeared in the polished glass. Their images were somewhat distorted, flickering and uncertain, as the figures passed in and out of it like spirits of the air.

'That's the mayor in front, Nick Brembre,' he murmured close to her ear so the guard could not hear him. 'At his heels comes his brother-in-law Harry Vanner. No, tilt it a little. That's it. The next fellow, see him? In the blue? That's Adam Bamme talking to Will Exton. And the last fellow? Hold still.' He adjusted the lens. 'He's a Bohemian called Petrus de Lancekrona. His sister is the Queen's first lady-in-waiting. They turn up every day about this time.' He let Hildegard take the lens and stood back. 'I guess Alexander Neville would like to know. Now you can tell him you've seen them for yourself.'

He took the lens and slipped it inside his pouch with an over-the-shoulder glance at his own guard. Edwin had engaged him in some speculation about bear-baiting and had made sure the man's back was towards them.

'Who are they visiting?' whispered Hildegard.

'I don't know but I'd say it was a Frenchman acting as go-between for King Richard. They'll be the ones doing the negotiations.'

Hildegard stared at him. 'You believe these rumours about the King fostering a secret agreement with King Charles?' She was shocked. 'But that would be high treason.'

'It's unfair to call it treason,' he replied shortly. He moved away from the window but Hildegard did not move. As Neville had told her, Richard's enemies were claiming that he wanted to make a secret treaty with King Charles to pre-empt defeat when the French invaded and save his own skin by offering certain high-born men as hostages. There was even a rumour that he would offer Calais to the French in his eagerness to keep them from his shores. She had never believed he would contemplate such acts. She did not believe it now.

'Why would they visit him in a group like this?' she asked.

'Talking money, of course. They're all wealthy guildsmen. They're the ones Richard has had to turn to for help now his coffers are empty. The French will be driving a hard bargain. Knowing them, they'll want to deal face-to-face with the city men.'

'It's hardly credible the city men will barter away the sovereignty of their own country. What evidence do you have for such a view?'

He shrugged. 'You've seen what I've seen. And you must have heard what people are saying. Do you have a better explanation?' He glanced over to where Edwin, with great resourcefulness, was engaging the guard in a game of dice. 'What else can they be doing in there?'

Hildegard was just about to turn away from the window when she looked back once more. What she saw made her stop.

She gripped the edge of the embrasure and peered down at another figure who had appeared. The way he walked was unmistakable. Long, swift, confident strides. He made no attempt to follow the others but went to shelter against the wall out of the wind. His white robe billowed in the eddies at the bottom of the tower but from where he stood he could observe the comings and goings around it without being too noticeable at ground level.

'May I borrow your glass again?'

Peering through it, she angled it so she could see his face. It was the same friar as before – her rescuer, his hood thrown back, looking up at the sky, a faraway expression on his face. He closed his eyes. It was strangely intimate to see him up close and yet be so distant. When he suddenly opened his eyes he seemed to look straight at her. She hastily handed the lens back to the prisoner. 'Useful object.'

'It's one of Roger Bacon's inventions. The glass has to be ground with great precision.'

'Who's the fellow in white down there?'

'Oh him,' said the prisoner, peering over her shoulder. 'Know him?'

'Not as such,' she replied. 'What's he doing here?'

'He has the freedom of the place, in keeping with the power of his lord and master,' the prisoner said in a scathing tone. He went over to the table and reached for the jug of wine. Edwin had thought to bring some provisions from York Place for him. They had not been told his name and he did not tell them it.

Ignoring his offer of a refilled beaker she sat down opposite and forced her thoughts back to the reason for their visit. 'Who else have you seen here?'

He downed a mouthful of wine, then putting down his beaker counted them off on his fingers. 'Only three your people might be interested in. One, the Marquess of Dublin, young Robert de Vere as was, and two, the Earl of Suffolk, the Lord Chancellor, Sir Michael de la Pole, and three, Chief Justice Tresillian – all King's men and as staunch as you'll ever find. Like Mayor Brembre down there.' He gestured towards the window.

'Anyone else?' she asked sharply.

He gave her a knowing smile. 'I am incarcerated here at the invitation of the Earl of Derby but he and the dukes of York and Gloucester have so far been absent.'

'I shall mention that to His Grace.'

'My thanks, Domina. I trust it will bring me his fond remembrance.'

'I believe it will.'

He bowed, sombre for a moment, then became cheerful again. 'I tell you, I don't relish spending the rest of my days in here. Nor do I look forward to the possibility of an interrogation by that fellow in the friar's habit you've just observed. Let Mr Medford know that.'

Hildegard looked at him askance. 'Your meaning?'

'The fellow's role is well known, surely?'

She shook her head. 'Forgive me, we are new to the city.'

'Well let me tell you this. He acts as an interrogator for the King's council. In other words,' he tapped the side of his nose, 'we know who fills his coffers and hence where his allegiance lies.'

'Where does it lie?'

'With the devil who runs the council now Lancaster's out of the country – with Woodstock, our glorious Duke of Gloucester.' He gestured towards the window. 'Despite his manner he's as lethal as a paid assassin, which, some say, he is. He's also said to speak a dozen languages, useful for the job no doubt, and he's a member of a dangerous

Castilian cult that believes in a saint you might imagine was pagan except that he serves to outwit the Moors.' He shook his head.

'I believe he follows the cult of St Serapion.' The friar had told her that much as he escorted her towards the quay and safety.

'Serapion.' The prisoner gave her a look full of irony. 'So far I've been lucky enough to escape his attentions since my first vetting when, I believe, I acquitted myself fairly well and only let him know what he already suspected. I can't say I feel confident in standing up to more rigorous questioning. Of course,' he added, hurriedly, 'I'll stand firm. You can tell Medford and his friends I say this in complete confidence.' He gripped her wrist in a convulsion of sudden fear. 'If I am racked, Domina, do not tell my wife. Keep it from her. She's tender and would not withstand the knowledge of it. Promise?'

'Of course, but—'

He shot a hurried glance at the guard and lowered his voice. 'I shall commend her to you and your Order if I may add a codicil to that effect in my will. May I do that?'

'It will not come to that. I'm sure Medford will do what's necessary to free you before they even think of the rack—'

'He will. I know that for a fact. But only when my usefulness as a spy within the Tower is ended.'

He gazed in a careful fashion at Edwin Westwode who was still throwing dice. 'Don't cross the friar's path if you can help it, Domina. Warn your friend here too.' He lowered his voice further. 'Warn Medford, the King is in imminent danger. Some plot's afoot and this friar, Rivera, is in it up to his neck.'

When he saw the guard get to his feet he whispered hurriedly, 'Something's going on in the Salt Tower and we can only speculate. You've seen the visitors for yourself. I don't know what they're doing. And neither does our mutual friend. This is why he is standing out there even now.'

He leant forward and spoke into her ear as if merely pouring more wine as the guard began to stroll towards them. 'The King is said to be paying us a visit—' He broke off and looked up with a cheerful smile. 'Now then, master, come and supplement your winnings with a stoup of this good wine our friends have brought us.'

They had to leave without any opportunity for further conversation. The guard was probably aware of messages being passed and had gone as far as he dare in allowing his prisoner this small freedom. Only when they were safely outside again and walking anonymously through the crowded streets did either of them make any comment. Hildegard feared for the prisoner, whoever he was, and believed his bleak assessment of his prospects was not far from the truth.

She told Edwin everything that had been said.

He shrugged off the warning about the spy, Rivera, but grimaced. 'Can we trust that prisoner?'

'I think we have to.'

'So, now for an audience with Mr Medford. He'll be interested in a coven of city aldermen visiting Frenchmen in the Tower.'

Returning to York Place Hildegard went in search of her new page. The Yeoman of the Wardrobe had fussed and fretted with the boy's hand-me-downs until he was pleased with the effect. He beamed at Hildegard and called the boy forth. 'Quite one of us now, isn't he?'

It was true. Young Master Turnbull was transformed and nobody, hopefully least of all Thomas Swynford, would have recognised him. He was all skin and bones, however, and, despite the empty platter on the table, looked as if he hadn't had a square meal in an age. It was decided he would do quite well helping the Yeoman of the Wardrobe with his chores until something more permanent could be found for him.

Archbishop Neville was still out on secret business for the King. His absence absolved Hildegard from having to confess to her changed status. To her relief it would have to wait for now.

After leaving Edwin she took a ferry back to Westminster and made her way alone along the public footpath towards the river postern. It was still daylight and there were several wherries disembarking passengers, the oarsmen shouting for more custom. They were doing brisk business.

Their shouts faded as she walked on and she was deep in thought, staring at the ground, when someone stepped abruptly into her path. Her head jerked up. It was Hugh de Ravenscar. So Ulf had failed to run him to earth. She spoke first.

'What do you want?'

'Greetings to you too, wife.' He smiled humourlessly. 'I've already told you what I want.'

'You'll get nothing from—'

'Not even that little you were willing to concede earlier . . .' He stepped closer, lowering his voice. '. . . before we were interrupted by that bloody mendicant?' He gave a leer that left her in no doubt what he meant.

A reply seemed unnecessary. She tried to push past him.

'There is something else.' He gripped her by the shoulder to prevent her leaving. 'It's Guy. He's at Westminster.'

'Guy?'

He let his hand fall when he saw that his news had surprised her. 'Didn't you know?' He eyed her suspiciously.

'How would I know? I haven't heard from your brother in years. Have you spoken to him?'

'I have not. I made the mistake of appearing to you without warning. I won't make the same mistake a second time. If you'd had chance to get used to the fact that I'm still very much alive I believe you would have reacted less obstinately—'

'You're deluding yourself—' she began but before she could set him right he continued.

'I thought if you could have a word with my beloved brother – prepare the ground somewhat – he will be more open to reason after prior warning from you. I've sent a message to let him know where he can find you.'

'You've done *what*?'

'The abbey fathers can't object to a visit from your kith and kin.'

'That's not my point. It's this: you cannot seriously imagine anything you say will make him view with favour your wish to take away his lands?' She raised her eyebrows. 'Knowing Guy he'll hang on to everything fortune throws his way. You'll never prise his inheritance from him now he's got used to it.'

'But it's my right! He's got to see the justice of my claim. He's only been called to Westminster because of me.' He brought his face down to hers. It was twisted with rage in an all too familiar way that repelled her. 'It should be *me* sitting in Parliament! *Me* called to advise the King! *Me* to be feted all over town instead of having to slink around like a felon. Not my upstart brother! Where's the fairness in that?'

'Whether it's fair or not, it was you who gave up any claim on your marcher lands when you pretended to be dead.'

'I'm not wasting my time arguing with you, Hildegard. In all these years you haven't changed. You still argue every damned point.'

'Only because you're so preposterous. Would you give up what you believed was yours by right of inheritance? Only if the very heavens fell in!'

'There's no discussing anything with you. You're as irrational as you always were. A nun? That's a laugh!' He gave her a look of undisguised hatred which was all the more shocking because he usually managed to hide his true feelings until his actions revealed them. He stepped right up to her and gripped her by the front of her garments. 'Is that your last word? You refuse me this one small service?'

'What do you think?'

'I think you're a bitch.' He crowded her off the path into the long grass. 'I hope you rot in hell!' He gave her a push.

She stumbled but managed to duck past him and this time he let her go, shouting only a warning. 'You haven't heard the last of this, you bloody woman. I want what's mine and I'll get it. You'll rue the day you ever crossed me.'

The injustice of his remarks ignited an ember from the past when their relationship had been all fire and pain. Before she could stop herself she swung round again. 'I rue the day I ever *came* across you. That much is true! Better you were still dead, Ravenscar! Better for everybody!'

By now she was at the wicket gate and the porter lifted his head in astonishment when he heard Hildegard shouting threats. It was a new man and he gaped as she hurried past. She heard Hugh utter some obscenity behind her back. But she did not care what he said about her, she was too angry and too shamed by her anger to give a damn.

Thomas was limping as he entered the cloister yard next morning. Hildegard went down to meet him, drawing him under a portico where they would not be overheard.

'My dear Thomas, how badly are you hurt?'

'Not so much that I have to lie in a bed in the infirmary,' he replied with a jaunty air.

'They told me you had a broken leg.'

'Exaggeration. I might have broken a few legs myself, though, as well as some heads.' He winced as he stepped forward and she took him by the arm.

'Let's sit.' She gave him an anxious glance. He had a black eye. 'What will the abbot think to you? Has he arrived yet?'

She had mixed feelings when he shook his head.

'Listen to me, Hildegard. Ulf sent me a message at St Mary Graces. That's why I'm here. I came as soon as I could. He told me what happened after we were parted by the constables. I'm at fault. I should have managed to stay by your side to protect you.' He gave her a searching glance. 'He told me the fellow must have roughed you up. Then he said I should come over and attend you – as if I needed to be told after hearing something like that!'

'He had no need to say anything. I only told Roger de Hutton about Ravenscar coming back from the dead because Ravenscar was his sworn knight. Ulf was present. He's been in the picture from the beginning. He knew him in the old days. I haven't told anyone else yet.' She gazed at him with a troubled expression. 'You know what it means? I shall be excommunicated.'

'Surely not?' His tone was serious, his eyes as clear as river water. 'Hildegard, I cannot advise you. This is far beyond my learning but I can assure you of one thing

– Abbot de Courcy will not hold you responsible for somebody else's deception. In fact he's more likely to see you as the victim.'

'I don't want compassion from him – to be seen as a helpless fool.'

'I'm sure that's the last thing he would say about you.'

'Oh Thomas . . .' She gripped his arm. 'On top of everything else I was worried about what had happened to you after I deserted you on Tower Hill. I thought my son might have been caught up in the fighting as well and went to find him. Now I realise he wasn't at All Hallows and never could have been there. The message was written by Ravenscar. It was a forgery. It took me in completely. Maybe I am a fool, after all.'

'So am I, then, because the note took me in as well. And anyway, it was a nasty trick to play. Who on earth would have expected a trick like that? I'm so sorry,' he added. 'I know how much you were looking forward to seeing young Bertrand again. But tell me something – was Ulf right when he said Ravenscar treated you roughly?'

'It's his usual way. He hasn't changed.'

'Ulf says they won't stop until they've tracked him down. I expect he's already in custody.'

'He was still free yesterday evening. He was lying in wait on the path by the river gate.'

Thomas's look of alarm was superseded by one of concern.

Hildegard laughed, enough to reassure him. 'I'm all

right. I shouted at him. I haven't shouted at anybody for years.'

Thomas got up. 'Let's take a beaker of wine in Abbot Lyttlington's kitchens. His servants will delight in offering us hospitality.'

The wind was getting up again and it was far too uncomfortable to sit in the cloisters much longer, so she accompanied him on the short walk towards the abbey's main buildings. He moved with a limp which he was vainly trying to conceal and she felt compelled to ask, 'Tell me the truth, Thomas, are you very much injured? No broken bones, are there?'

'I'll heal. The constables didn't get off lightly either.' He gave a rueful grin. 'It was madness. No one will listen to reason when their blood's up.'

As they went inside to find the refectory he explained what the fighting was about. 'It's over Mayor Brembre's desire to protect the city traders.'

At the mention of Brembre she pricked up her ears.

'One group of guildsmen want to open trade to everybody – but you can imagine what happens with no regulation. They undercut the locals and put them out of business as well as indulging in all sorts of sharp practice. Standards slip. They give false measures. Then refuse to appear before the courts. They ignore fines. It arouses a lot of resentment. Brembre's faction want to restrict trade to London guild members so it can be properly regulated.'

'It sounds like a minor squall.'

'On the contrary, it's a brewing storm. If it breaks it'll be with a terrible fury. You saw how enraged the apprentice boys are? Ordinary people are losing their livelihoods. Deaths have occurred. A man was executed not long ago. They see it as a battle between anarchy and order, or liberty and oppression according to your point of view. The city's going to destroy itself unless they can find a compromise.' He had evidently been listening to someone who knew all about it.

She brought him back to Brembre. 'Who are the mayor's opponents?'

'The ones who want a free-for-all? I don't know names yet. Their leader used to be the ex-mayor, John of Nottingham, but he's been put away in Tintagel Castle for extortion, and so far nobody else has risked sticking their heads over the battlements. Brembre makes sure of that.'

'How?'

'Don't ask. There's talk of men being rounded up and sent to the gallows without trial.'

'Can't anybody stop it?'

'The city has its own laws. Parliament and the King's writ have no power within the walls.' He looked bemused. 'Would you believe what started it?'

'What?'

'The price of fish!'

They were standing in line outside the refectory by now and when they went inside they were welcomed in as warmly as Thomas had predicted. 'I'll tell you more later,' he told her. 'Let's find somewhere to drink our wine in privacy.' He guided her to one of the long trestles and she noticed that he rested his wounded leg on a stool as soon as they were seated.

He filled their beakers and pushed the empty flagon to one side.

'Those who oppose regulation have the support of the Duke of Lancaster. He loathes Brembre. He'll do anything to thwart him.'

'Do you know why?'

'It's because Brembre gives the King financial support. It takes Richard outside the control of the council and gives him a power base within the city.'

She remembered the mayor and his secret visits to the Tower and was about to tell Thomas but he was still talking.

'There are other, more local reasons for the riots,' he explained. 'These secret affinities reach into every corner of London life. You can't buy a stoup of ale without a portion of the price going to pay a protection levy. Men are bought and sold for their affinity. I'm told a man can sometimes have two or even three masters, all rivals. Anybody clever enough to keep afloat in a corrupt set-up like that can end up rich.'

'Or, if not so clever, dancing on a gibbet?'

'That's true. I'm glad to say it's far less complicated at Meaux,' he smiled, 'praise be.'

He called for more wine.

Wishing to avoid discussing her own particular plight, Hildegard told him about her meeting with the two from the Signet Office, Medford and Slake.

'Apparently Medford believes that Martin and Willerby were attacked as a warning to Neville.'

'A warning? From whom? I suppose he means Harry Derby aided by his dancing dog, Swynford.'

She nodded. 'That's what they seemed to mean.'

'But? I can see you think there's more.'

'What puzzles me, Thomas, is how the attack on Willerby was managed – we're told his shouts brought the St Alban's man running, being on his way back from his false errand to Neville's cook. But how is it he didn't meet the attacker leaving the mews? He didn't mention anyone to you, did he?'

Thomas shook his head. 'The fiend must have been hiding somewhere.'

'But where? There's only a narrow passage between the racks of birds. And the mews itself only leads back into the stable yard. How could he get out without being seen?'

Thomas considered the matter before concluding that he must have hidden behind the door leading into the store and slipped out when the falconer ran to get help. 'He could have hidden inside the stables, passing himself off as a groom.'

'But somebody would have noticed an outsider. They would have said something. Where were you when you heard the commotion?'

'I'd just gone into the saddler's at the end of the stable block to get my sandals fixed. The saddler was in there with a couple of apprentices mending some harness. We all rushed out when we heard the shouts.'

'And you saw no one leave the mews?'

'No. I wasn't aware of anyone. People were pouring out of the stables to see what was up, just like us.'

'So there were plenty of people around?'

'It's a busy place. That poor falconer, though. He'd have done anything to save his precious bird. The fellow was grief-stricken.' He stared at her for a moment. 'Do you think Swynford had one of the St Alban's men in his pay?'

She didn't answer.

The kitcheners were beginning to bring in food and a hunk of bread was set down between them. After pushing it first towards Hildegard, Thomas broke a piece off and stuffed it into his mouth. Her head ached. Her bruises ached. Thomas was in a bad state too. She could see him guarding his leg from being brushed by people jostling in between the benches to find their seats.

'It was an awful day,' she reminded, 'rain bucketing down again. Just as it was in Lincoln.' She toyed with a piece of bread. 'Maybe little Turnbull will think of something else he can tell us.'

'Medford's going to need more than the word of a page if he wants to bring an action against Swynford.'

'I'm not sure that's how Medford and his friends do business.'

After eating a few oyster fritters and some watered wine they got up to go. There was a lot of activity around the entrance into the screens passage and when they craned their necks they discovered why. A retinue wearing the King's livery were swarming into the place. All the Yeomen of the Board were being lined up and inspected. One or two were singled out. The King's men went on into the kitchens and it looked as if they were going to repeat the exercise, kitcheners of every degree being marshalled for inspection.

It was nothing to do with them. They went outside into the windswept yard.

'Willerby might have bled to death if the head falconer hadn't cut short his discussion with Fulford about whether he sent that message or not,' Hildegard observed. 'Both times the attacks happened when we should have been miles away by the time the victims were discovered. But both times, by chance, they were discovered before we left.'

'Lucky I had to delay to get my sandals fixed,' Thomas observed. 'It suggests something hurried, though, perhaps unplanned?'

'Maybe.'

Hildegard looked up at the sky. Low rain-filled clouds were being raced along by the increasing strength of the wind. Flags cracked on their poles. Flocks of birds were being scattered across the wind like thrown grain. The air smelt fresh, with the scent of the river in it.

Thomas was considering the matter with a thoughtful frown. 'You mentioned the rain just now. And what I remember is this. You know how it releases the scent of things? There was a strong scent in the mews store. I can't place it. It was unexpected. I feel . . .' he looked puzzled '. . . I feel it might be important.'

Hildegard was reminded of Lincoln. It had been raining hard that day too and had sent most of the Bishopthorpe men into the cathedral. She recalled the venomous exchange in the chapel. The wet footprints of the two men on the tiles of the chantry floor. The smell of wet fabric, wool, worsted, leather. And that strange smell of pig fat and rosemary from the waterproofs Swynford wore.

She described it to him and he nodded his head in recognition.

Chapter Six

Aware of Hildegard's anxiety at the thought of Hubert travelling the length of England with only a small escort, Thomas suggested that she take the morning to escort him back to St Mary Graces.

'We might find that he's arrived while I've been over here. They were certainly expecting him at any moment. And,' he added, 'my leg's quite painful. May I beg you to see it as a reason to accompany me back to the abbey?'

Before she could set out she had to visit York Place. She had yet to arrange an audience with the archbishop. 'Neville's being most elusive. I haven't yet managed to inform him about Ravenscar's reappearance. He's going to fly into a rage when he does find out. It'll look as if I've been trying to deceive him. I'm not looking forward to it.' In addition, if Hubert had already arrived in London, he would expect her to have fulfilled her responsibility to the truth and would probably look askance at her failure to do so.

Almost as soon as they set foot inside the palace, Neville's page ran up. 'You're summoned to the audience chamber, Domina, Brother.'

'When?'

'Now.'

Here it comes, she thought. Neville must have learnt of her husband's reappearance. She climbed the stairs with her heart in her mouth. As she followed Thomas inside they were joined by the rest of Neville's inner circle, his close household staff.

There were grim faces.

Edwin was standing by the archbishop's lectern with his writing desk open and, it seemed to Hildegard, deliberately avoided her glance.

Expecting a showdown in front of the entire household, she prayed only that she would be allowed to defend herself before being condemned as a liar and a cheat with no right to the privileges of her Order.

The audience chamber was a large and splendid hall on the first floor, looking out onto the river. The shutters on the many windows were banging back and forth as the wind increased. As everyone had been saying that morning, as they struggled with flyaway cloaks and banging doors, the one good thing about it was that it was keeping Charles of France and his massive fleet of ships pinned in the harbour at Sluys.

Now the archbishop himself came flying in like a

219

hurricane himself. From the first moment it was clear he was in one of his famous rages.

Hildegard's breath stopped. Was her sin so great? She took a step forward ready to defend herself.

But she was mistaken. His anger was directed elsewhere, as he soon made clear.

'Everybody present?' He glared round. 'Well, people, we can sit on our arses no longer!'

Wondering what was coming next, everyone froze.

'On the first of October our most gracious Majesty, our beloved King Richard, will do us the honour of opening Parliament. Westminster will be flooded with dukes, earls, barons, bishops, abbots, shire knights, burgesses and every Tom, Dick and Harry in the realm who thinks he has the right to an opinion. And we have a task. We have to discover one thing. Our lives depend on it.' He glared round the group once more.

Still no one moved.

'Which way,' he growled, 'are the devils going to vote – with the King, or against him?'

There was silence.

'Will they cast their vote with their lord, King Richard, or with his uncle, Thomas Woodstock, the so-called Duke of Gloucester, and his lapdog, that bastard Arundel?'

The silence continued.

He glowered at his chamberlain. 'Do you know the answer, My Lord?'

'Not yet, Your Grace.'

'Do you, My Lord Steward?'

'I'm afraid not, Your Grace.'

'Do any of you sot wits know?'

There was a general agreement that no one knew.

'Of course you don't know. Are we astrologers?' He glared again as if the answer was being withheld. Hildegard, along with everyone else, waited to see what he expected from them.

'I tell you this, my dear friends, we cannot sit by and let the opposition destroy us. So what must we do? I'll tell you what we must do. We must obtain a list of names.'

He thumped his fist on the nearby lectern.

'Names! Names! Names! We must obtain the names of all the traitors who intend to destroy the King by voting against him.'

He walked to and fro for a moment then turned to glare round the group. 'Every man jack who intends to vote with the traitors must be found out. Then we shall persuade them to mend their ways. Names, my friends!' he repeated. 'Go out and find them. They will vote with us and the King – or be for ever damned!' He shooed everyone towards the door. 'Fence-sitting is not within our cognisance.'

With no opportunity to make her confession to the archbishop Hildegard went with Thomas to call a wherry to take them downriver to St Mary Graces where, another cause for alarm, Abbot de Courcy might have already arrived.

As soon as they began to talk to each other the boatman guessed they were northerners. He began to question them about life in 'the wilds', as he put it.

'Not as wild as you southerens imagine,' Thomas said, stretching his wounded leg on the thwart in front of him. 'The song school in Beverley, for instance, it's the best in the country. Most of the royal musicians are trained there.'

'I've heard tell of it,' agreed the boatman. 'But the weather? That must be a rare thing to have to contend with every day.'

As the wind was now howling up the Thames like a demon he had little to criticise, thought Hildegard. Waves were slapping against the sides of the boat with one or two spilling over the gunnels into the bottom and their boots were in a continual puddle of water. Fortunately, the tide was with them and they made good way towards St Katharine's where they were told there was a landing stage. From there it was only a stone's throw to the Cistercian headquarters just outside the walls.

Hildegard was relieved that she had not had to face the archbishop in his present mood. A word with the abbot first, if he had arrived, might clarify her situation.

'What are you folk doing down here, then?' the boatman continued as they scudded along. 'Here for this big Parliament King Dickon's calling?'

'We are,' Thomas confirmed. 'Although, of course, neither of us will have a vote in either chamber.'

'Who has?' he grunted. 'Of course, it's all about the subsidy again. Taxes, nothing but taxes.'

'Do you think they'll manage to raise enough?' Hildegard asked him.

'Aye, by fair means or foul.'

'I thought there was opposition to subsidising the King against the invasion?' she asked.

'They'd be mad to withhold their support. And face the cost of London under siege?'

'The French have been threatening to invade all summer. Surely it'll never get as far as a siege?'

'Course it will. The Frenchies are going to march right in. The door's wide open. Nothing to stop them. They'd be fools not to take the chance while they've got it. Then what?' He took a hand off an oar and drew it across his neck with a slitting sound and grimaced.

'The barons have got rich on the skirmishes in Normandy,' Thomas observed. 'Lootings. Ransoms. They could put some of it back now.'

'Aye, but pigs will fly, more like. They want their war profits but they expect us Londoners to pay to guard their backsides at home.'

The boatman was looking down the boat, able to gauge their agreement. When Thomas nodded he told them, 'It's down to private citizens to defend the coast. Like when Alderman Philpot got so pig-sick of the magnates' inertia he equipped his own warships.' He chuckled with mordant humour. 'That showed 'em! It narked Arundel and nearly gave Gloucester apoplexy!

"A commoner stepping in like that! Who does he think he is?" The answer came back loud and clear. He's a man doing your job, Your Grace.' He chuckled. 'You should have seen Philpot when he sailed back with loot from the two French ships he'd captured! We greeted him like a bloody hero. Cheering crowds. Flags flying! You've never seen the like.'

'We even heard about him up north.' Hildegard smiled. 'He must have been quite a character.'

'Pity he's dead, God bless him,' agreed the boatman. 'The ones that are left are of a different weave. Who is there now?'

'Who is left?' asked Hildegard.

'Mayor Brembre. Sir Nicholas Brembre of Smithfield fame.' He shut his mouth.

That name again, she registered. 'Who else?'

The oarsman looked off into the distance. 'There's Comberton, Exton, Vanner, one or two others likely to make a pig's ear of running the city.'

'What's this Mayor Brembre like?' she asked.

'There's one thing you can say for him. He puts his money where his mouth is – his coffers are ever open for the King's use.'

'So it's true, he makes loans to King Richard?' Thomas looked impressed.

'Lends thousands.'

'He must be rolling in it.'

The boatman gave a sardonic laugh. 'Beyond your wildest dreams, Brother.'

'The King has the combined opposition of his uncles, the dukes who run his council,' Hildegard pointed out, at the same time wondering where Brembre got his wealth from. 'It must be hard to have them holding the purse strings. He has no choice but to rely on personal loans from the city men. It's lucky such men as Brembre exist.'

The boatman was curt. 'You're right. The lad needs all the allies he can get. And that's a fact.'

Out in mid-river they were being drawn along on a frighteningly fast ebb. Great palaces behind high walls, pinnacles with flags snapping in the wind, and the squat Saxon towers of a hundred churches flew by in dazzling succession. They passed a burnt-out building by the water's edge.

'Savoy Palace, done for,' grunted the boatman. 'Inns of Court over there,' he nodded towards a cluster of buildings behind a wall, 'nearly done for. Bonfires in the yard of all their precious documents.' He was evidently referring to the riots during the Great Rebellion five years ago. A little further on he pointed, 'Baynard Castle, the Royal Wardrobe, where Princess Joan, God bless her, had to go into hiding.' There was a sardonic smile on his face. 'By, there's some stuff in that there tower I'm told. All their gold-caked robes. Which we're taxed to hell and back to pay for, I might add.'

Hildegard held on more tightly as the boatman dug one oar in hard to turn the bows towards the shore. Thomas surreptitiously clutched his bandaged leg as a crosswind sent them bouncing over the waves.

He completed his manoeuvre and brought them alongside the quay.

'A word of advice,' he announced as they prepared to disembark. 'Accept no invitations to Hatcham.'

'Why's that?' asked Thomas with interest.

The boatman's sardonic smile turned to an evil grin. 'That's where the mayor has his own gibbet – at the Foul Oak.'

The shore was swarming with people. Everybody was busy doing something. Stone cutters, carpenters, carriers. The thin and distant clamour of masons rose up from the walls. Their high-pitched whistles directed the massive loads of Caen stone cradled in the hoists as they were lifted into place. Men spidered over the wooden scaffolding built up along the walls where they were being extended.

Everywhere goods were being stockpiled in readiness for the expected siege. The warehouses along the quays were open even though ships could not put to sea because of the blockade.

They saw arms being brought in from the Midlands in hundreds of iron-shod carts, to be stored in the armouries. Wagonloads of arrows were coming in. Horses: destriers, palfreys, dray animals tied in teams of six.

Every habitation, where possible, was being fortified. Religious houses, and there were many, were paying good money to post armed guards at their gates.

Thomas was staring about him in consternation. 'All

this activity makes the invasion seem more real. I fear we haven't been taking it seriously enough.'

Hildegard gave a shudder as they began to walk up the lane alongside the wall of St Katharine's Priory. 'I keep thinking of the siege of Limoges.'

In that inglorious episode every inhabitant of the once large and wealthy town had been slaughtered by the Prince of Wales, King Richard's father, and his army.

Thomas was looking with scepticism to where a gang of labourers were deepening the ditch outside the walls to prevent them from being blown up by mines.

'It's nowhere near complete,' he said worriedly. 'Yet the French have been massing on the other side of the water throughout the whole of this summer past. I don't understand it. Why are we so unprepared? We've known for ages that the French have been busy, firming up their alliance with the usurper King of Castile. Ships have been requisitioned. Men conscripted. Do we have a death wish in this country? Do we want to be invaded?' He turned to her. 'You'll never believe what I heard the other day.'

He wore a look of innocent astonishment on his face. 'The French have devised a devilish plan to make their conquest more comfortable. They've had wooden castles designed which they intend to bring across on ships. Whole forests have been destroyed to supply the wood. They're going to stack them flat aboard the ships then erect them on the beaches when they land. Presumably they imagine they'll be safe inside to feast and drink after a day of slaughtering us English.' He sighed in disbelief and gazed round the work that was still going on. 'If they come this side of Christmas,' he muttered, 'God help us all. I can't see that half-built wall being a defence against their trebuchets.'

'Trebuchets are overrated,' Hildegard reassured. 'They take too long to get into place and even when the aim is good they take an age to do any damage.'

'Let's hope you're right.'

On their left rose the white walls of the Tower of London. Even from this distance three or four severed heads could be seen impaled above the watergate with swirls of birds shrieking above them.

Averting her glance, Hildegard followed Thomas into the narrow lane that ran uphill towards the abbey. For some reason she happened to glance behind them. A figure in white was just crossing the end of the lane. When she looked again, he had gone.

As Thomas predicted, Abbot Hubert de Courcy had arrived early that morning. One of the monks told them when they arrived that he had disregarded advice not to ride across the moor at night without an armed escort.

'He said he was in too much of a hurry to waste time in surrendering to imaginary dangers.'

He instructed a page to usher them into the private chamber traditionally set aside for the Abbot of Meaux. As head of one of the most powerful Cistercian houses in the north, the incumbent abbot there was a figure of importance. Hubert looked very much at home already, a pile of documents on his reading desk, a flagon of wine beside him and a modest fire in the grate.

His eyebrows rose when he saw Thomas walking in first and noticed his black eye.

'So, Brother. Did you break any vows while you were getting that?'

Hildegard was walking in behind her priest and now came to a stop near the door. Her knees felt weak. He was here. It seemed an age since she had last seen him. He had not noticed her yet. She would have to tell him the truth at once. But he had not yet noticed her and was teasing Thomas about his fighting.

The young monk stepped to one side.

Hubert's mouth opened. For a long moment she saw his glance linger over her and then Thomas was stepping forward and saying, 'My Lord, I praise St Benet you've arrived in good spirits. I beg leave, however, to attend to my duties – if not my wounds. Should you have no further need of me other than to chide me, I trust I may be excused?'

Hubert nodded as if a small problem had been lifted from him, and Thomas, with a kind glance at Hildegard, went out leaving them alone.

Hubert took a pace forward. 'I can't tell you how pleased I am to see you safe, Hildegard. What a journey! I gather you had a hard time of it?'

'Some unpleasantness. How about you?'

His face lit up in a smile. 'Nothing we couldn't handle.

I discovered that my page is surprisingly handy with his little knife.'

'He had to use it?'

'Only to set a few horses loose. But I have urgent news from Bishopthorpe.' He gestured to a bench under the window.

Sitting by his side Hildegard was conscious of the authority of his presence. To help concentrate she stared at a spot on the floor where some pieces of mosaic tile were arranged in a complicated pattern of lozenges and squares. All the time she was thinking about what she would eventually have to tell him and how it would change things between them for ever.

'Someone came to see me while I was making a brief halt at Bishopthorpe after you left,' he began. 'It was the wife of Martin, the man who was murdered in the brewhouse.'

Her attention was caught.

'It turns out that she was a laundress at Scarborough Castle when she met him.'

'I think somebody mentioned that,' she told him, not daring to look at him.

'What it means is that she's well placed to tell us about a rumour going round the castle.'

When she risked a glance his dark eyes were full of light, his lips softly mobile and, as she had expected, there was at least a day's dark stubble on his jaw, emphasising the curving line of his cheekbones.

'What rumour?' she managed to ask.

'About Sir Ralph Standish's death. You may have heard what they're saying?'

'What have you heard?'

'The official story is that Standish died from the bloody flux. The belief among the castle folk is . . .' he paused '. . . that he was poisoned.'

She jerked up her head. 'Is there proof now?'

'So you have heard the story?'

'There are always rumours,' she agreed.

'True. But his wife was distressed enough to convince me there may be something in it.'

She asked the question she had put to Edwin earlier. 'Who would want him dead?'

'Standish was given Scarborough Castle as a reward for his activities at Smithfield during the murder of Wat Tyler.'

'You mean—?'

'I mean this. When Tyler trotted out across Smithfield on his pony to speak directly to King Richard, it was Standish who accused him of being a liar and a thief—'

'He called him the biggest liar in Christendom if accounts are to be believed.'

'Yes. What's more, Standish would know a hothead like Tyler would not react calmly to a public insult like that.'

'So why did he do it if Tyler's reaction was predictable?'

'Because it was an excuse for Standish to draw his sword in a pretence at defending the King and give Tyler a wound—'

'Even though Tyler was only armed with his small eating knife?'

'True. It was a cowardly attack. There's no denying it. Tyler facing the King's men alone. One against many. Worse, Mayor Walworth drew his sword. They say he had taken the precaution of wearing a mail shirt underneath his mayoral robes. He struck a blow – for which he was later knighted on the advice of the council – and he and his alderman, Nick Brembre, couldn't or wouldn't prevent the men-at-arms finishing the job, for which Brembre was knighted along with Standish and one or two others. So Tyler died.'

'But are you saying it was a deliberate plot? There could have been a bloodbath!' Hildegard pointed out. 'All Tyler's men were drawn up in formation on the far side of Smithfield. Why would Standish knowingly take the risk of provoking them by killing their leader?'

Hubert frowned. 'This is only theory but, given the context, I believe they wanted an excuse to fight. The rebels, mostly bonded men, were unarmed except with makeshift weapons. They could have been slaughtered to the last man, like animals, just as the Flemish weavers in Bruges were slaughtered by the Duke of Burgundy. But there was a hitch – whoever put Standish up to it made a miscalculation. They reckoned without King Richard saving the day. Nobody could guess that a fourteen-year-old would act with such decisive courage. By speaking calmly to the rebels and leading them out into the countryside he saved many lives. The rumour

232

is the dukes and their allies wanted a bloodbath. They desired it. They knew, armed knights as they are, that they would win.'

'So they intended to provoke not only Tyler, so they could kill him, but also the men from the vills and manors waiting to hear what the King had to say about freeing them?'

'But according to rumour that wasn't the main purpose,' he continued. 'It's worse. What they really wanted, in the tumult and confusion that would have followed, was the opportunity to kill King Richard himself.'

'What?'

'The blame could have easily been put on the rebels. Standish, so they're saying in Scarborough, was assigned this task.'

She could find no words to express her horror.

Hubert added, 'He was well rewarded for what he did do. He was made constable of the castle a week after the rebellion.'

'Thank heaven he did not succeed in the rest of his commission.'

'*He* did not. But no doubt others are, even at this moment, being conscripted to do so.'

'You believe these rumours of a plot to assassinate the King, Hubert?'

'They are only rumours, true. Even so . . .' he paused '. . . on balance, yes, I believe them.'

'Do they say who's behind it all?'

'The Duke of Lancaster, maybe.'

'He's moved his attention to the crown of Castile.'

'Yes. Maybe Smithfield was his last failed attempt at regicide?'

'And now?'

'Richard has another uncle, equally ambitious, equally unscrupulous.'

'Woodstock?'

'With his elder brother out of the country, yes, Woodstock, the Duke of Gloucester. He now has a clear field.'

'Poor Richard. Nineteen years old. To be surrounded by such treachery from his own kin. It's enough to send anyone mad with fear. If this is all true he must live in constant terror of his life.'

'It's one of the perils of kingship,' Hubert said bluntly.

'My heart bleeds for him.' She must have given him a rather reproving look because he leant closer.

'We in my house are loyal, Hildegard. You may at some time have felt like questioning that?'

He gave her a full dark stare and her glance dropped in confusion.

'It's understandable,' he assured her softly. 'A foreign house – worse, a French one – with all our wealth and Continental connections, thriving in the very heart of England during such terrible times. Of course we are under suspicion. But I hope we are also above it.'

Relief flooded through her. She would trust him. She had longed for reassurance and now here it was. 'But Hubert, what else are you saying – that one of the King's supporters followed Standish to a remote Yorkshire castle and poisoned him to avenge the murder of Wat Tyler?'

'That's the way it looks.' He tightened his lips. 'There is another thing. This adept in the art of poison has been identified by the rumour-mongers. I'm told he turned up seeking work at Archbishop Neville's palace some time after Standish's death.'

'And he had been employed at Scarborough Castle?'

Hubert nodded. 'Yes. He worked in the kitchens. He drew attention to himself by his skill in ridding the castle of a plague of rats. It's a fellow called Jarrold—'

'Of Kyme?'

'You've come across him? Is he still a member of His Grace's household?'

She wore a horrified frown. 'He is here.'

'At York Place?'

'Yes.' She felt puzzled. 'But the rumours must be wrong. He's an unlikely avenger for Wat Tyler.'

'Why do you say that?'

'He has a connection with Thomas Swynford.'

Hubert looked startled. 'You mean he's maintained by him?'

She told him about the events that had taken place on their journey down to London and about the argument in the chapel at Lincoln. 'I believe it was almost certainly Swynford there, although I can't be sure as he kept his hood up.'

'Certainly Swynford wouldn't want an ally like Standish dead,' observed Hubert.

'It makes no sense.'

'Of course, it doesn't follow that Jarrold necessarily dances to Swynford's tune.'

'He could have an affinity elsewhere. I'm told men often serve more than one master these days.'

They fell silent.

Hildegard recalled the uneven relationship between the two in the chapel. Then she had not even known that the one calling the shots was Swynford. But it had been obvious that Jarrold was the hired man. She described this impression to Hubert and then told him about the testimony of little Turnbull and the messages he had been forced to carry at St Albans.

'But Swynford had already left when the falconer was attacked?'

She nodded.

'And Jarrold?'

'He'd also gone on ahead with the rest of the kitcheners. They can all vouch for him. I was late in leaving because of something Thomas had to do at the last minute.'

'Then it can only mean one thing: there must be a third man.'

'It couldn't have been Jarrold,' she repeated. 'He was in the yard helping out with the sumpter wagons until everyone set off together.'

'What were they arguing about at Lincoln before that?'

'It was difficult to tell. I wasn't really listening. It was only when I couldn't help realising that something was going on that I listened and then I only heard snatches of what they were saying. Jarrold gave the impression that Swynford had an obligation to help him. It was over something to do with a woman, he said. He seemed to feel Swynford had a duty to help him out. They're both from the same part of the country.'

'Does Jarrold have a tenancy in Kyme?'

'I don't know.'

'It might be one of the manors Swynford controls.'

'His mother owns quite extensive property in that area.'

Returning to the earlier topic, Hubert told her, 'The rumours at Scarborough do not mention Swynford.'

'In my opinion he would definitely not have seen Ralph Standish as an enemy.'

'We must look more deeply into the matter.'

She tore her glance from the pattern on the floor and turned to Hubert. 'How did you hear about Jarrold?'

'This again comes from Martin's wife. She's a local woman and, like herself, many of her kinsfolk work at the castle. Naturally, like all servants, they observe what is going on and discuss it between themselves. When I stopped off at Bishopthorpe Palace before riding down here she came to find me. She was in great distress. We've spoken in the past when she's visited Meaux to consult the Talking Crucifix and she felt she could trust me. She told me that she was convinced Jarrold killed her husband.'

'She said that openly?'

'Not exactly openly,' he chided. 'I tell you all of this in

the deepest confidence, Hildegard. But as it pertains to the health and welfare of the King and hence the entire realm, I cannot withhold what information I have.'

Reproved, she fell silent.

'I hope we can pool our thoughts on the matter?' he suggested in a softer tone.

Knowing what she had yet to tell him, she was unable to reply.

'Martin,' he continued, 'knew about the rumours concerning Ralph Standish's death as did everyone else at Scarborough. He hinted to his wife that he had proof that Jarrold poisoned him.'

'What sort of proof?'

'I don't know and neither, apparently, does she, but the two men worked side by side in the kitchens and something must have betrayed him. Given Martin's views he should have been pleased that Ralph Standish, a man suspected of being in a plot to assassinate the King, had got his just desserts.'

'And wasn't he?'

'She told me her husband was a man of some idealism and did not believe the rumours that rebels had poisoned Standish out of revenge. He felt the plotters must be finding it expedient to allow that belief to flourish. He wanted to confess what he knew to somebody in authority.'

'But he didn't.'

'No. He kept putting it off. He talked it over with her and, she suspects, with someone else, until eventually it must have got back to Jarrold. She told me they came to blows only a few days before the murder.'

'What were they fighting about?'

'She believes it was because Martin confronted Jarrold and begged him to confess to save his soul and exonerate the brotherhood of the White Hart.'

'And he would deny everything, of course?'

He nodded. 'But that wasn't the end of the matter. She knows Martin was worried about something the day before the retinue left Bishopthorpe but she put it down to unhappiness at having to go to London without her. Now she thinks it's because he wanted the matter with Jarrold to be resolved one way or another, but that when he confronted him again Jarrold threatened him.'

'In what way, does she know?'

He shook his head. 'It was enough to worry him but despite this, she believes, he decided to force the issue saying he would go to the archbishop himself and tell him everything. And he arranged to meet Jarrold before the convoy set out to give him one last chance—'

'And it turned out to be an assignation with his murderer?'

'So she believes.'

'Is this now the common view with those who remain at Bishopthorpe?'

He shook his head. 'If it is, it's not because of anything they know. She has told no one. She's too frightened to speak out.' His expression was bleak. 'Her fear seems justified. One of her husband's closest friends was John of Willerby.'

Hildegard felt a shiver go through her. She told Hubert about the argument in the chapel at Lincoln Cathedral again. '"I'll fix it," Swynford had vowed. "Show me the man." And Jarrold went up to Willerby in the queue and threw his arm round him in a gesture that was nothing like the friendship it appeared to be.'

'How appearances can deceive.' Hubert looked grim. 'Where is Swynford now?'

'With the retinue of the Earl of Derby, I expect.'

'With Harry Bolingbroke, heir to the dukedom of Lancaster.' His face was like thunder. 'Untouchable.'

Hildegard had been listening carefully to Hubert's story and although she had taken part, she had been in a dream. He was here, just as she had imagined him, his handsome face, the sudden sparkling warmth breaking up the austerity of his features. Despite the horrors they were exploring it brought such happiness to be sitting beside him again. She pulled herself together. 'Hubert, we have no sure motive for Ralph Standish's murder. Even his death by poison is based on rumour. It might be grief that makes his wife link her husband's death with his alleged poisoning at the hands of the same man. A way of making his death more significant. The obvious explanation is one Edwin came up with on the way down.'

'And what's that?'

'As Jarrold himself said in the chapel, a woman is

involved. Maybe it was the wife herself? Maybe she had an understanding with Jarrold before Martin appeared on the scene at Scarborough and she fell for him? Maybe Jarrold wanted rid of Martin for a reason like that?'

'I suppose it's a possibility.'

'We need to find out more about Jarrold of Kyme. And, as regards Willerby, we must find the third man, if there is one.'

Hubert's eyes were brilliant as he bent towards her. 'Let's work together on this, Hildegard. Justice must be done.' He gazed into her face. 'My dearly beloved, forgive me for mentioning this but I noticed as soon as I saw you – there's a bruise on your cheek.' His fingers hovered over it, not quite touching. 'In no way does it detract from your beauty, indeed,' his voice thickened, 'nothing could ever do that – but I'm afraid it must be causing some pain . . .'

He did not breach the physical barrier that must remain between them but his imagined touch was like a balm to her pain. But then he asked the question she had been dreading. 'How did it happen?'

Trying to gauge every nuance of his reaction, she told him quickly and plainly about the return from the dead of the Lord of Ravenscar. Her husband.

Hubert rose to his feet when she finished. Without a word, he crossed the chamber and gazed for an age out of the window as if unsure which way to turn. She thought he moved in anger. She could not tell.

She waited with a sense of dread.

It was over.

She had unwittingly deceived him. But she had been, herself, deceived. Surely he would understand that?

Nothing, however, could change the facts. She was not what she seemed.

It was over. His silence told her that.

It was over.

Now and for ever.

Chapter Seven

When Thomas came down again he met Hildegard in the lodge, where she stood alone.

He gave her a faint smile. 'They live in more comfort than we do at Meaux. I shall have to bring Hubert up to the mark when we get back to Yorkshire.'

In silence he escorted her as far as the landing stage. When they arrived at the boats Thomas turned with a look of deep concern. 'I assume you've told him, then?'

She nodded.

'May I be permitted to ask—?'

'Oh you may, Thomas. He took it as he always takes things. Enigmatically. He said nothing – only that he would need to see me more formally after he had consulted the proctor and the abbot.'

Hubert's cold face swam before her.

Thomas took her hand. 'If you want me to do anything, Hildegard, anything – anything at all – just say the word.'

After her outburst tears pricked her eyes. 'I will. Dear Thomas.'

He towered over her, his young face full of kindness, and said, 'I'll keep you informed. There's no rule I know that says I can't do that. Now I'm going to escort you back to York Place where you can seek Neville's advice. That's your best course. Turn to him. Let's go.'

'No!' She put out a hand. 'You've no need to come back again. You're wounded. I'll do as you say and go straight back to consult His Grace.'

'But—'

'Forgive me. I want to be alone.'

Thomas instructed the boatman not to pick anyone else up but to take the domina back upriver and see her safely ashore.

He was a cheery character. 'Never fear, Brother. I know the drill with you people. I'm so used to ferrying monastics about, I'm practically a monk myself.' The man, with a large wooden cross protruding from a forest of hair under his jerkin, grinned down the boat at Hildegard as she settled herself on one of the thwarts.

As he began to row strongly out into the stream she raised one hand to Thomas. He was hovering on the shore with a look of fierce concern on his face.

It took longer to row back against the tide, even though it was less strong as it approached slack water, and the boatman had to use all his energy rather than giving her the benefit of his thoughts like the other fellow.

It was just as they were approaching the burnt-out ruins of the Savoy on their right when Hildegard saw a boat leaving the shelter of the bank to head downriver. That was nothing. There were a lot of boats on the water at this time of day. What aroused her interest was the figure sitting in the stern.

It was the man they had been talking about, Jarrold of Kyme.

His hood had been blown back by the stiff wind and if he had looked across the water he would have seen her, but he was holding the gunnels of the narrow craft with white knuckles and staring into the bottom of the boat as if to avoid seeing the yellow water frothing on both sides.

On an impulse Hildegard leant forward. 'Boatman, can you turn here and go back?'

'Me, I can turn anywhere.'

'Then follow that boat!'

Catching the note of urgency in her tone, he gave a broad grin. 'With the greatest pleasure, My Lady. Hold on!'

She pointed to where the other craft was already slipping away. Deftly plunging an oar deep into the water and pivoting the craft by the sheer strength of his brawny arms, he set off in pursuit with long powerful strokes of the oars.

They flew along and almost caught up with the other boat but her man cunningly fell back far enough to make sure they would go unnoticed. Eventually Jarrold pointed to the shore and the bows turned in towards Tower Stairs.

Her own man followed, drifting to shore only when the other boatman had been paid off and Jarrold was striding up into a narrow cobbled thoroughfare. He disappeared between the two rows of tenements.

It was with some trepidation, quickly overcome, that Hildegard followed him into the labyrinthine streets off the quayside. It was thick with dock workers, porters, merchants overseeing their goods in readiness for the invasion and all the usual wharfside riff-raff that gathered in the hope of earning a penny or two. Suspecting that it was likely to be the district that catered for the needs of the vast hordes of sailors who peopled the riverside she pulled up her hood and kept her head down with only an occasional glimpse from underneath to keep Jarrold in sight. I'm wasting my time here, she told herself. He's probably going to find a woman.

But he did not stop. He ignored the calls from the girls sitting on the balconies above the lane and walked on.

When he reached the top of the incline where the street met at a junction with a wide thoroughfare she realised they were close to All Hallows by the Tower. She shuddered at the thought of bumping into Ravenscar again.

He had said he had not finished with her.

She assumed he meant that he would be applying through the courts for restitution of his lands – the ones that had now passed to his younger brother, Guy – and perhaps he had already begun to make approaches to the Court of Arches too to try to get back the dowry she had brought to the marriage. So, out of caution, she kept her head down.

By now Jarrold was crossing the road and heading up towards the great market in the Cheap. She noticed that he was carrying two empty leather bags over his shoulder. He came to a stop outside an ostler's. She watched him make payment and a horse was led out. Cursing under her breath she watched him ride on between the stalls towards one of the city gates on the other side. He joined the queue of people filing through.

She watched him leave.

An old man selling caged linnets was on the corner and she approached him. 'Can you tell me which gate that is, master?'

'That be Aldersgate, Domina.'

'And this thoroughfare?'

'Cheapside.'

'And the road outside the gate, where does that lead?'

'Out into wild country, towards Essex way.'

Deciding she could follow Jarrold no further she dropped a coin into the old man's palm and made her way back to the quay. Someone would know where the road from Aldersgate led. It might only be that Jarrold was on a legitimate errand from York Place. He might even be innocent of all their suspicions, the rumours about him misplaced.

They were on the Strand. Ulf had gone to buy them a couple of pies from a stall while Hildegard sheltered from the wind in the lee of a goldsmith's shop. Idly she peered in at the display of goods, then, losing interest, turned rapidly to scan the crowds for Ulf and the steaming pies. As she did so she caught sight of someone staring straight at her over the heads of the crowd from the other side of the street. He turned away at once but not quickly enough. She recognised him. So here he was again.

He was a fleeting figure now, weaving his way through the crowd. She thought she had seen him earlier but had been uncertain. Now there was no doubt. He could not slip away unseen. He was hemmed in by those going up Ludgate Hill towards the city and the ones coming down to Westminster. She watched to see if he looked back but he didn't.

Ulf returned.

He gave her a puzzled frown. 'Has something happened?'

'No,' she said at once, feeling flustered.

'If it's that bastard following you, you'd let me know?'

'That – oh, yes,' she recovered. That bastard Ravenscar. 'Of course I would.'

'I'll abide by your decision not to harm him but I swear I'll drag him in to face the music, you can be sure of that. He can't be allowed to get away with what he's done.' He lowered his voice. 'We've got news he's hiding out somewhere in Petty Wales. That makes sense, given that his lands used to be in the border country. He'll have contacts there because of the wool interests he used to have. He must regret losing the income from them.'

The reason they were standing in a blustering wind in the

lane called the Strand was because Hildegard had decided to call on Ulf at the de Hutton house on the way back, needing to let him know that Ravenscar was still around, had visited her at Westminster and uttered more threats.

Ulf had greeted her news with a curse, furious with himself for having so far failed to track him down. He was more determined than ever. With the allies Roger had been able to summon they had searched every likely tenement around the church of All Hallows, he told her; now they were turning their attentions to neighbouring parishes like Portsoken and the area around the docks.

'That wasn't him,' she added when she noticed him glance off across the street. 'It wasn't anyone. I'd tell you at once if it was him.'

Satisfied, he handed over one of the pies.

He threw his crust to one of the dogs roaming about and came to a stop. When he turned to face her he was looking serious. 'Hildegard, I have something to tell you. It may as well be now as later.'

'What's wrong, Ulf? You look terrible. Are you sick?'

He shook his head. 'Sick at heart, maybe.' His eyes were very blue. They bored straight into her. 'I'll come straight out with it. Since I was knighted Roger's determined I should marry. He's offered me a couple of women: one, his ward, a young girl with no sense, and the other a widow with sense and property.'

'Which one will you choose?'

He shook his head. 'The way I feel, it would not be fair to choose either.'

'But Ulf—' she bit her lip. 'For your own good, for your future happiness . . . ?'

He turned his head. 'So now you know,' he said gruffly and walked on.

By the time she returned to York Place it was a scene of organised, even military, chaos with servants hurrying in all directions in an atmosphere of grim purpose. The cats were receiving more kicks than usual.

'His Grace?' she asked of a passing yeoman.

'Gone to Westminster to confer.' Not even bothering to stop he rushed on.

Hildegard thought, I am reprieved. Again.

She recalled Hubert's reaction to her news and wondered how the archbishop would take it. Rage against the abbot made her kick the step where she was standing. Damn him. He had failed to show the slightest concern about what she was going through.

Edwin appeared, hurtling out of the chamberlain's office, and skidded to a halt when he saw her. 'Just off upriver,' he called. 'I'm late!'

'Wait a moment!' Pushing her own dilemma aside she said urgently, 'I've just had the most extraordinary conversation with Abbot de Courcy. Listen, Edwin, he has information that makes Jarrold sound dangerous. Can you warn the archbishop when you meet him?'

'What is it?' He hurried her into a corner of the yard where they could talk.

'Jarrold earned the reputation of being a poisoner up at

250

Scarborough. Warn Neville. He cannot know the sort of man he's harbouring.'

Edwin raised a fist as he hurried off, calling back, 'Priority, Domina. Tell me more later!'

Alone she went on into the kitchens.

This place was boiling with activity as well. Master Fulford sat high on his wooden throne barking orders. The minions scurried to obey and the kitchen clerk's quill flew over the pages as, standing, he wrote everything down.

Remembering that Neville had planned a great feast for his closest allies, she realised it would be useless to interrupt the proceedings at present. Later, then, when the feast had run its course and everyone was mopping up while Master Fulford basked in the afterglow of the performance.

The top table on the dais was piled with subtleties in the shape of gilded castles, silver swans and other fantasies the cooks had devised and an endless succession of platters was brought out to fanfares from the heralds. Sides of beef, mutton, venison, pork and all the edible birds of the air had been fried, baked, boiled, basted and trivetted, then decorated with pastes and sauces and creams and made to look like anything but what they were, and the same with the fish. Wars or not, the fishmongers had brought the best of their catch to the kitchens, harvesting both sea and river. Hildegard surveyed the ornate concoction placed in front of her. She was told it was hake. One jellied eye looked back through a trellis of pastry.

'Good stuff,' murmured Edwin, gnawing on a more prosaic chicken leg.

They were seated at the lower end of the main table, Edwin opposite with his page, and Turnbull standing smartly beside Hildegard, glorying in his new role.

'So Edwin, time to catch you on the wing. Events are overtaking us.'

'There's plenty happening,' he agreed.

'What did the archbishop say to you when you mentioned our mutual friend?'

'Most extraordinary,' he replied, mouth full. 'I plainly caught him at the wrong moment. He was just going in to see Abbot Lytlington and when he heard what I was saying he almost turned on me. He said, "We are involved in affairs of state, boy." He called me "boy"! How do you like that? "We have more pressing matters on our minds than the quarrels of servants. I trust you can bring the matter to a close yourselves." And then he was gone. I do understand,' he added, loyally. 'It is piddling stuff compared to what's about to erupt when Parliament meets. I hope we're going to survive.'

He looked worriedly along the table. On Neville's left was the chancellor, Michael de la Pole. On his right, Sir Simon Burley, the King's former tutor, and further down were others of the King's party.

'Alexander's in his most sumptuous garments,' he observed. Brocade, silk, velvet. His ring glittering. His head freshly shaven, giving him an even more pugilistic look than usual. Now he was booming something about craving their indulgence over the poor quality of the food. There was surely no room for complaint, thought Hildegard. Any one of the dishes would have fed a family of six for a week.

'And,' he continued, 'I offer my most contrite apologies over the matter of the sauces.'

De la Pole dipped his spoon into the sauce dish and inspected the contents with a mystified frown.

'Shortly before we left Yorkshire my best saucier met with a most unfortunate accident. He's a great loss. His fame was such that even the late Sir Ralph Standish invited him to Scarborough Castle to teach his own man from London how to make a good sauce.' He raised his goblet. 'To the memory of a good man.'

'Standish?' Chancellor de la Pole murmured flatly, draining his cup. 'What an unfortunate demise. The sweating sickness, I'm told.' He picked up a piece of pork from the communal platter.

'No. It was the bloody flux,' Archbishop Neville contradicted.

'I understand there were rumours,' murmured de la Pole as if the matter was of little concern to him.

'There are always rumours,' agreed Neville, smiling at his guest.

As if more urgently aware of the nature of the rumours, de la Pole's glance darted to the food that lay before him. 'The King's food taster works overtime these days,' he remarked. 'Dickon won't let Anne take a sip of wine without it being tried first. He's the same himself.' Then he chuckled, albeit with an air of bravado. 'I hear Mayor Brembre suggested inviting the dukes to supper and poisoning the lot of 'em in one fell swoop! "That would rid us of vermin!" he said.'

Neville chuckled at this too but, like de la Pole, even he eyed the shin of lamb in his fist with a sudden wariness. 'Call Master Fulford,' he instructed his page. The boy ran off.

Neville began to tell de la Pole about the attack on his falconer at St Alban's.

Hildegard's close questioning of little Turnbull, her new page, had brought no further information on this matter. All he had done, he had told her, was take a message to the falconer with the lie about Master Fulford wanting to speak to him, although, of course, he himself had not known it was a lie until somebody, Medford, had told him it was. And he had got a beating from Swynford anyway, although he didn't know what for. Hildegard fed the little lad venison from her own platter to comfort him.

He is as honest as the day, she decided. If he had seen anyone in the mews that morning who should not have been there he would have told her.

While Neville and the others began to discuss the subsidy the chancellor would shortly have to ask for, she leant forward. 'Edwin, about that matter at the Tower, did you get chance to speak to His Grace about that as well?'

He knew what she meant and nodded.

'What was his response?'

'He said, "Why the devil are they skulking round the

Tower? They'll be inside on the rack if they don't watch their step. Go back and find out." By which I take it the prisoner will have nobody to lobby for his release until we discover what they're up to.'

'We shall have to make greater efforts to find out, then, for that poor man's sake.'

'Neville doesn't seem to have an inkling what it's about,' Edwin told her. 'He thinks as we do, they're seeing a French envoy. But Brembre's vociferously loyal. His Grace can't believe he'd be involved in a traitorous deal with the enemy.'

'Might the King himself have sent for him?' Seeing his startled glance she added hurriedly, 'I don't mean in a spirit of high treason but merely as a diplomatic approach, to try to avert the invasion?'

'If that's the case he hasn't confided in the archbishop or any other advisors, as far as we know. Even Mr Medford knows nothing about it.'

'I've never met Brembre. Have you?' she changed the subject.

He shook his head. 'We shan't have long to wait. He's been invited.'

Just then Fulford, attired in his chef's garb, massive and red-faced, sailed into view. After a difficult bow to the archbishop and to the chancellor he asked, 'Is everything to your satisfaction, Your Grace?'

'We hope so, Jonathan, but a remark about the King's food taster put us in mind of poison . . .' He waved his shin of lamb.

'I would wish to burn in hell for all eternity should I poison you or your guests, My Lord Archbishop.'

'We, in turn, would lay down our lives should anyone be misguided enough to accuse you of attempting to do so.' Neville turned to his guests. 'Eat and drink, my friends, in the expectation of full and happy lives!'

Goblets were raised, refilled and, over the next hour, raised and filled again.

Meanwhile guests entered and others departed. Among those who arrived was Mr Medford with his shadow, Dean Slake, and a few other young men from the Signet Office. Mayor Brembre made a noisy entrance, accompanied by a large retinue, including his wife and her own body servants, and talk turned to the 'fish wars' as Brembre called them. Promises to string up a few traitors were made. Then talk circled back to the immediate matter of the forthcoming Parliament and what to do to protect the King from the plotting of his enemies.

The King's steward, Sir Simon Burley, genial with age and experience and the lustre of having once been among the victors at Poitiers, said, 'They claim Dickon's wrong in the head with his fear of assassins but to my mind he'd be wrong in the head not to fear them. The Lancasters want the crown and if they don't get it Gloucester will. That's the beginning and end of it for him. He has to defeat them. Or face defeat himself.'

'The danger comes from the fact that Bolingbroke was made second in line after his father if Richard doesn't produce an heir,' de la Pole broke in. 'I was there when the old King set his signature to a bit of legal chicanery thought up by Gaunt, naming them both. I wish to hell the lad would get on with it and produce an heir.'

'Is she barren, do you think?' Brembre broke in.

'I hear she did conceive but lost it,' Sir Simon answered smoothly with a covert glance at de la Pole.

'I expect he's going to make an announcement in Parliament when they're all gathered. Let's hope so.' The chancellor avoided everybody's glance.

The rest of them shook their heads and moved off the subject rather quickly.

'So who can he rely on?' asked one of the bishops in a helpless tone.

'Me,' said Neville at once.

'And me,' Burley spoke up.

'Me too,' said de la Pole.

'Certainly me,' agreed Brembre stoutly.

'And us,' cut in Dean Slake, indicating the rest of the Signet clerks.

Medford said laconically, 'We are all King's men. Trust on it.'

Neville turned to the chancellor and cocked an eyebrow. 'What are you asking for this time, Michael?'

He gave a rueful smile. 'Four-tenths and three,' he announced.

There was a stunned silence.

'You'll never get as much as that.'

'I'm aware of that, Alexander, but it's what we need if we're going to put up a defence against the French.'

'Let's hope the Commons see it that way.'

'You regard them as important?'

'With Woodstock and his faction against us, they could be crucial. Nicholas will have to keep the city on our side.'

The chancellor looked thoughtful. 'They can't get rid of us all. Should they desire a scapegoat on the first of October,' he glanced round, 'let it be me. If I'm going to ask for a massive tax and they squeal like stuck pigs, and we can't get the numbers on our side and they vote me out . . .' He paused. '. . . I can always go back to Hull.'

'You'd be best putting some gold into a secret place under the rule of Emperor Wenceslas against the day of defeat,' growled Burley. 'I know I am.'

Despite the gravity of his advice, both men smiled. 'I liked Prague,' admitted de la Pole. 'The Bohemians gave us a good time when we went to fetch the Queen to England. I hope to go there again some day. Preferably when they put the emperor's crown on Richard's head.'

Neville looked surprised. 'You think he'd want it?'

'He has as much right as anyone if Wenceslas has no issue. They offered it to his grandfather but the old fool declined.'

'If you think it likely, then I'll get my masons to set it in stone in York Minster so nobody will ever forget. A handsome stone head wearing the triple crown.' Neville raised his goblet in a toast. 'Richard! Bless him. King and Emperor.'

* * *

As Hildegard was leaving, de la Pole got up as well and came out into the corridor after her. 'Domina,' he called, 'I gather we're both from the same region of Yorkshire?'

'I believe so.' She stopped and turned with a smile. 'I'm attached to the abbey at Meaux.'

'So you answer to Hubert de Courcy, do you?' He laughed pleasantly. 'He's a rigorous and unforgiving fellow. He gives my clerks hell!'

'Why so?'

'He runs some of his flocks on my land. Never seems to be out of court over some dispute or other!' He moved closer and after a quick glance round spoke in an undertone. 'Alexander has told me why he brought you down here with him but I also understand you know something of herbal matters?'

'Not much. Only everyday cures. Why, is there—?'

'No, no, nothing like that. It's the Queen. You need to know that the rumours are true. She did indeed have a miscarriage. It was a few days ago. I was at Eltham Palace when it happened. As you can imagine it was a terrible shock. She was in the bathhouse when the King found her. I think he believed she had been murdered when he dragged her from the water. By the time we arrived it was a pool of blood. He had wrapped her in a cloak and was holding her in his arms, tears streaming down his cheeks. 'Find out who did this,' he kept saying. We called that Bohemian leechwoman and she reassured us that the Queen would survive but that the baby was lost. Richard was mad with grief and vowed he would never touch Anne again in case his brute lust should kill her.'

'I'm so sorry. Miscarriages are common. No one really knows why they happen. Thanks be that the Queen survived, although I know how important it is for the King to have an heir.'

De la Pole looked thoughtful. 'It would suit his enemies if he failed.'

There were sore heads, stone or not, next morning but Hildegard took the opportunity while the kitchens were quiet and Master Fulford was sitting in his private office to take along the cutting of the fern-like plant she had found at Lincoln.

He took it with a puzzled frown and after a pause shook his head. 'It reminds me of something but I can't place it. We don't use it in my kitchens. That's all I can tell you. Ask that Dominican out at Stepney, Magister Daniels. He's the acknowledged expert. He runs the largest herb gardens in the land. They say he imports magical plants from Outremer. Sells 'em for profit to all the necromancers. If he doesn't know what it is, nobody will.'

'Someone does know it,' she told him and she mentioned how she had seen someone picking the leaves in the Bishop's gardens at Lincoln. Later she had discovered from one of the Lincoln servants that the woman was Lady Swynford, who was renting a house within the bishop's enclave. She told him how she had seen her pull up enough leaves to fill two leather bags, which she had then handed to her escort – a youth who, it turned out, was the much-loved Thomas Swynford.

'It's probably an aphrodisiac for his lord then,' sniffed the cook. 'Every time Bolingbroke visits his wife in Monmouth Castle, she conceives.'

There was no news that morning from St Mary Graces. Hildegard had half hoped that Thomas would appear with news that the Chapter had come to a decision about her status. But it was not so.

I'll be far down on the agenda, she decided. The Chapter has enough to discuss at present. They'll be more concerned about the King's demands when he opens Parliament, and how the vote will go, than me and my predicament. On top of that there's the invasion threat. The unfortunate circumstances of one insignificant nun are nothing compared to all that.

A servant came to find her later that morning when she was leaving the chapel after Lady Mass.

'Someone waiting at the lodge, Domina. He has a message which he will impart to no one else.'

She hurried after him thinking it might be news from Ulf. But when she went into the lodge a page was standing there smartly attired in the old-remembered livery of the Ravenscars' ivory and green. He had no need to tell her who had sent him. A man stepped forward from out of the shadows and made a sweeping bow. 'My Lady of Ravenscar?'

'No longer.' She lifted her head in astonishment.

It was Guy. He had changed. It was called 'growing up', she realised as he began to speak. No longer a boy, it was not just the carefully groomed beard, he was a knight with the *gravitas* befitting such a position. He had taken a pace forward as if about to clasp her in his arms then drew back. 'It's good to see you again, Hildegard. Apart from your attire you haven't changed.' He studied her closely. 'Not a line on your face. And as fair as ever. Is your hair still long, or do they make you cut it?'

'Guy, we need to talk in private.' She led the way outside into the courtyard where they would not be overheard.

The porter followed, keeping an eye on this armed stranger who had entered the Abbot of Westminster's domain on an assumption of permission. He called out and with a sigh Guy unbuckled his sword belt and handed it over.

When he returned to her he asked, 'What's all this about?'

'How much do you know?'

He looked confused. 'How much is there? I tracked you down as soon as I got this.' He held out a piece of vellum.

She read it quickly: *Your sister-in-law is a Cistercian staying at the Abbey of Westminster. Consult her on a matter of grave importance to yourself.* It was signed simply 'H'.

'How like him. There's your clue. "H" for Hugh.' She hesitated, unsure how to break the news to his brother.

But Guy muttered, 'He's not dead, is he?'

'No. And he's here in London.' She told him quickly everything Hugh had said, including his vow to get his lands back.

Guy was different to his brother in one respect. He kept a tight rein on his temper. Less vitriolic. More thoughtful.

After a long silence his eyes narrowed. 'I always suspected the scoundrel of taking the easy way out. He never had the guts for a fair fight. Do you remember how he used to cheat me at everything? Chess, dice, fighting, swordplay. Even skittles. He cheated at every damned thing. Anything to win. Fair means or foul. Usually foul. And,' he concluded heavily, 'now he's here.' His hand strayed to the place where his sword belt usually hung. But he gave her a sudden sharp glance. 'It is true, isn't it?'

'I'm afraid so.'

'Does he want to meet me face-to-face?'

'I think so.'

Guy clicked his teeth. 'They say the past always comes round again. Things won't go his way this time. Be assured of that, my dear Hildegard.' His lips curved. 'I certainly remember your fights.'

'You do?'

'He did his best to break your spirit. Many a time I felt like stepping in to sort him out.' His hand moved again to where his sword belt would have been.

She had not got Guy's measure, she realised. He was the same in some respects but in others a complete stranger.

Underneath the urbane exterior there was something dangerous and unpredictable.

Now he gave her a disarming smile, flirtatious, pulling at the thin line of fair hair at the corner of his mouth. 'You must have known how I felt in those days?'

'What do you mean?'

'Think! I was a lusty lad of fourteen. What do you imagine? You were a prize and my bloody brother had won you. It wasn't fair.'

Now she remembered how surly he had been, forever moody and uncooperative, but Hugh had been a malicious tease, always trying to make the boy look like a fool in front of her.

The smile he gave her now had charm in it and lowering his voice he murmured, 'I remember you at the May Day celebrations. You must remember that? You wore a blue gown, your hair was the colour of silver birch flowing loose to your waist. You wore a crown of may. That scent still reminds me of you. Our women at home are all short and black-haired, Welsh, a little witchy, you can't tell one from the other except for their silver and gold. But you! You were so northern and wild. A fish out of water like me. We two, I thought, we two. Isolated in that big draughty old castle. It was like fate.'

'Guy, you were a boy.'

'I'm still that boy in many ways, Hildegard.' His voice had dropped to a level of intimacy she did not expect.

'My circumstances are changed now,' she told him.

'And so are mine. I'm called to Westminster to represent my shire in affairs of state.'

'He's desperate to regain his lands, you know. He's also after my dowry and the children's inheritance.'

Guy smiled faintly and smoothed the line of hair on his upper lip again. 'Then you'll want him alive as much as I do.'

After he left, Hildegard paced the yard deep in thought. He was a strange ally. Despite his apparent fond remembrance of her, she could only recall his constant quarrelling with Hugh and her need to mediate between them. Hugh had been cunning towards him, offering rewards for small favours and then withdrawing them when he got what he wanted. He accused the boy of pursuing her and had raged spectacularly night after night, accusing her of sporting with him in a licentious manner, which always drew a stormy denial until she eventually saw that he was testing her. He was like a cat with a mouse. Taunting both of them out of blind malice.

But now Guy was no longer a half-grown boy. Before he left he had reached for her right hand and made a promise. 'You can count on me. This is one I'm going to win.' When he had turned to go his face had split into a snarl. 'He wants to steal my lands? Over my dead body.'

The prisoner was sitting in front of a fire with his head in his hands and looked up with a hopeless expression to see who had been ushered inside, but when he saw Hildegard and her two companions he rose to his feet at once and came to greet them with genuine warmth. He poured them all beakers of wine and invited them to sit.

'I've nothing much to report. They still come every day, round about the same time.'

'Always the same men?'

He nodded. 'The only good news is that spy of Bolingbroke's seems no wiser than us. He's still hanging round – in between visits to other, less fortunate prisoners.'

'Has he been to question you again?'

'No, Domina. We can only praise St Benet for small mercies.'

'Brace up,' said Edwin, bringing out a cooked pheasant from the bag over his shoulder. 'His Grace is well pleased with you and sends this. As soon as Parliament opens he'll have you out of here and back home with your wife and children.'

'I'm supposed to be speaking for my shire. His Grace the Earl of Derby won't sign my release so long as there's a vote to be counted.'

They observed the evening visit of the mayor and his aldermen to their French prisoner but this time there was no sign of the spy, Rivera, in the Tower precincts, so, with nothing more to discover, Thomas escorted them both to the ferry landing before, still limping, he made the short walk back to St Mary Graces.

Edwin disembarked at York Place, leaving Hildegard to alight at the Westminster steps. An autumn mist had followed on the incoming tide. Now it was rolling over the waterside, deadening distant sounds and muffling those near at hand. It was that time between vespers and compline when everyone was in the feast hall. The thought made her feel hungry herself so she set off towards the great dark bulk of the abbey, using the frail light near the river gate as a guide.

She had not even got as far as the main path, however, when a man stepped out of the shadows. The small flame from the cresset he carried glinted off his mail shirt where it was partly concealed under a dark tunic. He wore a woollen capuchon pulled up over his head and had a copious black beard bushing over his shirt front.

In the moment she glimpsed all this she noticed no blazon on his garments. She stepped hurriedly back. A cut-throat.

But she was wrong.

'Domina, I carry a message from my master.'

Not a thief after her money pouch, then. She noted the word 'master'. Not lord. A commoner. 'And who is your master, sir?'

'I think you know that. He instructed me to tell you that he is consulting his lawyer in the morning. You might wish to attend?'

'Might I?' So he came from Ravenscar.

'And in order to ensure your attendance I was instructed to invite you to come with me.'

Before she could move he stepped forward, hooking one mailed arm round her neck and pulling her backwards off the path. Quickly trussing her arms behind her back with a rope that had been concealed under his cloak he grunted in her ear, 'You can guess the need for silence.'

'This is ridiculous!' she hissed, struggling to free herself. 'You must be from Ravenscar. Is he mad?' Don't answer that, she told herself. To my dolour he has always been mad.

'Shut your mouth!' the servant muttered, arm still round her throat but made suddenly nervous by her lack of fear. 'Come on! Get moving!'

'Why should I?' she protested, still grappling to free herself.

He tightened his grip. 'Don't start any trouble or it'll be the worse for you. I've got a knife here.'

'It'll be the worse for you if you harm me because then he won't be able to make me sign whatever bit of parchment he wants my signature on.'

'You think you're clever,' he snarled, losing his temper.

She kept her mouth shut. A malign brute with a knife and a bit of rope won't best me, she thought, but there's no point in provoking him.

Allowing him to bundle her down towards the shore where the river lay she was conscious of how wide and dark it was, like a roll of black velvet. The mist folded over the surface, opening now and then to reveal the blackness underneath then closing again as the wind played through it. Water lapped quietly against the sides of a boat secretly docked below the bank. When she caught sight of the sky it was a field of stars.

'Get in the boat,' her captor ordered.

'Where are you taking me?'

'Never you mind,' he told her.

By now the ferryman who had brought her to Westminster had sculled back downriver. There was no sign of life on the waterfront. Wondering if it was worth giving a shout to the porter in his gatehouse, she decided against. He would be too far away and it was likely this brute would think nothing of slitting her throat if she annoyed him. She allowed him to push her towards the water's edge and down the slippery bank into the boat.

The splash of a body falling into the water would alert no one. Sudden terror gripped her. Seen from the boat the bank lay in darkness. Further out in mid-river the mist was still rolling in. By the time the boat was only a few yards from shore not even the cresset light from the ferrymaster's lodge was visible.

The water might have been ink as she went in except that it was numbingly cold. After the first shock passed, the water closed over her head and she had to force herself back up to the surface. Gasping for air she thrashed about desperately trying to get her bearings.

Get back to the shore.

But she had no idea where it was and her boots were already filling, dragging her down, and she had to tear at the laces and kick out until they were grasped and drawn off by the current.

Somewhere out of the mist came a shout. Taking it as an indication of her abductor's position, she began to strike out in the opposite direction but was then confused by the subtle splash of an oar from somewhere ahead. She circled, trying to make no ripples that would give her away, the freezing water beginning to numb her.

In terror of being recaptured she began to strike out again, and then the mist rolled over her and spread its wreaths on the dark waters, and the cold snatched her breath and turned it to stone in her lungs and night came down as she slid beneath the black waves.

Chapter Eight

Some creature was lying next to her. She moved closer to share its heat. That was the first thing she noticed. The second was that she was unclothed. Spreading her hands over her breasts and down to her thighs she discovered that all her garments had disappeared, no shift, no breast band, no leggings, no belt with its pouch of herbs, and on top of her, pressing down heavily, was a fur of some kind.

Her fingers explored the edge where it covered her face. It felt like a wolfskin. Despite its warmth, and the heat coming from the creature beside her, she could not stop shivering. A deep coldness gripped her. Ice ached inside every part of her body. Only half conscious she moved closer to the source of heat.

Next time she woke up memories began to return to remind her how she had got here. At first disjointed, they were of water closing over her head, her determination to reach the bank and escape the brute sent by Ravenscar, the sinister creaking of the oars, the swirling mist. She remembered staring into a void, seeing nothing, fog on all sides, the river invisible, only its cold grip as evidence of its presence. She remembered the boat, water slapping against its sides, the oars again, as it drew nearer. A terrified phrase had hammered in her skull: *I can't make it*. Then the fierce will that made her keep on swimming returned.

Memory, still fragmented, brought back a sensation of being hauled from the water. A confusion of falling. Something caught at her clothes and she cried out. She was being dragged, remembered half crawling up a bank. She fell to her knees when she felt solid ground beneath her. Mud oozed between her fingers.

She must have slept again, the memory of mud and the iron grip of the river's reluctance to release her winding her dreams into nightmare.

Something was pressed to her lips and a warm liquid dribbled into her mouth. Honey. A deep tiredness overcame her and she surrendered to it.

When she came to herself again she forced her eyes open and watched the patterns dancing across an unfamiliar ceiling above her head. It was firelight. Without moving she watched the flickering red brilliance, the yellow, the gold, repetitive in essence but never entirely the same. It soothed her. She looked at it for a long time until she thought to wonder where she was. Still shaken by spasms in the aftermath of the great chill she had suffered she moved towards the warmth radiating from the source beside her and her eyes closed and she drifted into sleep again.

Eventually the realisation came to her that it must be a person lying next to her. It must be the one who had saved her from the river, removed her wet garments, dried her naked body, covered her with the wolfskin and now – as she saw when she did eventually manage to lift her head – lay beside her.

She stared at the almost familiar mouth just inches away. The half-moon shape of eyelashes, black as jet, the sharp high cheekbones.

Her pupils dilated. Lips parted. She made an involuntary movement to escape and his eyes opened. He put out an arm to detain her. A dangerous smile swam above her as he raised himself on one elbow and studied her expression.

'Awake?'

She dragged the fur over her breasts. She was shivering again.

The spy, Rivera, rolled off the couch and stood up. He was covered decently in a long night-shift but his arousal was obvious. He moved out of her range of vision and returned almost at once with a carafe and a sort of chalice. Figured silver glinted in the firelight. It had two handles like a loving cup.

Kneeling beside the couch he pushed one arm under her head to raise it and tilted the cup towards her lips.

He must have done this before, she realised, tasting the same honeyed drink. The sweet scent of herbs floated in the steam.

She jerked away, remembering to cover herself, and put out a hand to ward him off.

'It's not poison!' he laughed softly. 'It'll be good for you. Drink it.' He held it so she could take hold of the two handles herself.

Cautiously she took another sip. This time she did not drift off into oblivion but she felt disembodied. It was like a dream. The heat, the cold, the confusion. This man.

She drank some more then watched as he placed the cup on the floor. He went on kneeling at the side of the couch.

'You were so cold when I dragged you from the water, I thought you were dead. I believe you were very close to it.'

He noticed that she was shivering again and slid in beside her under the wolfskin and put his arms round her. His body heat was like fire. She was drawn to it but, shocked, tried to hold herself away. He moved back and patted the wolfskin more closely round her until she was inside a hot cocoon.

'The only way to bring you back from the dead was by sharing my body heat with you. This chamber's like a furnace,' he pointed out, 'it's a wonder the thatch isn't alight and yet you're still shivering. Here.' He reached onto the floor beside him and poured some more of the herbal liquid into the cup. 'Trust me. It'll help.'

Her lips felt stiff but she managed to croak, 'Did you pull me from the water?'

'I heard the splash as you fell.'

'Was I close to the bank?'

'No.'

She still felt dazed and did not ask whether he was in a boat himself and if so how he had been able to see her in the layers of fog and the unlit nothingness of the water or, indeed, how he had come to be there in the first place, as if by some necromancy. Instead she murmured, 'This is the second time you've saved my life. You seem to appear like a guardian angel when I most need you.'

The fiery heat from the drink surged through her body and her head sank back onto the pillows. 'How long have I been here?'

'All night. You fell in before compline and it's now nearly tierce.'

'As late as that? But I must go back to—' She struggled from under the heavy coverings over them both, trying to remember why it was so urgent to leave, then remembering she was naked, then trying to pull the blanket round herself and then, after that, attempting to rise to her feet. The effort was too great. Her knees buckled. As she made a grab to save herself Rivera was beside her at once, catching her in his arms, the fur slipping down, and, struggling against him, she felt his fingers on her skin like flame.

275

'Let me go, Rivera.' She uttered his name without thinking. It changed something.

He laughed. 'Rivera? Been checking on me?'

He stepped back, made no move to prevent her breaking free, but noticing that she was trembling again, pulled the wolfskin over her shoulders. He forced her back onto the couch.

'You're not well enough. Don't be in such a hurry. Your clothes are still wet. Your boots are at the bottom of the Thames. And besides all that, you nearly drowned. You've endured a profound physical shock. Rest a while. You can stay here as long as you need to.'

He went over to a shelf and took down a phial, unstoppered it and returned to the couch. 'Lie still.' He began to rub a fiery sweet-scented oil into her shoulders. She assumed he would stop there but he continued, methodically working the oil into her icy skin underneath the sheet with all the thoroughness of somebody who did it for a living until every inch of her body was glowing. When he finished he went to get an extra blanket from a chest and tucked her into it.

Knowing what she had been told, his tenderness disturbed her. He was a spy for Bolingbroke, an interrogator at the Tower, a man she had been warned against. He was an enemy of the King. She had been warned about him. And yet . . .

'Does anyone know I'm here?' she murmured from the depths of her cocoon when he had rewrapped her.

276

He shook his head. She noticed how his hair shone in the firelight. Long and untidy, black as night. When he looked at her his eyes seemed to drink her in as if he shared everything she had ever known. He came to sit on the edge of the couch.

'Do you feel like talking about it?'

When she made no reply he asked, 'Who was it in the boat?'

'Somebody sent by the man I was once married to.'

'The husband in the crypt. How did that happen?'

The directness of the question was an invitation. She told him how they met. How they parted. About the years of believing herself a widow. Of finding peace and eventually a purpose at the priory in Swyne. There was nothing to hide. When she finished he took one of her hands in his. 'But now he's back you're free of your vows to your Order.'

There was a little silence while she came to understand what freedom might mean.

He stood up. 'How did you get into the Thames? Did he push you or did you jump?'

'Ravenscar's man tied my arms behind my back then dragged me to the boat. When we got out into midstream he unloosed me. I thought it meant he knew I'd go without any fuss to meet my . . .' she hesitated '. . . but I was wrong. He untied me so that when he pushed me overboard and my body was found it would look as if I'd slipped on the river path by accident. That's what he told me. So I jumped—'

277

'Jumped?' he mocked. His dark eyes travelled over her face.

'I thought I'd have a better chance of swimming to shore than waiting for a crack on the head and being thrown in.'

'Why would your husband want you dead?'

'Because I'm in his way. He probably fears I'll refuse to sign anything he's got his lawyer to draw up. The Ravenscar lands passed to his brother but my dowry and any profit accruing from it went to our children and my Order. Now he wants it all back.'

'Your children?'

'A boy and a girl.'

'You're fortunate.'

She tilted her head. 'Does your Order forbid family life?'

'That. But the sort of life I have leaves no room for the responsibility of children either.'

'You seem surprised I have any.'

'My research into your background did not lead me into such detail.'

Their eyes met and his expression invited her to laugh but she felt a shiver run through her. 'You've been following me, haven't you?' When he didn't reply she said, 'It's too extraordinary that you should have been so close to where I was nearly drowned.'

He got up briskly, saying, 'If you want to show your gratitude, light a candle to save my soul.'

'I could light a cathedral full, but even that would

not be enough.' As she uttered the words she realised she meant it. She owed her life to him twice over.

He began to move briskly around the small chamber, looking for something, and then he picked up a roll of twine from a shelf next to a prie-dieu where a book lay open. He came back to the couch. 'Stick your foot out.'

'What?'

'You need new boots. I know just the fellow to make them in a hurry. He owes me a favour. You'll be trapped here for ever with nothing to wear on your feet. You don't intend to walk barefoot, do you?'

When she did as he instructed he stretched the twine from heel to toe and tied a knot in it to mark the length. Chancing to glance up from where he knelt, he held her glance for a moment then took her foot between both palms. After a short meditative pause he lowered his lips to it and pressed them against it. Soft as breath. He moved them sensuously over the arch to her ankle.

When his eyes met hers again she could see mirrored in them the battle she had faced in the past – between desire and the demands of their vows.

The twine with her foot measurement had fallen to the floor. He stood up hurriedly. She watched him go to a peg by the door, take down a thick cloak, put it on, go out, come back, pick up the twine, slant a smile then go out again.

She heard him call to his housekeeper. 'Matilda! Do not enter my chamber.'

A voice, distant, called up, 'Very well, magister.'

The door at the bottom of the stairs slammed.

She heard the housekeeper going about her chores, singing.

A promise was a promise. A vow was a vow. Of course, she knew some nuns took their vows lightly. They had long-term carnal relations with men, even bore children who became acolytes in their monastic houses. Such women and men, if also in orders, had no belief in the reality of hellfire. Hildegard had never been able to make up her mind about the existence of other worlds, heaven, hell, because where was the evidence?

On the other hand, she was brought back to the importance of keeping her word – and she had given it to her Cistercian superiors when they accepted her into their Order.

The canonical law upheld by Abbot de Courcy, the abbot and proctor at St Mary Graces, the Chapter at Clairvaux, even Pope Clement in Avignon, would not judge otherwise now Ravenscar lived. She was no longer a member of the Order. Her vows were invalid.

It changed everything.

As Rivera said, she was free.

When he did not come back, and with her clothes at present unwearable, she had no choice but to stay where she was. Now and then chill waves would shake through her and when she got up to use the bucket in the corner she felt dizzy and had to steady herself against the wall.

Pulling on a mulberry gown with trailing sleeves she found lying on a chest she opened the door and listened. There was no sound below. She took the bucket downstairs and went out into a yard at the back, where she emptied it into the barrel for the dyers to collect.

When she looked up someone was watching from across the yard. It was a very small man. No bigger than a child. He noticed she had seen him and made an ironic bow.

'Ave, *dulcissima*. Are you an angel sent from heaven to bring peace on earth?'

'I'm flesh and blood like you, sir.'

He acknowledged her remark. 'Then we are kin, Sister.'

'Indeed, Brother, God be praised.'

He walked back into a house opposite with an amused smile.

She might have slept. She had no recollection of doing so but when she opened her eyes Rivera was standing over her with a wooden bowl full of delicious-smelling broth. As she took it she noticed that he had rearranged her clothes in front of the fire. Her heavy worsted cloak was still steaming and there were puddles underneath it. Her linen shift drooped where he had spread it over the back of a chair.

He took his outer clothes off, pulled up a stool and watched her eat.

'Rivera,' she said as she put the emptied bowl to one side. 'Tell me truly, how did you come to be on the river at the time I went in? It could not have been coincidence.'

When he failed to answer she stared hard at him and asked outright, 'Why follow me? I believe I've seen you, here and there about the town, but I was never sure. It doesn't make any sense.' She wondered if he knew about her visit to the Tower. She shivered. The pause lengthened. Eventually he ran a hand through his hair. 'I'm clearly losing my skill. I don't deny it. How could I? I saw this beautiful woman in the crowd and had to pursue her. Of course I've been following you. I've been trailing you all over London like a lovesick swain.'

'You're being ridiculous.' He did not look at her. 'The truth,' she insisted.

He paused long enough for her to hear herself breathing.

Then he said, 'I learnt that you were the eyes and ears of Archbishop Neville.'

A chill spread through her that was nothing to do with her near-drowning. He was dangerous. She had been warned. He was an interrogator at the Tower. It was easy to forget when he looked at her with eyes filled with kindness and ministered so thoughtfully to her needs.

The truth was, she now realised, ever since being saved from drowning, she had been his prisoner. Whatever she told him, about the Cross, about the archbishop's guests and their business, could be used to further the conspiracy against the King. That was why he was keeping her here, taking advantage of her temporary helplessness to find out what he could about Bolingbroke's opponents. She would be more guarded in what she told him.

She watched, horrified at the way her thoughts were tending, as he took her bowl from her and placed it on the table.

When he returned to sit on the side of the couch it was as if a coin were spinning on its edge. It could fall either way. One push could set a different course.

Just one.

She reached forward, resting a hand on his shoulder, toying with the rough edge of his shirt. 'Rumours,' she murmured softly. 'This city runs on rumours. It's the same at home. I can scarcely set foot outside my grange without somebody whispering some nonsense about me. His Grace brought me down from Yorkshire to minister to his health needs.' She made a face. 'He suffers terribly from arthritis.'

He took her hand in his and held it. After a moment he pressed her fingers against his lips.

'The thing is,' he hesitated, avoiding her glance, 'I've been following you ever since I saw you in the crypt with what I took to be a French spy. I saw him arrive off a ship from France before the blockade came down.' He paused as if what he was about to say was difficult and kissed the palm of her hand. 'It made me suspect you and your lord archbishop of being traitors and, as such, opponents of My Lord the Duke of Lancaster.'

'The Duke?'

'And his son.'

'I am not a traitor to England and nor is the archbishop.'

'But the Duke is your enemy.' He pressed his lips into her palm again.

'Only if he is a traitor to the King.'

'He is not. The rumours about his aim to usurp the throne are exactly that. More, they're deliberate lies. Spread by the King's inner circle for their own ends.'

'That's a view, certainly. But his son? Are you confident he has no designs on the throne?'

Rivera did not answer. His eyes darkened.

The coin was still spinning. And she knew now what she must do.

She chose the words that would determine her fate.

'There is another rumour, Rivera. I'm sure you've heard it.'

He shifted his glance back to her face.

'They say King Richard is trying to arrange a secret meeting with King Charles of France. His aim is to do a deal to ensure his own safety. If that is true then we are best off if we let him go. We should choose another man, one who is worthy of the English people.'

She sank back onto the wolfskin and it slipped a little as she put a hand to her mouth. 'Forgive me! That must sound most seditious. I don't mean to speak against the King . . .'

He was staring intently into her eyes as if testing the truth of her sentiments.

She stretched out her arms. 'I feel so chilled. Will you warm me again, Rivera?'

Without expression he stood up, hesitated, and then, like a sleepwalker, unbuckled his leather belt and let it fall to the floor. With his dark eyes fixed on hers, he disrobed, pulled his shirt over his head and stood naked for a moment before climbing under the wolfskin and lying beside her. She matched her body to his and allowed her fingers to trail slowly over his chest, over the taut muscles of his stomach, lingering, then moving lower. It was no hardship to simulate desire, she discovered to her dismay.

He lay back on the mound of pillows with his eyes closed, his mouth set in a straight line.

Without his penetrating stare she could gaze at him without shame. His beauty moved her. It was full of contradictions. Harshness and tenderness. Eyes that could light up with humour, with warmth, or darken with secret danger.

In other circumstances and in less troubled times, she thought . . . if the world were different . . . She sighed, partly from regret, partly also at the reawakening of a pleasure long forbidden as he turned to her with that sudden smile that made her heart turn over and her limbs melt.

His tone was puzzled. 'Your prioress wouldn't agree with what you said earlier.' He watched her carefully.

'My prioress . . . ?' Sleepily, a brief image came to mind.

The prioress of Swyne. Ever faithful to King Richard. Upright, honest and intransigent. What would she think now?

She recalled her pragmatism and courage. Then she remembered the man beside her. 'You forget, Rivera, my Order, if I may still call it that, is under the rule of the Pope in Avignon.'

'She's a Clementist. Of course.' His expression changed. 'I made an assumption about you – travelling in Neville's household – forgive me. We have more in common than I guessed.' He was still looking thoughtful but turned and took her more firmly in his arms. 'I believe we shall soon have Richard where we want him.'

'What do you mean?' She stiffened.

'The evidence against him and his attempted private treaty with the French will be damning. Enough to give Bolingbroke his chance at the throne.'

'Evidence?'

He began to kiss her, lifting her hair and letting it fall. She was scarcely able to concentrate.

'We do have evidence. We have a sworn testimony from one of the servants who went to Paris with Lord Salesbury.'

She had heard the rumours about a secret mission to the French court but had not believed it.

Rivera began to push the wolfskin aside again. 'Soon it'll be common knowledge.'

'And is he to be trusted, this servant?'

'Indeed – he's retained by one of the city aldermen. Who in turn is maintained by Bolingbroke.'

As the wolfskin fell away and revealed her to his gaze she was aware that he did not trust her enough to name the alderman or the servant. Reluctant to give up any advantage, she ran her hands through his hair and pulled his head down to her breasts so that he could not see the alarm in her eyes and murmured, 'It is to be hoped his testimony will be enough to defeat a king.'

When he raised his head and smiled into her eyes he did so with such sweetness that it took her breath away. His words, however, sent shudders through her when he laughed and said, 'It'll be enough to start the rumour-mongers clacking and after that there'll be no stopping them.' His lips were on her mouth but he lifted them long enough to mutter, 'The London mob cheer anybody if they're handled cleverly enough. Or hang them. They're fickle rats. They're already beginning to doubt Richard's fitness to lead them, especially as he can't produce an heir. They're still in awe of his regality. But he can be made to seem anything his enemies want.'

'What do you mean?' She stopped him, bringing his face to hers so she could look into his eyes.

'He can seem extravagant while they starve. Partisan while they have to scramble for favour. Arrogant while they live lives of enforced civility. Once the mob has its views changed against him, it'll get rid of him. Bolingbroke will scarcely have to raise a finger, let alone an army. If he wants the crown enough they'll tear Richard apart and hand it to him on a velvet cushion.'

'But if Richard does have an heir . . .' she managed as his lips sank lower. 'The people would never support a usurper.'

'He will not have an heir. It will not be allowed. His offspring would be murdered in their beds.'

With a sudden savage gesture he pushed aside the last covering of the wolfskin and kicked it onto the floor. He knelt above her.

It will not be allowed.

What could he mean? Who would not allow it? He could only mean Bolingbroke or Gloucester.

As he closed over her she slid helplessly into the depths with the thought: *Save me from the fires of hell, save me from losing myself to this treacherous man. Save me.*

Rivera was lying back across the couch, his head cradled in her lap while she fed him blackberries from a wooden dish. The purple juice ran down and she bent her head to lick it from the corners of his mouth. The harshness had vanished from his face. His beautiful lips curved with pleasure. Unable to resist, she pressed kisses over his face until she reached his mouth, then, barely touching it, she listened to the soft rhythm of his breathing as it adapted itself to her own.

Wondering when she would have to leave she asked, 'Did they say when my boots would be ready?'

'Soon.' He opened his eyes. 'Never.'

'So I shall be a prisoner here?'

'Yes. Why would you want to leave?'

'I don't.' She kissed him again. He pulled her over himself, his mouth hot, searching for her own.

He said, 'You've heard all the noise in the street outside? That's because everybody's pouring out of the city into Westminster. King Dickon has opened Parliament. His chancellor is making his first speech even now.'

She buried her face in his hair. The moment de la Pole had mentioned had come. 'How is it being received I wonder?'

'I'll find out. I have to go out soon, work to do.'

The bell for nones had long ago faded.

'Work?'

He closed his eyes. 'I'll get Matilda to prepare some food for when I get back. I've told her not to enter my room. Don't let her know you're here or it'll be round town in no time, doing neither of us any good.'

'This housekeeper. I'm surprised she's a gossip.' She had heard his peremptory order from the top of the stairs. 'You speak quite harshly to her.'

'I do so to keep her from me. She's a widow. It would be her ruin if I allowed any intimacy.' He opened his eyes. 'She's not like you. She'd follow me like a faithful hound to the ends of the earth if I asked – even to the gates of hell.'

'And I would not?'

He studied her expression, eyes sombre. 'I know you

289

would not. You'd betray me on the slightest pretext if it could further your cause.'

'My cause? I have no cause!'

His liquid gaze swept her face, guarded and suddenly cold. 'I hope not. Or we should not be together.'

Later, before he went out, she leant against him, matching her body to his to bring her lips level with his own. They looked into each other's eyes. Rivera's were flecked with amber and jade. And then they became an endless black corridor leading into the abyss of his soul.

A street singer accompanied himself on a hurdy-gurdy directly beneath the window. He sang and played for some time. Jigs. Laments. A plaintive chanson that he kept coming back to. Maybe Rivera had paid him to play, planted him there to make sure she did not leave without being noticed. Her clothes had been moved somewhat further back from the fire and her cloak was still slightly steaming. Her shift was dry but she left it where it lay.

Warm underneath the animal skin she pondered the scene at the Tower, the one she had witnessed from the prisoner's window: Mayor Brembre, the aldermen and the Bohemian courtier, Petrus de Lancekrona, making their regular visit to the Salt Tower. She wondered if Rivera knew the Bohemian's name. He was well known even outside court circles for his extravagant behaviour, his devotion to Queen Anne. Rivera had been in the Tower enclave often enough to know about him.

She wondered if he knew the name of the person they were meeting, his allegiance, what the purpose of their meeting was, and whether it was knowledge powerful enough to bring the defeat of the King. She wondered about the aldermen, which one was a traitor, and the name of the servant who was supposed to have accompanied the King's envoy to Paris and how damning his testimony could be.

Rivera returned at last. It was late in the day. He seemed preoccupied. One sharp glance to make sure she was still there then a turning away of his head. The harshness was back, mouth grim, eyes hooded. He threw his cloak onto a chair.

Food, taken from his bag, he placed between them on the couch having climbed in beside her again, but although he urged her to start, he did not eat.

'Did you hear anything about de la Pole's speech to the lords?' she asked when the silence lengthened.

He looked up, startled, then shook his head. 'Only that he's trying to exact an outrageous tax which nobody will ever accept. Least of all the Commons.'

'Not even Mayor Brembre?'

He gave her a slanting look. 'Not even our illustrious mayor. Unless he's able to come to some secret exemption for himself and his cronies.'

'That's cynical.'

'I have no illusions – do you?'

'What do you mean?'

'Both sides are the same. Greed and ambition. Those who have power stop at nothing to keep it. Why should I respect them? It's only because of what the Duke has done for me that I'm on the Lancastrian side.'

'The Duke?'

'Forget it.'

'No, Rivera. Why should I forget it? How did you come to know him?'

'He had me educated and then gave me to the Benedictines. I asked to be released. You don't need to know all this.'

She said lightly, 'Your St Serapion is not very strict.'

'What do you mean?'

'You're insatiable.'

'I am! What about you?'

'I'm free, you told me so.'

'Do you believe everything I tell you?'

'Of course.'

'Then you're a fool . . .' He reached out for her. 'Except that I know you're not.' He whispered in her ear. '*Dedens mon livre de pensee, j'ay trouvé escripvant mon cueur—*'

'*La vraye histoire de doleu,*' she murmured in return.

'So you know it?' He looked at her with a quizzical expression. 'And do you know what I have written on my heart—?'

'The true history of grief—' she quoted.

'Grief at the falling of the prey,' he added with a touch of irony. He turned away.

Something had happened while he had been out.

He turned back. 'Now you've established I read poetry and found something out about my past, what else do you want to know?'

'Only what might be written truly on your heart,' she answered, referring to the lines he had just quoted.

'Doleur, death and dark deeds.' He gave a predatory smile.

'Tell me something true about yourself.'

'What do you want to know?'

'Anything.'

He looked thoughtful. 'When I was a boy I trained a hawk. It was a falcon. I used to think how she must grieve as she gyred in splendour towards the sun, knowing that she would have to return to earth.'

'What happened to her?'

'She flew off and didn't come back.'

He got up.

She asked quickly, 'What happened when you were out?'

He gave her a piercing glance. 'Interesting you should mention Brembre.' He returned to the couch.

When he hesitated she prompted, 'Why so?'

'I've just seen him at the Tower.'

As lightly as a zephyr she asked, 'Oh? What was he doing there?'

'He's there regularly these days.' He examined her expression as if it might tell him something. 'It can only mean one thing,' he said, still watching her. 'He's meeting someone on behalf of the King.'

'You think the rumour's true, then? This one about the secret French agreement?'

He ignored that, instead saying, 'I've also heard that something special is going on in the Tower the night after next.' He picked up a piece of bread and began to eat. 'Your new boots should be ready by then. Come with me. Let's catch the traitors in their nest.'

Rivera promised he would make sure she got back safely to Westminster. Although his small house was set in a jumble of similar unpretentious dwellings with only a view of the street, across the yard at the back was a narrow gap between the houses that in the north would have been called a laup. At the far end it descended in a dozen steps to the water. A narrow shelf of sand was revealed at low tide but when it came in the water reached the top of the steps. It was because of this that it was only possible to keep a boat on shore. There was one there now when they went out, a small clinker-built gig, hanging from a bracket on the wall.

Rivera manhandled it down onto the cobbles, dragged it into the narrow water-filled gap between the houses and handed her in while he steadied it. He climbed in after her, leant across and kissed her, then pushed it out onto the wide waters.

Hildegard felt a rush of fear as the tide broiled underneath the thin wooden shell and Rivera commented on her change of colour. He smiled warmly down the boat. 'Trust me.'

Before she alighted at the busy Westminster landing stage a few minutes later, nervous at appearing before the world again, he told her he would come to meet her in this exact spot at the bell for vespers the day after next.

'Don't draw attention to yourself. We'll go back to my place, have something to eat, then go on to the Tower after compline when it's dark.'

Chapter Nine

The cheerful porter was on duty when she reached the wicket gate. He looked at her in astonishment. 'Praise be, Domina! We'd given you up for dead. There's a reception committee waiting for you at the gatehouse. You'd best get on up there. Set Earl de Hutton's mind at rest.'

Ulf, with a posse of armed men in possession of the gatehouse, some scandalously playing dice in front of a couple of Benedictines, was pacing to and fro across the floor. Hildegard stood in the doorway until he noticed her.

When he eventually looked across he stopped in his tracks. 'Where the hell have you been?' He came towards her with a look of mingled relief and concern on his face. He looked her up and down. 'Are you unharmed?'

When she failed to answer straight away he went on, 'We got the message late last night about your accident.

Till then we'd been scouring the entire north bank for you, especially with these gruesome body parts showing up.'

She blinked. 'What are you saying? What message? What body parts?'

He in turn looked astonished. 'You know, the nailed hand and all that?'

'I don't know what you're talking about.' Rivera had mentioned no such thing.

'Don't worry about it now.' He put a hand under her elbow. 'Come and sit down. You look washed out. What the hell happened? Where've you been all this time?'

'I fell in the river. My rescuer took me in.'

'Fell in?'

'Careless of me.'

Ulf looked unconvinced but evidently decided to accept it. 'Who saved you?'

'A friar.'

'Roger will want to give him a reward.'

'No, he would not like that,' she said hurriedly, determined not to allow Rivera into the matter.

'These old mendicants who live by the river are ever vigilant,' Ulf began to say. 'They fish bodies out all the time. Compassion might come into it – but they make a fair living from selling the unclaimed cadavers to the surgeons.' He squeezed her shoulder. 'Lucky your rescuer didn't plan to do the same!'

'Maybe he did and was disappointed when I survived!'

She tried to smile but her face was stiff with the effort of lying to her beloved friend. His trustful blue eyes were a deep reproach if he only knew it.

'Two nights you've been missing,' he continued, turning his mouth down. 'I was going mad with worry, Hildegard. You can't imagine.'

Made more guilty by the fact that she had given no thought to the distress she might have been causing all the time she was in Rivera's arms, she could only murmur something about how sorry she was and beg his forgiveness. 'But what's this about a nailed hand?'

'The whole city's in a panic. Some madman nailed a severed hand to the door of St Paul's. It happened just before the King opened Parliament. Then, after the first session ended, a foot was found, nailed to the door of the Guildhall.'

'Why would anybody do such a horrible thing?'

'Speculation's rife, as you can imagine. There was no written message. But let's talk about you—'

She stood up abruptly. 'No, really – I-I think I'll go to my chamber and change my garments. They smell of river water and it's beginning to make me feel sick. I must wash . . .'

'Of course, I'm being thoughtless. Let me escort you. I warn you, from now on you won't be let out of our sight until we're all safely back in Yorkshire. This city's a nest of madmen. Even I'm having to watch my back all the time.' They moved towards the door and his men pocketed their dice and followed. 'When your friar sent that message to say you were alive and well, Roger tried to insist that you stay with us on the Strand. His Grace has other ideas, though. He's determined you'll stay at York Place. I'll send a messenger over to let him know you're back and then we'll get you over there with your things—'

'No!' She put a hand on his arm. 'It's best if I stay here for now—'

'But Hildegard—'

'Take my things over for me in the morning. There's a reason – I can't explain yet. I must speak to Medford first.' She straightened her cloak. 'I can't tell you more, Ulf. The offer of a message to Archbishop Neville to let him know I'm back would be helpful, though.'

'And an armed escort. I insist. You can't argue with that. I won't have a moment's peace otherwise, and I know Roger would give me hell if I failed in that as well.' When she lifted her head he told her, 'We still haven't found Ravenscar.'

In the solitude of her small chamber at the top of one of the tower staircases Hildegard called for water, and as soon as it arrived tore off her stained garments and stood naked for a moment. Then, slowly, she began to wash.

The promised escort was waiting in the yard when she went down. He was a young fellow, one she recognised from Castle Hutton, a four-square Yorkshireman in his early twenties with a broadsword at his side and a confident step that showed he would take no nonsense from anyone.

'Greetings, Haskin. You've been allotted this onerous task, have you?'

'I trust you'll make it light enough for me, Domina.'

Accompanied in this way she walked over to the Great Hall in the palace to seek out Mr Medford in his adjacent chambers.

'Go,' Medford encouraged as soon as she had explained Rivera's plan to get into the Salt Tower. 'You've done good work,' he approved. 'Let's see what you can find out. We've trusted Brembre so far but he plays a close hand. We need to know who he's got in there. He'll be worried about his future. Maybe he intends to sell the King down the river, like his own rivals with their fish! Of course, we have no jurisdiction over the Tower or the city. He can do what the hell he likes in there. He's King of London. It might be different next week, though.'

'What happens then?'

'His year's up. He has to stand for re-election on the thirteenth. The way things are it's touch-and-go whether he'll win.'

'So might there be a new mayor?'

'Yes, if he plays a poor hand. But don't ask me who it's likely to be. There's no clear runner. Everything's hanging by a thread.'

'So, for clarity, in a few days Brembre might lose his power over what goes on in the Tower?'

Medford nodded. 'He's adept at packing the Guildhall with his supporters but this time he might not be able to summon enough of them.' He laughed. 'Quite a force, our Nick Brembre. But nobody's invincible. Find out before Bolingbroke what he's up to.' He frowned. 'I wonder who the hell they've got in there? Some bloody French spy, I expect.'

'Maybe it's a mermaid,' suggested Slake with his usual strange humour

'Will you go, Domina?' Medford asked as if suddenly doubting her sense of purpose. 'We'll take care of Rivera.'

'Take care of him?'

'It's our job.'

'I won't go without your promise he'll come to no harm.'

He gave her a long look. 'I gather you were with him for a couple of nights.'

She said nothing.

Medford gave a quick nod of his head. 'Our gratitude. Have no fears for him.'

The bells of Westminster seemed to count the divisions of the day more slowly than she had ever known. Descending by candlelight to the half-built church for the night office with other hooded and softly shod worshippers she afterwards lay wakeful and impatient until lauds at the first glimmer of day. Then came prime, tierce in the teeming mid-morning when the whole abbey was alive with visitors, and then as regularly as sunrise and sunset, the office for the sixth hour, the ninth, vespers, until at last it was compline again and night folded everyone in its sacred embrace.

Before sending her clothes down to the laundry she buried her face in them, smelling river water. And the lingering scent of rose oil.

She had missed the opening of Parliament when Richard and his queen appeared with all the glamour of royalty. But she had been told about it by a couple of monks when she ate in the guest hall. The King had looked determined, she was told, the Queen frail and beautiful and frightened.

The Lords and Commons were in session every day by now. Only the representatives were allowed inside, but outside in the yard, waiting to hear what happened next, the entire population of London and the shires seemed to have gathered. Accents from all regions of the realm mingled in the general cacophony of musicians, food and ale sellers, and the endless singing of the pilgrims. The muzzled bear was made to dance to a piper and it did a sad shambling jig before sitting down again to look at its chains while its master collected pennies in a hat.

Every so often a herald would appear in the great arched doorway to make an announcement in a suddenly descended hush. Now shouts of astonishment were beginning to greet these announcements, arguments were breaking and fists flying, and by the time the latest reports filtered to the back of the crowd the facts were usually distorted and more arguments would break out about what was really going on. Hildegard listened to her neighbours. There was no doubt about de la Pole's predicament.

He had told the archbishop's assembled guests only a few nights ago that if a scapegoat was needed, it might as well be him. Now he was putting up a valiant defence against some outrageous charges being levelled against him. The barons were clamouring to impeach him on seven articles to do with rents and tolls in Yorkshire and other accusations of embezzlement and failing in his duty to the Crown.

Ulf sought Hildegard after he left the Commons. 'I've been in there all day,' he told her. 'I just want to check that Haskin is doing his job.'

The young bodyguard gave a smirk. 'I've got an easy task here, Captain.'

Ulf bent his head so Hildegard could hear him beneath the noise of the rabble swirling around the doors. 'There's a real clamour in there. They're now trying to blame de la Pole for that fiasco in Ghent. What more could he have done, I ask you? He raised ten thousand crowns in three days, mustered an army of three thousand including over a thousand longbowmen. The man's brilliant. It wasn't his fault that the French Flemings did a deal behind his back with the Duke of Burgundy and kicked their own countrymen in the balls.'

'How did de la Pole defend himself?'

'He said, "If I'm guilty – which I'm not – then so is the council for voting such a strategy." Then he laid the facts before them. It was enough. They had to shift around to find some other criticism – and all they could come up with was some nonsense about the renting of a parcel of land in the Riding and the profit he was supposed to have made from it.'

'Where is the land?' asked Hildegard, forgetting Rivera for a moment. It was her own territory, the East Riding, and might be something in which the Abbot of Meaux had an interest.

'It's on the bank of the Humber. Place called Flaxholme.'

'Nothing to do with Meaux, then.' She gave him a look. 'It's a hellish place, flooded half the year. I'm surprised he can make anything like a profit from it. What's their argument?'

'They say it was leased from the King in lieu of port taxes at Hull but the lessee was accused of murdering his wife's lover years ago and fled back to Middelburg. So de la Pole took it over. They claim he's taking an excessive profit from it that by rights should go to the King. As if he'd swindle the King!'

'So what did he do?'

'He dazzles them with figures and says, "With a profit like that I'll gladly sell. Any offers?" He looks round the chamber. There's dead silence. "No takers, then?" And he sits down in a storm of applause from our side and some snarls of rage from theirs.' Ulf grinned. 'He's quite a card. So far he's tying them in knots.'

Spirits lightened by this exchange she watched him leave.

The session had ended for the day and now it was between nones and vespers, still some hours before her meeting with Rivera. Having been pushed to the front of the mob outside the chapter house Hildegard had a good view of the rest of the Commons coming out. Ulf had been one of the first but now others followed.

No sign, she noticed, of the Abbot of Meaux. And no message about her legal status.

The guards started to force everybody back to make more room for the rest of the Commons to get out. It was then she found herself staring into the face of Guy de Ravenscar, her brother-in-law.

He was gaping, colour draining from his cheeks. 'Hildegard?' He pushed the bodyguards aside and stepped into the crowd, taking her by the arm. 'It is you?'

'Of course it's me, Guy. What on earth do you mean?'

'I thought you were dead!'

Her thoughts flew to the bearded would-be murderer who had tried to drown her in the Thames and she tried to pull away. 'Where did you hear I was dead?' she demanded suspiciously.

'From my bloody brother, of course.' Calling over his shoulder for his bodyguard to follow he put an arm round her shoulders and carved a path for them through the onlookers to the edge of the crowd where there was less noise. Haskin followed.

'The bastard said he'd got you out of the way and now it was only me he had to deal with. He seemed to think I was more easily persuaded to give up my land than you your dowry.' He gave a sardonic chuckle. 'He always underestimated me, the sot-witted devil. But how are you? He told me you'd slipped off the river path and drowned.'

'He hoped! He sent a man to take me to meet him. We went by boat. His instructions included pushing me overboard.'

'The murdering devil.'

'Luckily someone rescued me.'

'Tell me his name. He deserves a reward.' He looked intently into her face.

'I can't tell you.'

'Won't?' He gave a narrow smile. 'What is all this?'

'Nothing. He's a friar. He won't take a reward.'

'No matter. You're safe. That's the important thing. We'll join forces and take Hugh to court. We'll best him there, legally. We'll do him for every bloody penny he's got. We'll tie him in knots. He'll wish he'd stayed in Normandy with his French mare.' He chuckled darkly. 'He hasn't a leg to stand on – a bit like the poor fellow whose parts they're nailing up all round London.' He turned to his bodyguard. 'Let's go.' And to Hildegard, 'Coming to dine with me?'

'I can't. I have things to do.'

He nodded. 'I'm relieved to see you . . .' he searched for a word '. . . in bloom.' He bestowed a kiss on her forehead and with that he was gone.

Chapter Ten

Haskin was standing close, as ordered, and Hildegard turned to him, 'What's this about the nailed man?'

'They've found another part, Domina. His left leg nailed on a church door in Petty Wales near the Tower.'

'It's horrible. Why would anyone do such a thing?'

'They say it's a warning to Parliament, or to the King, or to Gloucester. They're not sure which way it's going yet.'

'A warning?'

'Haven't you heard the soothsayers? The corpse represents the body of the realm – the right hand is Calais, the left hand Aquitaine, the limbs are England and Wales, hence this latest, and the head is the city of London. The meaning to some is that Richard will hack his kingdom to pieces and hand the corpse piece by bloody piece to France.'

'Or his enemies will,' she replied sharply.

Haskin nodded. 'That's our view in the de Hutton household. Let's hope this broiling mob sees sense, votes for the right man and gives the Duke of Gloucester a kick up the arse.'

As a reliable bodyguard should, Haskin followed her all the way back to the staircase door leading up to her guest chamber.

'I'm not going to compline,' she told him with her hand on the latch. 'You can have the evening off.' Turning firmly she made her way inside.

Alone in her chamber she took off the familiar unbleached habit of her Order, and with a feeling that she might never be justified in putting it on again, threw it onto the bed. Removing her boots and the rest of her clothes she washed again. Twice in three days. After drying herself and patting rose water into her skin, she slipped into a clean shift and pulled on a plain woollen houpelande she carried as a spare. It fell to the ground in even pleats and she buttoned it up to her neck.

Instead of a wimple she unpacked a square of linen, rolled one corner to make a pad and fitted it over her brow. Then she tied the two corners in a knot at the back of her head, brought them round underneath her chin to be tucked in on both sides like a gorget, tucking the fourth corner inside the neck of the houpelande.

Over all this she donned a grey cloak, fastened it with a pin and pulled up the hood. Buckling on her leather belt with its attached scrip and a new knife to replace the one she had lost, she went barefoot to where her boots stood by the door. Thrusting her feet into them she tightened the laces and stood up.

He had warned her not to draw attention to herself. Now she looked like any other townswoman and not a nun at all.

With a swift glance round the chamber she descended the stairs, and with a furiously beating heart, stepped out into the mauve light of the October evening.

He is not here. Her heart lurched. The landing stage was bereft of life. The broad stretch of the Thames held the light long after it had faded from the land. It was like a sheet of gold foil stretching from one side of the river to the other. A few craft dotted the surface in midstream. The wind was still strong and came whining through the struts of the jetty, abrading the surface of the water and sending line after line of wavelets galloping onto the shore.

Unsure what to do she jumped down, her boots crunching in the shingle, but had taken only a couple of paces when a voice called softly, 'Hildi! Over here!'

Turning, she saw a movement a little way along the beach. A distance of three or four yards separated them. It was a yawning gap. A space they simultaneously hastened to bridge and then they were in each other's arms, his mouth hot against her own. 'It's been an age. I thought you'd changed your mind,' he murmured.

'I thought *you* had.'

* * *

They were lying on the couch in his chamber again, with only the glow from a cresset outside the window to cast light over their entwined limbs. The street singer was back, ignoring curfew like everyone else on this night of premonitions and change. Meteors had been seen, confirming the invasion and the dangerous brink on which England stood. The sweet and plaintive voice carried up to where they lay and gave expression to all the longing one human being can feel for another.

When he stopped Rivera opened the casement, throwing out some coins and calling down, 'Play on!' The music started again.

Rivera was encouraged to talk more intimately than usual, telling her things he wanted her to know about himself. 'We have so little time.' He lifted her hair, planting kisses on her hot skin. 'We have to leave for the Tower soon.' He looked tenderly into her face. 'Whatever happens, this is true, isn't it?'

She reached up to touch his lips with her fingers. 'Yes, this – whatever it is.'

'To be drawn down into the flames together.'

'Regrets?'

'None.'

'Nor me. But I feel there's something . . .' she glanced round his room '. . . there's something in the air tonight . . .'

'The invasion? Or are we back to the exalted spirit and the sinful flesh?' He looked at her with the sort of expression that made her heart turn over.

Nothing will happen to him, she thought, shivering with revulsion against Medford and Slake and the rest of the Signet clerks, the shadowy figures whose function was to further only the wishes of the King.

He rested her palm against his cheek. 'The poet tells us there is no greater woe than to remember past bliss in times of distress. May your woes be small, Hildi. Soon I shall have to take you into a place of evil. You know it.'

'Believe in your saint. He'll protect us.' When he smiled with a glinting irony, she asked, 'Who is he, St Serapion?'

'He was a Castilian. He offered himself as ransom for the release of a friend during the wars with the Moors. They took him in exchange, then tortured him to death as he knew they would. An uncle of mine, my father's brother, was one of his followers. He offered himself in the same way in a time of war. He was my hero when I was a boy.'

'Did you live in Castile?'

'I was born here. My father was an ambassador for King Pedro and married an English woman in the household of the Duke of Lancaster.'

'Was this when he was negotiating for the hand of Pedro's daughter, Constanza?'

'Yes, the second Duchess. When my mother died and my father decided to go back to Castile the Duke made me his ward. He promised me to the Benedictines but afterwards I asked him to allow me to leave them to establish a shrine in honour of St Serapion.'

'You owe the Duke a lot.'

'The Duke, yes. Pray he does become King of Castile and end our war with Spain.' He lifted his head towards the rattling casement. 'Still the wind blows . . .'

He took her in his arms and held her as fiercely as if the army was already at the gates. His voice was no more than a whisper. 'I have certain information that the French will sail this night. Their prophets say the wind will drop. Then nothing will stop them.'

His words sent a chill through her.

'It makes it more urgent than ever to find out who Brembre visits in the Tower and whether he's a traitor to the King. Or,' he added, 'whether the King is a traitor to his people.'

They had a strategy worked out so that when they arrived at the ward bridge they would do so separately. 'I have free access here,' Rivera told her superfluously as they approached the grim walls of the Tower's outer defences. 'You have a prisoner to visit. Go and ask for him. I'll meet you at the Salt Tower when the vigil bell sounds.' He gave her a small push in the direction of the guardhouse.

Before she left she asked, 'Are you armed?'

He gave her a slanting smile. 'Are you?'

When she spoke to the custody serjeant he frowned. Beckoning, he led her outside into the great yard on the other side of the bridge and with nobody to overhear him asked, peering into her face, 'Didn't anybody tell you he's been moved?'

'Where to?'

The man gazed worriedly off across the yard. 'All I know is, after his interrogation, they come in, they move him, they tell nobody what they're going to do with him.'

'Interrogation?' Her breath was held until he gave her a bleak look that said everything. As if to confirm it he nodded towards the distant figure that was crossing the bridge. It was Rivera.

'Who moved him?' she managed to ask.

He scratched his head. 'You might go to a private chamber in the White Tower. Tell the guards there I sent you. Here,' he rooted in his coat for something and handed her a well-thumbed pass. 'Show them this.' Before he turned away he said softly, 'I only do this because you folk do good.' He looked her up and down in her commonplace disguise. 'You Cistercians,' he added, to make it plain, 'as I know you to be.' He crossed himself.

Rivera was to meet her outside the tower closest to the river where the aldermen made their visits. Deciding to try to seek out the prisoner after they had done their task with regard to the mayor she set off towards it under a sinister cloud of ravens that fed on the severed heads of the condemned.

'Moved him?' Rivera's face turned cold.

'Didn't you know?' She searched his face for the truth.

He was shaking his head.

'Why would they do that, Rivera?'

'There's only one reason. But I told them they'd get nothing more from him. There was nothing more to give.'

He gripped her fiercely by the shoulder in the shadow of the tower. 'He was Swynford's prisoner, acting for Bolingbroke. I told Swynford he had nothing for us.'

'Is he . . . did they rack him?'

Rivera turned away. 'We can't stay here all night. Let's do what we have to do.' He turned back. 'Or would you rather keep out of it?'

'I'll come with you.'

He looked surprised but simply turned on his heel and went in through a small unguarded door that led into a corridor. Hildegard followed. By the time she reached the end, the one guard, who had apparently been half asleep when Rivera burst in, was groaning with a bruised jaw while his arms were being trussed. Rivera did a professional search for all the keys, found them with no difficulty, then locked the man inside his own cell.

'Come on.' He led the way to a set of narrow stairs that spiralled up round the inner wall of the tower. On the first level the stone gave way to wood and they trod more cautiously over the boards until they reached a stop at a locked door. Rivera tried various keys until he found one to fit. Before shouldering it open, he whispered, 'We don't know who or what's on the other side. If necessary I'll give you time to get back down below. Don't argue.'

He inched the door open without a sound. A bright glow of light issued from the chamber beyond. It was brilliant, like sunlight, unearthly after the darkness of the stairs.

Rivera stepped through the door onto a gangway that ran round the inside of the tower. Hildegard followed then stopped with a gasp. There was no chamber beyond. Instead there was a yawning pit.

They were staring down several floors to ground level where a massive furnace belched out tongues of flame and a dozen men stripped to the waist were feeding it with fuel, wielding bellows and pouring molten metal down a gully into a series of moulds. The heat, even from the height of the gangway where they stood, was intense. It was like a scene from hell: the heat, the flames, the clanging of metal, the raucous shouts in some foreign tongue from the sweating labourers.

The closer she looked, the more she noticed. A dozen men were dousing the hot metal with cold water from a massive barrel. Steam rose up, hissing and spitting. Others broke metal pipes from the moulds and stacked them in orderly rows, others wrapped sacking round the finished objects in a further part of the arena.

Rivera turned to her. 'Not *who* but *what*! He's making weapons.'

'What are they?' she whispered.

'Firing machines of some sort.' He peered over the edge again. 'They must be what the French used when they attacked Southampton decades ago. "Ribauldequins" they called them. I thought they'd given up on the idea. It didn't work.'

'I heard some mercenaries talk about this sort of thing when I was travelling in Italy.'

He gave her a sharp glance.

'They thought the problems could be surmounted. It was to do with the explosive they have to use. Sulphur, saltpetre . . .' she remembered the mercenary, Jack Black '. . . and the charcoal to ignite it. Once they get the proportions right they can project a bolt further than a longbow. Or so they expect.'

'There's also the problem of how to hit a target with any accuracy. The French failed to solve it.'

'Do you think these men have found a way round it?'

He gazed down at the arena below. 'If they have done, they'll be invincible.'

She drew in a breath.

In her interest in the scene she had temporarily forgotten that Bolingbroke would delight in having discovered the secret of the Tower. Now, even if he didn't know already, he soon would because Rivera would inform him of the fact.

'I think,' Rivera broke into her thoughts, 'those iron workers down there must be Bohemians. I know they've been working on the idea in Prague for some time. The Castilians are still working on it as well. So far nobody seems to have solved the problems. Eventually, I suppose, they will do so. Men are always trying to invent the ultimate weapon of destruction.'

317

She stepped back from the immense heat that was rising from the furnace. 'I can see how Mayor Brembre got involved – the Powder Makers' Guild must supply the gunpowder. They're one of the guilds he supports.'

'So much for the so-called fish wars. They're not fighting over fish at all.'

'I suppose now we've learnt the secret, we part,' she said in a clipped tone. 'You to inform your Master Swynford, lackey to the Earl of Derby, and—'

He gripped her by the shoulders to make her stop but before he could speak there was a commotion down below and when they peered over the rail of the gangway a group of men were entering the workshop through the doors immediately below.

Brembre himself, his blue hood pushed down round his shoulders, his cap deferentially held in one hand, was immediately recognisable. He was pointing out the various aspects of the works to someone as he came into view and a crowd of people were jostling in behind him. At the appearance of the visitors, the labourers stopped what they were doing and stood mopping their brows. The ironmaster ordered the metal gate on the furnace closed. Cressets were brought in to light the sudden darkness.

Visible in the glitter of the flames a tall, handsome, athletic-looking young man strode into the middle of the foundry and looked round. Even in the wavering light, when he pushed back his hood to reveal his red-gold hair he looked every inch a king.

Hildegard had never seen him before. She turned to Rivera. 'Is it . . . ?'

He nodded. 'Striking, isn't he? It's called "regality".' He watched through narrowed lids as the King began to explore every inch of the foundry, turning his attention with particular acuteness to an examination of the finished weapons.

Now that the roar of the furnace was shut down his voice reached clearly to the balcony. 'Petrus, are you sure they can't show me how they work?'

One of the courtiers brought the foundry master forward. He pulled off his sweatband in place of a cap and bowed. 'Best off in the open, My Lord King. Such is their firepower. And more space, should an accident occur.'

'When can you show me?'

Brembre stepped forward. 'In time, My Lord.'

'We have no time. When the French arrive our enemies will swarm in like rats. Nothing can stop them. My people have been told I'm going to abandon them. I must show them otherwise.'

The captain was heard to explain in a mixture of English and his own language the difficulty of controlling the aiming of the weapon and Hildegard caught the word 'ribauldequin'. She exchanged a glance with Rivera.

The King was able to discuss the matter in the ironmaster's own language and Brembre stood by, unable to follow more than a few words, while the King went over and hefted one of the firing tubes onto his shoulder and peered inside the hollow. The royal retinue, wearing plain cloaks with hoods concealing their faces as if in disguise, now began to fling them back in the heat and explore for themselves. Hildegard gripped the edge of the balcony when she saw Medford and Dean Slake in the group. The King, however, had turned to a young man by his side.

'What do you think, Robert?'

'That's de Vere, the new Marquess of Dublin whom Gloucester hates so much,' murmured Rivera.

De Vere put down the iron casing he was examining. 'I think this is the most significant advance in the art of war ever made. It will end the use of horsemen and sadly make a nonsense of our greatest strength, the longbow.'

'I agree. The black art of war has turned a shade darker. And it's our decision whether we take advantage of it or not.' The King patted Brembre on the shoulder. 'You kept the secret well, Nicholas. Even Mr Medford here did not know what was going on, did you, Medford?'

'I am remiss in my duty, Your Grace.'

'No, the mayor here was following my instructions to the letter. I still wear the Signet.' He lifted his hand and a ring caught the light and shone like fire.

He beckoned to the foundry master. 'I want this place cleared by morning. The weapons must be taken upriver to Windsor Castle. My men will be ready to receive you.'

There was no discussion about whether this would be possible in so short a time. The Bohemian did not question the order either but set to at once barking out instructions to his men who got onto the task with alacrity.

The King turned to leave saying, 'Medford, make sure these men are well rewarded.'

In moments the whole retinue had swept from sight.

Rivera's face was like a mask.

Below, in the guttering light, the job of putting out the furnace was started, while others gathered up the implements of their trade, and the metal tubes, the so-called ribauldequins, were rolled in sacks. A man was sent to organise transportation.

Then, as Hildegard and Rivera stood on the balcony, something happened that took them both by surprise. The door through which they had entered suddenly opened. There was a shout. Hildegard saw the gleam of weapons in the half-light. A man with a pike materialised and began to walk towards them.

Without speaking Rivera pushed Hildegard behind him. She saw the knife in his hand as he stepped forward to meet them.

She caught at his sleeve. 'No, Rivera, don't!'

The pikeman came on, backed up by half a dozen more. Grinning in triumph he beckoned to Rivera with one hand, 'Come on, Brother. Let's have you. You're not going nowhere now. Might as well save your skin and come quietly.'

'He's right,' said Hildegard. 'Don't fight them. There are too many.'

Rivera seemed to agree. He pitched his knife over the

321

edge of the balcony and spread his arms by his sides as if in surrender.

The pikeman went back to the door to allow them to follow him along the narrow walkway. When the man was bending his head to duck under the lintel Rivera suddenly grabbed him by the shoulders and pushed him headlong down the stairs, scattering like skittles the rest of the detail standing lower down. In the confusion Rivera managed to grab Hildegard by the arm and drag her with him. They managed to get halfway down the stairs, half falling, pitching headlong, leaping three steps at a time in a welter of arms and legs until a second group of pikemen materialised at the bottom.

They wasted no time in talking but simply stormed up, grabbed Rivera by both arms and hauled him bodily down to ground level. He fell to his knees and they kicked him in the ribs with their metal boots until Hildegard came tumbling down after him and then they made a grab for her too until an authoritative voice called out, 'I said let the woman go.'

It was Medford.

Rivera was dragged along the passage, blood pouring from his mouth.

'Rivera!' Hildegard gave a scream that echoed to the height of the tower. Before it died away he was in chains and being hauled roughly out of sight.

She turned on Medford in a fury. 'You promised him no harm!'

'I did no such thing.'

'You said—'

'Yes?'

He was right. He had made no promise but he had allowed her to believe he had.

'Affairs of state, Domina,' he said coolly. 'We must keep clear heads. The King's life is at stake. And we are still no nearer to discovering the nature of the plot against him, nor what form it might take. Rivera will tell us what he can if he knows what's good for him.'

Hildegard was allowed to leave. All she saw in her mind's eye as she trudged across the green towards the White Tower was Rivera's bloodied face and his dark eyes turned towards her in disbelief. They said as clearly as words: *You have betrayed me.*

As the bridge warden had told her, the prisoner she and Thomas had been visiting had been moved. When she eventually found him in a cell at the end of a dreary passage he was lying in a wooden chair, limbs lolling helplessly, his pupils dilated with pain.

'I shall rest here until I'm fit again,' he muttered hoarsely when he recognised his visitor. 'Remember your promise to my wife?'

Hildegard took his broken fingers in one hand as gently as she could. They were swollen to double their size, blue-black with bruises, his nails ripped out. 'You must let her know what has happened. She'll care for you.'

'I fear she will not when she sees I'm no longer any use to her.' He closed his eyes in defeat.

Hildegard did what she could to mend him. She applied salves and tinctures to his broken sinews and she paid his guard to follow her instructions on how to treat him after she left. Then she leant over and whispered, 'Did you have anything to tell Rivera?'

The prisoner lifted his head, sweat standing on his brow with the effort, and was about to speak when the guard called out, 'No more time, Domina! Quick! Out of here! The guards!'

The tramp of heavy boots could be heard in the passage as another watch came on duty.

As soon as Hildegard stepped outside onto the green she noticed something different. It was the uncanny silence. The wind had dropped. It was just as Rivera had told her. When the wind dropped, the last barrier to the invasion would fall.

Outtside the great walls of the Tower the city was in uproar. An atmosphere of panic had taken hold. A fever of fear and excitement was bringing people out into the streets. Groups of men were going from door to door selling cudgels that somebody had had the foresight to stockpile over the preceding weeks. The sound of swords being belatedly sharpened filled the air as every rusty blade was dragged out.

'Arm yourselves!' went the cry. 'The French are coming! Protect your families!'

The street traders were out in force, selling anything that might conceivably be needed for a siege: food, ale, weapons. It looked as if every household had come outside to stand in the open under the stars.

'Better out than being trapped in our houses like rats,' she heard somebody say as she passed. As well as fear and an air of panic, a feeling of relief – the day of doom was here – brought a mood of festival, as if force of numbers and their own strong will would be enough to outface King Charles and his terrifying army.

Out on the river small craft were being loaded with kindling, ready to be turned into fireships when the enemy fleet hove into view. The city walls glinted with cohorts of armed men. Every tower had its longbowmen. Fires burnt at the end of every street. There was a smell of naptha on the air.

Hildegard, her mind filled with dread about what would happen to Rivera now Medford had him in his clutches, allowed herself to be carried along by the crowd. Soon she found herself on Cheap and found they were making for the Guildhall.

After his meeting with the King, Brembre was back among his people. As she arrived in the square outside he was standing on the steps coming to the end of an oration. Part electioneering speech, part rallying cry, he was summoning every last man and able-bodied woman and child to the defence of the city.

'London will never surrender! Let them burn us, let them send their trebuchets to batter our walls, let their armed knights strut and stamp. We will never give in!' His words brought roars of support from the crowd. Many of them must have felt it was hopeless. Some were in tears. But their defiance was solid.

'On this night of nights we are tested,' Brembre declaimed. 'And, dear friends, we shall not fail. Victory! The King wills it!'

'Engelond! Engelond!' they roared back.

Some, who in previous years had caused the streets of the city to run with blood, now openly sang the forbidden rebel anthem of the Brotherhood of the White Hart. Defiant, fated, their idealism brought tears to Hildegard's eyes and she learnt again that there was nothing more certain to break the heart than a lost cause.

The mob, however, forgetting the past, were ebullient, ready to cheer to the skies anybody who appeared on the steps to shout defiance at the approaching enemy. Aldermen, maybe courting votes, added their own voices to Brembre's. London would not fall. They vowed it to God and all the saints. They vowed it especially to St George. And they vowed it on their own lives to the King. 'Dickon! Dickon!' they shouted. 'Save the King!' Nothing could defeat him. Nothing could defeat them. Prayers were offered. The *Te Deum* was sung. Penitents screamed and thrashed themselves. The doomsayers predicted only partial defeat. The alehouses filled with defiant drunks. Others knelt quietly before the shrines with lighted candles in their hands. The churches threw open their doors to allow the blessing of incense into the streets.

Hildegard returned eventually through these scenes of

resistance to the stoical calm of York Place. Fortunately she found that her things, few as they were, had already been sent along and a chamber made ready for her. It was past midnight. Here the gates were barred, the guards on full alert, and she had only been allowed to enter the deserted precinct by the night gate after she had been thoroughly scrutinised by the porter on the other side.

She sat at the window, fully clothed and with her knife by her side, watching for the French ships and seeing in her mind's eye Rivera, chained, inside the Tower.

Part Three

*H*e was allowed out to take some air as soon as it was daylight.

'If you want to escape, Brother, you're welcome to jump.'

Rivera gazed down from the top of the tower and gave a wry smile.

His guard was smirking. 'I understand you folk believe in miracles. As do many now!' He chuckled. 'Maybe an angel will swoop out of heaven and take you in her arms?'

Rivera, glance fixed on the sky, said, 'I fear there are no angels, not even in heaven.'

He could see the Thames clearly from up here and noticed that the tide was on the turn. It was suspended in perfect equilibrium like a spinning coin, impossible to predict its new direction.

Effluent from the night-soil boats swirled behind the markers until, it seemed, the coin fell, the tide began to pour more strongly in one direction, and the human detritus was coaxed with its scavenging rats downriver towards the sea.

Chapter One

When she woke up she was still sitting, albeit more stiffly, in front of the eye slit. What had roused her was the wind whining between the towers of the palace, howling over the slant roofs, snicketting inside her room through the window slit and making her cloak lift and shiver on the floor where she had dropped it the previous night. She could see the archbishop's banner on the tower opposite. It was taut on its pole as the wind raked through it.

Out on the sliver of Thames visible between the buildings there was no sign of a war fleet.

Hastily throwing on her cloak she ran downstairs into the yard.

'Did they come?' she demanded from a passing servant.

His face was alight. 'Did they heck! Turned back, didn't they, the lily-livered losels! Blaming it on the wind again. Have they no oars?' He raised a fist. 'Engelond!' and ran off, chortling with glee.

Relief flooded through her. They had turned back? It was impossible. Why would they do that? She would go to the Tower and try to get in to speak to Rivera.

After that, to Medford.

The streets were unsafe, the porter warned when he saw her leave. Ignoring his advice, she fought her way through a jostling crowd to reach the landing stage and managed to hire a wherry as far as the Tower.

With nothing to lose or to gain they were able to talk openly now and with a naturalness that in better times would have led to greater closeness. It could lead nowhere, however, and for that reason they held nothing back. Rivera was direct. With his familiar slanted smile that seemed to imply so much he asked, 'So you're interested in Sir Ralph Standish?'

'Who told you that?'

'My neighbour, Jack Kelt.'

'How on earth would he know?'

'Gets everywhere, Jack. We play chess. He talks. I talk. Then he makes a move and takes my queen. He was allowed to come and see me this morning.'

She was surprised by that. 'However he got his information, he's right. It's far from your territory, though. Standish's death was in Scarborough Castle. It strikes us as ambiguous. We're looking into it.'

'Why so?'

'I'm surprised you don't already know, as you seem to know so much else.'

'Rumours about poison, then?'

She nodded. 'We even have a suspect. But the evidence is only circumstantial and there's no real motive, given the man's allegiance to the same master as Standish and yourself, of course. It's not our real concern. The coroner was satisfied. It's only rumour from the household at Scarborough that prompts our interest, and the fact that before we left Bishopthorpe Palace one of the archbishop's kitcheners died. It was only when we were on the road that we discovered that he'd been murdered and that he'd had a connection with Standish.'

'Two deaths. And the link?'

'Who knows? But there was almost a third death.' She told him about the attack on John Willerby at St Alban's.

'A link there too?'

'We can't prove anything.'

'So we're talking here about the activities of Thomas Swynford?' Rivera looked thoughtful but said nothing more.

Hildegard turned the conversation to other things. 'Your informant was wrong about the French invasion.'

'The fleet did set out. He was right about that. They were halfway across the Channel when something stopped them and they turned back.'

She risked the question that Rivera could have no interest in avoiding now and asked, 'Did you tell Swynford something was going on in the Tower?'

'He knew it was. That's why he wanted me there.'

'Did you have any idea they were making weapons?'

335

He shook his head. 'Not until that moment when we stepped through onto the walkway and looked down.'

'I wonder if Swynford suspected what was going on?'

'He mentioned nothing of it to me. He thought they had a French go-between in there. I doubt whether he'd have been able to keep a secret about weapons to himself.'

'Maybe he heard something in the last few days? When did you last report to him?'

He ignored the latter question. 'I doubt he could have known what was going on,' he repeated. 'Brembre even managed to keep the secret from Medford.'

She smiled somewhat ironically. 'Medford certainly thinks he knows everything. There was a grim pleasure in seeing him wrong-footed by the King. But I wonder . . .' She bit her lip. 'I wonder who else knew?'

When he made no reply she said, 'If word got back to any of the King's enemies about a secret weapon you can be sure they would use the knowledge to their advantage. They might even use it to do some sort of deal with the French. "We'll give you the secret if you take care of Richard." Something along those lines?'

'That would be high treason.'

'Do you imagine Gloucester or Bolingbroke care about that? They think they're above the law.' She looked steadily into his eyes. 'Outside the circle of the King, who else could have known? Can you find out?'

He laughed. 'In here? What sort of visitors do you imagine I have?'

* * *

336

Before she left, Rivera came right up to the window of his cramped cell. It was unlike the comfortable quarters of the nobleman he had interrogated: no fire, no chair, no bed, no table, just an overflowing bucket in the corner and enough room to take two paces before turning. But at least, so far, he had suffered no physical torture.

He brought his face close to the bars. 'You betrayed me.'

The stale smell that wafted from within could not prevent her from moving closer. While the guard was looking away she whispered, 'I did not intend that, Rivera.'

His eyes were bleakly compelling so that she was drawn to press her lips to his through the bars.

She was handing in her pass at the lodge when a servant caught up with her. Taking her at face value he addressed her as he would any townswoman. 'Mistress, a missive from prisoner Rivera.' He pushed a leather pouch into her hand. 'Money for his housekeeper so she can eat. And would you also fetch him clean garments from his lodgings.' He added, 'It's allowed for you to take it. We had it checked.'

The two men were sitting in the window casement when she was ushered in. They were playing chess. It looked as if Slake was losing.

'Domina.' Medford came forward, bowing, smooth as

ever. 'I understand you've just come from the Tower and have something to tell us?'

She had sent a note ahead of her arrival to make sure he would see her.

'I believe you should free Rivera.'

'Hah! I've no doubt you have personal reasons but do you believe we've got anything from him yet? He's as close as an oyster.'

'What you want from him is not what he yet knows. My view is this. The French turned back for a reason. It must have been a good one. The change in the weather is a poor excuse.'

Medford listened carefully but he still shook his head.

'Domina, we are ahead of you. The reason they turned back is from fear, because their spies discovered we possessed the secret of the ribauldequins. King Richard knew this.'

'But,' she cut in, 'haven't they known about them for some time? Haven't they had ships specially built to take them back when they capture them, as they hoped? What if they realised they could not get their hands on them, wouldn't that deter them? It would have been a wasted effort if they had no hope of getting hold of them. Should our question be: who told them they'd been moved?'

'You imagine someone warned them, last night after the King gave the order?' He looked askance. 'Someone in the King's party?'

'Not necessarily.'

338

'Not the Bohemians. They're utterly loyal to Queen Anne. You mean somebody in Mayor Brembre's circle?'

'It seems so.'

Having been caught out once, Medford evidently decided he ought to listen. 'Do you have a name?'

'I believe if you free Rivera he'll be able to find a name for you.'

'Have you so beguiled him he's chosen to come over to our side?'

She ignored that. 'Set him free. It's the only thing to do. There are contacts who trust him. They can know nothing of any changed allegiance, if it exists. If he can find out who warned the French that the weapons had been moved it might lead you to the faction in the city who are plotting against the King. It might be one of Brembre's aldermen, someone he trusts. So far the city has supported King Richard. Maybe now there's a group gaining the ascendancy who intend to place their resources with the King's enemies. Find the traitor. It will be proof of—'

'Treason.' Medford concluded as Rivera had done. For once his composure seemed to have been disturbed. 'What do you think, Dean? Shall we allow the domina to loose her bloodhound?'

Slake got up and strolled over with a chess piece in his hand. He was smiling and in his crumpled velvet looked as benign as a well-fed cat. 'That's a very good idea, Domina. You believe your man will lead us to someone we would very much like to meet? Good.' He grinned in a friendly fashion at Medford. 'When the traitor tells us who his master is, all we have to do is get a nice sharp axe and chop off his head. Chop! Chop! Yes, let's do that.'

Roger de Hutton. Unmistakably. Surrounded by his men, he was emerging from the Great Hall and came to a halt in Palace Yard. It was after midday and the first session had just ended. Hildegard could hear his voice from where she was crossing the yard some distance away and when she approached she could almost see his red beard bristling with rage.

His rant was directed at the behaviour of the dukes, especially Gloucester. His fellow barons also came in for a tongue-lashing. When Hildegard greeted him he swivelled to acknowledge her, then, beckoning her closer, launched back in.

'The fools can't grasp it, Hildegard! Gloucester's trying to bring the chancellor down so he can get at the King. Can they see it? No they can't! It's nothing to do with rents and profits. The Ghent fiasco. All that. They must be blind not to see it – or are they just plain stupid?'

'Both, I would imagine,' agreed Hildegard to placate him. 'What's happened?'

'Their arguments are ground so thin they're near transparent!' he continued in astonished anger. 'Don't the rest of those sot wits understand they're a step away from deposing the King? What's bloody wrong with the stupid oafs?'

Hildegard stopped him long enough to ask again what had happened.

'They've just impeached de la Pole! Can you believe it? The King's chancellor, for God's sake, thrown into prison like a common criminal!'

When he calmed down enough to tell her more she heard that although de la Pole's nimble brain and knowledge of his own innocence had given him hope that he would prevail over his enemies, the chamber was deliberately packed with the King's opponents and he had no chance when it came to a vote. The indictment was couched in such apologetic terms, however, even the law lords knew they were on thin ice.

'While the city of London celebrates survival, Gloucester and his cronies are destroying England! They've got rid of the treasurer as well, Fordham, the Bishop of Durham, poor sod.' Roger seemed torn between helpless rage and astonishment that they could get away with it. 'Then if that's not enough,' he continued, 'Gloucester's had the audacity to demand that all the King's household should be dismissed and reappointed by the King's own council – of which he's now the head! Can you believe it? You can imagine what Dickon said to that.'

'What did he say?'

'After a few honest oaths he said, "I shall not allow the lowest scullion in my household to be dismissed at the behest of the council." Then he walked out. He's in the royal apartment at present with de Vere and Burley and a few others, deciding what to do.'

Roger gripped her convulsively by the hand. 'At least the bloody French changed their minds, hey? I wonder how that came about?'

'I'm told it was because the weather turned against them.'

'Weather be damned. They can sail their own ships, can't they? They're bloody big enough!' He gave her a long sceptical look. 'The word is they were given a promise somebody couldn't keep, then took fright at the reception they might be in for.'

'Promise?'

'King John of the French? That's what I'm hearing. Remember what happened to the poor devil? Captured by us and then stuck in the Tower of London for years on end because his dukes wouldn't pay his ransom? It gave Burgundy and his cronies free rein to run the country to their own advantage. I bet Gloucester wouldn't turn his nose up at an opportunity like that.' He called to his guards. 'Attend me! We leave!'

'Wait, Roger—'

'Can't. Got another blasted meeting.'

Ulf had been hanging around on the edge of the group listening to all this, and now he stopped long enough to tell Hildegard that de la Pole had had his lands declared forfeit and his title stripped. 'Nobody's safe,' he warned as he turned to follow his lord. 'I hope Secretary Medford isn't asking you to do anything dangerous? He's as much at risk as all the King's party.'

They were just about to say goodbye when a herald appeared. The yard was full of people but everybody fell silent as he shouted, 'Make way for the King!'

The same tall, fair, handsome young man she had seen in the Tower the previous evening came striding down the path in the direction of the royal barge. The yard rapidly emptied as the crowd followed. Ulf and Hildegard joined them.

The deck master had started shouting for the lines to be thrown off as soon as he saw the King approaching and by the time Richard stepped on board with a small entourage the barge was already on the move, ripped into motion by the power of the tide. The oarsmen fell into place. Moments later the long sweeps were sending the barge swiftly downriver towards the palace at Eltham.

Rivera's lodgings were outside the city walls on the Westminster side, not far from Roger de Hutton's town house.

A woman with a worried-looking face answered her knock. 'News of the master?' she asked before Hildegard could open her mouth.

'Let me in.'

She handed over Rivera's pouch with the coins in it as soon as she stepped inside. 'I've come to fetch clean clothes.'

'So it's true? He's in the Tower? Jack Kelt said so.'

'May I go up?'

She was nearly at the top of the stairs when the housekeeper called, 'So you know where to go?'

Hildegard turned. Their eyes met and, with the look, understanding flashed between them.

His melancholy chamber. It was more empty than seemed possible from the mere absence of one man. Everything was as they had left it. The mulberry-coloured robe hanging on the door. The couch with the rumpled wolfskin. The two indentations in the pillows where they had lain their heads.

She found a chest with his clean linen in it and put a few pieces into her bag, folding on top a white habit with a hood. There was the badge of his Order, red and gold, lying on a book on the table and she carefully pinned it to his shirt.

When all was done she went over to the small shrine above the prie-dieu. Matilda must have been the one to light the candle in front of the image. A face with a resigned spirituality gazed out on the world from within its border of gold leaf. The painter had managed to catch a look of compassion in the face that recalled the way Rivera sometimes looked.

When she went down again Matilda came through from the back. She opened the door for her but before Hildegard went out she said hurriedly, 'He's a good man. You need to know that. He always denied it. He hated what he had to do but he's good in his heart where it matters.'

Hildegard held out her hand. Matilda gripped it. Tears stood in her eyes. 'They won't rack him, will they?'

* * *

The city's night of panic and defiance had given way to relief, thanksgiving and eventually debauchery. The air was filled with screams and shouts and the sound of things being broken. Before she set out even to Westminster to see Medford, Hildegard had heard the warnings to stay within the enclave of York Place. 'The scenes out there are like Armageddon,' opined the porter.

But she had her own view of defiance. There was too much to do. And anyway, Westminster had been safe enough.

Now, after leaving Rivera's lodgings, which she had reached by asking the ferryman to drop her off at the narrow laup at the back of the house, she had to pass through crowds of exultant citizens spilling outside the walls into the fields and pouring in a noisy flow down Ludgate Hill to the Strand, where they would eventually fetch up outside Parliament. News of Gloucester's insulting demands that sent his royal nephew marching out of the Great Hall had spread. Richard had acted with the sort of defiance everybody understood.

It looked as if they were going to celebrate but, knowing how volatile they were, it was easy to detect an undercurrent of violence in their behaviour. Civic authority had no control outside, nor even, at present, inside the walls. In the interregnum before the new mayor was sworn in nobody seemed to be in control. All along the route any taverns with ale left in the bottom of their barrels after the previous night were full of people nursing hangovers and doggedly drinking the dregs as if their defiance against the enemy had found another purpose.

As she hurried along Hildegard gathered that the annual election to choose the mayor had taken place earlier that morning in a rabble of fist fights, abductions, threats and the buying and selling of favours, and that the votes to elect the new mayor had already been counted. At the loser's insistence they were being counted again.

When she eventually reached the Guildhall Brembre and his allies were standing around with expressions of dumb shock. She waited along with a massive crowd until the result was ratified, when a quietly thoughtful man called Exton took his place.

St Mary Graces. It looked as well fortified as the Tower.

'Any news?' she asked as soon as the door closed and they were alone. Thomas, his wounded leg resting on a padded stool, shook his head. He dipped his fingers into the sweetmeats Hildegard had brought him. 'I have a feeling the abbot is avoiding me.'

'Why would he do that?'

'Because he has nothing to tell me about what he knows is uppermost in my mind – your fate at the hands of the Chapter.'

'Thomas, in this turbulent time my personal problems cannot be uppermost. I mean to say—'

'I'm not pretending I wasn't worried last night when we expected the French to come roaring in. We're on the front line here and would have had to deal with their wounded. It would have been a sore trial of our consciences. Even so, my thoughts are ever with you.'

Hildegard gazed at a patch of sky framed in a square of lattice. 'My prioress is always warning me to be less impatient. The patience required to wait for their verdict is sent as a lesson to me.'

'We all have to learn something—' he broke off. 'There is news. You got my note?'

'Yes. That's why I came over. I thought it was to do with the decision of the Chapter.'

'It's news from St Alban's. Prepare yourself.'

'What is it?'

'The falconer, John Willerby. He was found dead three days ago. The news has just come through.'

'But he seemed to be on the road to recovery when we left—'

'He didn't die from his wounds. He was poisoned. You remember that kindly monk who was attending him? He wrote to me in detail describing what happened. He was full of remorse that he had allowed it. He said the smell made them suspicious at once, that mousey smell of hemlock, and then before they could set their minds to the problem a man made a full confession to his priest. And then hanged himself.'

Hildegard took the seat Thomas offered. 'Go on.'

'The story is that he recognised Willerby from years ago when, so he said, Willerby had accidentally shot his daughter, a child of ten, when she was playing in the abbot's chase. We can imagine the man was doing a bit of poaching at the time and took the child along with him. Such would be his guilt at being the cause of his own child's death, when he saw the instrument of his guilt he decided on revenge.'

'I see.'

'I'm told Willerby was apprenticed to the St Alban's falconer in the old days. Not the same fellow we met but the previous one. The bereaved man couldn't believe his eyes when he sauntered in soon after we arrived. He blurted it out to Swynford who was in the mews at the time. Swynford told him there was only one thing he could do. If he was ever to call himself a man again he should get rid of him. I have this verbatim.' He showed her the document in his hand. 'Would you like me to read you what it says?'

She nodded.

'Swynford says, "I don't like that fella either. He's done me and my master a great harm. Let's put the rat out of his misery and I have a sure way of putting him down," and he comes out with some plot to make the new bird attack him so it looks like an accident. "Frighten the bastard," says he. All I have to do is go into the mews while their men are out and whack the fellow over the head and tie some carrion to him then get out. "Leave nature to do its course," says he, "Let God decide." Then this other fella come to me: "You heard what my master said – put the rat out of his misery. But keep it simple. You can do it with this if that first plan fails," and he shows

348

me some hemlock and says, "Do it with this for a safe job but only make sure I'm well down the road before you give it him."' Thomas frowned and lowered the pages. 'So Swynford was away on the road to London when the attack occurred and so was the man who suggested hemlock.' He indicated the pages of the confession. 'He's described here as Swynford's retainer—'

'His retainer being . . . ?'

'Jarrold of Kyme.'

He gave a grim smile. 'When Willerby did not perish from his wounds, this poor grieving fellow,' he waved the sheets of vellum, 'took the opportunity to get inside the infirmary and gave him a lethal dose of the hemlock Jarrold had supplied. End of story.'

Not quite the end, thought Hildegard. She said, 'We always guessed Jarrold was more than Swynford's tenant. Alexander Neville will not be pleased to find a member of his household has allegiance to anyone else, especially the vassal of one of the King's enemies.'

After she left Thomas she went to the Tower and tried to get in to hand Rivera his things but the custodian shook his head. 'No visitors, mistress.'

She went cold. 'What are they doing to him?'

He shook his head again. 'If that's stuff for him you can hand it to me. I'll make sure he gets it.'

Aware of the unlikelihood of breaking through the security that surrounded the Tower, she was forced to turn back.

* * *

There were no ferries to be had at the Tower steps. By now swarms of people were flocking round the landing stage, trying to get home, but with so many out on the streets and the increasing danger of violence after the election result, the pressure to get away had forced an unusual number of ordinary citizens to try to escape by water. All the boats were full and many ferrymen were refusing to come back into town because of the violence. There were no horses for hire either. When she approached a nearby ostler he told her, 'All gone, mistress. Stay in your house and barricade the door. It's going to get worse.'

'I can't stay in my house. I'm far from it,' she told him, turning away.

She would have to walk. She pulled up her hood, checked that her knife was in reach, and set off.

The Tower, with its secret torture chambers, now lay behind her. It dominated the tenements around it, a white and deathly place against the darkening sky. She felt full of foreboding. The custodian had not confirmed that he was being tortured. In that, she told herself, was comfort. Medford had said he would get him released but then Medford said many things, or at least, allowed them to seem to be said.

It took an age to negotiate the teeming streets. Doing her best to avoid the unlit alleys and the most raucous mobs out looking for trouble, by the time she left the city gates on Ludgate Hill and had crossed the Fleet by its wooden bridge it was late afternoon and already getting dark. The prospect of night enticed rougher elements from their lairs, professional pickpockets and cut-throats, revellers drunk on ale, all were emerging from the backstreets, shouting obscenities as they reeled along looking for entertainment. There were women among them, young and old, children even, mindlessly hurling stones into the crowd.

She saw for the first time what it must have been like here in London during the Great Revolt, the hurling time, when the ideals of the leaders were brought into disrepute, compromised by the violence of the undisciplined mobs.

The air was thick with smoke from their naptha flares and in the light of the flames hundreds of faces passed before Hildegard's gaze, looming out of the shadows with a lurid prominence – faces pockmarked, distorted by open sores, mouths lolling open to reveal blackened teeth, leering and graceless. But not their fault, she reminded herself; forced to live like brutes, they behave like brutes, their lives as hopeless and fractured by pain and poverty enough to send them mad.

The best of them had been exterminated in the great bloodletting that followed the Revolt. Now it had all come down to an undirected frenzy of hatred. Crazy on strong drink, they spilt over the paths, gesticulating and threatening anyone who fell foul of them. One of these gangs objected to Hildegard's presence as she tried to walk past and they shouted some insult, but she ignored them and hurried on. One of the men, however, followed her.

'You, bitch, are you French?' He stabbed his finger into her shoulder.

She lifted her head long enough to assure him she was as English as he was, adding, before she could stop herself, 'Sad be the day.'

'Here!' He gave her a push. 'What did you say?'

Wishing she had bitten off her tongue, she tried to walk on but he stepped in front of her.

'Bloody bitch!'

A group of four or five horsemen were riding up the street towards the city. They were about to pass as the man tried to pull at her headscarf and their leader brought his small cavalcade to a halt with a raised hand. 'Hold it! Who's this?' he called out. Looking down at Hildegard he said, 'I know you, woman. You're that whore nun of Alexander Neville's!'

Hildegard felt like sinking into the ground. His words had drawn in the rest of the drunk's cronies. Now, high on a horse and with his massive war sword and glittering breastplate, the banner of the Earl of Derby cracking in the wind beside him, he momentarily managed to transcend his usual insignificant demeanour.

Before she could reply, her loutish attacker stepped up. 'She calls herself a nun?'

'She does indeed, master.' His tone was unctuous. 'We can imagine how rigorously she keeps her vows, eh?' Swynford looked down at her. 'Plying for trade in the stews, Domina?' He laughed and his own men followed suit as if he had cracked a particularly witty joke.

'Keep a civil tongue in your head, Swynford,' she replied.

'Or what?' He gazed down with contempt into her face.

The lout had stepped up behind her and now, encouraged by Swynford's manner, put an arm round her waist. 'Come on, bitch, show us what they teach you in that nunnery of yours.' He tried to drag her into his foul-smelling embrace but she slipped her knife from her sleeve and held it in front of her.

'Try it!' she warned.

He stepped back with an oath. 'You, a nun? You're no nun, you're a bloody witch.' He glanced back for support from his accomplices who were now beginning to goad him on. 'We know what they do with witches in Paris!' he shouted for their benefit. When they staggered closer, asking what the fun was, he shouted to them, 'What do they do? They burn the bitches!'

One by one they took up the cry. 'Burn! Burn! Burn the witch!'

Hildegard stood her ground with the knife still in her hand but Swynford drove his horse right up against her so she was trapped between the two groups. He snarled, 'Neville's not much use to you now, is he?'

She tried to duck under his horse's head to make her escape but he drove the animal forward again and she stumbled back to avoid being trampled and bumped into the drunk, giving him the opportunity to grab hold of her round the waist.

'Come on, lads!' he bellowed. 'Let's have a bit of fun. Let's burn the witch!'

They began to drag her back the way she had come, up Ludgate Hill towards the city. Swynford, roaring with laughter, shouted encouragement. His men, a gang of ill-kempt ruffians, their livery typically obscured, started up an excited chant and began to follow. It was plain they had been riding out looking for trouble and now they had found it. Swynford took out his sword and held it aloft.

'A witch! A witch!' he roared. 'Let's make this city clean! Out with witches!'

His yells, augmented by those of his henchmen, brought people running. Soon there was an excited crowd. Some took up the chant, not caring what it was about so long as they could join it; others stood dumbly, staring with a kind of horror at the witch who had been caught and was now being dragged along the street towards her just desserts.

The gates of the city lay in the distance but it was a place where the King's writ did not run. And far behind, receding, lay the fields, gardens and orchards of the great houses along the Strand and, even more distant, Westminster, the seat of government where the rule of law was supposed to hold sway, and close by, on both sides of the lane, were the shuttered houses of the friars, the courts of the lawyers, the scribes and clerks, and no help anywhere.

A cart was found and was being dragged into the arena

that had formed round her. She looked at it in horror. She knew that if she allowed them to force her into it she would be as good as dead. They may not be able to build a fire before help arrived, as it must, but they could tie a rope around her neck, sling one end over the nearest branch then whip the horses on.

This is the end of my life, she thought in cold fury. Among a rabble of drunks urged on by a traitor to the King. She turned on her captors. 'You'll regret this to the end of your days and beyond! Take your hands off me. At least permit me to walk to my fate!'

The idea of prolonging her ordeal appealed to Swynford and he encouraged them to make her walk step by step up the hill, and as they goaded her with jibes of witchcraft and naked orgies at the full of the moon and other obscenities their thwarted lusts could summon, the crowd grew so dense they had to use cudgels to carve a path for her. 'Here comes the Queen!' went the shout. 'Behold the bitch, the Queen of Hell! Make way!'

People pinched her and snatched at her clothing, and tried to tear it. They crossed themselves, gazed in horror at what they saw as the embodiment of their worst fears. They spat and pulled her hair, the headscarf long since lost along with her knife. And she thought in despair: This must be my punishment for loving Rivera.

They were nearing the summit now, in a tumult of noise, when she felt someone hanging onto her sleeve, and glancing down, with the intention of shaking herself free, she saw that it was the very small man, Jack Kelt. He had wriggled his way to the front of the mob and was clinging onto her arm, and such was the pace that was being forced, he was having to run to keep up as Swynford's henchmen quickened their speed in their eagerness to reach the top of the hill where the old gods were worshipped at the ancient place of sacrifice dedicated to the pagan king, Lud.

Now her captors were further pleased to discover that she was to be accompanied by a creature spawned by the Devil, as they saw it, and it confirmed their view that she was a witch, unnatural, a monster, and deserved to die.

The chanting increased to a frenzy.

Kelt was unbothered. The kicks and shoves now bestowed on him as well as on Hildegard were received as if to lighten her punishment. 'Do not despair,' he shouted above the tumult. The separate elements of the mob had meanwhile turned into a single entity, a devouring beast, a dragon with its head approaching the top of the long slope, its body bulging as more and more people flocked to join it, its tail tapering back down to the Fleet.

Then Kelt shouted, 'Look!'

She followed his pointing finger.

Where the crowd opened out, there, striding down the hill, came a figure in white.

Without altering his pace he broke through the vanguard like a spear, scattering folk right and left, driving straight towards her through the thickest part of the crowd until he was brushing aside Swynford's men-at-arms, shouting, 'Back! Get back, you bloody animals. I claim this hostage!'

He grabbed the reins of Swynford's horse and dragged him to a halt. Swynford still held his sword and was about to bring it lashing down when he realised it was Rivera who gripped the reins. 'What the hell do you want, Brother?'

'Listen to me!' Those nearest fell silent. 'I claim your hostage,' he repeated in a strong voice that carried deep into the crowd.

The men-at-arms came to a confused halt. People began to quieten down to hear what was going on and their silence rippled all the way back to the most distant fringes of the onlookers until there was scarcely a sound. 'What's happening now?' somebody asked.

Hildegard stood trembling with astonishment. Jack Kelt held her sleeve.

'You owe me a debt, Sir Thomas,' said Rivera in a voice loud enough for everyone to hear. 'I've done you good service. Now I demand payment.'

'Service?' Swynford's glance darted from side to side and he looked as if he was about to deny it but then he lowered his voice. 'I've paid you—'

'There is still one account outstanding. If you want blood in payment, take mine. I demand the release of this woman in exchange for myself. My saint commands and expects it.'

'Rivera, no!' Hildegard pushed forward.

He ignored her.

To Swynford he said, 'I have your secrets. Release her or take the consequences.'

Swynford was busy working it out. His secrets? The look of fear on his face was abruptly replaced by cunning. 'If that's your wish. You? Instead of her?'

'A heretic,' one of his men helpfully suggested. 'May as well burn one as another, Captain.'

Swynford glanced nervously at the crowd. Their mood was on a knife-edge. Outrage that their bloodlust was to find no outlet was simmering dangerously beneath the surface and Swynford was quick to read it. He made the decision to save his own skin, shouting, 'You heard the heretic! His life for hers! What shall it be? Yea or nay?'

'Death to the heretic!'

Swynford smiled. 'So let it be!'

Raising his sword he spurred his horse forward, making sure his men had grasped what was happening. 'Drag the heretic to the block!'

'Death to heretics!' came the response.

They held a more illustrious scapegoat now. Swynford began to lead the procession to its destination.

The crowd had started braying for a victim again and when news that the witch had been bartered for a heretic friar reached the outer fringes they howled with the desire to see his blood. No mere witch for them. Now they had a bigger prize. And the Pope had ordered heretics to be burnt and the King had taken no notice, but now they could put the matter right. Superstitious fervour drew in the doubters. Their own sins could be wiped clean by doing the Pope's will. If he willed it, they would fulfil it and make sure of their place in paradise.

Hildegard stumbled, picked herself up, ran alongside Swynford on his horse, grasped the saddle. Her voice was harsh with fear. 'You have no right of life and death, Swynford. You'll hang if you do this. The law will punish you!'

'There is no law.'

'Then you'll burn in hell! He's innocent. You know he's no heretic.'

He sneered down at her. 'The Londoners, it seems, think otherwise.'

Hildegard turned to the people nearest. 'Stop him, someone!' But their bloodlust was not to be thwarted. There were jeers, more vicious jostling. Swynford rode on.

It was then Rivera turned back and reached out through the crowd for her, pulling her to his side. He put his arms round her and for a moment they seemed to stand in a vortex of silence with themselves at its centre. Nothing could touch them.

'Rivera, he'll take you at your word!'

'Yes.'

'You are wronged,' she whispered passionately.

'I am doomed,' he replied.

The crowd churned on all sides but he seemed oblivious to them. 'Medford released me. The name you want is Harry Summers. Follow the trail. It leads to the Queen.'

Oblivious to the jeers, he held her tightly in his arms. 'Forget me, Hildegard. Don't grieve. Death is the purpose of our existence.'

With one hand he quickly unpinned the red and gold emblem of St Serapion from his cloak and folded her fingers round it. He rested his lips briefly on her mouth. The mob forced itself between them. He looked back over their heads as if he wanted to say more but they were pulling him away up the hill.

Their hatred was redirected to a better target, to an alien friar, a man who could read books, who spoke languages, who probably practised the black arts and wove spells to destroy his neighbours. He was everything they were not.

Rigid with dread, Hildegard tried to find a way along the darkening street to summon help.

'Where are they taking him?' she shouted to someone being carried along in the surge beside her.

'To Ludgate block.'

'Axe the bastard, whoever he is!' a voice shrieked.

'He's a French spy, like as not,' another one claimed with malevolent satisfaction.

'No!' Hildegard's voice was lost in the tumult.

The sun appeared in a lurid slant of light between the narrow tenements, painting everything the colour of blood. Armed gangs with lighted torches were still forcing a path up the hill but the procession had come to a halt there, people pressing so thickly to see what would happen next they formed a wall, blocking the street and allowing no one past. Jack Kelt had vanished long ago. Hildegard fought and shoved to get as close to the front as she could. She could just make out the figure of Rivera across a sea of onlookers. His white garments blazed against the deepening shadows as the sun sank behind the rooftops.

The torch-bearers were gathering round the place where he had been dragged by the guards and she thought some of them were trying to build a fire but then she saw Swynford, still astride his horse, gesture to one of his followers. A burly man built like a blacksmith stepped out from among the rest of them and drew a war sword.

Rivera seemed not to be aware of anyone. He was staring out across the heads of the crowd towards the river. He was standing quite still.

While the onlookers chanted and jeered and told them to get on with it, Swynford was giving instructions, nervously looking up and down the street. A lawyer's clerk was found from somewhere, a priest was pushed to the front of the crowd. Rivera seemed oblivious to everything and went on standing without moving. Then she realised he was praying.

His expression transcended the hellish scenes around him. She remembered the icon in his chamber and realised she was seeing the same look of resigned compassion.

Swynford reached down from his horse and tapped him

on the shoulder but even then it took a moment before Rivera made a move.

'God's will be done!' somebody shouted from the crowd.

Rivera turned towards the sound. The words floated clearly in the deathly quiet that descended. 'I am absolved. May you be absolved also.'

Hildegard began to fight her way towards him, but no one would let her through and the guards held her back with their pikes and she had to watch as he turned to the swordsman. In a nightmare she heard him ask, 'Is the blade sharp?'

'Sharp enough, magister.'

Swynford, detecting a note of doubt in his man's voice, snarled, 'Get on with it.'

Rivera raised his right hand. 'So be it.'

Hildegard watched in horror as he knelt and rested his head on the block. She saw him make a small movement with one hand to push aside his hair.

The swordsman lifted his massive blade. As one, the crowd drew in a breath of expectation. Hildegard reached out. Help must come.

Then the blade swept down in a brutal arc. The crowd groaned. There was the crack of splitting bone. The sword rose and fell again. And for a third time it made its descent.

The chaos of public spectacle was reduced to the most intimate moment of death.

The crush of onlookers at the front fell back, scattering those behind, and the crowd like a wave, without a mind, moving on instinct, drew in on itself, away from the horror. And then a roar broke out and cries of release rent the air.

Hildegard uttered one howl of grief and loss.

It was Ulf, holding her protectively in his arms, and they were somehow free of the passers-by and standing lower down the hill in the shelter of a building. He was murmuring, 'I'm sorry, I'm sorry, I didn't realise who he was.'

Chapter Two

The de Hutton house on the Strand. Night.

Hildegard felt as if she would never sleep again. How could she? When, around prime, the noises from the chamber below convinced her that the household was awake, she somehow prepared herself for whatever was to come. In her hand, she found Rivera's red and gold emblem, its shape indented into her palm. She pinned it underneath her shift and went down.

'I have to see Medford,' she announced when she came face-to-face with Roger de Hutton on the way into the hall. Ulf was beside him and stepped forward.

'I'll be ready shortly.' He turned to Roger, 'If I may be released for an hour, I'll escort her.'

'I've sent a message across to York Place to tell them you'll be staying here when you get back. You'll be safer.' Roger led her in to break the night fast.

She sat in the hall and stared at the bread and wine

put in front of her but did not touch it.

Ulf returned to tell her he was ready to leave when she was.

She lifted her head. 'What happened afterwards?'

'Some Dominicans came out of their priory and took him into one of the chantries along there. Swynford and his accomplices had disappeared by the time we arrived. The crowd handed over half a dozen of the ringleaders. We took them to the Fleet. They'll hang this morning. We came as soon as that little fellow, Kelt, alerted us.'

'Why did the rats not try to stop it?' demanded Roger.

Ulf took her hand. 'He was the one who saved you from drowning, wasn't he? The one who looked after you. I'm sorry.'

When she came down carrying her cloak, Edwin Westwode had arrived. The look of concern on his face showed that they had explained everything. Together they left for Westminster with Ulf and a couple of bodyguards.

Hildegard had no fear of being waylaid by mobs or cut-throats on the way there and would have gone without an escort. It didn't matter one way or the other now. Nothing mattered. She was seeing everything through a heavy gauze. It absorbed her grief. She felt nothing could get through it to touch her. She lived lightly behind it.

Medford. In black velvet as usual. A white linen shirt with elaborate cuffs. More than ever he looked like a tall child in its best clothes. Now, she knew, he was a child who pulled the wings off flies.

Dean Slake was by his side as usual.

Medford was expatiating, uninvited, on his reason for living.

'To protect my liege, His Grace the King, from the machinations of his enemies. To maintain his glory and splendour, to increase profit and establish peace in his realm. Richard is our anointed king, our one hope for victory against the French. Without him we are nothing. We exist solely to do his will.'

He turned to Hildegard.

'You have information for me?'

'The name you want is Harry Summers.'

Edwin made an exclamation of surprise. 'Harry? But I know him!'

Medford swivelled. 'Go on.'

'He was my predecessor at Bishopthorpe Palace. He was Archbishop Neville's private secretary.'

'Where is he now, do you know?'

'He's with the Earl of Northumberland. I haven't seen him for ages.'

'Northumberland's staying up near Clerkenwell,' broke in Ulf. 'Roger de Hutton was dining there a couple of nights ago.'

'What are we waiting for?' Dean Slake was at the door.

Medford gestured to the others to follow, calling, 'Horses, Slake! And armed guards!'

* * *

Northumberland had an imposing house and was famous for barring the Duke of Lancaster, Gaunt, from the gates of his castle during the time of the Great Revolt, when Lancaster had been booted out of Scotland and feared to return south until the troubles had died down. By that time news had already reached him that the mob had burnt his Savoy Palace to the ground. The north was safer.

On the ride over to Northumberland's, Slake mentioned this insult to Gaunt and his continuing opposition to Gloucester, but Ulf was of the opinion that he was a slippery customer and said he wouldn't trust him as far as he could throw him – and given his girth that wouldn't be far.

Hildegard listened but felt no inclination to add anything. The streets seemed abnormally quiet now. The new mayor, Exton, although he had not yet received his chain of office, had sworn in dozens of new constables and given them broad powers to clear the streets. Curfew was enforced once more. The void that had been filled by men like Swynford with their own militia was now filled by the official forces of law and order. Even Gloucester, seen parading around with his army, the fox's brush swinging from his lance, was now asked to stay outside the walls.

When they arrived at Northumberland's stronghold Medford pushed in straight past the guards on duty with a peremptory 'King's business!' Slake followed. It was up to Ulf to explain that it was nothing to look affronted about but rather a matter for pride to be visited by the King's secretary, abrupt of manner though he was.

Hildegard followed the men up to the solar.

The Earl was truculent and as irascible as Roger de Hutton but ten times more powerful, owning vast tracts of land as one of the marcher lords in the border country between Scotland and England. He was known to have got rich on running arms between the two old enemies.

Slake, smiling despite the frosty reception, introduced them. 'Mr Medford, the King's secretary. And I'm Will Slake, Dean of the Signet Office.'

'What about it?' asked Northumberland in his strong northern accent.

'We understand you retain a clerk called Harry Summers?'

'What if I do?'

Smiling peacefully Slake said, 'Mr Medford and I would like to speak to him.'

Without taking his glance off Slake, Northumberland cuffed a page on the head. 'Fetch him.'

While they waited Northumberland looked his visitors over and seemed to find nothing to like. He grudgingly acknowledged Ulf but had nothing to say to Hildegard.

It was surprising that he was so vastly popular with the Londoners but it was entirely because of his insult to Gaunt and he rode his popularity as if by innate right.

A young man came in, hair somewhat tousled, and, still tying the laces of his shirt, bowed elaborately to his lord.

Northumberland merely growled, 'Playing skittles again, you bloody wastrel?'

When Summers looked round at the visitors his glance alighted on Edwin and his face lit up. 'Westwode, you old devil. What are you doing here? How are you, fella?' He strode forward and clapped Edwin on the back.

Edwin shot a glance at Medford but was clearly pleased to see Summers. 'Going well, Harry?'

'Still keeping the old quill sharpened.'

Medford looked irritated. 'We have some questions for you, Summers.' He turned to the Earl. 'Is there a privy chamber where we might conduct this business?'

Northumberland nodded towards an inner door and they all trooped inside leaving the Earl glaring after them.

'Well,' asked Summers with a bright smile, 'what brings you here? I don't understand. How can I help?'

Slake was at his most affable. He got into conversation about skittles and when Summers was off his guard he slipped in a question about allegiance, but Harry Summers, his face lacking any trace of guile, affirmed outright his support for the King.

'We're all King's men in the north, everywhere but Pontefract, Pickering, Knaresborough and Scarborough.' He listed them on his fingers. 'Lancaster's got them in his iron fist. You should hear the Earl fuming. "He's placed his bloody castles so he's got me cut off from the south of my own country. Is he trying to throw me into the arms of the Scots?"' A look of alarm crossed his face. 'I don't mean to imply . . . not that he would—'

'You mention these Lancastrian strongholds,' Slake cut

369

in with a disarming smile. 'Did you and the archbishop visit many of them?'

With a puzzled look at Edwin, whose master the archbishop now was, he shook his head. 'Why would we? We'd enough to do with church business. Oh, except of course for Pickering Castle. His Grace loves to hunt, and of course we sometimes ended up at Scarborough after a day out.'

'Tell us about it.' Medford spoke for the first time.

'About hunting?'

'About Scarborough Castle. You must have been there when Sir Ralph Standish was constable?'

'We were, as a matter of fact.' Summers looked bewildered but evidently believing there was no harm in it answered in a straightforward manner. 'His Grace thought he'd better have a look at this new placeman of Gaunt's, so we went over there after a good day out. They spent the evening in discussions up in Standish's solar. It was at the top of a tower looking out over the sea one way and the moors the other. Amazing place. You could hear the sea booming on the rocks way below.'

Hildegard heard Medford sigh but he allowed Summers to continue.

He was saying, 'I have good cause to remember those steps leading up to the top.' He grinned. 'Standish had a flaming temper, even worse than Neville's. He threw me down them and I had a bump on my head for a week.'

'What made him do that?' asked Hildegard while

370

everybody stared at Summers as if they couldn't believe their eyes.

'He thought I'd been listening in. I was astonished that anybody should harbour such suspicions about an archbishop's clerk. It's outrageous. But here I am, going up the stairs to give His Grace a message, when the door at the top suddenly flies open. It's Standish. He's shouting something over his shoulder like: "I'm owed! Get it? It's not my fault things went arse over teat. They owe me!" And a voice comes from inside: "And if they don't pay their debt?" Standish again: "I shall take the truth to where it will do most harm!" Then the archbishop: "And where is that?" And then Standish mentions you, Mr Secretary. He says, "Ask Medford!" And then he comes flying out, knocks me over, picks me up and gives me a great shove sending me back down the stairs. I was never so astonished in my life.'

'And, apart from Archbishop Neville, do you know who was inside the chamber at this time?' asked Medford.

On the way back they had to ride down Ludgate Hill. Hildegard found her cheeks were wet as if a shower of rain had passed over without being noticed.

'So did Standish have something to tell you?' Slake asked Medford.

'Don't you think I would have informed the King?' Medford stared straight ahead.

'It's to do with the rebellion,' announced Slake, continuing, 'we know Standish was one of the traitors at Smithfield.'

Hildegard wiped the back of her hand across her cheeks. 'The Abbot of Meaux heard a rumour along those lines.'

'Go on,' said Medford.

'Apparently Standish was paid to get rid of Tyler. He was also instructed to assassinate Richard in the confusion they expected to follow. Standish was rewarded with Scarborough Castle by his master—'

'Lancaster,' put in Slake.

'And,' she continued, 'maybe he thought he had a right to the rest of his payment, whatever it was, despite the fact that he failed in the final detail. Maybe that's what he was so furious about when Summers was there. Neville must know.'

Medford looked furious.

Slake gave Medford a glance. 'If Standish had come to you with a story like that, names and so on, and you'd told the King, then all hell would have broken loose. There might even have been a second rising.'

'It would have been a clear case of treason and would have led to civil war. Richard would not have wanted that.'

Hildegard stared at Medford.

His tone was clipped as, avoiding her glance, he added, 'Not after the vengeance brought down on his people after the rebellion with those endless executions. He would not want to be the cause of more bloodshed.'

'He wouldn't,' agreed Ulf, not having observed the expressions on the faces of the two men. 'Good Queen Anne earned her name by stopping the executions. It was her first request to Parliament after being crowned. Obviously Richard would be behind it, knowing what we do about his distress at seeing the rebels hang without trial.'

'Just think, if you'd known about Standish's role,' observed Slake to Medford, 'you could have quietly got rid of him. Events up there filter down to London at a snail's pace. Luckily for us the bloody flux did it instead.'

'How is little Turnbull getting on?' Hildegard asked Edwin as he was about to leave them outside York Place. Ulf had already had to peel off at the de Hutton house but Haskin and the rest of the group, including the bodyguards from the Signet Office, had remained. Now they came to a halt.

Edwin gave a half smile at her mention of the boy. 'I hear he's doing well. Apparently Swynford taught him nothing. But they've started from scratch and feel they'll make something of him even yet. He has the will, they say.'

'I've neglected him. Maybe I can take him out so he can see something of London.' Medford moved his horse on impatiently at what was nothing to do with affairs of state. Hildegard leant forward with a quick glance over her shoulder. 'We could visit that herb garden at Stepney His Grace mentioned?'

Poison. Back to that.

Before she went on to her guest lodgings at the abbey to pick up her things to take them over to Roger de Hutton's place, she asked for a private word with Medford. Slake was in attendance, of course.

'It's this, Mr Medford. I'd forgotten it until now. He told me the trail leads to the Queen.'

'What do you make of it?'

She shrugged.

'So is that all?' His brooding glance sent spiders up and down her spine.

'That's all. I thought it might make sense to you. Maybe I'm missing something?'

'I would imagine that's a rare occurrence.' His dark glance followed her to the door as she took her leave.

From Standish to the Queen. He knows I'm getting close, she thought without any feeling. Am I in danger?

No time to ponder the issue. It was of no interest one way or the other. The purpose of life is death. That's what he believed. She remembered his little chamber. The wind rattling the casement. The street singer with his melancholy lament. And firelight. The way his mouth curved when he smiled. Wolfish, she had once thought. *I am being devoured.*

They set out next day shortly after prime to get the best of the morning, little Turnbull on a pony, Haskin on a tough old warhorse, Hildegard riding astride a palfrey, and a couple of silent men-at-arms from Medford's Signet Office. Keeping an eye on me, she guessed. But when the secretary had offered them he said, 'We don't want you to come to harm, do we, Domina?'

* * *

The old friar who ran the gardens was a spry eighty-year-old with a shock of white hair. Once a successful merchant, he had made a fortune in his retirement for his adopted Order by importing and selling herbs and medicinal plants. He was said to possess the widest variety in the kingdom. They were sent from all over the world, more than one hundred and forty-two different kinds, all named and described together with their virtues in a book he had just written.

When he noticed Hildegard and her escort outside the lodge he walked up towards them with a hoe over one shoulder, a smiling figure at home between his sparkling beds of plants. After a formal greeting he offered her bodyguards some refreshment with his own servants in the lodge, then turned to little Turnbull. 'Now, young master, do you know your plants?'

'Not all, magister,' the boy admitted with beguiling honesty.

'Well, take this trowel,' he fished one from his pouch, 'and go and find some mint, parsley and chives. Dig up a little root of each to take back to York Place with you. Your gardener there can make use of them and you can watch them grow.'

After he ran off the old man turned to Hildegard. 'So, Domina. What can I do for you?'

'I crave a remedy for grief, magister.'

'I can see that. Have you tried a warm fireside, a glass of honey in wine and some friendly conversation?'

'I fear I need stronger treatment.'

'Follow me.'

He led her to a lean-to at the side of the lodge. Inside it was perfumed with bunches of sweet-smelling herbs hanging from the rafters. Along the back wall were rows of tinctures and other cures in blue and white pots, sealed and stoppered to maintain the potency of the contents. He took one down, uncorked it and poured a quantity into a phial and put it into her hand.

'For the torments of the body brought on by despair. Best applied by a loving friend but failing that it will still work its magic if you give it time. And this,' he continued, taking down a glass flagon filled with a dark liquid.

After pouring some into a clean bottle he turned his kindly scrutiny on her as she tucked both physicks into her bag. His kindness made it easy to ask him the question that had been puzzling her.

'It's this plant,' she explained, pulling the stems she had picked in the bishop's garden in Lincoln from the container in her scrip. 'I cannot identify it nor work out what its virtue is.'

He took the now-dried leaves, sniffed them, crumpled one between his fingers, then gave her a shrewd glance.

Just then little Turnbull bounded up, calling, 'I have them, magister. All correct.' He was about to show them his gatherings when he saw the leaves in the magister's hands.

'Ah, you've got some of that as well.'

'Do you know what it is?' the old man asked him.

'I do. It's hart's tongue.'

'It is indeed, young fellow. At least, that's what some call it. How do you know it?'

'My previous master had some in Lincoln. It's like gold, he said, paving our way to fame and fortune.'

'He said that, did he?'

'And he called it "white hart physick".'

The white hart.

King Richard's emblem.

'Right,' said Medford after Hildegard told him what she suspected. 'We'll bring him in. See to it, Dean.'

Hildegard put out a hand. 'Will you grant me a request?'

Medford raised his eyebrows.

'Allow me to speak to him first?'

'I'm looking for Jarrold of Kyme.'

'Try the buttery, Domina.'

It was the quiet time, after the first sitting of the day and before the second and the kitchens were empty, floors swept clean, the pots and pans in gleaming rows, the knives, ladles and other utensils hanging from hooks. Shadows and silence. A cat sidled round a door. Rats defeated. Hildegard walked through the labyrinth of passages until she found him.

He appeared to be busy, stuffing things into a hempen bag.

'Leaving?' she asked.

He looked up. 'What if I am?'

'Going anywhere interesting?'

'I am, Domina, as it happens. For what it's got to do with you,' he added.

She waited to see if he would expand on his boast.

He did.

'I've been commanded by the Great Council to attend the King in his kitchens as master herberer.' He smirked.

She reached forward. 'And is this one of the herbs you'll be using?'

He snatched it back. 'Plenty more where that came from if you want some.' The idea made him snigger but he said no more, merely tightening the strap on his bag and offering her a challenging look.

'Do you plan on ever going back to York?' she asked.

'I've wiped the dust of that bloody hole from my boots. Me, I'm staying put.' He made as if to push past her. He smelt of sweat and decaying leaves.

She stood her ground. 'It's a pity about Martin.'

He jerked to a stop. 'What about him?'

'Being dead.'

Neither of them made a move to cross themselves.

'He had it coming.'

'Why so?'

He shook his head. 'I'm saying nothing against him. He wasn't a bad lad, just misguided.'

'In what way?'

'Leave it.'

'I don't feel like leaving it. I feel I owe it him to find out why he died.'

'Why ask me?' he sneered. 'I'd think it was bloody obvious to a halfwit. You'd die if you were hit on the back of the head and chucked in a vat of ale.'

'Is that what happened?'

'I can think of worse ways to go.' He began to laugh then stopped when he saw her expression. 'What?'

She continued to stare at him.

'What are you looking at me like that for?'

'What did you hit him with?'

Jarrold looked astonished for a moment then gave a snarl. 'Don't think you can pin it on me.'

'Only His Grace, his clerk, the bailiff in Bishopthorpe and myself know he was hit on the back of the head. And you.'

'Piss off out of my way, you bloody nun.'

She barred his way as he tried to barrel past her from out of the buttery and there was a brief struggle in the doorway when she thought he was going to hit her but she clung onto him and said fiercely, 'You could not know he was hit over the head unless you did it, Jarrold! You could not know!'

'So, who's going to listen to you?'

'Why did you have to kill him? Was he about to announce what he knew about Standish?'

'What about Standish?'

'What did you use to get rid of him? Hemlock?'

'So obvious! I'm a master of my trade. Credit me with some skill! I'd use something more subtle.'

'Such as?'

379

He considered her for a moment but was unable to resist the temptation to tell. 'What Martin saw me feeding to the rats. He guessed I'd used it on Standish as well.'

He took out his knife.

'That Scarborough lot were glad Standish was dead – being rebels as they were. I knew they wouldn't let on. On the contrary,' he smirked, 'they were cheering me, just like they were the other day at York Place when I killed some more rats. It was only bloody Martin, sanctimonious sot wit. Then when he saw me turn up at Bishopthorpe he was scared shitless . . .'

'So who paid you?'

'Paid? What makes you think I was paid?'

'You surely didn't do it for nothing? Who paid you?' she insisted. 'Was it Swynford?'

'Don't be stupid. He didn't want Standish dead, why would he?'

'So who was it?'

'You wouldn't believe me if I told you.'

'Try me.'

He gave a derisory laugh. 'You mad bitch – I'll tell you who it was. Then this! See it? What is it?'

'It's a knife . . .'

He waved it in her face. 'The mastermind who set it—'

'Hey, that's no way to treat a lady!' It was Dean Slake, jaunty as ever, suddenly materialising as if from nowhere.

Hildegard turned in astonishment to see Medford as well, strolling in from the storeroom next door. The storage spaces were divided by wooden partitions with bars up to the ceiling to allow air to circulate but to prevent theft. Every word must have been audible on the other side.

Slake had picked up a cleaver from the kitchens at some point and was beating it against the palm of one hand as he approached. 'Now then, Jarrold of Kyme,' he said affably. 'Why don't you come with us?'

Before Jarrold could move Slake went right up to him, put him in a headlock and, before their eyes, slicked the cleaver down Jarrold's front from ribs to belly. It made no sound but left a red trail under the ripped fabric of his shirt. Jarrold's expression was one of astonishment. Hildegard saw him stare down as Slake twisted the cleaver and his guts began to spill out into his hands. When Slake let go he staggered forward a pace or two, reaching for the wall opposite, leaving streaks of blood down the white lime wash as he clutched for support. He began to slide slowly, slowly, to the ground.

Medford stood over him when he was still. 'Dean Slake. I've said it before, you're a hasty fellow. Now we'll never know what he wanted to tell Hildegard.'

Chapter Three

'Slake has blocked off the trail that leads from Scarborough by way of Bishopthorpe and Lincoln.'

Edwin and Thomas were gaping at her as she told them what had happened. She began to believe they thought, as Jarrold had, that she was mad, but then Edwin got up to pace about Thomas's chamber and he was firm. 'I didn't tell anybody how Martin was murdered. And of course His Grace would not do so.'

'It sounds as if Jarrold has got his just desserts.' Thomas made the sign of the cross. They had told him about their meeting with Harry Summers and now he asked, 'Jarrold seemed about to tell you he was acting on instructions from someone you know, Hildegard. So who was it? Someone who was at Scarborough Castle the same time he was working there?'

'Was it the unnamed guest in the chamber with His Grace when Standish had his outburst and pushed Harry down the stairs?'

'Can we find out?' Thomas looked from Edwin to Hildegard and back.

'By necromancy probably.' Edwin got up hurriedly and went to the window. 'I can't see me going up to His Grace and asking outright.'

'Best to leave it for now,' Thomas suggested. 'Maybe we're not meant to know.' He looked troubled.

Hildegard persisted. It was no time for avoiding the truth. 'Jarrold was adamant he was not acting on Swynford's instructions. He took pleasure in hinting that it was someone else. It was his big secret. But who was it? Things happened too quickly. I'd no idea Medford and Slake were listening in. It was stupid of me. I should have expected that.'

'Only someone as devious as they are would think along those lines,' Thomas assured her. 'Did Medford give any excuse for what Slake did?'

'He tried to suggest that he acted on impulse. To protect me. Impetuous Slake.'

Edwin gave a snort. 'Like hell he is. I hope Harry's going to be safe. He didn't say anything that would make him seem dangerous, did he?'

Hildegard shook her head. 'Medford thinks he's a fool. Slake said, "I do believe I could beat that fellow at chess," and Medford replied, "I'm sure you could. And so could a babe in arms." He's safe, Edwin.'

'I'm going to call in at Northumberland's place and warn him anyway. He's one of the best. A bloody good chess player as it happens.' He stared moodily into the fireplace. It contained a small lick of flame, the most the monks would permit.

Thomas looked at him with kindness. 'Don't despair, Edwin. Trust in God. Things are not always what they seem.'

'I'll be glad to get back home to Yorkshire. I'm sick of this snakepit. You can't trust anybody.'

Medford had shattered his illusions, Hildegard realised. She put a hand on his shoulder. There might be an even worse disillusionment to follow.

Edwin was about to continue when the door opened and a page thrust his head round it.

'His Grace, Abbot de Courcy of Meaux.'

Hildegard stiffened in alarm. But then Hubert came striding into the chamber, coming to an abrupt halt when he saw Thomas had visitors.

'Brother, forgive me – I had no idea—' He broke off as his glance raked the room and came to rest on Hildegard. His eyes lit up. 'My messenger surely can't have reached you already? He must have wings!'

'Messenger?' She remembered to make a small obeisance.

Hubert's face was sparkling with pleasure. 'I sent him out straight after tierce with instructions to inform you we have a judgement.'

'Judgement?' It seemed she could only repeat his words like a fool.

'On your divorce.'

She held the word back and simply stared at him. She had forgotten that.

He came over to her and she was aware that Edwin and Thomas had tactfully turned away to continue a separate conversation.

Hubert looked carefully into her face. 'You look ill, Hildegard. I hope you haven't been worrying about this issue?'

'No.'

There was a pause. She could think of nothing to add.

He lowered his voice. 'You're being very brave about it. The Chapter took their time, I'm afraid, but they agree that it should be possible. They say you're free of any promises made to Ravenscar. You'll have to reaffirm your vows to us. But that should be no hardship.'

She could only stare at him. Hubert had none of the louche sensual pragmatism of Rivera. His austerity, his air of authority and straight dealing were like fresh rain on the confusion that had gone before. He was smiling with great warmth, plainly concerned by her appearance, searching her face for an explanation. She felt suddenly tired. She swayed and he jerked out a hand. 'Are you ill?'

'I fear so.'

'Thomas!' he called over his shoulder. 'Have you no page in attendance? Can't you see Hildegard needs help?'

Thomas sprang to his feet, winced when he leant too heavily on his injured leg, then plumped down again as Edwin got up instead, saying, 'Let me.'

He gave Hubert a reproachful look. 'You cannot know what Hildegard has been through, My Lord Abbot.'

*   *   *

'There was no need to tell Hubert all that, Edwin.'

'He would have had to discover it some time and it was best coming from me.'

'My gratitude, then.' The abbot had said nothing when Edwin told him about the mob's violent attack and the subsequent beheading of one of Swynford's spies. He had looked at her with concern when the clerk had gone on to tell him about Jarrold's gutting, right there in front of her, and his anger was at once obvious, forcing Edwin to remind him, with many apologies for being so forthright, that even he could not stand against the King's secretary without calling down trouble on his own head and probably that of his Order.

'He will claim that the Cistercians are traitors and only here on sufferance. He'll persuade the King to clear you out, just as they've cleared out so many other alien monastics.'

'Close St Mary Graces?' replied Hubert robustly. 'I'd like to see him try.' But it was true. They all knew Medford could persuade the King to do it in the interests of the state.

Now Hildegard drew her horse to a halt and called Edwin to stop. 'There's a little chapel here,' she told him. 'I'd like to go inside for a moment. Do you mind waiting?'

Haskin and the two Signet Office guards drew up behind them. When Haskin saw what she was going to do he said he would come inside as well. Just to be on the safe side. He swung down from his horse.

* * *

386

It was a small place, dark, its coloured glass letting in little light and the frescoes of St Margaret emerging in triumph from the belly of the dragon, the Devil in disguise, visible only dimly. The colours swam out of the shadows, ochre, black, purple, and a red pigment like dried blood.

A few candles were guttering under the east window where a coffin stood with its lid closed. She went over and looked at the flames. They were dancing like things living and taunting her with their vitality.

There was an inscription on the coffin lid, written in an educated hand. *To our dearly beloved brother and martyr in Christ, Francisco Rivera.*

Of its own volition her hand dashed forward, scattering the candles. Wisps of smoke rose and vanished followed by the smell of singed fabric.

Haskin touched her on the shoulder. 'My Lady, come away now.'

The King, it was announced, was refusing to leave Eltham until a delegation of forty aldermen, including the new mayor, would come to hear his side of his grievance against the Duke of Gloucester. It was contrived, however, that the Duke with his two allies, Arundel and Edmund, another of the King's uncles, turned up instead. Armed to the teeth. Insolent to the point of treason. Laying down the law as they intended to interpret it.

They claimed that if the King did not return to Parliament within forty days, it was written that it should be dissolved. Then he would certainly not get any money.

This was ancient law, they lied, and if he did not do their will he could be deposed and another member of the royal family would rule in his place. King or not, he had to obey the law of the land or lose his crown.

Unable to get any sort of legal advice that would have satisfied his opponents, Richard, nineteen years old, with no money and no army of his own, conceded. He arrived in the royal barge at Westminster quay on the twenty-eighth of October, the Queen, pale and plainly ill, by his side. They held hands like children. Richard put his arm round her when she stumbled and the Bohemian, Petrus de Lancekrona, helped him carry her into the palace.

Gloucester, fox's brush swinging on its lance, followed, smirking. The Earl of Derby was not far behind. Attired from head to foot in green and gold, looking like a king himself, he crossed the yard to a storm of applause. The cheers followed him inside, where the King would hear the level of the crowd's support.

Later that day King Richard made a surprise announcement. He had decided to name his heir. For the security of the succession and the peace of the realm he had chosen the one who would next wear the crown. It was to be a cousin, the Earl of March, thirteen-year-old Roger Mortimer.

The severed limbs nailed to the doors of various strategic buildings and symbolising the body of the realm had been forgotten in the more pressing and unsymbolic drama taking place in Parliament. Now the mystery of the body parts was brought back into public awareness when one of the hands was discovered shortly after lauds on the feast of Saints Ethelred and Ethelbert.

It had been thoughtfully stuck on a pike above London Bridge on the side facing out across the Thames to Southwark, so that anyone entering the city as curfew was lifted that morning would be sure to see it.

News of its appearance swept through the cobbled streets where the market was being set up, and down to Westminster almost as swiftly as a hawk could fly.

If the perpetrators of such barbarity intended to clarify their gruesome message, it was still at best ambiguous. Was it meant to represent the hand of God, the saviour who had caused the wind that drove the French from English shores? Or was it meant to affirm the power of the King – bow down all ye who enter here – and offer a warning to his enemies? Was it meant as instruction to the city men to give the King their support against his enemies? The discussions went on with varying levels of acuity in all the taverns, at all the stalls, in the streets and byways and the courts and yards and ginnels, until Hildegard thought she would be driven mad by it.

'It's a civic matter,' Thomas told her with conviction on the day he happened to be allowed to walk again. He had arrived by wherry at Westminster, discovered she was still staying with Roger de Hutton, and had made his way, limping, and with waning confidence in his infirmarer, halfway up the Strand.

'It stands to reason,' he said over a beaker of wine

in Roger's solar, 'the other parts have all been posted up at sites within the city walls. It's meant to scare the apprentices into obedience. Exton has already started to root out anybody who doesn't agree with him.'

Roger growled something about the monk's strange idea of reason and pointed out that the rest of the body hadn't shown up yet.

Shortly after midday his complaint was satisfied. The head, wearing a makeshift crown of willow wands, was discovered nailed to the broken gates of the Savoy Palace.

A terrified servant brought the news. 'It's just across the street!' he bawled out, tumbling over his own feet and throwing himself in front of the first figure in authority he could find. It happened to be Ulf, just then crossing the courtyard with a message to the vintner to bring up extra supplies to the solar. The steward followed him out into the street.

'Show me,' he commanded.

The frightened lad led him along until they reached the small crowd that had already gathered and were gaping up at the bloodied human remains with its crown awry.

'Hildegard must not see this.' Ulf dragged the boy back with him and handed him over to the under-kitchener. 'Give him something to steady his nerves then tell him to shut his mouth. I'm going up to inform His Grace right this minute.'

It was impossible to keep something like this a secret for long. After a mumbled explanation to Roger, Ulf approached Hildegard where she sat in a niche. Everything about him showed that he had news he was reluctant to impart.

'You'll find out sooner or later, Hildegard. Somebody else is bound to recognise him. It's Hugh de Ravenscar.'

She stood up.

Roger had sworn to kill him. Ulf too. Now they both looked stunned.

'It's justice,' said Ulf. 'Don't waste tears on him.'

'Tears?' She had forgotten what tears were and now merely groped for her goblet and took a sip.

Ulf had heard a few murmurs from the onlookers outside the Savoy and now told her, 'It's being seen as a warning to the King's enemies.'

'Some good may yet come of it, then,' Thomas said after a pause. 'It might deter the Duke of Gloucester and his cronies from trying to steal what is not theirs.'

Thomas was somewhat optimistic. Another view was soon sweeping London. The severed head was a warning to the King himself. Obey your subjects or you'll finish up with your head crowned with thorns and stuck on a pole like any other traitor.

'Who would like to accompany me to Westminster?' Hildegard asked. It was nones. Parliament would soon rise for the day.

Ulf offered at once and Roger, strapping on his sword belt, got up as well. Thomas, unable to hide his limp, said he hoped a horse could be found for him, if Roger would be so kind.

With an armed escort, the three of them set out and arrived in Westminster shortly after the doors of the chapter house had been flung open.

'I should have been in there this morning,' remarked Ulf without regret.

'And I should have been in the other place,' Roger pointed out. 'To hell with the bastards.' He shot a glance at Ulf. 'What's she brought us here for?'

Hildegard rode alongside him. 'There's someone we need to see, isn't there?'

One of the shire knights was leaving as if he couldn't get out fast enough. He recognised Ulf and came over. 'You missed nothing, fella. The carve-up is now complete. I abstained. I doubt they'll ask me again. I'm off to the country to save my life.' He reached up to grasp Ulf by the hand and the steward got down off his horse and gave the man a bear hug. 'Watch your step, Geoffrey.'

When he was out of earshot Ulf said, 'He's a rare bird. He's called Geoffrey Chaucer. He's Richard's court poet but he's retained by Lancaster on account of his wife. She's the sister of the Duke's mistress.'

'Which one?' Roger asked.

'Katharine Swynford.' The Duke had countless women but his liaison with Thomas Swynford's mother was the longest lasting and most fertile in terms of the children she had borne him outside the law.

'I saw her in Lincoln.' Hildegard commented. There were other concerns on her mind at present.

A figure she recognised left the chapter house with a

crowd of other men and she watched as they swarmed across the yard, some elated, others with grim faces. They disappeared into the nearby tavern.

'That's that, then,' observed Roger with a covert glance in Hildegard's direction. 'What are we doing next?'

'I understood you'd offered to escort me?' she replied with something of her former spirit. 'Now I'm going to go over there,' she gestured towards the tavern. 'You can accompany me or not, as you please.'

'I've got better wine in my slop buckets than they'll have in there,' Roger began to point out when Hildegard dismounted and threw him the reins of her horse. 'Come on, Ulf. I'm going to fetch him outside.'

When she looked back Roger was holding the reins of two extra horses in his hand with the possibility of a third as Thomas gingerly dismounted.

The tavern was bursting at the seams with the sort of people who like hanging around anybody with the lustre of political power about them, and as well as them there was the big crowd from the Commons who had just come in. Guy de Ravenscar was easy to spot. He stood head and shoulders above most of the local men.

Hildegard went straight up to him. 'Was it you?'

She didn't offer any of the usual greetings and when he saw her face he peeled off from his companions and asked, 'What's the matter?'

'Come outside.'

People were staring as she pushed her way back through

the crowd to the door and somebody shouted, 'You're doing well there, Guy.'

But then they were outside and she was turning on him shouting, 'Did you do it?'

'Do what, my dearest—?'

'Don't give me all that. The head. It's horrible – that thing! Is it your doing?'

'What is this?'

She took him firmly by the arm. 'Did you, Guy. Tell me! That head, nailed to the Savoy gates. Who put it there? It was you, wasn't it?' Tears suddenly welled up and she felt she was having to fight for breath. She slapped his face and began to punch him. A crowd formed. Nobody interfered. Guy gripped her by both arms.

'Steady on! What's happened?'

Ulf stepped forward and explained, succinctly, adding, 'I know I vowed to deal with the bastard but I would never have done anything so barbaric.'

Guy's jaw seemed to sag. He released her and she stood panting for breath, shouting, 'I don't even care what happens to him! I don't care! Don't you understand? I can't breathe.' She was choking. 'Did you, Guy? Was it you who nailed him up there?'

His strange reaction made her falter. He was staring at her with his mouth open. He looked back at the tavern then turned to face her. 'I think I must have.'

'What?'

Ulf took a step forward.

Guy suddenly seemed unsteady on his feet and groped his way to a nearby wall and sat down with his head in his hands. Hildegard and Ulf followed.

After a moment Guy rubbed his hands over his face and lifted his head. 'My men are loyal to me and I to them. I hated Hugh. Everybody knew that. I'd no idea how much I hated him until I met him again in the city. Didn't you hate him, Hildegard, truly, in your heart? You have as much reason as anybody.'

She shook her head. 'He was as he was. My only ambition was never to set eyes on him again. I don't hate him. There's too much sorrow in the world to make room for hatred.'

'I don't have your nature. I hated Hugh and despite that . . .' he gestured vaguely in the direction of the Savoy '. . . I still do. I feel no sorrow. If that's what's happened then he's got what he deserved. But I fear I may have brought him to such a hideous end by allowing my men to think I would welcome it. I fear they have fulfilled what they see as their duty to me.'

He stood up. He seemed dazed. It was easy to see that he believed what he was telling them. Somehow he pulled himself together and managed to explain. 'They're wild border men. Used to everyday brutality. It's how they survive. They live by simple rules. If they see that I'm dishonoured, they'll take revenge on my behalf. Their allegiance to me is absolute. They know no other law.'

He took an unsteady step. 'The city is no place for them. They are too savage, too free. Parliament is finished.

I'm going back to Wales to raise men for King Richard. He's going to need longbowmen. I beg you, do not detain them. My wild Welsh archers may yet save England.'

He went back into the tavern and Ulf and Hildegard were returning to where Roger was still waiting with the horses when they saw him emerge with half a dozen subdued but rough-looking men-at-arms. A few girls from the tavern straggled out after them with lewd comments and invitations to return.

Their horses were brought up. Guy swung into the saddle, the raven still hanging by its neck from his pike, and began to lead his men in the direction of the horse ferry. When he drew level with the de Hutton group he raised one hand in salutation and one or two of his men glanced over and then quickly away.

Ulf helped Thomas into the saddle. Hildegard leant her head against her horse's neck for a moment and closed her eyes.

When she looked up, her brother-in-law's small army had gone.

Later they discovered that before he left the city for good, Guy had made sure the head was taken down and he paid for a mass at All Hallows by the Tower, the little church where his brother had attacked Hildegard in the early days of her stay in the capital. Appropriately it was near Petty Wales, between the river and the Tower, where his men had hunted down their liege lord's inglorious sibling and dealt him their own form of justice.

Hildegard doubted she would ever see Guy again. She had failed to get his measure. He had looked pleased enough when he set off with that jaunty salute. It was clear he was going home to consolidate his claim on his lands and not to mourn but to celebrate.

After compline later that day, when the kitchens at Roger de Hutton's town house were quiet, Hildegard went down to boil some water. In her hand were some fresh leaves of hart's tongue, a gift from the old gardener, Henry Daniels.

While she waited for the water to boil she thought of the wasted man-hours spent poring over arcane legal texts as the monks at St Mary Graces discussed her situation. She had been a widow before and she was a widow now.

The water began to bubble and she poured it over the crushed leaves, stirred them, watched small flecks rise to the surface, and let it steep. Old Daniels had told her what the plant's virtue was before she left. Turnbull's master had called it white hart physick, so pure the hart will never breed. Daniels' words had been more prosaic. It's a spleenwort, he told her, to promote women's courses. When it was ready she strained it into a cup then lifted it to her lips and drank.

Chapter Four

These days it was easier to get a ferry now that Parliament had ended. Most of those called had returned to their manors in the shires or to their great castles in far-flung corners of the realm.

Westminster Hall was again peopled only by the shadowy figures with business at the court of Chancery or the King's Bench. The sightseers and the pilgrims in Palace Yard had found other places to visit, and after they departed the food sellers, the jugglers, singers, card sharps and other mountebanks had no trade so they too left, and even the chained bear no longer sat outside the tavern. That once boisterous place was again host to no more than a few regulars who regained their former positions by the windows and went back to watching the world go by.

The abbey, too, lost its guests and resumed the ancient pattern imposed by the followers of St Benet. Choirs of monks sang, undisturbed, the offices of the day from matins to nightfall and the only ripple on their serenity was the sad and sudden death of their abbot, Nicholas Lytlington. His legacy, his precious Missal, was hoped to outlast the plotting of the city men, the chicanery of the barons and the rise and fall of kings. He had voted for King Richard. The abbot's death was sudden but he was, as Ulf told Hildegard, a very old man, an alleged son of Edward the Third by one of his mistresses. He would be missed for many years and no one thought his death in the slightest degree sinister.

The shrine beside one of the abbey bridges in honour of St Margaret, the helper of women, was empty too, although the altar was decked with late roses from the gardens at Eltham. Queen Anne and her entourage had just left when Hildegard reached the threshold and looked in. A sacristan was dousing candles.

She walked on towards the landing stage where Thomas and Edwin were waiting. There were several ferrymen to choose from, but as they strolled along the quay to make their choice one of them called up to them. He knew them, he claimed.

It was the same man who had taken Hildegard and Thomas downriver shortly after they arrived in London.

He asked what they thought now to the great capital.

They were polite and non-committal. In response he told them he had made a small fortune over the last few weeks and would be sorry to see the last of the outsiders leave.

'By, you wouldn't believe the passengers I've had in my boat while Parliament's been on,' he told them, pulling strongly from the shore as soon as they were aboard. 'Magnates, burgesses, knights; I even had the King's secretary in here the other night. Took him all the way down to Eltham, I did, when Dickon was refusing to come out.'

Thomas murmured his interest. Encouraged, the boatman continued. 'Aye, and he knows your part of the world. How about that? Says it's rough country. He was up there a couple of years back, he says, on king's business.'

Hildegard sat up. 'Whereabouts was he? Did he say?'

The boatman allowed the craft to ride the tide with only a token pull on the oars. 'A wild place, he says, by the sea. A great castle high on a cliff.'

'Scarborough, maybe?' she suggested.

'Aye, that's the place. Been there yourselves?'

'So everything is clear,' Hildegard frowned. 'Or is it?' She got up to pour some of the archbishop's Gascon wine into their beakers, then sat down in the corner of the cloister where they had gone to keep out of the wind.

The talkative boatman had dropped them off at York Place, where Edwin had to make some final preparations before returning north and Hildegard, belatedly, had been granted an audience with His Grace. Thomas was planning to leave with the Meaux contingent just as soon as Abbot de Courcy gave the command, but for now was not needed.

Many in Neville's retinue had already packed up and the wagons, surrounded by prowling cats, were being loaded with baggage and filled the main yard amid all the mayhem of departure.

She waited for her companions to say something. Edwin spoke first.

'It was Medford in the tower chamber with Archbishop Neville when Standish had his outburst and threw Harry down the stairs.'

'Medford who sealed the butcher of Smithfield's fate.' Thomas frowned. 'No doubt he would claim that Standish had to be silenced to avert civil war.'

'And it was Jarrold, the poisoner, who was commissioned to do the job,' Hildegard added. No wonder he had given that knowing smile when he had taunted her with the name of his secret master. Afterwards he must have found refuge at Bishopthorpe where Neville knew all about him. But then Martin got into the picture.'

'He must have threatened Jarrold with the rumours over Standish's sudden death. And, of course, he may have known something more specific, like what poison was used, working side by side with him in the kitchens there. Jarrold must have been desperate to shut him up—'

'Then Martin made the mistake of trying to warn him off by telling him that he'd already confided his suspicions to his friend Willerby, the falconer.'

'Frightened that everything was spinning out of control, Jarrold must have acted out of desperation. Later he appealed for help to the lord of his manor at Kyme, Sir Thomas Swynford.'

'That's what the argument in the chapel must have been about,' Hildegard suggested. 'Not about a woman at all. I thought Jarrold was lying when he said that to Swynford. And of course, he couldn't tell him the truth.'

Rain, falling in the garth, the smell of wet fabric, puddled footprints on the floor and then that sign, his arm round Willerby, this is the man. And Swynford devised his devilish plot.

'It's a lord's duty to protect his tenants just as it's their duty to serve. You understand that too, Edwin.' Thomas turned to the clerk.

Edwin was staring across the yard to where, his own master, the archbishop had appeared. He jerked round. 'Quite right, Thomas. Quite right.'

They agreed that fate had offered up the perfect instrument to finish the job of obliterating the trail that led from Standish, through Martin, to Jarrold – the grieving father at St Albans.

'Jarrold might have got away with it even then. He seemed to have no real motive for being involved. In fact, quite the reverse.'

'But then Rivera perceived a wisp of smoke that led us to Harry Summers.' Rivera's name caught in her throat. 'And there we got our motive,' she continued. 'To prevent Standish from revealing the entire conspiracy to assassinate the King. Who better than a master in the art of poison? Now only one mystery remains.' She hesitated. 'Medford believes the conspiracy continues—'

'But where's the secret in that?' asked Edwin. 'Gloucester, Arundel and Bolingbroke are open about their enmity.'

'Couching their ill will in the hypocritical tones of men who pretend to be acting from altruistic motives,' Thomas agreed. 'When we all know they're driven by greed and the lust for power. Indeed, where is the mystery?'

'Even the secret of the Tower is out. The King's cracker gun did its job. It kept the French away and now it's safe in Windsor Castle where it can be perfected by the Queen's compatriots.'

A final feast, lavishly augmented by all the leftovers, the scraps, the sudden gifts of venison and birds of the air from other barons with too many vittles uneaten in their larders, was set.

Brembre, ex-mayor, but still accompanied by his overlarge entourage, was howling with rage about the Duke of Gloucester. 'Whoever heard of a king being overruled by his council?' he fumed. 'But without an army or the money to raise one what can he do?' He patted his bulging money bag. 'But we must not despair. I may not be mayor but I've still got the power of gold to offer.' He turned to the archbishop. 'And you've done well to get yourself elected onto the council, Alexander. You can safeguard Richard's interests from there.'

'I fear I've been invited merely as a sop to Gloucester's

critics. He's making it as difficult as he can, demanding that we remain in London throughout the year of the council's term. As if I can leave my northern flock for a year. He knows it's impossible.'

Neville, unlike Brembre, had the look of a man who had lost the fight. A realist, thought Hildegard, or was Brembre the realist when he imagined they could still fight back? She recalled Guy de Ravenscar and his promise of a Welsh contingent of bowmen.

'Others will rally to the King's support, will they not?' she asked Brembre.

'Most certainly. Sir Simon Burley, Robert de Vere, Michael de la Pole when he's sat out his prison term, all as loyal as you want. They'll muster their forces. I'll back them.'

'I hear Richard insisted that he should be the one to supervise de la Pole's sentence. The upshot is he's invited him to Windsor Castle for Christmas as his honoured guest!' Neville suddenly smiled. 'He has style, our beleaguered King. I applaud him.'

'You'll be at Windsor as well?'

Neville nodded. 'But I shall stay in London in the meantime to see which way the wind sets in.'

'I'm invited,' Brembre told him. 'I'm keen to find out how far these Bohemian lads have really got with their firecracker experiments.'

'What are they calling 'em, tarasnishs?'

'Some Bohemian word like that. I prefer "bombard" or "firecracker" myself. It certainly sent Charlie boy scurrying off home with his wooden castles and his Spanish warships! The wind's changed, oh dear! Down the market they're claiming it was the hand of God came down to save us, the sot wits!'

'If somebody from our side told him they were more advanced than they are, I'm not surprised he ran for it.'

'Exton,' said Brembre with satisfaction. 'An old ally of mine.' He chuckled and exchanged a knowing glance with Neville.

'It was a clever bluff.' The archbishop smiled. 'Let them think the King would meekly offer them the keys to the city along with the fort of Calais the minute they showed up. Then hint that it was a trap to lure them in so they could be blasted to kingdom come by our secret weapon.'

'Exton's servant did a grand job. He put the wind up Charles and his dukes all right with his hints to their spies. The ultimate weapon of destruction!' Brembre roared with laughter. 'I don't mind losing my mayor's chain to Exton. We city men are in it together. If the dukes won't save our skins, we can do the job ourselves. Hand of God, my arse!'

'How far have they got with their invention?' Neville asked.

'Not far, although they're experts at this sort of thing, they tell me. It stands to reason. Prague's known as a city of alchemists. They understand gunpowder. Richard's brother-in-law Wenceslas fosters their researches. What we need now is for our own merchants to put their hands in their pockets.'

'City of alchemists?' Neville raised a smile. 'Is that why de la Pole's so fond of the place?'

'He likes it for the dancing and the good times. He says those Bohemians are more like Yorkshiremen than his own countrymen here in the south. When he was there with Simon Burley to bring the new Queen back he said they had a fine time. Music and merrymaking, he says, with a bit of alchemy thrown in.' Brembre lifted his goblet. 'Here's to the cracker guns, real or imaginary. Let's hope they blast the King's enemies to kingdom come!'

Neville invited Hildegard into his privy chamber later. He seemed vague, as if something had shaken his confidence and was unsure how to proceed.

His falcon was sitting on a perch draped in scarlet cloth with the gold chain round her leg, and he went over to her and ruffled her feathers. 'It's the sweetest thing to watch a falcon stoop to her prey. Not sweet for the prey, of course.' He glanced up. 'I thought you were going to bring us down.'

'My loyalty would have prevented it.'

He gave a sad smile. 'Yes, I believe it would.'

He left the falcon and came to stand close so he could speak more confidentially. 'I had to send you and Edwin to talk to that fellow in the Tower to keep you off the scent. We didn't know what was being cooked up there, of course.' He gave a tentative smile. 'We're living in uncertain times. Gloucester's hatred for Richard runs deeper than you can imagine. He and Bolingbroke are determined to pursue him to the end. He is not mad.

They really mean to destroy him. We know greed drives Gloucester, spite is Arundel's motive, Bolingbroke thrives on jealousy and ambition, and poor Edmund tags along not quite sure what's happening. I'm on the King's council and I'll do my best to protect Richard's interests, but how long I can play both ends I don't know. They'll be coming after me next.'

Hildegard remembered the journey down to London, the attack on their convoy, the attempted theft. 'You still have the cross?'

'They will no doubt send hired men after it again. But they'll never find it. I'm the only person who knows where it is and nothing will ever prise the secret from me. Not even you, Hildegard.'

He wore a disillusioned smile. 'If it had any real power we would know it by now. It possesses only the power we ourselves invest in it. In these end days nobody gives it credence. We live in a godless world.'

He put a hand on her arm. 'Jarrold came to see me, you know. He told me what he'd been paid to do. I said I would hear his confession but otherwise he was on his own. I had no idea it had led to murder.'

'No one could have guessed that.'

'That may be so. But what about you, Hildegard? I know where my path leads. Don't be brought down with me when I fall. Go back to your grange at Meaux and live there in seclusion doing good and humble work. Live like that for the natural span of your days.'

* * *

If his death was not to have been in vain she had to solve the enigma of his last words: *Follow the trail, it leads to the Queen*. It could not simply imply that there was a plot – everyone knew as much – so might it be better to ask: what form does the plot take?

Thomas sent a messenger inviting her to St Mary Graces to say farewell until they met again at Meaux. Aware that the abbot would be present, and suspecting that perhaps he was the instigator of Thomas's invitation, she made some feeble excuse and instead Thomas, alone, came down to the de Hutton house on the Strand.

'I'm travelling back with Hubert tomorrow,' he told her. 'He was disappointed you were unable to come over. He's flooded with last-minute obligations to his hosts and couldn't get away. He sends his greetings and says he's looking forward to meeting over a flagon of wine when you get back to Meaux. There's talk that he's going to represent us at the general synod in France next year,' he added.

'Will you go with him?'

'I would deem it a great honour but am hardly worthy.'

Hildegard smiled.

When he asked her how she was travelling back she told him Roger was insisting she travel with his entourage.

'You'll be safe enough with those men-at-arms of his.'

'What about you, Thomas, are you able to ride?'

He nodded. 'I'll manage. I just hope I can keep up with Hubert. He rides like a madman.'

* * *

She was no nearer making sense of Rivera's words when the time came to say goodbye. Roger, Ulf, even Haskin, stood about in the yard looking uncertain.

'It would take too long to explain. But it's something I need to do. I've already been to see the abbot at St Mary Graces. He gave me his permission and his blessing.'

'So you're travelling down to Canterbury when?' asked Ulf.

'Tomorrow.'

Roger looked sceptical. 'And then across into Normandy, over the mountains and down into Spain? Well, the saints preserve you, Hildegard. You wouldn't catch me going on pilgrimage to Santiago de Compostella.'

Ulf looked troubled but said nothing to add to Roger's verdict. He came over to give her a hug. 'I'll be married when you next see me.'

'I hope you have every possible happiness and the joy of many children.' She returned his hug.

'Steady on,' he said. 'I've got to take a second look at her first.'

'I'm sure she's beautiful.'

The boat drifted towards the gap between the houses and the ferryman rested on his oars while his passenger took her time.

Moving, shifting, magical. She saw him coming out of the house, holding out his hand to her.

Rivera.

She blinked the image away. She would never come to terms with it. His eternal absence. The loss.

At her sign the boatman allowed the boat to drift back into the outgoing tide.

Turning away, she caught a sudden sight of Jarrold. He was back, then.

Standing at a bench at the far end of the kitchens, he was on the point of turning out one of the leather bags she had seen him with earlier. A servant was picking up a sharp knife to begin work on the herbs that came spilling out. Jarrold reached into another bag at his feet and made a second pile further along the bench where someone else could get to work. Then he came towards the door carrying the two empty bags.

As he passed she took the opportunity to detain him. 'I need some herbs for my cures, master. Can you tell me where you obtained those?'

For some reason he looked affronted. 'They're not cures. Who said they were cures?'

'Most herbs can be considered as such.' She withstood his belligerent stare without flinching.

Observing that she was not going to be put off, he lied. 'Brought them from Lincoln myself.'

'They look fresh.'

'If you want fresh, try Henry Daniels.' He walked off.

When she woke up her entire body was weeping. She lay puzzling over the dream until it was time to leave.

* * *

Abbot de Courcy came flying up the road from London on his black destrier, galloped under the stone arch into the courtyard at Meaux and dismounted in a billow of dust. He threw his cloak to a nearby servant. A few moments later Thomas followed. When he dismounted, his leg still encased in bandages, he was less agile than the abbot and gave a bemused smile at the monks who had gathered in the yard to welcome the travellers home.

'Well ridden, lad.' Hubert clapped Thomas on the shoulder making him wince. 'I hope you'll ride like that when you come to France with me next year.'

'You mean I'm coming to Clairvaux?'

'I do.' Hubert swept on into his private lodge leaving his servants to follow with his things.

Despite his obvious delight to be back in his own domain, over the next couple of weeks the abbot began to walk more frequently to the bridge across the canal dividing his abbey from the adjacent grange, where it had been his practice to meet Hildegard after vespers to discuss matters of mutual concern to both establishments.

Now he stood alone, staring down into the darkly flowing water until the winter sun slipped behind the bare-branched oaks and he had to find his way back to the abbey by starlight.

After a few evenings of this he made his way to the bridge as usual, but then, instead of staring at the water as it rushed underneath, he strode across to the building on the other side and rapped peremptorily on the door.

A face appeared at the grille.

'Is Hildegard back from London?'

There was a moment of confusion in the darkness inside. 'She has left England, My Lord.'

'What?'

'She has gone on pilgrimage.'

'I gave no such permission.'

'I understand she obtained permission from the Abbot of St Mary Graces, My Lord.'

Hubert made his way back to the bridge. He halted halfway across and put both hands on the parapet and stared into the water without moving.

There were running footsteps and a servant from the grange appeared. 'My Lord Abbot?'

He turned almost savagely. The servant ran up, placed a small vellum roll into his hands and fled back to the other side.

Only when he was alone in the privacy of his chambers did he rip the seal off and read the message: *When you receive this I shall have set out on the road to Compostela. Forgive me. It is not, as you believe, an easy matter to reaffirm my vows. Hildegard.*

Eventually he went to the window where he used to watch the light from her chamber window until it went out after vigils.

Compostela. The field of stars.

Outside, a lantern. The high walls. The drifting sound of nuns singing the night office.

In his mind's eye he saw a figure clad in white receding down a long straight road under a high sun until it became one with the horizon.

Epilogue

Hildegard made a sudden stop so that the group of pilgrims walking along beside her were momentarily thrown into disarray.

Hart's tongue. *So pure it will never breed.*

Now she saw it.

Swynford. Jarrold his carrier and go-between. And the King's council issuing their edict that all King Richard's retinue down to the meanest kitchener should be appointed by them.

The royal food taster was an old man in his eighties, never likely to feel the effects of a concoction of hart's tongue. Nor would the King. A goblet of jasper would not detect it either.

Only the Queen would suffer.

Mortimer was heir.

But Mortimer would die.

When the Duke of Lancaster's requiem was played, his

son Bolingbroke, the Earl of Derby, would have only one obstacle between himself and the crown.

His childless cousin, Richard.

The pilgrims had moved on up the road, not breaking step now the confusion was over. One of them called back to her. 'Keep up, mistress. St James is waiting!'

It was too far-fetched. It would require cunning and immense patience. Was he capable of it?

She considered turning back. The long miles over the mountains to England, the difficulty of getting close to the King, of informing someone who could be trusted.

She remembered her intention to light a cathedral full of candles.

She fingered the emblem under her cloak.

The pilgrims called again. 'Widow! Do come on!'

And then she knew. The decision was made.

One step after another.

Like all the days unfolding towards the end.

ALSO BY CASSANDRA CLARK

Summer, 1384. Hildegard of Meaux – sleuth, spy and now an abbess of the powerful Cistercian Order – has found refuge from a world of violence and blood-feud at her new grange in Yorkshire. But by taking a bonded maid into the fold, Hildegard has made a dangerous enemy, an enemy who thinks nothing of destroying her little sanctuary to further his own ends. Meanwhile her own history, and her possession of a priceless relic, threatens to drag her into the schemes of traitors, among them the ruthless Henry Bolingbroke, who seeks to overthrow King Richard II. Can even the resourceful Hildegard unweave the tangled skein of conspiracy?

To discover more historical fiction and to
place an order visit our website at
www.allisonandbusby.com
or call us on
020 7580 1080